The Vampire King

Book #3 of the Horn King Series

BRAE WYCKOFF

Know you are loved!

B Wyckoff

The Vampire King
The third book in the Horn King series.
©2015 Published by LR Publishing

ISBN: 1514296020
ISBN-13: 978-1514296028
Library of Congress Control Number: 2015946138

Editor: Penelope Bartotto
www.penelopeannebartotto.com

Map created by Michelle Modifica-Nichols
Cover art by Jill Wyckoff and
Sharon Marta of Marta Studios
http://www.martastudios.com

DEDICATION

This book is dedicated to all things true, noble, reputable, authentic, compelling, and gracious. The spirit of adventure brings out the best, not the worst; the beautiful, not the ugly; things to praise, not things to curse.

"There is someone greater who makes everything work together and will form you to become His most excellent harmony."
The Vampire King

Table of Contents

ACKNOWLEDGMENTS

Thank you to my beautiful wife, Jill, who captured my heart at twenty and said, "Yes" when I was twenty-one.

We have had 22 brilliant years together since that glorious day of December 11, 1993. Thank you for bringing the best out of me, for loving me for who I am, for encouraging me like no other person could, and letting me hunt down these adventures walled up inside my mind, and for letting me release them upon this amazing world we live in.

Blessings upon you and our family!

<u>The Heroes of Ruauck-El</u>

Bridazak Baiulus – An orphaned Halfling (Ordakian or Dak for short) who was the Carrier of the Orb of Truth and the leader of his friends, Spilf, Dulgin, and Abawken. He is now in search of Manasseh in the Underworld.

Spilfer Teehle – Spilf is also an orphaned Ordakian that Bridazak and Dulgin found on the streets of Baron's Hall and has travelled with for years.

Dulgin Hammergold – This red-bearded surly dwarf is stubborn and always looking for a fight, but deep down he has a heart of gold and will do anything for his friends. He favors an axe that was gifted to him by his father.

Abawken Shellahk – He comes from the Province of Zoar in the East. He is a human fighter that wields a magical scimitar called the Sword of the Elements. He is now married to Raina.

Raina Sheeldeen – Raina is an elf mystic that was lost for centuries to a curse called The Burning Forest. She is a powerful wizard that fights alongside the King of the Dwarves, El'Korr. She is now married to Abawken.

El'Korr Hammergold – El'Korr is the older brother of Dulgin and was also lost for centuries within The Burning Forest curse. He is now the King of the remnant of dwarves fighting for freedom against the Horn Kings.

Xandahar Sheldeen – Xan is an elven fighter cleric that has lived over 700 years. He is a great and powerful healer.

Jack – A rescued teenaged human trying to find his way in the world. He feels lost without his family and feels the heroes that he looks up to have also abandoned him.

Rozelle –Gnome druid who is in love with Trillius the thief. Rozelle has the ability to shape change into animals.

King Morthkin –Frost Dwarf King who reins from Te Sond—The Shield.

Geetock –Wild Dwarf bodyguard to King El'Korr. He recently took the place of Rondee the Wild who fell during the battle within the Chamber of Cleansing versus the Dragon God.

Neutral Persons of Ruauck-El

Romann de Beaux –Vampire leader of Pirates Belly in search of freeing his lost love from the evil ruler of the West.

Daysho Gunsen – Hired assassin that made a deal with Romann de Beaux after beheading the evil mystic Veric and delivering the head to Ravana.

Trillius Triplehand –Gnome thief who was taken over by an evil blue dragon spirit called Dal-Draydian. Set free from the dragon he now experiences withdrawals of the memories left behind. He recently befriended the young boy, Jack.

The Villains of Ruauck-El

King Manasseh – This human lived over three centuries and was the ruler of the Northern Kingdom. He was known as the North Horn King and was raised from the dead by an evil mystic and black dragon to reveal to them the location of the five dragon stones. Manasseh wanted revenge against Bridazak.

The Dark Lord – This deity is the ruler of Kerrith Ravine, a doorway to the Underworld.

Reegs – Shadow creatures that are demonic spies for the Dark Lord. Reegs are used to report their findings to the Dark Lord and are spread throughout Ruauck-El.

Ravana –West Horn King and rules from the city of Tuskabar.

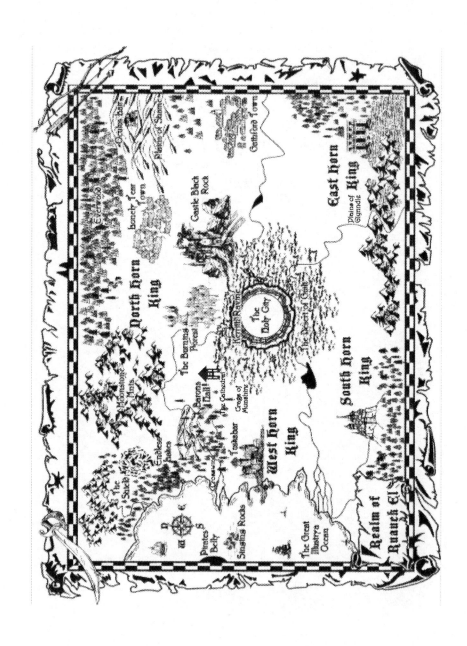

Prologue

The Countessa

Romann de Beaux, the vampire leader of Pirate's Belly, and sworn enemy to the West Horn King, Ravana, exited his anchored ship into the darkness of night. Like a whisper he moved gracefully over the breaking fluorescent waves toward a faintly outlined island. The coldness that emanated from this place was as frigid as himself—the grip of death.

Before long he entered a temple at the top of the low rocky ridge. The cracked pearl-like pillars and faded pigment of the natural coloring revealed its age—older than ancient.

A single source of light came from the back recesses within the one roomed chamber. It was a rectangular shaped structure with a steeple roof. The pillars were on the outside leading to the open entryway, and in all regards this place resembled a tomb.

As he entered he said out loud, "I wish to parlay and come humbly before you, Countessa." He bowed as he swooped his swashbuckler hat off of his head and fanned it outward in the purest etiquette.

A chilling female voice resounded all around him, "Good to see you, Romann."

The red, fiery hair of the human slightly fluttered behind her from the breeze off the ocean as she revealed herself. She had olive colored skin and her eyes yearned to suck the very life from all who looked into them. They were steel blue and cut deep to the heart of one's greatest fears. Her red robe draped to the floor and dragged behind with slight pause as she ever so slowly stepped toward Romann.

"What brings you here to my island sanctuary?" she said.

"Forgive my intrusion, my lady. I wish to call upon my request," he remained bowed.

"Stand," she commanded.

Romann slowly did as ordered and looked into her gaze.

"I gave you one favor to call upon in your time of need and it is now, you say, after all these years?"

"Yes."

"Speak."

"I wish for you to train someone in the art of the Vemptukai royalty."

"Vemptukai?" she laughed. "Royalty is inherited not trained. I have waited centuries for the Vampire King, but we have not heard anything, not even a whisper. It is not possible for whomever you speak of to be *trained* in the Vemptukai."

"I beg of you, Countessa. Just your wisdom and guidance in the ways will fortify this candidate."

"Who do you speak of?"

"His name is Daysho Gunsen."

"Ah, the infamous assassin. A strange request coming from you." She paused for a long moment and then in surprise asked, "Did you turn him, Romann?"

Reluctantly he said, "Yes."

"Impressive. This is your first?"

"And my last."

"Mmm, we will see about that. If I agree then this will be my repayment, you understand?"

"I do."

"It amazes me that you would waste such a gift for another's benefit."

"I see this as a benefit to me, not to anyone else."

"You love her that much?"

Romann looked hard into her eyes and nodded, "Yes, with all my heart."

"Well, that is an odd statement for a vampire since we are in essence heartless. Your request intrigues me. I have been meaning to get out and see what has been happening in the realm. I will teach your barbaric assassin the ways, but if he does not fall in line then I demand he be enslaved to me for all eternity."

"Agreed."

Chapter 1

The Lily of the Valley

Abawken and Raina, newly wed, held each other as the bronze dragon, Zeffeera, glided above the billowy clouds. They had been flying for many hours and the sun waned on the horizon. The beautiful rays igniting the wall of clouds below them in pinks and oranges, gave them a glimpse of what they personally experienced in heaven.

"We are almost there, Raina," Zeffeera said within her mind.

The female dragon soared through the buttermilk sky and broke through the canopy to the realm below. An enchanting valley laced with streams, trees, and green grass came into view. Birds of all types flittered to and fro, buckhorns grazed in the green meadows, and the smell of fresh spring rain permeated the land. Zeffeera descended rapidly toward a massive tree without branches. Completely covered in green moss and vines, the true nature of the spectacle became clear when Abawken realized it was not a tree but instead a tower; a mystic's tower.

"Welcome to Teras di Kimli; The Lily of the Valley, my home."

The bronze winged creature gently landed in front of the covered tower. White flowers dotted the outer wall amongst the green foliage, birds chirped songs of delight, and a cool breeze rolled through, bringing the many fragrances of the land with it.

Abawken, adorned in his regal wedding attire, and a long ivory colored jacket tail, slid off the dragon. He turned fluidly while raising his hand to assist his new bride. Raina took it and slowly fell into his waiting embrace. The billowy sleeves of her white wedding dress caressed her arms and her sleek shape underneath the satiny material lent much to the imagination. They stared into each other's eyes for a long moment.

Zeffeera telepathically projected, *"I will leave you two alone."*

They never took their eyes off of one another and did not respond to Zeffeera. Abawken swept his bride off her feet and walked to the tower. He stopped when he realized there was no door. Raina giggled as she watched her husband's face scrunch in confusion. She then said, "Kali," and the network of vines untwisted and separated, revealing an entry. The human walked through the threshold and stepped into no ordinary tower, but instead an extra-dimensional space that harbored a palace inside. Wood floors with intricate etchings no human or other race could have designed laced the grand entryway. A dual staircase ran on either side and met at the upper level. Plush couches and chairs lined the walls. A sunken bathtub, steam slowly rising from the surface, snared his eyes from perusing any further.

Abawken tried to speak but was interrupted by a kiss. He passionately returned it and walked toward the water. He slowly took the steps leading into the bath, clothes and all, still kissing. As they submerged together, locked in passion, they began unclasping belt buckles and stripped their tunics and robes off.

The next day, Raina gave her husband a tour through the valley, showing him the marvels of her home. Abawken was in awe of how the land and the creatures in it responded to her and now to him. Flowers were more vibrant, the water clearer, the animals attentive, following them in nearby groups. They sat amongst a grove of trees and shared their pasts with one another, delving deeper into the relationship.

As they laughed together, Abawken heard a third voice, giggling, in the thick of the trees. He suddenly stopped and stood in a defensive posture and the mysterious noise went silent.

Raina smiled and dryly said, "Oh, my great protector."

"Did you hear it?"

"Hear what, my love," still playfully smiling.

"Come out, whoever you are!"

Another giggle erupted within the grove. It sounded like a child.

Raina responded, "It is safe, Neph. You can show yourself."

"Who dis dat?" the immature voice asked.

"This is my husband."

"Oh, but whad dee do?"

"His name is Abawken. Come and show yourself."

A creature, an arms-length, darted out from the shadows of the trees and landed on Raina's shoulder. Glasslike wings fluttered from the back of the naked, hairless being. A trail of glitter evaporated in the wake of its path.

"Hid dame di Dawkin?"

"Yes, Neph. He is a human, not elf."

"Dooman?"

Abawken stepped toward her and Neph sprung and hid behind Raina's neck, then peeked over her head, shyly.

"Hello, Master Neph. Pleasure to meet you."

The winged sprite, smiled, and then flew in front of his face, hovering. "You dunny dookin."

Abawken looked at Raina and slightly shrugged. Neph turned toward her and said, "Wherd do go, Daina? I wa donely."

"I am sorry Neph for being away so long, but I am back now. Thank you for taking care of the Valley."

"Do good?"

"Yes, you did great."

Neph instantly skittered back inside the grove, an echoed giggle fading along with the sparkly trail left behind.

Raina snuggled into Abawken's arms, "Neph was gifted to me by the King of Sprites within the Everwood Forest. He has never seen a human before."

"I have seen his kind within the forest you speak."

"You are full of surprises, what else have you done, in your short life?"

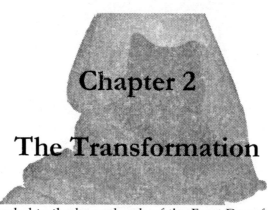

Chapter 2

The Transformation

Jack descended to the lower levels of the Frost Dwarf castle, where tooled stone and ice gave way to natural tunneling. The diamond ring vibrated slightly in his grasp whenever he came to a crossroads requiring a decision. Choose the wrong way and the gem remained still, but when choosing the correct way, it pulsated. The lower he traveled, the colder and more isolated he felt. Shivering, he watched his breath rise in front of him. No matter how deep and dark the tunnels became, he could still somehow see. Jack would look at the gem and then revert back to his surroundings. He understood in his mind that the ring was giving him the ability to see.

The jewelry piece vibrated suddenly, bringing him to an abrupt stop.

"There is only one way to go," he whispered. Confused, he peered back and forth down the corridor. He leaned against the wall and sighed heavily. The diamond pulsed sharply, startling young Jack and almost dropping the valuable item. A single word entered his mind. Jack stood upright and repeated it aloud, "Vemptukai."

Shifting stone resounded abruptly behind him, causing Jack to freeze in pure fright. He slowly turned, terror gripping his young mind, and stared into a strange hallway that wasn't there before. The ring pulsed. Jack took his first step inside and flinched as torches sparked to life along the walls as far as he could see. Cobwebs dangled from the sconces and a strong musty odor assaulted his sense of smell. Each step he took echoed and the hissing sizzle of the flames grew increasingly louder the further he entered.

"Hello," he nervously called out. He jumped when the secret door closed behind him, sealing him inside the corridor. Jack ran back, but it would not open. He clutched the edges and strained to move it. His fingertips turned white in color, his eyes closed tight, and his face grimaced trying to open the door. The breath he held was released along with his struggle. He turned to face the empty corridor. Bridazak's words entered his mind just then and calmed him, *"I tend to think of risk as faith."* This was something he heard from his hero. Jack's heart rate settled a bit and then he began to creep further, following the endless torches.

Hundreds of feet proceeded, until finally, Jack spotted an open room ahead. The light ended at the opening, but shadowy illumination informed him of the chamber beyond. He grabbed one of the ignited torches, sliding it out of the iron sconce and burned away the dusty cobwebs in the entryway.

A thirty-foot circular room came into view, with twelve stone sarcophagi perched against the wall at a slight angle. There were no exits, except for the door behind him that he had cautiously entered. The unmarked graves had layers of dirt covering them. A stone pedestal with etched runes stood at the center of the chamber.

The mysterious hollow voice returned to Jack's mind, now stronger, *"Place the ring upon the altar."*

The frightened, but determined fifteen-year-old, bent on adventure, did as instructed. The clear diamond abruptly flared into a bright light, causing the shadows in the room to elongate, and then slowly fade. Jack investigated his ring, but before he could touch it, a blast of energy shot toward each of the stone lids, forcing Jack to fall to the ground to dodge the beams. He watched from his sitting position as the rays caused the covers to crumble, revealing the corpses within.

Rotted flesh dangled from sunken faces. Arms crossed over their chests lay against tattered clothing that hung from their six-foot frames. Their eyes, that sprang open in unison, were black as night.

Jack scrambled to his feet and clung to the pedestal, trying to distance himself as much as possible from the beings. His shaky voice asked, "Who are you?"

They spoke aloud, their unified voice, haunting and hypnotic, "We are the Twelve." They stood motionless and resolute, arms still crossed over their chests.

"What do you want?"

"We want you, Jack."

"Me? I'm just a boy. I don't understand. Did the ring call you?"

"Not the ring, but your soul. We walked your realm two-thousand years ago until we were not needed any longer and here we have harbored ourselves, entombed for all eternity. New evils have surfaced. Darkened hearts have invaded the land once again, but entrapped by our own demise, we are unable to stand against the threats."

"But what can I do? I don't even know how to fight properly with a sword yet."

"What we offer will not require a blade."

"But why me?"

"Your strength is beyond measure, Jack. We sensed it when you arrived at this place. We used the ring in your possession as a conduit to contact you. Your soul is the strongest we have ever felt before."

"What is it that you want from me?"

"You have been touched by the hand of Adonai and thus your spirit rests in his hands, never to be taken."

"Adonai?" Jack questioned.

"Adonai ha'adonim—The Lord of Lords, God Almighty, Ruler and Creator of All."

Stunned, Jack responded enthusiastically. "You know God?"

"Yes, but it was too late for us. We condemned ourselves to being forever separated from Him."

"But why? What did you do?"

"It matters not, but what does matter, is the choice set before you. Help us or remain a child, learning in your way, until united with God once again."

"Help you how?"

"You can save us, Jack. We have longed to be in the arms of Adonai, but our souls are no longer ours to give to him."

"Who has your soul?"

"We made a deal with darkness. At the time, we were human, living a finite timeline, but we longed to live forever to battle the evil of the land. We were paladins, determined to vanquish all impurities from the realm. We have lived with regret ever since which has been more painful than this tomb we have been trapped in. You are different Jack, someone to be trusted, someone we can trust. It is not by chance you are here. You have a calling on your life for greatness and we want to help you achieve this calling of yours. Will you help us, Jack?"

"What is it you need me to do?"

"We need you to seek out an ancient artifact, the Mirror of Lost Souls. Once procured we will need it returned to us here."

Jack chuckled, "I don't know, maybe this is too big for me. I don't have the experience."

"We will bestow upon you powers. Each of us will gift you a strength; what we give will forever change you."

"Powers? What kind of powers?"

"Strength, knowledge, wisdom, speed, endurance, and more. Jack, do not solely be enticed by these gifts. Your transformation will be severe and beyond legend of anything the realm of Ruauck-El has ever seen before. The land is groaning for what we offer, but you will not be able to go back to being a child."

"You mean, I will get older also?" There was fear in his question but also a tinge of excitement deep within.

"Twelve years, one for each power granted by the Twelve, added to your life. It saddens us to burden you with the loss of your childhood. We will not be angered if you choose to ignore our plea."

Jack paused, thinking over his life thus far. He no longer had his family. Bridazak was gone, and he longed to contribute more in helping those in need. Jack's mind raced. Images of his father flashed in his mind and he heard his words ring in his ears, *"Stop thinking, just do it!"*

Softness lacked in his childhood home, his father's form of upbringing was harsh; having to raise his son alone, amongst the military might of the fallen King Manasseh. Jack had no memories of his mother, who had died when he was very young.

Bridazak, his hero, then entered his mind. The ordakian had ensured him that his father was safe when he encountered them the first time. How he cherished that day at Black Rock Castle and playing a small part in helping them. He just wanted to be like his heroes. They inspired him to be a better person, simply by being who they were. His insides churned as the choice loomed bigger and bigger at each passing moment, a decision that would change his destiny forever.

He peered up and said confidently, "I will help you."

A silver, engraved chalice materialized on top of the pedestal next to the diamond ring. An eerie feeling encompassed young Jack. The cracking of bones resounded around him, snapping his focus away. Each resident of the ancient crypts woke from their slumber and took their first rigid steps toward the center. Dust billowed from their bodies as they each extended their right arm to grasp the decorative grail. Jack slunk down to dodge the crowding undead. Unintelligible words were chanted in unison as Jack watched, wide-eyed, unable to move.

"Sheomin theokvoo kaminval. Sheomin theokvoo kaminval." They repeated the phrase over and over. Jack found himself mouthing the words himself as it continued, but caught himself, stopping abruptly. He refocused on the fallen paladins of long ago, and once again the haunting words that took shape, mesmerized him. Entranced by the melodic voices, his lips began to follow along until finally he spoke them in conjunction with the undead beings. "Sheomin theokvoo kaminval." Jack's shaky voice strengthened upon the repeated utterance of the words.

A deep red, almost black, viscous substance, appeared inside the chalice each time the phrase was spoken. The liquid rose inside the silver container, slowly reaching the brim. Just before spilling over the edges, the chanting stopped. Eleven decaying hands let go and backed away.

The twelfth soulless warrior turned to Jack holding the chalice out toward him. "Take it."

"What is this?"

"It is your destiny, young Jack. Drink and be filled with power."

Jack whispered, "My destiny."

He reached for the cup, hands trembling. A strange warmth raced through his hands when he touched the cold silver. The paladin assisted Jack in bringing it closer toward his lips. Everything slowed for Jack as the surreal moment locked him in place. The drink was now almost upon his lips. Jack smelled the strong scent of iron mixed with the distinct odor of blood. It jolted him back to reality but before he could move away the undead paladin grabbed hold of the back of young Jack's head to hold him in place. Jack tried to resist but it was futile. He gasped as a tendril formed from the swirling liquid and then formed into the shape of a spear. Jack could do nothing but look upon it in horror and then it shot into his mouth.

The cup fell and clanked loudly against the stone floor, rolling to a stop, as Jack stumbled backwards, falling to the floor, gagging. His chest heaved forward as the blood from the Twelve ran its course through the boy's body. He screamed in agony as the tendril now laced through his veins and could be visibly seen through his outer skin, branching out in all directions. Dark splotches, like a disease, came and went on his skin, pulsing like the rhythm of a heartbeat. The gurgled screams ended and soon Jack settled and lay motionless, eyes closed.

"Awake, young Jack," the raspy voice said.

Eyes, black as night, shot open. Jack sat upright and slowly surveyed the room. He held up his hands in front of his face inspecting them. Jack's fingers were numb as he slowly wiggled them. His vision was blurred and still adjusting through the transformation but he watched his fingers elongate and his fingernails protrude into sharp blades. A sharp pain stung his left side and shot down his leg. It didn't stop there as his entire body was racked and a blood curdling scream echoed through the chamber as he convulsed. Jack arched his back in agony, yelling for it to stop.

"It is too late, young Jack. You are now the Vemptukai."

Jack lunged forward baring his teeth. Two prominent fangs elongated on the upper row as he hissed in anger. Not a speck of white could be seen within his pitch black eyes. Bones cracked and popped inside his body. Excruciating pain brought a grimace to his face and more screaming.

The Twelve slowly retreated, returning to their former resting places, standing at attention within their lidless sarcophagi.

Jack settled onto his back, a single twitch sparked here and there, until finally no movement came from the newly formed adult. His clothes were stretched and torn along the seams. No breath came from his body as he stared without blinking at the ceiling above. He was entranced by the visions in his mind.

Images of lost memories flooded his thoughts, not his own memories, but the Twelve, as each member introduced themselves to Jack and each of them anointed him with their specific power. The first was the known leader of the Twelve, *I am Ferum Saracen and have granted you the strength of giants of legends past.* The face of the paladin, well groomed dark beard and mustache and perfectly combed hair, slowly faded away and was replaced with a new warrior.

"I am Obier the Bishop and I impart the wisdom of an immortal." The tips of his red bushy mustache descended below his chin and his left eyebrow raised high on his forehead.

"I am Ganelon."

"Rinaldo."

"Maugris."

One after the other granted him the twelve powers, one from each member, until there were no more to give. Speed, sword, magic, hand-to-hand combat, knowledge, royalty, endurance, vision, illusion, and armor were all passed onto the new creation lying motionless in perfect stasis.

The Twelve said at once, "Rise, Vemptukai."

Chapter 3

Where Out Thou Trillius?

Trillius moved hastily down the dwarven cut corridor. Heavily armed Frost Dwarf guards were placed strategically along the way, nestled in hidden alcoves. This was the King's hall before entering his private war chamber. Trillius kept his head down as he passed the sentries who glared at him as if he were guilty of something.

Muffled conversation echoed from the ice covered door ajar at the end of the hallway. Firelight shadows cascaded out of the crack. The largest Frost Dwarves the gnome had ever seen stood at attention at the entrance. One pushed the door open as Trillius zipped past.

The gnome entered a group of arguing dwarves and scuttled to the side in hopes that no one spotted him. The Frost Dwarf King sat at the head of the ice carved table, hand on his chin, contemplating and listening to his arguing kin. Trillius had grown accustom to the stench of dwarves while spending weeks within the castle, but in this chamber, it reeked of something else he couldn't quite place his nose on. Not only was the smell different, but a strange foreboding within sharpened his senses to be on the alert. He listened in on the dwarves sitting at the table as he leaned his back against the wall, uncertain as to why he'd been allowed in this meeting to begin with.

"While the Horn Kings of the West and East are distracted we need to strike!"

"Nay, we should wait and hold our position. We are stronger as a solid force, but if we move out then we are more vulnerable."

"Vulnerable, my dwarven ass! We strike now and show them what we dwarves are made of—iron!

"You speak of iron, yet you hid in the mountains like goatals scared of the lion."

"Step outside and I will show you scared."

A hovering hammer formed of ice suddenly materialized at the center of the table and slammed down, cracking the frozen top, ending the arguing sharply. All attention turned to Morthkin, King of the Frost Dwarves, Ruler of Te Sond, Protector of Guul-Fen. His blue, ice crystalized skin shimmered and his eyes blazed a brilliant orange before fading back to the normal soft, blue hue. "I have sat here for the last hour, listening to your endless squabbles, but none of you have shown the respect of the one sitting at this table who brought down the North Horn King with nothing but a handful of the bravest warriors. Not one of you has stopped to ask his opinion. You came to my kingdom in search of hope and yet you fall back on old wounds. The times have changed and now we need to unite more than ever. Old words need to be buried in the old world. Good people suffer outside these walls as we argue. Our strength comes from unity and from a single voice." Morthkin paused, looked hard at everyone around the table and beyond and then said, "It is time that I invoke Giimtock."

Trillius saw this single dwarven word bring uncomfortable shifting of seats at the table. Eight dwarves looked around the room while two bearded clan stared into each other's eyes. Sitting across from King Morthkin was King El'Korr of the Hammergold clan. Trillius noticed the ever so slight nod these two burly members exchanged.

"Agreed," El'Korr responded.

A dark haired dwarf, sitting closest to El'Korr stood, "Giimtock has not been invoked since the Unknown Age and can only be broken through death of the one that is chosen."

"Bailo speaks truth," another spoke.

"Silence!" Morthkin stood. "It must be done. Giimtock has been called and there is no going back. On this day, there will be one Dwarven King and one voice to unite all dwarves."

El'Korr stood and slowly walked to the fireplace with his arms locked behind his back. A heavy fur wrapped over his shoulders and clasped around his neck as a cloak. "Sound the call and let all dwarves cast their vote and let it be done."

King Morthkin joined El'Korr by the fire while the others exited the room to inform all the clans.

El'Korr whispered, "Are you ready for such a change?"

Morthkin placed his hand on El'Korr's shoulder and they both stared into the yellow and orange flames.

Trillius spotted Dulgin approaching him from across the room.

Dulgin stated, "Any luck?"

Trillius raised his eyebrows, "Luck? Please, Dulgin, I do not require luck. I have skill."

"So you didn't find him."

Trillius paused and then his prideful stance slinked back, "I have not. I have searched high and low for the lad and fear he is not within this walled fortress."

"Where could Jack have gone off to? It doesn't make one bit of dwarven sense."

The meeting chamber had cleared, all except Trillius, Dulgin, Xan, and El'Korr.

King El'Korr said, "Trillius, what have you found out about Jack?"

"Not much. He has literally vanished, but being a boy with no experience, my instinct says something else."

"Like what?" Dulgin asked.

"I believe Jack was taken."

"Taken by whom and why?" El'Korr said.

"What someone would want with a teenage human child I have not the foggiest idea. Whoever took him, they are very good. There are no signs indicating any struggle inside his room and I've asked hundreds of patrons inside the keep and not one of them have seen him. With so many, someone should have witnessed something."

"On the contrary, it might be easier for someone to come in unnoticed due to so many," Xan pointed out.

"A valued point, Xan, but the question comes back to why Jack?"

King El'Korr took in a deep breath and exhaled, "Keep searching. I'm tired of losing people."

Trillius spoke before they disbanded, "I have another thought."

"Yes, what is it?"

"Perhaps young Jack fell into the hands of goblins."

El'Korr looked at each of them as this thought elicited many variables inside their minds. "Goblins? The horde is back in their hole where they belong."

"Yes, but perhaps he wandered to the lower levels and a small band of rovers captured him."

"Impossible. Frost Dwarf sentries are posted at every corner leading below. One human child would not be able to circumvent them. Besides, we can't go into the horde on mere guesses. Report back when you find something of substance." King El'Korr left the room. Guards closed the door behind him.

Trillius and Xan stared at the ground in contemplation.

Dulgin blared, "Well, we can't be finding the young lad staring at our feet."

The red-bearded dwarf opened the door and ushered each of them out. Xan exited first, but Dulgin halted Trillius, grabbing his shoulder. The dwarf leaned in, "I am uncertain as to why you have suddenly taken an interest in young Jack these last couple of weeks. Be certain that my dwarven eye is watching you."

Trillius peeked at Dulgin and saw the dwarf's greyish-green eye protruding a little further out to emphasize his point. "I only wish for Jack's safety. The boy is my friend more so than yourself, be assured of that, One-Eye." Trillius pulled away harshly and exited.

Trillius had literally searched every crevice of this fortress, even the parts of the castle forbidden for anyone else to enter and he had a few trinkets to prove it. He was in a portion of the keep that had few souls and he found it to be a place of solitude for him to think through his thoughts. *"What are you doing here, Trillius? Is this about a diamond ring or is it about Jack?"* He shook his head trying to get the thoughts out of his mind. He growled in anger and kicked a loose rock down the shadowy hallway while saying out loud, "Dammit Jack, where are you?"

He pushed his wispy hair from his silver eyes, leaned his back against the wall, and slid down. He let his head slump as he brought his arms to rest on his knees. Hours passed.

The gnome shook himself from his half-slumber as a distinct odor reached his senses. The same smell he encountered at the dwarven gathering of leaders. He stood and then scuttled to each shadow along the torch lit hallway. Trillius was certain he was being followed. This could be his chance after weeks to discover who was behind Jack's abduction.

Trillius thought, *"It had to be about the diamond ring, but why take Jack, and now why follow me? They must not know who I am."*

He scampered to the turn at an intersection and darted around the corner. Trillius quickly hid within one of the many alcoves the Frost Dwarves had crafted throughout their kingdom to strategically position troops to lay in wait. Whoever was following him would soon be revealed. It was time to unmask this mystery. He slowly pulled a dagger from behind his back.

Trillius stilled himself and his thoughts slowed as well, *"A little closer. That's it. You are about to encounter the Great Trillius."*

A single lit torch in the corridor fluttered slightly. Trillius slowed his breathing. He blocked out the sight of the flickering flame. One more second and the mysterious person would be under his blade and the culprit would be revealed. He sensed the presence as he pressed closer to the side wall within the alcove.

Before the assailant came into the light, the torch snuffed out with a sharp gust of wind, casting the hall into total darkness. Trillius' eyes adjusted and he shot out into the cold corridor with his dagger leading the charge, but there was nothing.

A haunting whisper echoed and reached the Gnome's ears, "Trillius." The 's' extended into the air as a hiss.

"Who are you? Where is Jack?" Trillius demanded.

Again, the whisper returned, but further away, "Trillius."

"I have powerful friends. Return Jack unharmed." There was no response and Trillius in desperation yelled, "Don't mess with me!"

A third calling of his name barely audible, dropped like breadcrumbs leading the gnome. Trillius slid along the wall in pursuit and finally reached an intersection where light mingled with the darkness in the hallway. He halted, waiting to hear a sound to alert him which way to go, but nothing came forth. Trillius took in a deep breath and exhaled, "Dammit."

He thought, *"I know this trick and I am not going to be the hunted."* Trillius retreated back the way he came.

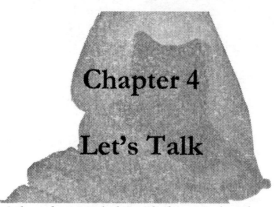

Chapter 4

Let's Talk

Trillius' thoughts swirled inside his mind as he unlatched the door to his room. He snagged the loose string he had placed within the jam before it fell to the ground, bringing him confidence the kidnapper had not gone into his abode. The gnome smirked as he entered and closed the door, latching it locked. A red glow of dying embers in the fireplace cast a dim light.

He unclasped his cloak and threw it upon a chair in the corner. Trillius made his way to grab a piece of wood from a small pile on the left and tossed it into the fireplace. A flash of invigorated sparks rose as the new log crashed into the charred debris. Trillius knelt down and used a fire poker to move the embers closer to the wood. Flame soon sprouted and licked away at the fresh food it received. He set the prod to the side and warmed his hands.

Trillius sat on the fur rug and laid down, clasping his hands behind his head. He remembered kissing Rozelle at this very spot and sighed.

He said aloud, "I need to get out of this place."

Just then his poker stick toppled. The ping of the iron on the ground startled him, making him sit up.

Trillius spoke as he let out a held breath, "Aren't you a little jumpy?" He stood to retrieve the item, continuing to talk to himself, "What the hell are you doing here, Trillius? Since when did you become an investigator? There is no reward in this place."

The same distinct odor hit his senses before he heard the shuffling behind him. He immediately spun with the iron poker in one hand and his dagger in the other. A figure sat at the far edge of his bed. The shifting, sparse light of the fire shadowed the being in front of him.

"How did you get in here?" Trillius asked.

A deep voice, with a strange echoing reverberation, replied, "Is that how you greet an old friend?"

"I don't have friends. You best tell me what you want before I skewer you."

"Trillius," it said, trilling out the s.

"It's you? Where is Jack?"

"Jack is..." he paused.

"You better not have hurt him."

"You care for this Jack, don't you?"

"I care to find out that he is alive, and he will be returned unharmed."

"It is difficult to answer if he is alive or unharmed."

"Seems pretty simple to me. Yes Trillius, Jack is fine," the gnome mocked.

"Yes, Jack is fine." The figure did not move and remained at the edge of the bed.

"Unless the boy is some long lost relative of a rich noble that none of us are aware of then why take him?"

"Take. Interesting word choice."

"Yes, stolen, kidnapped, taken. Why did you take him?"

"He went willingly."

"That is not true."

"Truth is what you seek and truth I have given. Jack knows what he wants and he has chosen his path."

"Path? You speak as if you know him, but you don't."

"And what does the Great Trillius know of the young boy in search of his destiny, in search of himself, in search of someone to care about him?"

"That is between him and me." Trillius slowly backed toward the wood pile, placed the iron rod down and grabbed another log, placing it gently into the fire.

"You will need one more in order to get the right lighting," the being stated.

Trillius grabbed another and placed it on top at an angle, all the while keeping his eyes on the mystery person. "What are you? You don't sound human."

"No? Perhaps I sound orc or goblin?"

"No, more like a demon, I would say."

"Demon? That is a bold statement, Trillius."

"Are you a demon?"

"To some, perhaps."

The light in the room increased as the fire strengthened. Trillius could see the faint outline more clearly and noticed bare feet with torn beige pants that stretched tightly around his calves, frayed at the ends.

"You look human."

The brightness of the room spread and Trillius was able to finally see the eyes. Two prominent colors, grey and red, swirled like a whirlpool around the black pupils. Shoulder length hair, brown with silver streaks, fell slightly in his face. Strange tattooed markings were laced around his eyes and forehead, but the face was oddly familiar to Trillius. He felt as if he knew this person from somewhere in his past. The distinct swirling eyes he knew though—a vampire, Romann de Beaux had those same swirling effects. This was not Romann, however. He waived the thoughts of the swashbuckling leader of Pirate's Belly away as he noticed the tunic this one wore was shredded around the arms and neck and fit snugly around the chest, many sizes too small. *What is this thing?* Trillius thought. *It is different. Not a vampire I had seen before, though I had seen only one other. I don't recall the markings on its face. Those I would remember distinctly. Where have I seen this?*

"Do you recognize me, Trillius?"

"Have I seen you in court?"

The human stood, towering over Trillius. Arms and broad chest were one flex away from ripping the rest of the tunic away. The skin color of the human was a strange ashen grey. He took a step closer to Trillius. The gnome reacted by bringing his weapon up to bare.

"Not in court, Trillius. Do not be afraid."

"I'm not afraid. I'm the one with a weapon here, remember? You should be afraid," Trillius said, while his eyes darted to the exit of the room.

"I can feel your blood racing." The human stretched its bulky arms out wide and took another step closer.

The mystery man suddenly changed his voice to that of a young boy, "It's me, Trillius." He stepped closer to the bright light of the fire and the gnome gasped at what he saw.

"Jack?"

"In the flesh," he bowed, arms still out wide. His swirling eyes returned to his normal grey coloring.

Trillius scrunched his face in confusion, his head slightly tilted. "How is...," he fumbled, "What happened to you?"

"I met some new friends."

"Don't mock me. This is a ruse," Trillius shook his head in disbelief.

"I assure you that I am quite real. Touch my hand." He stepped forward and extended his hand.

Trillius scooted a step backward, "Get away from me you shape shifter. Return the young boy at once."

"I realize this is a lot to take in, but we have work to be done. I am Jack."

"It's not possible."

"I have found my destiny, Trillius. I wanted to find my place in this realm. Bridazak has fallen, my father waits for me in heaven, and you were the only one who spoke to me when I needed someone most."

"How do you know these things?"

"Because I'm Jack."

"What delusional creature are you?" Trillius suddenly ran for the door. The human materialized instantly in front of him, stopping his hasty exit.

The twisted being said, "Your friend, the dragon Dal-Draydian, gave you information about hidden treasures."

"How do you know this?"

Jack raised his voice and the booming tone forced Trillius to step backward, "Answer me!"

"Yes, yes he did. Why?" Trillius cowered.

"Have you heard of the Mirror of Lost Souls?"

"Yes."

"Can you take me to it?"

"Not without proof of who you are."

Jack glared at Trillius, "So be it." The creature vanished and reappeared behind the gnome in a flash. He grabbed Trillius' head, hands covered his ears, and spoke an ancient dialect, "Vee-noosh Cal-eem."

Trillius' body began to spasm, flailing about, but his head remained secured in the hands of Jack. Visions pummeled the gnome's brain. Trillius watched what happened to the young boy, watched the diamond ring leading him deeper into the dark, watched his transformation, and then it ended. Jack released him.

Trillius stumbled away, leaning against the wall trying to catch his breath.

Jack said, "Now you see the truth. I am the Vemptukai."

Trillius slumped down and placed his back to the stone. He peered up and said, "A vampire? I don't understand. You were just a child and now look at yourself. How do I get myself into these situations?" He shook his head. "Rozelle is going to kill me."

"Are you ready to leave?"

"Leave? Now?"

"What are we waiting for?"

"Just give me a moment to think. You blasted my brain with disturbing images that I would like to forget."

"You know where the mirror is. Let us think on the way."

"You see, that is the problem. I know it exists but I don't know the exact location. Dal-Draydian gave me all kinds of images of great trinkets across Ruauck-El, but he never gave me directions."

"Then I will find it on my own." Jack's body turned into vapor.

"Wait!"

Jack morphed back and stared at Trillius.

"I have a proposition," Trillius grinned.

"Speak."

"There is an item that can help me, I mean us, find what you are looking for. I require you to assist me in getting it and then we can retrieve your mirror."

"What item?"

"We can talk along the way, but first let's get you some clothes. You look horrible, now that you are all grown. We need to get you cleaned up—make you a presentable vampire to meet some old friends of mine."

"You don't have friends."

Trillius smiled mischievously as his plan unraveled inside his mind and thought to himself, *I am the most blessed gnome to walk the realm of Ruauck-El. The God of Luck is truly with me.*

Chapter 5

The Truth

The tan, muscular human glistened as the waterfall splashed around him. He stroked his long, shoulder-length, light-brown hair back under the torrent. A misty vapor surrounded him and the sun reflected off the finite droplets casting scintillating rainbow colors swirling about. The water roared overhead and thundered below, as it relentlessly slammed into the large boulders under his feet.

Amongst the noise of the crashing fluid, he suddenly heard the whisper of God trickling into his consciousness, *"Help him."*

Abawken closed his eyes and focused, answering in his mind, *"Who, my Lord?"*

A flash of Bridazak hit his thoughts and Abawken's eyes sprang open.

Raina splashed water below him in the turquoise pool and playfully called, "I'm waiting."

Abawken stared at her for a long moment, unable to shake the image of his lost friend.

"What is it?" Raina asked.

"Nothing," he finally managed to say.

"Your wife calls upon her husband. Why are you not by my side?" she toyed.

Abawken half-smiled, "Forgive my manners." He dove into the pool below and glided under water. She wrapped her arms around him as he came to the surface and they embraced in a passionate kiss.

A sprite with glass-like wings fluttered around the couple. They heard the beating wings, but still continued to kiss, ignoring it. The creature asked, "Why do dat?"

They slowly parted lips, gazing into each other's eyes while resting their foreheads against one another.

"Daina, did dear me?"

"Yes, Neph, I heard you, but I don't want to talk right now. Go play."

"Dokay, dut why do dat ding?"

"What? Kiss?"

"Des."

"Because we love each other."

"Dwhat dis dove?"

"Love is when you care for someone so much that they become part of who you are."

"Oh, dis Dawkin dow Daina."

Raina giggled, "No, Neph. Abawken is still Abawken, but we are now connected like you and me."

Neph lurched backward and yelped, "Dwee don't diss!"

"I know we don't kiss. We can talk later about this, Neph."

"Dokay, dut me don't dunderstand." The sprite shrugged, soared away, and darted into the tree grove surrounding the majestic pool.

Raina refocused on her man, "Where were we?"

Abawken beamed with joy and said, "You are good with Neph."

She raised one eye-brow. Abawken quickly answered her confused look, "You will be a great mother of our child."

She then narrowed her eyes. Abawken quickly said, "I mean, when we decide to have children you will be a great mother."

"Abawken, we have a lot to figure out in nine-months time. You sound as if I'm going to raise our child alone."

"What do you mean nine-months time?"

She smiled.

Feeling suddenly overwhelmed, Abawken sputtered, "Are…are we…I mean, are you…?"

"Yes," she nodded, "I'm with child. Our child."

Abawken's knees buckled under the water. The buoyancy was the only thing that kept him standing. He was in shock and then wonderment soon befell him. Pure joy gripped his heart, soul, and mind. He suddenly grabbed Raina and lifted her high up into the air exposing her body half-way out of the water and twirled her about. She laughed with him. He slowed and brought her back down.

He said, "You blessed me by taking me as your husband and now have fulfilled my final dream of becoming a father. I am overwhelmed, my love."

Again she smiled and did not say a word.

Abawken looked at her and then quizzically asked, "How do you know you are pregnant? We have only been married for a short time."

"Because I asked God to reveal it to me. He gave me a vision of his birth."

"His birth?"

"Yes, your son."

In a shocked whisper Abawken managed to say, "I'm having a son?"

Raina smiled and nodded. "Are you pleased?"

"Pleased? I am beyond words." Abawken slowly reached out and touched her belly. Raina kissed him and he kissed her back.

Just then a flash of Bridazak entered Abawken's mind, jarring him backwards.

Raina asked, "What is it?"

"It's nothing. I am overwhelmed with joy, tis all."

"No, you saw something. Speak."

"It's..."

"It's what?"

"It's Bridazak."

Raina pushed away slightly and a serious demeanor encompassed her, "What did you see?"

Abawken pulled her closer to try and resume what was interrupted, but Raina forcefully pulled away, speaking her words slowly and authoritatively, "What did you see?"

"His face surrounded by darkness, but it was only an instant, nothing more."

His wife looked away, contemplating his words.

Abawken continued, "I also felt the impression that I needed to help him, but that is impossible."

Raina swam to the shore and Abawken treaded after her.

"Raina, what is it? Do you know something?" he asked.

She climbed out of the water, her skin glistening as she grabbed her robe and put it on. Raina turned and stared intently at Abawken who had followed her to the edge of the pool, "There is something you need to know. Something I discounted when it was originally revealed to me."

The tan fighter exited the pool and gently grabbed her shoulders, "What is it?"

"Your Bridazak purposefully fell into the vortex at the Chamber of Cleansing on that day."

"What? Why and how did you come by this information?"

"Xandahar had a brief exchange with the ordakian. Nothing verbal, but Xan told me that Bridazak mouthed the words 'I will be back'. Xan believes that Bridazak was trying to save Manasseh."

"Save him? It doesn't make sense."

"I agree, but now you are given a vision and an impression. It is not a coincidence."

"It must be just my subconscious. He is gone, Raina."

"Gone where? You of all people shouldn't discount these leadings. God led you to Bridazak and you travelled for almost a year before finding him."

"Are you saying that Bridazak is still alive?"

"That, I do not know."

Abawken said, "I need to talk with your brother about this."

Raina looked on her husband lovingly, placed her hands on either cheek, lightly caressing him and said, "It appears our honeymoon has come to an end. Let us return to the real world and see what has become of it."

"We? You should stay—"

Raina cut him off, "Stay? You think that I am bound to be your housewife and take care of our child in seclusion?"

"I wasn't saying that. I just wanted you and our child to be safe."

She chuckled, "My dear husband, I am the Sheldeen Elf mystic. Everyone is much safer when I'm around."

He smiled, "I love you."

"I know," she said.

Chapter 6

We Found Him

"**W**hat in orc hell is going on around here?" Dulgin shouted, downing another mug of ale, the liquid dribbling down his beard.

Spilf kept his head low at the table they were sitting at while his dwarven friend walked to the keg to get a refill. Xan grabbed a bottle of wine and emptied the remainder into his wooden cup and then sat next to the ordakian.

"Spilf, you remember seeing Jack at the wedding, right?"

"We have already gone over this, Xan. Jack ran away, plain and simple, just like Bridazak," his voice trailed off.

"Snap out of it, Stubby," Dulgin charged.

Spilf planted his hands on the table firmly and stood, "Why? What does it matter? Maybe I should just go back!"

There was silence as Xan and Dulgin exchanged a glance as they knew what their hurting friend meant—going back to heaven. Each of them thought about this moment in their life. They envisioned the bronze dragon, Zeffeera, punching through the hole of Kerrith Ravine and entering a new world. It was like a rebirth to them when they had entered heaven's domain those many months ago. A moment hadn't gone by that each of them wished to be there. Xan took a large swig of his wine and retrieved another bottle from a crisscross rack along the wall. The elf brought it back to the table and while pouring he said, "What about your parents, Spilf? You just found each other. I realize you are in pain, we all are in pain, but Bridazak would want us to move forward."

"Move forward? Is that what we are calling it these days, Xan? Let me ask you, why haven't you moved on yet?"

"What are you inferring?"

"I have never seen you as quiet or distant as you have been these passed weeks. You among all of us have been drinking quite a bit more and even in private I have seen of late. Is that your version of moving forward?"

Deep down Xan had been harboring a dark secret from everyone. He role-played scenario after scenario of what would happen if he told his friends sitting before him the truth of what had happened at the Chamber of Cleansing. He found the numbing effect of the drink to lessen the sting of the truth he carried. His thoughts weighed heavily and he battled his heart and mind on whether he should tell them that the fallen hero, Bridazak, might still be alive in the Underworld. Truth can be dangerous when wielded incorrectly and it has killed many of men. All the realities of Ruauck-El, the foundations of history, spoke to him that Bridazak was dead. The ordakian being alive was an impossibility, but something deep inside of him raged to differ.

Xan resigned himself and said, "Each of us is processing in our own way, Spilf."

"Are you going to talk about my drinking, Stubby?" Dulgin said. "Cause I haven't been drinking enough."

"Let us return back to the subject of Jack and now Trillius disappearing," Xan said.

"Good riddance to the gnome. There is no loss there," Dulgin growled.

"It is no coincidence that days ago Trillius was here looking for Jack and now he is suddenly gone. Something is clearly amiss and King El'Korr has charged us to find out what has happened."

"Great, my brother gets all the war glory, bashing heads, while we get to Gnome-sit."

"We need to find him first before we can 'Gnome-sit'."

"That's why we have Stubby, Xan. He knows the way this Trillius thinks, don't ya?" Dulgin smacked the ordakian on the shoulder.

Spilf stood up and walked to the door, opened it, and left while muttering, "Yeah, guess that is all I'm good at now."

Xan took a step toward the door, but stopped and sighed heavily.

Dulgin said, "It's no use chasing after him. This is a deep wound that won't heal overnight. He will come around. Finding Trillius and Jack is the perfect distraction."

"I hope you are right."

"C'mon, this Dwarven Ale is lonely and needs company." Dulgin nudged Xan to come back to the table. Xan downed his wine and gave the dwarf a half-smile.

"That's the spirit, Elfy!"

They sat and drank together.

Xan asked after a while, "Do you think it might be possible to survive the Underworld?"

Dulgin nearly choked mid-swig, "What are you talking about, ya blundering fool? It's impossible."

"Yeah, I keep hearing that, but what if God made it possible?"

"Spit it out, Xan. You've been holding onto something for weeks and this must be it."

"I have been waiting for the right moment."

"Well, there is no right moment when it comes to dwarves. We don't take kindly to surprises. We drink and speak what needs to be spoken." Dulgin took another gulp.

"I believe Bridazak is still alive," Xan blurted.

Dulgin sprayed his drink in shock. "What?"

Xan slowly wiped his face but stared stoically at the dwarf.

"You are serious about this? What makes you think of such a tall tale?" Dulgin took another swig.

"Because Bridazak told me."

Again, Dulgin spewed his drink. "What? When?"

Xan wiped his face and answered, "In the Chamber of Cleansing, just before he fell."

"Why didn't you tell us before?"

"Because I didn't want any one of us to take that leap of faith and chase after him."

Dulgin glared and nodded, "That makes sense. I'm sure Stubby would have dived off the edge to save him. Heck, I might've done it myself."

"I thought the same and weighed it best to wait."

"Well, what did he tell you?" Dulgin lifted his cup to take another drink, but Xan held his arm.

"I don't wish to waste anymore of your drink, nor do I wish for another ale bath."

"Bath or not, you best be speaking. What did he say?"

"Bridazak mouthed the words, 'I will be back'." There was a

pause.

"That's it? That is all he said?"

"I had to read his lips and I'm certain that is what he said. He chose to fall into the pit."

"He chose to?"

"Yes, and while he battled Manasseh, I could tell he was resisting killing him. They spoke to one another, but I could not hear their conversation. It was as if he…"

"As if he what?"

"As if God had instructed him to do it."

"God? Why on Ruauck-El would He do that? That don't make one bit of dwarven sense."

"I agree, but if he is alive down there, then perhaps we can help from this side to aid him."

"Aid him, how?"

"I have heard of an item that can look into the Underworld."

"What item?"

"It is called Akar's Looking Glass."

"Akar? That be an old tale to scare children. Who told you about this?"

"Raina."

"She only told you to point out that it is impossible since it doesn't exist."

"How do you know?"

"My dah searched for the legendary item to help him find a mountain."

"Just because he didn't find it doesn't make it non-existent. I think Trillius might know where it is located."

"Trillius? That gnome doesn't know anything but trouble."

"Granted, but his time with Dal-Draydian gave him insight into lost treasures. Trillius mentioned a couple times the blue dragon's knowledge, and that he imparted bits of this knowledge into his own mind."

"Wonderful. We have a thief that loves treasure more than himself now gone missing."

Xan placed his drink down, "Let us find Spilf and start our search for Trillius again, but let us keep our additional information to ourselves for the time being. Spilf is in a fragile situation."

Dulgin downed his drink and slammed it on the table, "I don't like keeping secrets. I'll let you tell him and if you don't then I will."

Xan exhaled a held breath and said, "Agreed. He will be informed soon."

"Spilf wouldn't agree with soon, but I will follow your lead."

"Thank you Dulgin. Shall we find Spilf?"

"Why not? I'm ready to get out of here anyway. I'm sure we will find something that I can bury my axe into along the way."

Xan chuckled but caught his breath when the door behind him suddenly burst open. Spilf, exhausted, chest heaving deep intakes of air, slumped against the frame and said, "We found him!"

Dulgin stood, "Found who?"

"Trillius."

"Where?" Xan asked while standing.

"In the caves outside the Chamber of Cleansing." Spilf still fought to catch his breath.

"In the caves? What is he doing out there?"

"I don't know. A Frost Dwarf patrol spotted him. They gave pursuit but couldn't find him. They said it looked like he was heading for the west exit."

"The west? That is where Raina teleported us in," Xan stated.

"Well, he can't get far. I don't think he is a mountain climber," Dulgin said.

Spilf suggested, "Maybe he is on the trail of finding Jack."

"Gather your equipment and weapons and meet me at the Great Door of Morthkin leading out to the caves beyond," Xan said.

"Everything I need is right here," Dulgin said as he grabbed his father's axe and rested it on his shoulder.

The three friends met at the massive double-door. The iron portal, layered in melded gold, formed intricate designs and images of dwarves holding shields. White gold, emblazoning the trim of the pictures, brought an aura of power to the depictions. The Great Door of Morthkin was open as Frost Dwarf patrols came and went, protecting the outer area and the Chamber of Cleansing, which held the precious Sky Diamond.

"Lead on, Stubby," Dulgin said.

Spilf entered first into the frigid cavern and heard the echoes of armored Dwarves marching through the jagged complex. The blue ice glowed from the power of the Sky Diamond and the strange phenomena of the Frost Dwarves' strength shone through.

They traversed the gigantic stalactites and the ice encrusted boulders until finally reaching the snake-like tunnel that led to the outside.

"We will eventually come out to an open platform overlooking the Shield Mountains," Xan stated. "I have prepared a spell that will aid us in our search."

"Cast away, Elfy."

Xan closed his eyes, raised his arms high and spoke the incantation, "Sheek-nok-vo-tu-kee-omin." He opened his eyes as he finished and lowered his arms back to his side.

Dulgin waited and then said, "Did I miss something? I don't see what your spell accomplished."

"There," Xan pointed. "Do you see it?"

Dulgin and Spilf looked down the cavern entrance and then spotted tracks glowing and becoming more vibrant.

"Well done, Elfy. I'm impressed."

"Thank you," Xan smiled.

Spilf said, "Why are there two sets of tracks?"

The others looked and also spotted the larger prints. They walked closer to investigate.

"These look human sized," Spilf announced, while bending down to feel the lip of the barely crushed ice.

"Human? Could it be Jack?"

"Nay, too big. This is an adult."

"Enough talk, let's find out who the gnome-skull is traveling with," Dulgin said as he walked deeper into the tunnel.

The glowing tracks eventually led to the icy ledge overlooking the Guul-Fen Valley. Howling bone-chilling air whipped around them as they peered over the edge. A light flurry of snow swirled about them.

"The tracks end here!" Xan yelled above the wind.

"Did they jump?" Dulgin asked.

"They are gone. C'mon, let's head back before we freeze to death out here," Spilf said as he wrapped his cloak around himself.

"Do you have any other spells, Elfy?"

"No, nothing that will assist us any further."

"What else can we do?"

Xan stared out into the open air beyond, "We need to find Rozelle. She might know where Trillius is going."

"Going? That is assuming he was able to get down from here," Spilf indicated the drop off.

"Trillius is with someone and whoever it is must have some ability to fly or feather fall to the valley floor below. What other options do we have?"

Dulgin said, "Let's find the druid gnome and give her the wonderful news of her misbehaving boyfriend."

Chapter 7

The Underworld

The gurgling pockets of mud and sludge enclosed in various craters went on as far as Bridazak could see which wasn't very far in the dark realm of the Underworld. The glow that emanated from the ordakian abruptly ended twenty-feet from him in all directions. A shield of black encompassed his aura. Bridazak had torn a piece from his cloak and wrapped it around his head to cover his mouth and nose from the rancid smell of sulphur mixed with fecal matter.

It had been a day of travelling from what he could surmise and still no change in the terrain.

Bridazak spoke aloud to make light of the situation, "I shall call this place 'Sludgeville'."

A crater to the left belched loudly, spitting the vehement porridge at his hairy-bare feet. He stepped to the side to avoid stepping in it.

Bridazak sighed and said, "Where are you, Manasseh?"

A voice responded—a voice outside of the light, "I didn't believe them." Then it chuckled.

Bridazak froze in place and waited.

The mysterious voice echoed again around him, "What brings the famous Bridazak to the Underworld? Are you lost?"

"Who are you? Show yourself."

"I'm intrigued once again by your choices."

"If you are another drone of the Dark Lord come to toy with me then move on. I'm in no mood for games and you cannot enter the light."

"I am no drone." A dark brown-skinned creature, pure white hair, gray-blue eyes, with a plump nose; pitted and almost three inches in length, entered into Bridazak's sanctuary. The Deep Gnome stood three-feet-tall, much smaller than the ordakian. It wore earth-toned clothing, leather boots adorned with strange writings, shiny gold bracers around its arms, and a small thin dark brown cape slung over his left shoulder. The deep gnome gazed at him with a cocky confidence.

Bridazak instantly recognized the individual from their first encounter in the town of Lonely Tear before they had unveiled the Orb of Truth. Bridazak said his name aloud, "Mudd."

"Yes, in the flesh."

"What are you doing here?" Bridazak asked.

"I would ask you the same, but alas I will answer first. This is my home."

"Your home?"

"Well, an aspect of it. What you see before you is a pocket of the Underworld. There are many levels to the darkness you freely roam."

"I don't feel so free down here. I have been travelling all day and this is all I have seen."

"Oh, are you site seeing?"

"I'm looking for someone."

"Oh, the Manasseh you spoke of. And what will you do when you find him?"

"I'll let you know when I find him. Care to give me directions?"

"I'm no tour guide, but I will give you information."

Bridazak's eyes squinted in contemplation, "I don't understand how this is your home. You are no demon or undead."

"No. I am something else entirely."

Mudd walked closer to Bridazak and the only thing separating them was a small bubbling crater of the toxic thick soup churning inside. The gnome said, "I was cast down from heaven with the one you call the Dark Lord."

"Why?"

"The simple answer is we rebelled against God."

"You were an—"

"Yes, an angel. I chose my path and now have the consequences of my choice."

"You said we. How many fell?"

"A third of the host. The Underworld was birthed for us and when the fall of man occurred we were granted access to your realm."

"The fall of man? You are talking about the Tree?"

"Very perceptive, young soul."

"So you follow the Dark Lord then?"

"Originally yes, but no longer. He is powerful, don't get me wrong, but I keep to myself and stay clear of his schemes. Unfortunately, our own kind interacted with the races of Ruauck-El and ended up becoming gods to the simple minded. Abaddon has grown fond of the new religions that followed and now we understand why he allowed it to happen."

"Abaddon is the Dark Lord's name?"

"Indeed. Not many know it."

Bridazak's brow furrowed, "Why did Abaddon allow you to be worshipped? That doesn't make sense."

"From your perspective yes, but Abaddon's goal is to separate mankind from the true God of Light. Having multiple religions confuses the absolute truth and creates barriers of spiritual blindness. Many fall victim to the lies which incites infighting, rebellious hearts, and those who would rather not believe in anything but themselves."

Bridazak plopped to the ground to sit, his shoulders slouched, and his head hung low, "Mudd, what am I doing down here?"

"You heard the call."

Bridazak peered up, "I know I have been called, but—"

Mudd cut him short, "No, you heard the call. All have been called but few heed it."

Quizzically, Bridazak said, "God told me to go to the Underworld and I obeyed."

"More emphatically, He gave you a choice, for He would not force you or anyone to come. He is bound by free will."

"I don't understand."

"Bridazak, God will love you no matter what. You can do no wrong as long as your heart is focused on Him."

The gurgling sounds increased around them as if the craters were pots of food placed over a fire.

"You must continue to move, Bridazak. Come," Mudd extended his arm to help him up.

"If I had chosen not to come to the Underworld and let Manasseh go, then—"

"Then God would still love you and He would create another

path. It is difficult to comprehend His ways. He is the creator of everything."

"Where do I go from here?"

"The same belief you felt when you chose to come here is the same belief you will need in order to find Manasseh. This dark world you walk in bases everything off your desires. The Lake of Fire will be the marker to indicate you are close. Be careful what you desire in your heart as you will be misled in the Underworld. There is nothing good down here."

"How do I protect myself with no weapons?" Bridazak asked.

Mudd smiled and began to fade away before his eyes. Before he completely vanished, a distant, hollow voice said, "You are the enemy of darkness." Then Mudd was gone.

Bridazak was once again alone and he whispered, "Enemy of darkness?" Bridazak's bow pulsed in his grasp. He inspected it but nothing stood out to him. The ordakian instinctively raised the bow and pulled the string as if an arrow was notched. A bolt of light ignited and strengthened the further he pulled the line. He let it loose. The sizzling bolt of light pierced the dark shielding beyond and ignited the endless silhouettes of what he called 'Sludgeville'. The bright aura glowed like a brilliant flare. He strummed another shot, and then another in various degrees of separation to try and find anything to give him a sign as to where to go. Then he recalled Mudd's message of desires and belief.

He whispered, "I believe." Then he fired another shot into the darkness. This time the arrow of light sunk into a dungeon wall, something he had not seen before. He quickly moved toward it and discovered a door ajar. It squeaked as it opened. Rust had taken over the hinges. Beyond the opening was a long corridor. Grey bricked walls and cobblestone floor brought the gloomy familiarity of Manasseh's dungeon that he had seen at Black Rock Castle.

The hallway was deathly quiet as he entered. Bow at the ready. He looked both ways into endless darkness and then released the bowstring, sending an ignited arrow. It soared beyond view until finally diminishing hundreds of yards into the gloomy corridor. Bridazak turned to look behind him at the door, but found it had disappeared and only a solid wall remained.

"I guess I will go this way," he whispered.

Bridazak cautiously walked for hours. There were no sounds to alert him of any change, only silence. The corridor continued on the same and the ordakian began to wear down due to the unchanging environment.

"Will this ever end?" he said.

He fired another shot and still it went beyond vision. The zap of energy echoed down the dungeon hall. Bridazak stopped walking and then placed his back against the wall to rest. He closed his eyes and thought, *"I could use some help right about now."*

The Dak's eyes flared open when he heard the faint sound of dripping water. A wooden door, not seen before, was now visible a short distance away.

"Thank you," he whispered as he looked toward heaven. Bridazak placed his ear against the wood to listen, but only heard the echoed plops hitting the floor. He twisted the lever and the door popped open. A shove of the portal and in he went. Now inside, the chamber had a blue aura which created a shadowy haven of indiscernible dimensions.

"Let's shed some light in this place." Bridazak fired an arrow of light toward the ceiling. The brilliance filled the room and there before him, chained to the wall, was Manasseh. His head hung low and his shackled wrists held up his body. His clothing was torn and blood stained.

Bridazak approached the human but halted when a demon creature materialized in front of Manasseh. Spikes protruded from its muscled body and its skin glowed a darkened red as if it showered in blood itself. It stood ten-feet tall with four arms and had claws as razor sharp as any magically enhanced weapon ever created. The teeth were black and pointy and pupil-less eyes revealed no life behind them.

"Bridazak," it said in a deep, husky, demonic voice.

"And you are?"

"Pain," it hissed.

"Right, I should have guessed," Bridazak quipped as he backed away bringing his bow up to bear. "I want Manasseh."

"Come and get him."

Bridazak fired his arrow. It slammed into the monster, scorching its skin but doing very little damage. He fired again with the same result.

It laughed heartily and then a new voice shouted from behind Bridazak.

"My turn, beasty."

"Dulgin?" Bridazak yelled in surprise.

The red-bearded dwarf charged with his axe, swinging at the demons leg. It connected and took out a chunk of its armored flesh. It howled in pain and then grabbed the dwarf with one of its four appendages, then another latched hold of his axe, taking it from Dulgin. Its other arms skewered and ripped Dulgin in half. Blood spewed out in all directions.

"No!" Bridazak yelled and fired a volley of arrows.

"You are next, halfling."

Abawken suddenly sailed through the air over Bridazak and slashed with his scimitar. The human fighter severed the beast's upper left arm. Black blood sprayed out of the open appendage. Abawken landed behind it and then swiped his sword across its back. The creature lurched in pain and fell to one knee.

Abawken shouted, "Bridazak, get Manasseh!"

Before the ordakian took his first step, the demon phased away and materialized behind the human. Its sharp claws sprouted through Abawken's torso. The human heaved forward and he gasped for air. Blood gushed from the fatal wounds as he slumped lifeless, sliding forward from the sword-like claws.

"Your friends have failed you," it growled.

Bridazak was stunned at what had transpired in mere seconds. His friends had died before his eyes. It was his fault. Anger welled up inside and he yelled in horror as he fired arrow after arrow. Each shot pushed the hideous monster back. His anger charged each arrow with tremendous power. Black blood splashed against the walls and floor. The final shot pierced its left eye, puncturing through the back of its skull and blowing it apart. It fell to the ground, toppling over like a stone pillar, dead.

The ordakian heaved with heavy breaths as he looked between his shredded friend Dulgin and the corpse of Abawken. Their lifeless eyes stared back at him.

A slurred whisper came from Manasseh, "Bridazak, help me."

He took a step toward the chained human. His feet seemed like they were encased in mud. Another step and then another.

"What have you done," a voice said from behind him.

He turned to see Spilf at the doorway looking at the carnage.

"Bridazak, this is your fault." Spilf glared at him.

"I-I," he stuttered.

"Why did you leave us? We came to rescue you but we have found only death in the Underworld."

"Spilf, I'm sorry."

"Sorry? You are sorry? That is not good enough. Look at what you have done. Dulgin and Abawken are dead because of you."

Bridazak looked down at his deceased friends. Blood pooled around them.

Manasseh moaned. Bridazak said, "Spilf, help me release Manasseh."

Spilf responded by moving toward the human. Bridazak watched his friend retrieve what he thought was Lester and Ross, his magical thieves tools, but instead Spilf produced a dagger and quickly sliced Manasseh's throat and said, "This is what you deserve, Manasseh. This is what Bridazak should have done."

"Spilf, no!" Bridazak grabbed his friend's shoulder, looked into his friend's hatred burning eyes and then felt the sting of Spilf's dagger plunge into his stomach. He gasped for air, shocked at all that had happened.

"It's your fault, Bridazak. But I will save us all. We will reunite in heaven."

Blood gushed out of the wound. Bridazak clutched his gut but his life was quickly slipping away. He watched in further horror as Spilf, both hands on the hilt of his blade, thrust it into his own chest.

Bridazak slumped to the ground and Spilf keeled over dead next to him. Bridazak coughed and gave short inhaled and exhaled breaths as his own life faded away. His friend's blank and soulless eyes stared back at him. The last haunting image he remembered as the darkness of death fell upon him.

Chapter 8

The Caretaker

Daysho Gunsen held his gaze upon the Caretaker of the Thieves Guild. Daysho's eyes were covered by the hood of his cloak, a sharp line of light revealing only the bridge of his nose down. He showed no emotion toward the scrawny human who sat upon a maroon upholstered chair flanked by half-a-dozen black leather armored guards, swords and daggers drawn. The Caretaker's thinning hair accentuated his shiny scalp and the dark bags of skin hanging beneath his eyes. A red shirt seeped sloppily from under his half-buttoned, leather tunic. The glossy, charcoal grey breeches were awkwardly skin tight and his high black boots were scuffed and in need of a polish.

The Caretaker's high pitched voice resounded in the meeting chamber, "You make me laugh, Daysho. You step foot into the Judgement Chamber of the Guild and give me an ultimatum? This is Tuskabar and I rule here. Perhaps in other cities the guild leaders bow to the assassin, but here, well, here we do things our way." He scoffed, "I have waited years to have an excuse to put you down and this betrayal to the Guild of Tuskabar is all I need."

Daysho held out his hands to his sides, palms up, "Guilty as charged. Then you refuse to step down?"

"Of course, you idiot!" the Caretaker yelled, his face flushed with anger. He stood and placed his hands behind his back, calming himself. He waltzed around to the back of his chair and then rested his arms.

Daysho smirked and whispered, "Good."

"I've had enough of you. Kill him," he ordered his men.

Before they reached him, Daysho uncovered his head and the advancing men halted, fearful of the assassin's eyes, which swirled black and grey.

51

Daysho said calmly, "No harm will befall you if you surrender."

"We don't bow to demons. Kill it!"

Daysho smiled, revealing his white fangs. At that very moment, a surprise counter attack launched as six vampires materialized behind the Caretaker's guards, grabbing hold of them and sinking their teeth into their necks. Blood gushed out and ran down the guards shoulders, soaking into their undergarments.

The Caretaker yelped in shock and backed away.

"Where is your resolve now?" Daysho asked.

The Caretaker's lips began to quiver and his eyes darted to and fro, seeking an escape route.

Daysho suddenly appeared behind the human and whispered in his ear, "I asked you a question."

The Caretaker screamed, but halfway through it turned to a gurgling whimper, as Daysho sunk his pearly whites into his flesh. The human slumped to the ground as Daysho wiped the edges of his lips. He then ordered his men, "Take them to the holding cells while they go through their conversions."

Daysho took his place and sat upon the chair in the room while his minions dragged the bodies off. The sliding of boots on the hardwood floor faded away and then he was alone. He rested his head against the back of the vaulted seat and closed his eyes.

A new voice echoed from behind the assassin vampire, "You have been busy, Daysho."

Daysho stood and saw Romann de Beaux walk out from the recessed shadows.

"Yes, my master. The plans are in motion and—"

"No need to explain to me the plans," Romann cut him short and then placed his hands behind his back. Romann wore a red velvet jacket that covered his entire torso down to his knees. The gold buttons gleamed brilliantly off the flickering torchlight. Black leather pants melded into his high boots. The most distinguishing adornment was his sea foam colored, wide-brimmed hat with a frazzled yellow plume that lightly fluttered as he walked. "Do you find it necessary to be so dramatic with your takeover?"

"Dramatic?" Daysho inquired. "If I wanted theatrics then I would have changed the Caretaker while in high court with the entire Guild as a witness."

"Well, that would have been entertaining, I'm sure. It appears there is a vacancy for this caretaker position," Romann amused. "I wonder who will fill this most important role."

"Yes, I wonder," Daysho grinned.

"Where do we stand with containment of this quite drastic change in the hierarchy?"

"I have a contingent of vamps stationed in the surrounding towns. We will dominate the region in weeks and be ready for an assault on Ravana's Tower in due time."

"Remember not to kill Ravana. I need her to release Kiratta from the curse of Oculus."

"She won't do—."

Romann, in the blink of an eye, grappled Daysho, pinning him to the chair, clutching his throat, "Your response to me will always be, 'Yes, master.' Is that understood?"

Daysho, barely able to speak gasped, "Yes, master."

Romann let go and then straightened his jacket, "Now, I have someone for you to meet."

The vampire assassin sat upright, chagrined, "Whom might that be, my master?"

"May I introduce to you Countessa Penelope De Luz," he swept his arm out to the back of the room.

Emerging from the shadows was a pale, olive skinned female with red hair. Her curls bounced on either side of her shoulders as she walked forward. Hollow clicks of her heels echoed as she took each step. Green, sparkly eyes penetrated Daysho's soulless being and with a royal authority she approached. Her voice was smooth and perfect in tone, "I now see what you meant, my Grace. This one will take some work. How much time do I have?"

Romann answered, "A week, perhaps more."

"Mmmm, so little time, but I like a challenge."

Daysho coughed, "My master, what is the meaning of this?"

The Countessa turned to Romann, "He is barbaric. Are you sure he is the one to fulfill my repayment?"

"Yes, he is the one. Do what you must." Romann looked at Daysho, "You will follow her instructions, and if you do not then the Countessa will take you as her slave for all eternity."

"I do hope you disobey, Daysho," she quickly added.

The assassin stood stunned, uncertain about how to respond. Penelope paraded around him, scrutinizing him from head to toe. Daysho kept his face down, not wanting to gaze into her piercing eyes. She wore a maroon ballroom dress and she slowly plucked at her long pearlescent silk gloves until they came off of her hands.

Daysho looked up and caught Romann's eyes. He silently pleaded with his master, longing for answers.

Romann said, "Listen to her Daysho. Trust me and your future will be greater than you can possibly imagine. This is a gift." He then blended into the shadows and disappeared, leaving Daysho and Penelope alone.

She said, "Yes, Daysho, I'm a gift."

"May I speak?"

"Permission granted." She waltzed behind him.

"Help me understand what this is all about."

"This is all about you, Daysho. You wanted this position, this status, but you have not the proper skills to hold it."

"With all due respect, I have many skills."

"Ah, yes, the art of assassination, the skills of reading people, of anticipating moves, and so on. But you lack the greatest skill of all."

"What is that?"

"Character."

"I do not understand."

She lightly caressed his shoulders with her index finger as she circled him, "You lack understanding, but after I am done you will have the character to lead."

"I am sure you will see how capable I am of bringing Ravana down," Daysho retaliated.

"But how will you lead after that? Others will challenge you."

"And they will die."

"Mmm, a true leader does not waste what he has been given."

"And what is it precisely that you will give me?" he mused.

"I have been in the counsel of kings for thousands of years."

"Always a Countessa and never a queen," he quipped.

Suddenly, Daysho found himself pinned to the ground. His left cheek shoved into the cold floor. He tried to resist her strength but found it to be futile.

Penelope whispered in his ear, "You will show me respect,

Daysho. I will teach you the necessary character talents to perfectly lead an army of undead. You will be the Vampire King, or my slave. The choice is yours."

Chapter 9

Jack and Trill

Trillius could see the first twilight of dawn approaching. They had travelled throughout the night, heading southeast. The mountains of the Shield quickly morphed into open plains and then changed into sparse woods, thickening the further they went. Periodically, the gnome turned around to see if his new vampire toy followed. The fifteen year old boy, now a six-foot-two hulk of ashen flesh, glided in his wake. Trillius admired Jack's new attire. It gave Jack the look and feel of mystery, shrouded in a black hooded cloak and wearing dark leather underneath. He could easily be mistaken for an assassin which wasn't a bad thing in his eyes. The gnome smiled as he thought of what was to come.

Trillius stopped, breathing heavily, "Well, it's almost dawn."

Jack responded, "Yes, of course, you need your rest."

"My rest? I'm stopping for you."

"Why me?"

"You see the orange ball of flame coming up?" he pointed. "Remember, it kills vampires? Ring a bell?"

"The sun is not my enemy. We can continue."

Trillius held up his hand, "Wait, are you telling me that you won't die in the sun?"

"That is correct."

"What kind of vampire are you?"

"That remains to be seen."

"So I could have slept last night?"

"I am following your lead, Sir Trillius."

"Don't sir me. I just lost my beauty sleep."

"My apologies."

"Yeah, you better be sorry," he sat on a nearby rock.

"Shall we continue then?" Jack proposed.

"Not yet. I might as well eat something before we continue." Trillius reached into his bag and fetched the dried rations. He proceeded to take a bite before noticing Jack staring at him, emotionless. Trillius froze mid-chew and said, "Do you want...," he hesitated to say it.

"Want what?"

"You know."

Jack grinned.

Trillius chewed and pointed off into the forest, "I'm sure there is a fluffy babbit out there for you. Why don't you go and do what you need to do, just don't do it around me. I get queasy."

"I don't eat fluffy babbits, Trillius."

The gnome froze mid-chew again and peered up at Jack, "You're not going to...well, okay, there is a small town several hours away and you can feed there."

"Feed?"

"Yeah, you know, suck blood? That is what those fangs are for, isn't that taught in vampire school, or something?"

Jack chuckled, "You are very entertaining, Trillius."

"Oh, I was always meant to be the Vampire Jester, don't cha know." He went back to eating his rations while rolling his eyes.

Trillius felt uneasy beneath the swirling eyes of Jack, "Do you really have to stare? Look over there or something. Your eyes are creepy."

"Where are we going, Trillius?"

"I told you already, we need to see an old friend of mine and get the information we need about your trinket."

"You don't have friends, remember?"

"Yeah, well, that was a figure of speech. This guy used to be a friend so that is what I meant when I said 'old friend'."

"Then this old friend will be surprised to see you then."

"One can only hope," Trillius whispered to himself as he chewed the last piece of dried meat.

Trillius jolted forward with a yelp when Jack appeared next to him and whispered in his ear, "Yes, one can only hope."

"Dammit, don't do that!"

"Trillius, I need to find the mirror and I am not to be used by you. Especially to gain you ground within your empire of shadow thieves."

"I'm appalled young Jack that you would think so little of me. Of course I will get the mirror. Dal-Draydian showed me it exists. I just need to find a way to get to the location."

"And what is your way?"

The gnome paused, "Trade secret."

Jack glared at him.

Trillius held up his hands to placate the vampire, "You need me and you are going to have to trust me."

"Who are we seeing Trillius and what shall we expect when we find him?"

"He is another gnome that I travelled with in my early years. He stabbed me in the back and betrayed our friendship. He has something that I need in order to help us."

"Something?"

"It's a ring, alright?"

"What does this ring do?"

"It is called Krinka."

"Again, I ask what does it do?"

"The Krinkans were a group of assassins in the Bronze Age that were masters of disguise and stealth. This ring aids those who wish to not appear as themselves."

"Trillius," Jack slightly raised his voice, "We are not on some treasure hunting scheme of yours."

"It's no scheme. We need it."

"Why? A disguise will not help us to find the mirror."

"In order for me to travel out in the open, then we most definitely need this ring. I'm a wanted gnome. My face is plastered in every establishment from the North to the West. Without it we will have others interested in our business and that is something we don't want, is it?"

Jack paused, morphing his eyes from the swirling colors back to his normal steel grey orbs. Trillius squinted and wrinkled his brow as he watched the transformation.

Jack said, "Then let us get this ring of yours so we can blend in."

Trillius smiled, broadened his chest and placed his thumbs inside his belt. "That's better. We should make it to Glendale by this evening. We can rest there, or I can at least."

"We should stay away from populated areas as you suggested."

"Glendale is deep within the Amber Woods. We will be fine. Them folk don't get out much, trust me. Besides, I need a hot meal."

The quiet town of Glendale was nestled in the Amber Forest, north of the border leading into the West Horn King territory. This location, formed by the huntsmen, was a place they controlled. Those few who knew about it kept it to themselves and the patrolling militia to the west saw no gain in having the forest and those who resided within the timbered confines.

Trillius strolled down the only path of Glendale, passing the weathered dwellings and shops. The sound of stringed instruments strengthened as he approached the only tavern in town.

"Let's see what 'Toad Stools' has to offer. Hopefully the food is better than the name of this establishment," he spoke quietly to himself.

The smell of smoked mutton, mixed with rotting vegetables assaulted his senses. His face scrunched in distaste, "Maybe not." He turned to look out into the night, eyes searching to the left and to the right, before entering alone.

Every soul within the tavern wore different shades of green attire—the woodsman's preferred color. Three tables were packed to capacity and the forest trackers laughed and told their tales while sharing pitchers of mead. Trillius scanned the bar and located a vacant spot between two men leaning over the dark wood top with their arms surrounding their drinks. The fireplace cracked and popped. To the right, the local minstrels sang of the wood gods and quests of mighty rangers.

"Interesting place," he said under breath walking to the bar.

Trillius looked up at the four-foot-high perch, an arms-length higher than himself, and then tugged on the cloak of the man on the left. The human glanced downward, glaring at the gnome.

Trillius said, "Would you get the bartender's attention for me?"

The man turned back to his drink, ignoring the gnome's plea. Trillius tugged again.

"I will keep pestering you until you get his attention."

He slightly shook his head and then called out, "Max."

A thick-boned, heavy-set man, with a grizzly beard and a brown rag slung over his shoulder leaned over the bar-top, spotted Trillius and said, "Yeah, what do you want?"

"Maybe a drink would be nice."

"Got any money, gnome?"

Trillius jangled his pouch and the burly human disappeared and a minute later produced a tankard of ale.

"Two silver."

"That is absurd, it should be two copper," Trillius responded.

"Suit yerself," the bartender pulled away.

"Wait, fine." Trillius laid two silver pieces on the counter and then took the large stein of ale.

The gnome asked, "By chance, do you have a section for my height?"

He chuckled and pointed, "Yeah, its outside. Find yerself a tree stump, little-one."

Trillius raised an eyebrow, half-smiled, and then raised his drink, "Thanks for the help." Trillius turned to face the room, noticing a few stares in his direction, and made his way toward the center table of men.

Trillius stood on the outside of the six-man hunting party and took a sip of his drink while raising his eyebrows in delight. *"Not bad,"* he thought.

The gnome's loud slurping sip hushed the table in front of him. They all turned in unison to address Trillius. A curly dark haired human with a short non-manicured beard asked, "What are you all about?"

"Oh, me?" he pretended to be surprised.

"Yeah, you."

"Well, I'm all about having a drink and finding good people that I can buy a round for."

The man turned to face his buddies, "Well, we can be good people." Laughter burst from the others. "Kam, fetch a chair for our new friend."

"Coming right up, Tel."

Trillius climbed into the human sized seat and placed his drink on the edge of the table. "So, whatch ya'll talking about?"

"Sharing stories of the forest."

Trillius noticed each of them making eye contact with one another. He knew something was amiss. "What kind of stories?"

"Ghost stories is all, but never mind that, where you headed?"

"Just passing through, making my way to the Borderlands."

"Tucker just came from there. Didn't you, Tucker?"

A younger and more slender man, brown hair and eyes to match said, "Yep. Not a good place to be these days."

Trillius raised his eyebrows, "Oh really, why is that?" He then grabbed his tankard and sipped.

"Rumors of swelling armies on both sides."

"Well, not to worry gents of the forest. These armies you speak of won't bother with your precious woods." Trillius took another sip.

Tucker lowered his head and voice, "We are more worried about the vampire sightings."

Trillius coughed, eyes flaring wide, "Vampires?"

The table, in unison, shushed him.

"Vampires, are you certain?" Trillius whispered.

Several of them nodded while Tucker said, "We found our good friend old-man Timber drained at dawn today."

Trillius thought, *"Dawn today? It wasn't Jack then."*

"Yeah, and Kam spotted someone suspicious in the woods but they left no tracks."

Another man, his voice deep, added, "We have all noticed a shift in the woods. Something dark and evil has come."

Trillius drank many sips as he sat and listened to the humans bantering back and forth about their precious woodlands falling victim to an evil presence. He glanced periodically out the windows in search of Jack, hoping he had listened to his instructions to wait outside the town.

A high-pitched scream suddenly jolted everyone in the tavern. A young serving maid let go of a wood tray filled with drinks. It crashed to the floor as she brought her hands up to her face, still screaming while entranced by a sight out the window. Men instantly stood and grabbed for their weapons. The bartender came out from behind the counter and wrapped his burly arms around the frightened child.

The girls lips quivered as she cried, "I saw it. It's out there." She pressed into Max's gut while several men approached the door and window. Their swords and bows were at the ready.

All the men at Trillius' table were standing. He glanced to his sides while sipping his drink and noticed leather coin pouches dangling in his face. Trillius raised one eyebrow and looked around. All eyes were focused on whatever lurked outside. He smacked his lips, while setting his drink down and pulled out his trusty dagger. One snip and a quick tuck of the pouch within his hidden pocket inside his cloak. Another quick glance and then he cut his second pouch. *"Becoming a profitable evening after all,"* he thought and smirked.

A brave soul pulled down the latch and swung the front door wide open. The wind caught it and slammed it against the outer wall. Some flinched, while others gripped their weapons tighter. The night was cold and damp and a strong breeze blew amber colored leaves the size of a human's hand past the opening. The door rattled back and forth against the wall as the wind kept it pinned. No one made a sound inside the tavern. No one blinked. Not a soul moved an inch.

"There!" someone shouted and pointed out the door.

A silhouette of a man masked in the shadow of night came closer. It appeared to be hovering off the ground, covered by a dark cloak. Trillius heard the bowstrings stretch and then the twang of release as a volley of arrows impacted the skulking figure. Whatever it was vanished, a deep laugh resounding from outside.

"That's Wild Willy's laugh," a man from the back shouted. "The creature got Willy!"

Another woodsmen said, "If it got Willy, then why is he laughing?"

A face suddenly appeared in the light of the doorway, grinning from ear to ear and eyes bulging out. "Gotcha."

An eruption of sighs filled the room and men relaxed their weapons as the gangly Wild Willy entered the establishment, dragging the brown cloak he used in his ruse behind him. "What's crackin?"

"Your face in a second. You scared young Ginny dammit," the bartender barked, still holding the girl.

Men grumbled and dispersed back to their tables. Wild Willy

approached the young lady and bent down close to her face. His eyes bulged out so much she thought they might fall out at any second. He smiled through his grizzly brown beard, baring his uneven tarnished teeth. "Sorry about that, lass. Just getting the boys all razzed up is all. No harm done."

Max pulled her away and escorted her behind the bar.

Trillius hopped down off his chair and said, "Well, I need some fresh air after that one."

"Don't be wandering off on your own this night, little-one," Tel said.

"I think I can manage." Trillius leaned in and whispered, "Looks like Wild Willy scared the vamps away."

A few of the men chuckled as Trillius headed for the open doorway, but halted when one of the humans called, "Hey, what about that round of drinks you were talking about?"

"Oh, yeah, um, I will be right back. Why don't you all decide what you want and then place your order with Max. I'll pay him when I return." Trillius tapped a coin pouch on his belt to assure the men he had the money.

They nodded their approval and Trillius melded into the shadow of night as he exited.

Trillius' eyes adjusted to the dark. He stayed close to the wall of the last building leading out of the tightly confined village. He wrapped his cloak around him tightly to prevent the chill of the windy night from penetrating his bones.

"Jack," he whispered harshly into the dark. Leaves rattled in the trees around him as a strong gust of air passed by kicking up the amber petals and tossing them to and fro down the dirt path. Trillius crept to the back of the darkened home to get off the street and was quickly immersed into the woods.

"Jack," he said more firmly in a hushed tone.

Trillius heard a jostle to his left and turned sharply. A silhouette of a human stood between two trees, twenty paces away.

"C'mon Jack. I don't have time for your vampire tricks. We have to get out of here."

The figure didn't move and Trillius thought he heard whispering mingled in the wind. The gnome took a step toward the man but quickly halted in place when he spotted a second assailant, who stood motionless, covered in the shadow of night amongst the trees.

"You're not Jack," Trillius said under breath.

"No we are not," a voice said calmly into the gnome's ear causing Trillius to jump in fright.

Standing behind him was a six-foot human as pale as a ghost, eyes swirling grey and green. The creature bared his fangs. Trillius stumbled backwards and bumped into another vampire. He yelped.

Trillius held up his hands crying hastily, "I'm not worth the effort. I'm full of air mainly."

Sinister chuckles oozed out of each of the creatures.

Trillius quickly responded, "I can help lure the humans out for you."

A raspy voice said, "We don't need your help, Trillius."

The gnome froze and gazed long and hard at the vampire who spoke his name, "I recognize your voice. How do I know you?"

It scoffed, "Because you wanted my help in Tuskabar not too long ago."

"Reese? Is that you?"

"It is I."

"What happened?"

"It is a new era and the great shift in the North with the fall of Manasseh has brought its contagion to the West."

"To the West? You speak of King Oedikus."

"Oedikus is a corpse. No, I speak of Ravana, his daughter and true ruler of the West."

"Does the Caretaker know of your fate?" Trillius asked pointedly.

Reese snarled, "The Guild has a new leader and he will soon be the ruler of the West Kingdom."

"New leader? Who?"

A vamp from behind spoke, "Can we kill him now?"

"Nay," Reese held up his pale hand. "Trillius will help us with delivering a message."

"Yeah, a message," he half-smiled in response and then whispered, "What message?"

"Not to worry little Trillius, none of us fancy the taste of a gnome."

A sigh of relief registered on his face, "Well, that's good. You had me going there."

"But we will use your blood to deliver our message," he smiled menacingly while the others snickered behind him.

"What? No wait!"

The vamps slowly moved in. One grabbed his left arm, the other snatched his right and stretched him wide, hoisting him into the air, eye-level with Reese. They sniffed his wrists, smelling the blood flowing through his body.

Trillius yelled, "Jack! This would be a good time right about now."

Reese cocked his head slightly, "There is no one else here, poor Trillius. Vamp senses can smell life a mile away." Reese opened his jaw, fangs extended out, and he hissed.

Jack suddenly appeared behind him, grabbing hold of Reese's hair and pulling his head back, saying, "I'm not alive." Jack ripped the vamp's neck open, unleashing its blackened blood, before twisting the head clean off causing a geyser to darken the leaves on the ground and in the low branches above.

The two other vampires released Trillius and came at Jack in a flurry of claws and teeth. Trillius rolled away and turned just in time to see Jack holding a lifeless heart of one creature in his grasp. Jack's arm extended through its chest and out its back. His other hand held the other high up in the air gripping its neck.

Jack retracted his bloody appendage and squashed the heart in his clasp. It gushed through his fingers like soggy fruit. He turned toward the remaining vamp and brought it close to his face, still holding it above the ground.

It scratched out a question, "Who are you?"

Jack's swirling eyes intensified and spiraled around his iris's faster. "You will obey me." Jack lowered the vampire to the ground and released him.

"Yes, my master."

Trillius scoffed under his breath, "You can compel vampires?"

Jack kept his gaze, "You will return to your hive and report what you have seen today. Give your new leader this message—the

Vemptukai   has   returned."

Chapter 10

The Giimtock

A rapid knock resounded on the door to the private chambers of King Morthkin. The Frost Dwarf leader looked over at King El'Korr who turned around at the knock. They connected with their eyes and El'Korr pursed his lips and nodded. "It is time," he said.

"Enter!" yelled Morthkin, a trail of visible breath from the cold fading into the air.

Geetock opened the door and took a step inside, "My lieges," he bowed, "the time has come. We wait for you in the Great Hall."

The two kings did not respond and Geetock left hastily, closing the door behind him. El'Korr approached Morthkin and extended his hand and arm out. The Frost Dwarf grabbed hold of El'Korr's forearm and they embraced a warrior's embrace.

Morthkin said, "The Dwarves will move in unity whatever the decision."

"Agreed," El'Korr responded, "My knee will be the first to hit the ground upon the utterance of your name."

"As will mine if it is your name called and between you and me I hope it is you."

Both of them exited the room and in seconds were looking upon a sea of dwarves crammed into every available space in the Great Hall of the Shield. The loud voices stilled to murmuring upon seeing them enter. Each of the kings stood on either side of the throne. Dwarven magistrates, dressed in royal robes of blue with gold stitching, were standing next to wooden chairs fanned out behind the throne.

Groups of gathered Dwarves represented their clans, some small, while others grand, not only in numbers of Dwarves but also in armaments. Armor was polished, shields sparkled, and weapons gleamed in the blue hued lighting of the Frost Dwarf keep. Each

67

section had a banner that waived the insignia of that clan. Hundreds of flags were laced throughout. There was strong tension in the air. This ceremony had not been seen by many of the dwarves gathered and had only been called upon two other times in their entire history. The Giimtock was, in all regards, something invoked only due to extreme circumstances. An underlying threat to all clans, in this pivotal moment in time, necessitated having a single voice to bring unity and strength to the dwarves.

A frail dwarf sitting in the center of the magistrates stepped forward in front of the throne and brought up his hands to usher complete silence. His raspy voice echoed for all to hear, "Let it be known by all dwarves assembled here that the Giimtock has been called upon. The laws state that the clan members of the nominated kings are not allowed to vote, thus all other clan members will place a single named king onto a ballot. Now then, the votes have been cast and counted. Once the name is read aloud then every knee will bow to the Giimtock and follow one king as one body, moving in unity and strength for the survival of the dwarves. The only way to end the Giimtock is for the appointed leader to fall in battle, or for the leader to end it once the threat against survival has passed and there is peace in the land. Consequently, all other king candidates will lose their title and will be given a new rank from the Giimtock." A hush fell over the waiting dwarves. "We have tallied the votes and will now announce the Giimtock."

A voice yelled somewhere amongst the crowd, "El'Korr!" This elicited a loud uproar of those in agreement and those opposed. There was no telling who was on what side.

Others yelled, "Morthkin!" Pushing and shoving matches ensued in several areas.

"Silence! Quiet the Hall!" the panel of magistrates yelled as they stepped forward. Several minutes passed while the frenzies dwindled. Frost Dwarf guards had to step in and quell a few squabbling clans but no bloodshed occurred.

The old white-bearded dwarf was handed a single folded parchment sealed with wax. Everyone knew the time had come and the most important name of all dwarves was about to be revealed. The honor that this single dwarf would receive and the sheer responsibility of the one called would be beyond measure for the ordinary person.

He popped the seal. Not a sound other than the sliding fingers across the parchment could be heard. Everyone seemed to be holding their breaths in anticipation. He opened the folded paper, quickly closed it back, and then gazed up, looking at those gathered. His white bushy eyebrows scrunched together and his face hardened in seriousness.

"Let the two candidates step forward," he announced.

Morthkin and El'Korr strode forth and stood next to him, one on either side. Each of them was resolute and prepared to bow to the other. Each of them could not fathom being the chosen one, the third Giimtock, and perhaps the last Giimtock for all time.

The venerable dwarf called out, "The new Giimtock is..." He paused. A pause that seemed to go on for eternity and then it happened, the name was uttered. It took a long second for it to sink into the hearts of all the dwarves.

"El'Korr is the new Giimtock!"

The dwarven king blocked it out and only knew it was him when he watched King Morthkin step in front of him and bow to one knee. El'Korr was in shock. The cheering grew distant and the flags waving rapidly slowed within his mind. He felt his knees buckle but then the noise flooded into his consciousness and everything suddenly lurched to real time speed. He found his resolve once again.

El'Korr was startled when someone from behind him placed a crown on top of his head. He peered back to see one of the magistrates stepping away and bowing. The new Giimtock leaned down and grabbed hold of Morthkin to have him rise. The Frost Dwarf leader did as instructed. They locked eyes and each saw the moisture of emotion seeping in along the edges. They nodded to one another ever so slightly. Morthkin stepped aside and made way for El'Korr to address everyone.

He took a deep breath and exhaled slowly as he walked to the edge of the steps that led down to his people. He brought up his hands to quiet them.

El'Korr said, "Thank you for your vote of confidence. For centuries we have called each other by our clan names. I have been Hammergold. Others are known as the Redhearts, the Bluefists, Irongut, Smasher and more. But now, at this time, in this place, we are the same—we are Dwarves!"

An eruption of cheers like no other caused the ground to rumble.

Morthkin raised his hands and silenced them once again, "We follow you El'Korr, King of all Dwarves, the Giimtock. What is your first command?"

El'Korr bore his eyes into them. He studied their faces. They were eager to hear his first order. He said, "We march on the West Horn King!"

Raina and Abawken sat atop Zeffeera as the bronze dragon elegantly landed on a ledge outside the Frost Dwarf kingdom, the Shield. The wind was calm and the air not as cold as usual. They were below the freeze of the Guul-Fenn Mountains in the more temperate climate. Abawken slid down and then helped Raina.

"It feels strange to be back," Abawken said.

"How so?"

"It is the loss of Bridazak. It feels like I'm visiting his tomb."

"Come. Let us pay our respect then."

Raina turned to address Zeffeera and said telepathically, *"My dear and loyal friend, thank you. Go home and I will call upon you when needed."*

"As you wish, Raina." Zeffeera jumped from the perch and soared backwards down the mountainside before unfurling her wings to catch the air. She gracefully glided away into the distance.

Before Raina and Abawken walked into Te Sond, they gazed upon the valley below and watched the thousands of people of all backgrounds milling about like ants. Formations of military men, row upon row, marched in unison. It was an army ready to unleash itself upon the Horn Kings.

"I can feel the pain and the anger in them," Abawken whispered.

Raina grabbed his hand and squeezed it, "They will fight for all the injustice caused to them and their families. Come, let us announce our return."

They turned to find King El'Korr with his Wild Dwarf bodyguards flanking him. "Good to have you back," El'Korr said.

Abawken and Raina walked hand-in-hand toward him. Raina said, "You look well. I sense something different about you. What is it?"

El'Korr responded, "Much has changed. I will explain inside."

Raina acknowledged Geetock with a nod, "I see you received my message."

The Wild Dwarf winked and then wedged both thumbs into his belt.

"We have much to discuss," El'Korr stated while turning to walk back inside the keep. "Strange happenings have taken place and we are planning to march within days."

"Strange happenings?" Abawken said.

A new, yet very familiar dwarven voice, chimed in from the back of the group. The bodyguards parted to reveal Dulgin with Spilf and Xan right behind him, "Strange, as in weird, not right, and upsetting me greatly."

"Master Dulgin!" Abawken quickly embraced his dwarven friend in a warrior's hug.

"Good to see you, Huey."

"Well met, everyone," Raina said. "Let us divulge our information inside."

El'Korr agreed, "Yes, come this way. I have a feast prepared to celebrate your return."

The aroma in the chamber was so tangible that you could taste the air. Servants came in, delivered a platter of cooked elsh and steamed vegetables, and then quickly departed after bowing to King El'Korr. Others roamed around the table to pour Dwarven Ale or Elven Wine.

El'Korr pushed away from the table. His chair legs screeched on the floor. The room quieted. "Let us pray. Dear God of all gods, we thank you for your provisions. Bless our coming days and bring us favor. We submit ourselves to the laws of heaven. Ka-leema."

Everyone echoed the closing prayer in unison, repeating the dwarven word for 'let it be so', "Ka-leema."

"Clear the room. It is time we discuss our plans," El'Korr announced. In an instant, all non-essential staff exited between the three doors, leaving the heroes of Ruauck-El alone with the Wild Dwarf, Geetock, and the former King Morthkin of the Frost Dwarves.

Abawken said, "I apologize for moving hastily in this conversation but I want to inquire about the strange happenings you mentioned."

Xandahar quickly answered, "Young Jack went missing right after your wedding and we have been unsuccessful in finding him. I am hopeful that Raina can assist in locating him."

"What would be the motivation for anyone to take Jack?" Raina asked.

"We have asked the same question, Mistress Raina," El'Korr answered. "You and Abawken have returned early. We were not expecting you back for another seven days-time but are most grateful for your timely arrival. Your assistance in this matter will be called upon."

Raina almost seemed to be scrying the minds around the table but looked curiously at El'Korr, so much so that it made the king uncomfortable.

He said, "I don't like your long stares, Raina."

"Mmm, my apologies, but something has changed amongst you. I have noticed the servants more attentive and the other dwarves bowing lower than before."

El'Korr took a deep breath and exhaled while saying, "Very perceptive. Yes, something has changed. We called upon an ancient law of the dwarves called the—"

She cut him off in surprise and sudden realization, "Giimtock?"

"Yes, it was announced the day prior to your return."

"Well, this is quite a change. I can only say congratulations and raise my glass to the choice made."

The others grabbed their drinks and hoisted them high into the air, "To the Giimtock!"

"Abawken and I have news of our own," she gripped her husband's hand under the table. "I am with child."

Faces and voices ignited in exuberant joy. Everyone stood instantly and raised their goblets to toast the good news. Congratulations echoed up from the table accompanied by thankfulness from the newlywed couple.

Abawken noticed Spilf's low demeanor and understood that the loss of Bridazak weighed heavy on him still.

King El'Korr raised his hands to get everyone's attention and to settle the separate conversations that had evolved from the announcement. The voices hushed and they sat in their chairs.

"We are in a time of transition and in days we will march our army to the West Horn King's border for a full assault on the capital city of Tuskabar. Along the way we will set up outposts in surrounding towns and villages to protect the innocent people. I have appointed several leaders and given them sole instruction on what and where they will go. No single leader knows the other's plans so our enemy could only receive partial information if they were ever captured.

"I will appoint Abawken as Commander of the human army to set up these outposts and be our voice of peace. This will be a—"

Abawken stood and said, "I apologize King El'Korr for my interruption but I have come by other news that will direct my path elsewhere."

"What news is greater that will detract you from our mission?"

"I have heard the voice of God and He has given me insight that will affect several people in this room."

Spilf's face looked up from his somberness, "From God? What did He say?"

"He simply told me this, 'Help him'."

Xan and Dulgin exchanged glances. Xan then looked at his sister who was staring directly at him, a calm composure of strength plastered on her face.

"Help who?"

"Master Spilf, I believe Bridazak is still alive in the Underworld."

Shocked voices ignited at the statement. Spilf stunned, tried to grasp what Abawken had said. His surroundings faded away as if he was in a dream. The voices became distant, the blood drained from his face and he felt like he was going to pass out.

Xan's voice silenced everyone, "He speaks the truth!"

El'Korr said, "How do you know this Xan?"

"Before Bridazak fell into the vortex he mouthed the words 'I will be back'. He willfully fell and I believe he was going after Manasseh."

"Why can we not be rid of that evil king's name and why would our beloved Bridazak willingly go where only the tortured and wicked reside?"

Spilf said, "You knew this the entire time? You didn't tell me? Why?"

"I was waiting for the appropriate time. I am sorry."

"Sorry? You know that I would do anything to help my friend."

"Exactly the reason he did not tell you, Spilfer Teehle," Raina said.

Spilf chimed, "We need to go after him through the vortex then!"

"Wait!" Xan held up his hands. "We cannot help our friend on the inside of the Underworld, but there is another way." Xan looked at his sister.

Raina nodded, "Xan is right. Legend speaks of an item that could search the depths of the dark realm. It is called Akar's Looking Glass."

El'Korr responded, "Legends are just that. There is no way we can chase after myths nor do we have the resources and time. I cannot leave my army, Raina."

"You will continue your campaign but will have to make adjustments as we decide our next recourse."

"Dulgin and I have come up with an idea," Xan said.

"Let us hear it, Master Xan."

"Trillius had intimate knowledge of hidden treasures throughout the realm from his connection to Dal-Draydian. The ancient dragon's knowledge could be our way to find Akar's Looking Glass.

Dulgin followed up, "We have a little problem however."

"What is that?"

"Along with Jack we are now missing Trillius, but we feel that Trillius is either working with the assailant who took Jack or he was gnome-napped. We don't know which but we tracked Trillius to the upper west entrance leading to the Chamber of Cleansing before losing the trail."

Xan jumped back in, "We did not find any evidence of a struggle from Trillius and his tracks suggested he went willingly. Our plan is to travel to the nearby grove of Firbelg to find Rozelle. She might have information on where Trillius might have gone. At this point it is our only course of action."

El'Korr issued instruction, "Abawken, you will take Spilf and Dulgin to find Rozelle. Xan and Raina will remain here within the castle as a central source of information. You will funnel your findings to me as I lead the army to the west. All in agreement say aye?"

In unison the room said, "Aye!"

El'Korr added, "Geetock, our time table just moved up. We march tomorrow. Alert the Commanders."

Chapter 11

The Discovery

"Have I ever told you how much I dislike the woods?"

"No, Dulgin, why is that?" Spilf asked as he pushed through a set of whipping branches.

"Cause I don't like the color green."

Spilf timed the release of the flimsy wood. It smacked Dulgin in the face. The dwarf stopped and glared at Spilf who shrugged and said, "Oops, sorry about that."

"Whatever, Stubby."

Abawken led the way and smirked as he listened to his friends back and forth antics, all the while, keeping his mind alert for what lie within the Firbelg Grove.

Spilf said, "Well, I actually enjoy the forest because of its scenery and the wonderful fragrance it elicits." The ordakian took in a deep breath of the earthy but sweet smell, closing his eyes as he took in the air through his nostrils.

Dulgin tugged free some leaves of a bush next to him and shoved it hard into Spilf's face. "How do you like that smell?"

"Ah, Dulgin, that is rank," Spilf retracted while spitting the wet leaves away and scraping his hands across his face.

"That is troll-zett."

"Smells like poop," Spilf continued to wipe his soured face.

"That is what I said, troll-shit."

Abawken stopped, "How do you know this plant, Master Dulgin?"

"Dwarves train to fight trolls. We discovered this plant by accident when I was but a child. My brother and I were dared by the others to sleep in a forest, similar to this one, for an entire night. Hammergolds don't back down from a challenge. El'Korr discovered it when he cut through a patch with his blade. He got the juice of the plant on his forearm and wiped the sweat off of his face," Dulgin chuckled, "He thought I had zett my breeches. It is something you can't smell until it is under your nose and it reacts to the skin."

Abawken asked, "How does it help with fighting trolls?"

"I was just getting to that, Huey."

"Are we going into Dulgin's history time?" Spilf mocked.

"You best be paying attention Stubby cause it can save your arse when Forest Trolls are about. As I was saying, my brother and I ended up wrestling each other amongst these bushes when we suddenly heard a gurgled roar through a thicket of trees. We silenced ourselves and remained still, hidden within the shrubs. The smell was so bad it numbed our senses and our vision blurred. A critter approached, but we were uncertain as to what it was, but it sounded big."

"Let me guess, it was a troll," Spilf chuckled, looking at Abawken for support.

Dulgin punched Spilf in the meat of his shoulder, deadening his arm. Pain wracked Spilf's face and his hand rubbed the area to try to lessen the effect.

"Good guess, Stubby. This is a troll story don't cha know. Now shut yer trap and listen."

"You didn't have to hit me."

"If you were a dwarf, I would have punched you in the face."

"Go on with your story, Master Dulgin."

"A Tree Troll had heard our scuffling and they can smell meat within a hundred yards. This one was twenty paces away but did not charge us. It lumbered right by our position. We could hear it sniffing the air. Needless to say we stayed there in the exact spot for the entire night, not moving."

"So you discovered this scent masked the senses of the creature," Abawken concluded.

"But why stay the entire night? You could have snuck away," Spilf offered.

"Actually, we passed out from the fumes and woke hours later," Dulgin laughed then patted Spilf's injured shoulder as he walked past him. "C'mon, time to find the Druid Gnome."

Dulgin took two steps and abruptly stopped, bringing his hand up to signal his friends to hold their position. Each of them froze and scanned the woods. The birds stopped chirping. There was a haunting silence. Dulgin slowly pulled out his axe and gripped it tightly. Abawken unsheathed his scimitar and Spilf withdrew his dagger.

A minute elapsed with no movement. Spilf broke the silence with a whisper, "Is it a troll?"

Dulgin turned and glared at the ordakian. A loud series of grunts came from beyond a thicket of trees and bushes. Dulgin said, "Run!"

They instantly heard the thrashing and stomp of something charging them followed by an ear splitting squeal. Abawken grabbed hold of Spilf and took flight using the power of his magical weapon and flew into the upper branches of a larger tree.

Dulgin held his position as any true dwarf would, "C'mon, time to meet my axe!"

Bursting through came a gargantuan beast moving at tremendous speed. It plowed the smaller trees aside like twigs. Dulgin rolled out of the way at the last instant to avoid being trampled. He couldn't see what it was but knew it wasn't a troll. He stood back up.

Abawken saw the true nature of the creature. It was a massive tusked boar, the size of a small cottage. Its coarse hair resembled the spikes of a porcupine. It clipped their tree, shifting it enough to knock Spilf out of his perch. The ordakian plummeted to the ground and landed in the bushes below, flat on his back. He gasped for air, holding his chest. Abawken caught himself and held on to another branch. He heard the cracking of the wood and knew the tree was not stable.

The monster turned around sharply, much quicker than normal, and was upon Spilf. He hulked over the halfling. Its menacing ivory tusks, the size of a giant's arm, descended upon him.

Dulgin charged and shouted, "Over here, Ugly!"

Abawken jumped and dodged the falling debris.

The boar paid the dwarf no attention as its mouth came closer and closer to Spilf. Its huge nostrils sized up its meal with quick intakes of air.

Spilf's vision was blurred, either by the fall or the smell of the troll-zett bush, he wasn't sure which. He saw a brown mass approaching him like a cloud. He suddenly felt the hot breath of the creature on his face followed by the wet saliva of its tongue.

Abawken and Dulgin watched the beast lick their fallen friend and looked at one another in confusion.

A new voice echoed around them, a female voice, "Poi likes him."

The two adventurers turned and saw the gnome, Rozelle.

"This thing belongs to you?" Dulgin asked.

"This thing is my friend and his name is Poi."

"Your pig could have killed someone."

The creature squealed loudly toward the dwarf.

"It's not a pig, it is a boar. It's okay Poi. Don't mind the dwarf."

It went back to licking Spilf, pushing through the ordakian's hands trying to defend his face. "Stop it."

"That is enough, Poi. Patrol the area my friend."

The huge creature bolted over Spilf and plodded off into the grove. Spilf slowly stood up with help from Abawken. He checked his limbs to make sure nothing was injured while Abawken held his arm and wiped off the vegetation that clung to his body. A few twigs were nestled in the ordakian's hair.

Spilf said, "Rozelle, your friend could have killed me."

She responded, "I had the plants cushion your fall. You were safe. Poi was just having some fun."

The heroes looked at where Spilf fell and realized the bush and other vegetation was no longer plastered to the ground but fully sprouted as if the ordakian never fell on top of it. They moved in one accord, shifting to and fro.

"Why have you come to Firbelg? I was about to return to the Shield."

"Mistress Rozelle, we have grave news and need your help."

"Let me guess, it has something to do with Trillius?"

"Good guess," Dulgin mocked.

"What happened?"

"It appears Master Trillius has gotten himself mixed up with a kidnapping of young Jack and has left the confines of the Shield."

"Trillius? Kidnapping? That is ridiculous. He hates children."

"Listen here Rozzy, Trillius is up to something and I can feel it in my dwarven bones. I don't know his role with Jack but I know something is wrong and he is a part of it in some shape or fashion."

"I don't wish to argue with you Dulgin. I want to help but I am uncertain as to what you need from me."

Spilf interjected, "We think you would know where he went."

"Went with Jack? I have no idea. I am at a loss as to what he is thinking, but I know he would most likely be looking out for himself."

"Where would he go then if not with Jack? You know him better than any of us. What would Trillius do on his own accord?"

Rozelle pondered the situation, thinking, and then she looked up at the heroes with a glint in her eye, "He talked a lot about an old associate of his and how this person owed him. Trillius always told me that once he acquired what was taken from him that the realm would once again bring favor upon him."

"Who is this associate?" Abawken asked.

"His name is Smitty Bigglesworth."

Meanwhile, back at Te Sond, Raina and Xan sat in a private chamber from the main hall, talking over the happenings within the castle since the wedding. They were both interrupted when a Frost Dwarf knocked twice and then entered the room.

He reported, "Mistress Raina, we found something that needs your attention."

"Found what?"

"General Morthkin waits for you to join him in the lower levels of the keep. I was sent to guide you."

Raina looked at Xan, "Come brother. Let us see what has been uncovered."

The icy-blue skinned dwarf led them deeper and deeper into the keep to an area clearly not travelled by the kin. They passed through sentry guards stationed at the entrance prior to an unkempt corridor. The rock walls were less ice covered and ran more natural than the smooth walls of the Shield in the upper levels. Raina could feel a strange presence in the area and her stomach knotted as she approached Morthkin and his guards waiting for them.

"Well met, King Morthkin," Raina said purposefuly.

Morthkin tensed at first but relaxed understanding Raina's inflection was to honor his former position. He nodded his thanks.

"What is this place?" she asked.

"We stand in the Lost Halls—a place designed in the ancient days to hold evil at bay."

Raina understood the sick feeling now, "What did you find?"

"This," he pointed to a wall next to him. He uttered a command word, "Gielmon." A sudden flash of a symbol materialized. The single letter 'V' marked a secret door now highlighted. "My team found dust prints leading out of it." He knelt down to show her. He looked back up and said, "A human's print."

"Jack?"

"Nay, it is an adult."

"What is this place?" Xan asked.

"It harbors the Twelve," Morthkin answered.

"The Twelve? What or who is that?"

Raina delicately touched the secret door and uttered the word, "Vemptukai." The secret door opened.

General Morthkin quickly commanded, "Seal the door. We don't want to release them." His guards took a defensive posture with weapons at the ready.

"They are still here and still trapped. I can feel their presence. I must investigate the tomb."

"Is someone going to explain what is happening?" Xan raised his voice.

Raina answered as she looked down the dark passage, "The Twelve are fallen paladins. They walked this realm over a thousand years ago."

"Paladins? But why are they here?"

Morthkin answered, "Te Sond is a prison for the worst offenders of the realm. Much like the Dragon God you battled, the Twelve, are another entity held for all eternity."

Raina said, "Wait here. I will return."

"This is not a good idea, my sister."

"Someone opened the entrance but the Twelve are still here. We must find out what has transpired. I will be fine, trust me."

Raina entered the darkened tunnel and torches instantly ignited to reveal the passageway. She ascertained another set of footprints, much smaller than the prints outside the entrance. They were child's prints heading in and an adult's heading out. She contemplated what it meant as she walked in further. Up ahead lay the entrance to the tomb. The seal was broken and her elven eyes, laced with the sparkle of magic, penetrated the darkness beyond to see sarcophagi lining the walls. Opened sarcophagi. Each Paladin, lay back in their stone beds with crossed arms over their chests and a smirk upon their faces.

"Where is the boy?" Raina asked.

There was no response. Raina uttered a single word and stretched out her left hand toward the darkness. The incantation ignited a brilliant light into the room. Raina spotted the sparkle of a gem in the center on top of a pedestal. A diamond ring and one she recognized.

"Jack, what have you done?" she whispered.

Chapter 12

On The Road Again

D ulgin stomped ahead of the others. His pace quickened and he sniffed the air in rapid succession, pulling in strands of his red mustache.

"Dulgin, slow down? I don't smell anything," Spilf said while hustling to keep up with his friend. Rozelle and Abawken were right behind him.

"Shut it, Stubby. I can taste it. It's my Mah's food, I'll bet my dwarven beard on it."

No one else dared to speak as they followed. The trees were like a blur and the layers of pine needles underfoot caused a spring in their hastened steps.

Spilf announced, "Hey, do any of you hear whistling?" The ordakian didn't wait for anyone's response and chased after Dulgin who moved ahead.

Rozelle whispered to Abawken, "Are your friends okay? I can smell and sense things a mile away and there is nothing but the forest and the creatures that inhabit it."

The human shrugged and said, "Be my guest to argue with Master Dulgin."

She raised her eyebrows, "Good point."

"Rozelle, what makes you think Trillius will be after this Bigglesworth?" Abawken continued to walk with the gnome right behind him.

"There is no guarantee that he is, but Trillius spoke of him often enough."

"What happened between them?"

"To be honest, I don't know exactly. Trillius never divulged the entire story, but apparently Smitty stole something from him and framed Trillius which sent him on the run ever since."

83

"I take it you don't know what it is they stole or what he was framed for?"

"No, but I do know that Trillius is wanted by two Horn Kings, although one has fallen. The other is the West King Oedikus."

"Smitty's place is on the western side," Abawken surmised.

"Exactly, but with the border falling and the uncertainty of all-out war, I don't think anyone will pay much attention to Trillius."

"It seems Master Trillius brings attention to himself no matter what."

Rozelle went quiet and then asked, "What was heaven like?"

Abawken halted and turned toward the gnome. He looked into Rozelle's dark green eyes and stared for a long moment.

Rozelle looked away and said, "What are you looking at?"

"Where I come from it is important to look into someone's eyes as we believe it reflects the soul. When you ask me what I am looking at, I can tell you your heart is pure and you long for peace in the realm. The war that approaches burdens you greatly and you dislike taking sides. You only travel with us now because your heart is for Trillius."

Rozelle said, "How do you know these things by just looking at someone's eyes?"

"There are many things you can learn by watching. We have a saying, 'thelos-ki-ma', which simply translates, 'even a blind man can see'."

"You didn't answer my question though, what is heaven like?"

"Though I was physically there and the beauty of it is beyond description, I can tell you that we are closer to heaven than you think."

"I don't understand."

"I believe heaven is coming to Ruauck-El and has already come. We just need the eyes to see it."

Rozelle looked around, "I see the trees, feel the breeze, and smell the vegetation. I can hear the forest talking to me. All of nature points to the Goddess of Growth."

"Where does this Goddess reside?"

Rozelle swung her arms out and indicated the area, "All around us. Each plant lives and breathes because of her breath of life."

Abawken stared at her. His ocean blue eyes showing no contempt; only love.

"You want to say something, Abawken. I can tell. Why do you hold back your words?"

Before the human fighter could answer, they heard Dulgin and Spilf call their names. Abawken and Rozelle moved quickly through the woodlands, following the dwarven tracks left behind. They pushed through a dense wall of brush, bumping into Spilf and Dulgin who stared at an old man in dirt smudged beige robes, stirring a wooden spoon inside an iron pot dangling over a small fire.

"That is not your Mah, Dulgin," Spilf said.

"Oh, we have visitors. Grand, grand," the old man said excitedly as he tasted the dark stew bubbling inside the pot. "I knew it, I knew it."

"You knew what, old Huey?"

"Oh, a mighty dwarven warrior has graced us. Come, come sit. The food is ready." The wizened man's white hair reached his shoulders and his long white beard draped to his neck.

"Us?" Spilf questioned. Spilf whispered to his friends, "I think this human is crazy."

"Oh, I'm not crazy. Come and sit everyone."

Rozelle stepped forward, "He seems harmless, let's join him." She sat on a log around the fire.

Abawken joined, followed by Spilf. They all turned to look at Dulgin.

"I'm wondering what you all are going to eat?" Dulgin asked. "There is clearly only enough in that pot for me." Dulgin smiled and sat next to the old man.

"I have plenty for everyone." The frail human pulled out an old leather sack and rummaged through it, producing wooden bowls and handing them out to the adventurers. Then he brought out a silver ladle to scoop the stew out. He poured heavy helpings into each member's dish.

Moans of joy rumbled through camp as they ate and delighted in the food.

"This is great," Dulgin mumbled between a mouthful. He was about to finish but the old man tugged his bowl away suddenly.

"Hey, I'm not done yet."

"I know and that is why I'm filling it back up my bearded friend." The old man ladled in more and then handed the bowl back.

Dulgin beamed with joy and began to slurp and shove the stew into his open mouth.

"What is your name?" Abawken asked.

"Oh, I'm just an old man passing through."

"We are not around anywhere close to be passing through. It is dangerous to be walking about on your own out in the woods," Spilf said.

Rozelle quickly responded, "I'm sorry for my friends, old one. We are grateful for your invitation and this gift of food. We are only curious."

"Oh, nothing to apologize about. My name is Ish Za-Kane. I'm a wanderer."

The group of adventurers introduced themselves.

"So, Ishy, what are you doing out here in these parts?"

"Well, Dulgy," the old man responded coyly causing Spilf to almost choke on his stew in laughter. "I'm on an adventure."

"Bah, you are no adventurer, unless you're a wizard," Dulgin chuckled and then froze, "Wait, are you a wizard?"

Ish smiled, "No, I am no wizard but I can see things time to time."

"I can see things too. I can see my bowl is empty," Dulgin jabbed his empty dish out for another refill.

"That's what I like to see, a hungry dwarf."

"I like you, Ishy. You aren't like these other Huey's out there, no offense Abawken."

"None taken, Master Dwarf."

"What can you see?" Rozelle asked.

As the old man spooned more stew into Dulgin's dish he said without looking at Rozelle, "You seek love, young gnome."

"Go on."

"Your love for others is beyond measure, but what you must understand is that love is pursuing you and will not relent until it has found you."

"But I am not hiding and will accept this love you speak of with open arms."

The old man stared intently at Rozelle. She gazed deeply into his almond colored eyes and was entranced by the depth. She saw the sparkles of reflected light twinkle and begin to move around in a spritely dance. Rozelle was suddenly standing on the shore of the ocean. She looked down at her feet and saw millions of diamonds covering the ground like sand. A presence stood behind her but she was afraid to look. The sound of the waves crashed and then the rushing ocean shuffled the diamonds to cause a beautiful resonating sound like broken glass tinkling in harmony. The water receded back and the choir of diamonds shifted their sound once again.

The presence behind her spoke soothingly, "You are the diamond I seek."

Rozelle blinked and she was instantly back at the campsite. She looked around at the others who continued to listen and eat. It was as if no time had passed. Rozelle hid her face from her friends as a single tear dropped from her eye.

The old man turned to Spilf and said, "I have a gift for you, little-one."

Spilf looked around at the others and brought up his hand to his chest, "For me?"

"Yes, yes, for you. I have been waiting to bump into an ordakian." He dug inside the leather sack, his facial expressions ranging from confused, to that is not it, until finally his face brightened with joy, "Ah, here it is." He produced a strange pair of goggles with rose quartz lenses. A leather strap was tied to each end and a buckle in the back was there to adjust them to the size of the head it would be adorning. He handed them to Spilf.

"What is it?"

"These are called 'Goggles of Seeing'."

"Woah, what do they do?"

"Well, they help you see of course. Now, I have something to give Abawken as well."

Abawken smiled and said, "I have all that I need, Master Ish."

"Of course you do, but the gift I give is, well, you will see. Now, hold out your hands and close your eyes."

Abawken hesitated.

"Come on, come on, I'm not going to hurt you."

The human fighter held out his hands palm up and slowly closed his eyes.

"Good, now relax and tune your mind to receive. You always give but you have difficulty in receiving."

Abawken began to protest and open his eyes, but the old man quickly smacked the top of his head and said, "Keep'em closed."

Abawken smirked and then relaxed.

"Excellent, I will now deposit my gift into your hands." Ish Za-Kane placed his index finger pressed against his thumb as if pinching something and then slowly touched the open palm of the fighter. He then did the same in the other open hand. "There. You can open your eyes."

Abawken looked at his hands and then at the others who shrugged, unsure of what just happened. Dulgin brought up his stubby pointing finger and twirled it next to his ear, the common sign that someone was crazy.

The old man turned abruptly toward Dulgin and the dwarf turned his twirling finger into scratching his ear. "Now, what do I have for you?" Ish contemplated for a second and then his face lit up like he just discovered a lost treasure. "I have the perfect thing."

Dulgin responded, "Okay, Ishy, I'm not as tolerant as the others and there is no dwarven way that you, being a human, have anything that I would wa–"

"Here it is." Dulgin stopped short and caught his breath when he saw the gift produced from the leather bag. A wooden pipe carved from top to bottom with images of craggy mountains and swirls representing wind. The dark sherri wood gleamed like it was just finished by the carpenter himself. Ish handed it to Dulgin, who slowly reached out with one hand in awe of its craftsmanship.

"Where did you get this?"

"Trade secret, I'm afraid. Now this is a special pipe my bearded friend."

"How so?"

"Well, go ahead and try it and you will see."

Dulgin began to reach for a pouch of some tobacco he had, but Ish grabbed his hand and said, "You won't be needing that. Place the tip in your mouth."

Dulgin hesitated but Ish encouraged him with nods until he finally did as instructed.

"Give it a good tug."

The dwarf sucked in the air through the piece and instantly white plumes of smoke billowed out of his nostrils and the pipe. The robust smell that emanated seeped into everyone's lungs.

Rozelle began to cough, "That smells horrible."

Dulgin pulled the pipe away and smacked his lips, "This is the grandest tobacco I have ever tasted."

"Ah, good, I knew you would like it. It is called an 'Ever-burning Pipe'."

"Where did you come by this?"

"I acquired this some time back and for the life of me I can't remember but always knew that I would give it to a dwarf and now here you are."

There was an awkward silence from the adventurers as they were overwhelmed by Ish's hospitality.

The old man stood, "Well, the day is getting long and I'm sure you have a destination to get to."

Rozelle agreed and also stood, still avoiding eye contact with anyone, "Yes, yes, we should be going so we make the next town by nightfall."

One-by-one they gathered their belongings and then thanked Ish Za-Kane for his kindness.

"No thanks necessary. I love to give to others."

The adventurers turned and began to head out when Ish said, "Dulgin, one more bowl full for the road." The old man handed him the filled dish and the dwarf eagerly accepted it. Dulgin noticed that the iron pot seemed just as full as when they first arrived, but shrugged it away as he received the generous amount of stew.

They pushed through the heavy wall of bushes and began their journey once again. Spilf suddenly stopped and said, "Oh wait, I forgot my goggles." His friends waited for him. Dulgin continued to slurp the stew and paid no attention.

Spilf quickly entered the campsite and discovered no campsite at all, but instead an overgrown patch within the forest. Things were undisturbed. The worn logs where they had sat just moments ago were now moss covered and flowers grew out of the cracked bark. The trampled vegetation and exposed dirt earlier were now completely covered with shrubs. Vines with tiny white flowers encompassed what used to be the fire pit where the old-man Ish had been cooking just moments ago.

"Guys?!" Spilf called out in shock.

The others rushed back, emerging to see exactly what he saw. They stood there stunned.

Dulgin whispered, "Who was that Huey?"

Spilf spotted his goggles dangling off of a branch. He hesitantly fetched them and said, "Didn't the human remind you of someone, like he was familiar to me somehow."

Abawken nodded, "He did."

"He was strange indeed, but there was something familiar about him," Dulgin added.

Rozelle remained quiet, contemplating the vision she had seen, and the immense amount of love she felt from the presence who spoke to her. Then she remembered Abawken stating heaven would be coming here to the realms. Again, she asked inside her mind, *"What is heaven like?"* Rozelle looked up, regaining herself, and said, "If we hurry, we will make Glendale by nightfall."

Chapter 13

Smitty Bigglesworth

Trillius and Jack kept their faces hidden under the confines of their hooded cloaks. Human patrols marched to undetermined destinations and paid no heed to patrons scurrying across the dirt road in front of them who sought shelter in dilapidated buildings. This was Crosswind, a border town controlled by the West Horn King's militia. The army proceeded in setting defensive barriers in preparation for war, but there was no opposing Northern army in sight. Citizens, mainly from the north, fled King Manasseh's territory in a mass exodus once rumors spread that he had fallen.

"Smitty is in the next town, a few miles further. It's time I introduce you to my old friend," Trillius smirked. "It might get a little rough in there but I'm sure you can handle yourself."

"Once we get you your ring then you will take me to the mirror."

"You are one pushy vampire. Yeah, we get the ring and then we will be one step closer to the mirror. Now, don't rush the meeting. I want to gloat a little over Smitty if you know what I mean."

"Halt!" a stern voice sounded from behind them.

Jack and Trillius froze. Trillius turned slowly while Jack remained steadfast. A pair of guards approached.

"Well met," Trillius said.

"You came from the north," the militant voice did not ask but stated instead.

"Uh, yes, we did."

"You are a gnome," he continued.

"Uh, yes, you are a perceptive one, aren't you? What is this all about?"

"We wanted to get your take on the happenings to the north. What have you seen?"

"Oh, you seek information on King Manasseh."

"That is correct."

"Well, my friend and I just escaped the clutches of that vile human, no offense, I like most humans, just not that one."

The unshaven guard, wearing leather armor and helmet glanced at his partner, "What do you mean by escaped?"

Trillius took a step forward and ushered the man to lean down to hear him, "Manasseh has indeed fallen."

The guard stood upright, "So, the rumor is true then."

The other sentry said, "How do you come by this information and what's wrong with your friend? He is not looking at us. Hey you, turn around," he ordered.

Trillius stepped in the middle, "He is a deaf one. Someone I rescued in the forest. Don't mind him."

The guard ignored the gnome and grabbed Jack's shoulder, turning him to face them. Jack turned but kept his face hidden beneath his cowl.

The first man stared intently at Trillius while his partner dealt with Jack, "Gnome, you look familiar to me."

"Oh, seen one gnome, seen 'em all. We must be going now," Trillius began to back away while tugging on Jack's cloak.

Jack spoke, his voice deep yet soft, "His name is Trillius."

"Wait, I've heard that name before."

The other guard said, "I thought this one was supposed to be deaf."

There was a long pause as the registration of the name Trillius was processed through the human's mind. He squinted in contemplation causing the chapped and dry skin around his eyes to wrinkle. Trillius' eyebrows raised a bit as he held his breath waiting for what was to come and then there it was. He spotted the recognition on the guard's face. The wrinkles lessened slightly, just enough to give him tell that he was known. The guard went for his sword hilt and his comrade did the same, not certain as to why, but knowing full well to support the offensive move none-the-less. Jack pulled his hood away and the guards stopped and stared at him. The vampire's eyes flared in an amber glow and Trillius watched the men fall victim to his trance.

"You will not remember this encounter. Go back to your post and wait for your next assignment."

The guards turned and walked away like mindless drones.

"Why did you tell them my name?" Trillius demanded.

Jack pulled his hood over his head and ignored him.

"I asked you a question. What was that all about?"

Jack turned sharply and hissed, "I wanted to see how famous you truly are." Then he slightly smirked and turned to walk.

Trillius caught up to Jack, "Now you see why I need the ring. Pretty nifty trick you can do. Does that work on everyone?"

"Are you nervous, Trillius, that I might control your mind?"

"Should I be? I already had my mind controlled by another once."

"You speak of the dragon."

"Yes, Dal-Draydian," Trillius' voice softened and his mind drifted longing to see the ancient wyrm. He desired the creature's power coursing through him again, as when they were linked.

"You miss it, don't you?"

Trillius refocused, "Miss Dal-Draydian? Never," he lied. "That scaly beast haunts my mind to this day. The only benefit I received from him is the knowledge of the many marvelous trinkets scattered across this realm. Items I very much wish to acquire."

Jack remained silent as they walked but he knew that Dal-Draydian's link to Trillius left a scar within the gnome's brain. To be under the control of such a powerful ancient dragon would have left a hole so deep that it would be near impossible to climb out of.

"What scar do I face within my own mind? I have almost forgotten my true self having only lived fifteen years. The memories of the Twelve conflict inside me. They consume me," Jack thought.

He watched Trillius and knew the gnome had a deeper motive than just this ring. Both of them were using each other and yet in all facets of this adventure they were partners. Jack had to be certain he was first to his prize. Trillius could not be trusted.

"Welcome to my old stomping ground, Shade Haven. It's a small town of a few thousand residents, but caters to the many travelers passing through each day. It is a great location for a business gnome such as myself. Can you smell it?"

Jack did not respond but instead gave a quizzical look at Trillius.

"Gold, my friend. The sweet smell of gold."

The sun was setting on the western horizon and golden hues of the fading sunlight glistened on the top of the sparse trees and the sides of closely built buildings.

"It appears the thought of war has brought even more people and money to this lovely place," Trillius commented. "C'mon, Smitty is this way and I'm anxious to see him."

Many vendors lined the streets selling what they could well into the night. With the influx of people the businesses flourished, but there seemed to be a panic just below the surface of the vendors. Those who sold knew this swelling mass of coin would eventually cease once the war started...if the war started.

With each step Trillius took, he felt his heart flutter and race faster and faster. It wasn't nerves but instead excitement. He could never have gone against Smitty alone, too many followers, but with a powerful vampire by his side his chance of survival was practically guaranteed. He strutted, a smirk plastered on his face, and nodded to strangers as he passed. Trillius' face soured when he saw the name of the upcoming street. A decorative sign with intricate design work burned into the sherri wood dangled and swayed in the cool breeze of the evening. The sounds of the vendors and patrons were now distant and the singular squeak of the metal chain echoed in his ears. He felt his skin boil in anger. The sign read, 'Smitty's Street'.

The gnome's eyes narrowed and he thought, *"He has a street named after him?"*

"Calm yourself, Trillius," Jack said while placing his hand on the gnome's shoulder.

Trillius slowly relaxed, "Oh, I am so looking forward to this." The gnome looked at Jack and stated sternly, "Now remember, be patient when stepping in to help, I mean it."

Jack nodded, "As you wish."

They turned down the lane and could instantly see a shift in wealth. The street was paved with cobblestones and the shops were cleaner. Guards were more plentiful and citizens more regal in their attire.

"My, how things have changed, my dear Smitty," Trillius said under his breath.

The melodic sound of a minstrel and a band originated from a single structure straight ahead. Glowing lamps dangled on hooks all along the railing and a supernatural soft blue hue sprang to life off the sign above the swinging saloon style doorway, "Smitty's Place". The two-story tavern was packed with more people entering than leaving. Small clusters of patrons stood outside holding drinks and conversing. Shuttered windows were wide open, revealing more jovial customers inside the establishment.

In the center of the street just before Smitty's Place stood a bronze statue of a human, one hand on his hip, and the other holding high into the air the image of a torch. Magical light emanated from the beacon showcasing the brilliance of the polished metal.

Trillius' attention focused on the monument and he slowly walked toward it. He came to the base and read the plaque.

Trillius whispered it aloud, "The founder of Shade Haven stands as a beacon of hope to all that understand loss. Smitty Bigglesworth will be in our hearts for all time for the love and sacrifice he gave in saving the children of our town and repelling the Hill Giants of Cobblestone Mountains."

Jack softly said in Trillius' ear, "This Smitty used the ring to be portrayed as a human. Your so called friend appears to be dead."

"Things are not always what they appear, young Jack. C'mon, let us reveal this ruse."

The bard strummed his lyre and belted out the rhymed lines of his song as citizens of Shade Haven slung tankards of ale back and forth and joined in the singing.

"Riches and wealth come and go,
But our heroes remain in the show
Smitty is our hero
Let us celebrate his name
Smitty-smitty-hi, smitty-smitty-ho..."

"Oh brother," Trillius said under breath.

He scanned the room but saw only throngs of the tall-folk—humans. Jack stood behind him, keeping the shadow of his hood covering his face. Trillius darted between drunks and partying patrons, wading deeper into the establishment. It smelled of fresh licorice mixed with the scent of tobacco, sweat, and alcohol.

"You still have old habits, my friend. You were always a sucker for that licorice," Trillius said to himself, heading toward a vacant table just to the left of the minstrel. Trillius glanced back and then realized that Jack was gone, but he knew he was there, ever watchful and ready. The gnome broke through a barrier of humans clustered in front of the bard and found the empty table. He quickly realized why no one occupied it when he read the placard on top, *"Reserved in honor of our fallen hero, Smitty Bigglesworth."*

Trillius tugged on a nearby waitress's skirt. She turned, looked around and then went back to what she was doing, not noticing the three-foot-tall gnome. Another tug came quickly after. She turned sharply, her face perturbed at the childish joke. An expression of surprise replaced her irritation when she spotted Trillius.

"Hello, yeah, I'm down here. I'd like that special drink you serve here. It's called Glabra Root."

Her brown hair, pulled back in a pony-tail, frizzled around her forehead from a long day of work. The sheen of sweat glimmered on her skin off the lamp light. Her grimy face contorted as the gnome requested the drink.

"Something wrong my dear? Move along, I'm thirsty." Trillius turned and climbed into the single chair at the reserved table.

The waitress back peddled into the crowd and disappeared, clearly dismayed at the gnome's request and action.

Trillius smiled at the humans glaring at him, nodded his head in acknowledgment and pretended to be unaware of the unspoken rule, "Do NOT sit there." There were two sets of stairs leading to the upper sitting area. The railing was lined with customers and every table packed to capacity. Guards were positioned in key quadrants of the building and Trillius made mental note of them, all the while smiling and nodding to those he made eye contact with—eyes that wished him dead for sitting here.

"Wow, these humans are serious about their precious Smitty," he thought to himself. Trillius noticed the bard glancing his way uncomfortably and his tune faltered a bit.

"Are you taking requests, minstrel?"

The singer's eyes flared wide, unsure how to respond. He continued to strum his lyre and quickly looked away.

"What da ya think yer doin gnome?" a drunk hollered from the second level, spilling some of his drink in the process. His group of cohorts followed with a slurred, "Yeah!"

Trillius smiled, waved, and then rolled the tips of his fingers along the table edge. He noticed guards being told of the gnome's disregard and the small posse banding together in the back of the room.

"Let the fun begin," Trillius said as six hired hands speared their way through the crowd.

"Excuse me gnome, but that seat is taken," a guard said with a raspy voice.

"Taken by whom? I don't see anyone."

"Well, it is the owner's table. You understand."

"I don't understand. The owner is dead, so how can he be in need of a table?"

The guard took a deep breath and exhaled while peering at his band of men and raising an eyebrow.

"Looks like we have to do this the hard way." The human reached to grab Trillius but the gnome slinked below the table and appeared on the other side of the three-foot wide round top.

"Why don't you have the owner come take the table from me himself?" Trillius chided.

"Listen here, little-one, we don't want to throw you out but we will."

Several patrons yelled, "Hall his ass out of here!"

"Yeah, take him and throw him out!"

"Grab his nose!"

"His kind doesn't belong here!"

The human leader issued commands for his team to move around both sides and capture the gnome, but Trillius hopped onto the stage, eluding his captors. The bard yelped in horror and the music abruptly stopped as the musician nearly fell off the platform. The jovial laughter resided and changed to murmurs of, "What is happening?"

Trillius raised his hands and yelled, "May I have your attention?"

"You can stick it!" one bellowed.

"I'm not sure what that means but I will take that as a yes. My dear misled patrons of Shade Haven, the feared Trillius has returned."

Gasps moved in waves around the room while others questioned what a Trillius was. Voices escalated throughout.

"Calm down everyone!" Trillius fanned his hands downward.

The guards moved and surrounded the stage. Others came to support.

Trillius continued, "I came to pay homage to your beloved Smitty. Where can I find him?"

"He is dead cause of you, gnome!" one shouted with others in agreement.

"Well, what a shame," Trillius mocked. "Who runs this fine establishment then?"

"Ricshar!" several collaborated.

"Oh, and where is he?"

"I'm right here, Trillius," a deep and hoarse voice carried from the back of the building.

The crowd slowly parted and standing with hands on his hips was a fat human wearing baggy pants and a tight tunic, sleeves rolled up.

Trillius instantly spotted gold rings on this person's fingers, "Ah, there you are," he whispered and smirked. "I wish to speak to you in private."

"By all means. This way," he waved his arm back, indicating an open door behind him.

The guards grabbed Trillius but the gnome easily slipped from their hands by way of his magic leather armor which created a greasy substance on the outside of his body. The shine dissipated when he was out of reach like a drop of water in the heat of the desert. The guards that attempted to apprehend him were befuddled and looked at their hands. Ricshar chuckled. "Nice trick, gnome."

"I have lots of tricks," Trillius said as he passed him.

The hired hands followed Trillius and Ricshar into the back room and closed the door behind them.

Trillius perused the room, noticing the dark sherri wood desk, a set of red velvet upholstered chairs in front, and a huge painting of the fake human-formed Smitty battling a Hill Giant on the back wall.

"Please have a seat." Ricshar waddled to the brown leather chair behind the desk and plopped down.

The gnome continued to scan the room. A couple guards flanked their leader while the rest stood behind Trillius. Another door to the left opened and a skinny older human with wispy hair and metal rimmed spectacles wedged on his nose, entered.

"Oh dear, I didn't know there was company. I will come back later," the old man said.

Ricshar said, "No, don't go Timmy. I want to introduce to you the infamous Trillius."

The venerable man paused, "Oh dear, Trillius? He is the one who…" he stopped when he made eye contact with the gnome who glared at him.

"Go on, Timmy. I'm the one who what?"

Ricshar interjected, "What is it that brings you to Smitty's Place, gnome?"

"Well, Pigshar, I mean Ricshar, I'm here to collect what is rightfully mine."

"And what might that be?" he chuckled.

"You want to play dumb? I can understand since it comes so naturally to you."

"You understand gnome that your insults only quicken your time of death. I'm an entertainer and love to be entertained which is why I granted you an audience in the first place."

"Then I'm one lucky gnome. I'm an entertainer also so we have something in common, old friend."

"You are no friend of mine, I can assure you. Guards, let's be done with this one."

Two men instantly snagged Trillius' arms. The gnome's smile quickly faded when he realized his magical armor did not function. He attempted to pull free but was held fast.

"The minute you walked through the threshold of that door was the minute your magic got given a time-out."

"Nice trick," Trillius gulped.

"I've got lots of tricks," Ricshar mocked.

"You went through that door as well so how is it that your ring continues to function?"

Ricshar squinted, "My rings are not magical. Let's get to the issue, shall we? You betrayed Smitty after leading him into a trap with those Giants of Cobblestone. The town of Shade Haven will have your head, tonight."

Trillius began to panic, looking around the room for his back-up. This was not Smitty and now he was without an immediate escape and in a situation he preferred to be out of. Ricshar stood and walked to stand in front of the gnome.

"Hoist him up, boys."

Trillius was now eye level with the fat human and he could smell the foul odor of Richshar's unwashed armpits.

"Before we march you out to the townsfolk, I thought I would introduce you to my fist." Ricshar punched Trillius in the stomach and the gnome grunted and gasped for air.

In a raspy whisper, Trillius said, "Is that all you got?"

Another fist slammed into his gut.

"Boys, why don't you each introduce yourselves to Trillius' nose."

Menacing chuckles resounded and one by one they hit and smacked the child-sized gnome, breaking his nose, knocking a tooth out, and splitting a deep gouge under his right eye. Blood trickled down from the cut nose and lip, and his eye began to swell.

"You are looking much better now, Trillius," Ricshar commented.

Trillius' voice scratched as he spoke, "Help."

"Help? I'm sorry but there is no one here to help you. The only gift forthcoming you is death but first some more pain." Ricshar nodded to his men and more slugs swept in, breaking ribs and bruising his body.

"Before you go, Trillius, I think I would like to have a souvenir. Your nose stuffed and mounted on my wall will be a grand trophy." Ricshar unsheathed a dagger from one of his guard's belts, grabbed the gnome's meaty nose, and positioned the blade.

Trillius had no fight left and his head only stayed in place because Ricshar held him. His body hung limp and barely conscious. He groaned in pain. His good eye fluttered, blind in the other. Trillius felt gravity take his body and he fell to the floor, numb. *"Just kill me,"* he thought. *"Jack, you betrayed me."*

Chapter 14

Time to Gloat

The darkness was serene to Trillius. There was no chaos within the dark depths that his mind drifted in. *"I must be inside the veil of death,"* he thought. *"Am I dead? I must be. I don't feel anything. I don't sense anything. I'm alone in this dark place but strange I still have my thoughts. Why wouldn't I have my thoughts? How fitting that I should now discover the mystery of death. It appears to be nothing more than eternal darkness. This is truly damnation. Not a soul to pilfer from. Is the final destination when your mind succumbs to the reality and ceases to think? Perhaps I am still in the throws of death. My body is still within the realm and my mind has gone ahead."* Trillius felt himself smirk. *"What does someone do within this lifeless state? Do I now haunt those who still breathe the air of Ruauck-El? Where is Ruauck-El? Fitting that I'm on my own once again. I have always been alone except for one soul. The dragon. He knew me. He understood me."*

Trillius heard a distant voice in the pitch black call his name. It startled him and yet the voice was familiar.

"Trillius," it called again.

Thoughts flooded his mind of Dal-Draydian, the ancient blue wyrm who had bonded with him. Could it be his friend had returned? He tried to call out but no words developed. He yelled inside his mind, *"I'm here, Dal-Draydian!"*

"Trillius." His name was clearer and closer.

"I need you," Trillius continued to say within his brain.

A sharp pain stung his back and he flinched. Shattered light infiltrated his solitude and more pain wracked his face. His eye fluttered open and a blurry image hovered above him. He smelled a sweet fragrance of spices and oils after feeling something wet hit his face. He heard the faint sound of flesh sizzling and then his swollen eye opened.

Trillius' voice crackled, "Dal-Draydian?"

"Trillius, it is me."

The image of a dragon within the gnome's mind shattered before him like a stained glass window. Trillius flinched and he could see Jack standing over him. He looked around to see the wood ceiling of Smitty's Place and then the painful memories of Ricshar suddenly flooded back. He sat upright and began to check himself. An empty vial rattled hollowly next to him.

"A healing potion, Trillius," Jack said to calm him.

Trillius' senses came back and the pain subsided. He checked his nose to see if it was still there, "Thank the nose-god," he sighed in relief.

Trillius stood. Jack attempted to help him but was swatted away, "Where the hell were you?"

"I was here."

"Do vampires understand directions or the word 'help'?"

"Your direction was to be patient and allow you to gloat."

"Yeah, gloat over Smitty, not dumb-ass Ricshar. By the way, where is he?"

Jack looked past Trillius and the gnome spun to see the guards gagged, tied, and surrounding Ricshar who was also gagged.

Trillius straightened out his tunic and approached, "Well, I guess I had more tricks than you, Pigshar!"

Mumbles and groans exuded from the gags and eyes darted from Trillius back to the vampire.

"Where the hell is Smitty?" Trillius yelled at Ricshar.

"I'm right here, Trillius," a faint, defeated voice, came from behind him.

Trillius turned and saw the scrawny human named Timmy sitting in the chair behind the desk.

"It was you?" Trillius suddenly realized. "Now I understand. Pig-man was your decoy. Does he even know who you truly are?" Trillius smirked.

"Trillius, I didn't think you would stoop so low as to work with undead."

"Anything to dethrone you, Bigglesworth. Where is it?"

"Where's what?"

"Don't do the 'what' thing, just cough it up." Trillius looked at

Jack. "Do you mind assisting my tied up old friend here?"

In the blink of an eye, Jack materialized next to Smitty, ripped the rope away and placed the man's frail hand firmly on the table. A prominent gold band glimmered on his middle finger.

"Ah, there you are. Such a prize," Trillius wet his lips with his tongue. He then turned to face the captive audience of Ricshar and his hired goons. "It is time for you to see the truth."

Trillius stepped toward the desk, leaned in and tried to slide the ring off, but it would not budge. He pulled harder but still it did not move.

"It is magically in place," Smitty stated.

"How about over your dead-finger?" Trillius nodded toward Jack. The vampire understood and reached out his index finger toward Smitty's hand. Jack's nail supernaturally extended, an eerie sound of stretched bone echoed, causing Trillius to squirm a bit and sour his face. Jack stabbed the base of Smitty's finger, cutting through the bone and severing the appendage. Blood sprayed the desk. The skinny human screamed and then the magic of the ring wobbled and his true nature was revealed—a gnome.

"Smitty Bigglesworth in the flesh," Trillius waved his hand in presentation to the others. The humans' eyes flared wide in surprise.

Trillius plucked the ring from the still warm finger and watched it revert to a stubby gnome digit which he dropped it to the floor in disgust, "Yuck." He then slid the magical item onto his own finger and instantly felt the power of the relic. "Mmm, that feels good."

Smitty held his hand snug inside his shirt, grimacing in pain. The gnome nemesis was a little taller than Trillius. Grey hair speckled within the brown and a crooked nose bent inward, almost touching his upper lip.

"I panicked, Trillius," Smitty said, gasping for air.

"Is that what you call it? You betrayed me. We were supposed to be partners."

"Trillius, I'm sorry."

"Funny, I didn't hear any apologies when your goons were showing me their kindness." Trillius took a long pause, then looked at Smitty, "I should have known not to trust you when we arranged the two Horn Kings to hire us to get the ring for them."

"It was the ring, Trillius. I couldn't help myself."

"Well, you had your turn and now it is mine. You squandered this power, but what I will do with it will rival anything you could ever imagine."

"Then you will let me live?"

"Of course I will Smitty. You need to witness this new era we are coming into. The humans of Ruauck-El will fall out of power and that means one thing," Trillius leaned in and whispered, "opportunity."

"I can help you, Trillius."

"I know you can. You made a friend over the years that I need to meet."

"Who?"

"The Madame."

"No, Trillius. She will kill me."

"How is that any concern of mine?"

Jack interrupted, "Trillius, we have your ring. No more side adventures."

Trillius half-smiled, clasped his hands behind his back, and said, "Jack, might I have a word in private with you?"

Jack followed Trillius to the edge of the room.

"There is one thing remaining that I did not tell you about. Something we need to acquire to get the location of your mirror."

"Trillius, my patience is thin," Jack whispered.

"I know and I am sorry for not walking you through my entire plan but I thought it would overwhelm you with all of the vampire stuff you are going through. You know, just recently changing and what not."

"Speak Trillius, what is it?"

"I'm getting there. We need to acquire a special quill from the Madame."

"What is this quill?"

"It is called the Quill of Fate."

"No, we will get the mirror and that is final."

"But you don't understand."

"Enough! We are leaving." Jack grabbed Trillius and lifted him off the floor with one hand.

"Dal-Draydian!"

Jack froze and then slowly brought Trillius face-to-face, "Dal-Draydian what?"

Trillius gulped, "Dal-Draydian knows the location of your mirror. I only know it exists."

"The dragon is dead."

"There is a way, Jack."

"What way? And no more lies."

"Let me down so I can think clearly."

Jack dropped the gnome and he landed hard on the wood floor. Trillius stood and dusted himself off.

"I guess I deserved that."

"You deserve more, now speak."

"Well, we need this Quill of Fate."

"Why?"

"If Dal-Draydian knows the location of the mirror then the Quill of Fate will grant us access to his spirit and we can commune with it and get the information."

"Why would the evil spirit give us this?"

"We are friends, Jack. Trust me on this."

"Trillius, this creature used you. It dominated your mind and the residual feeling you have of it is not the truth." A sudden memory flash of the Twelve pounded Jack's mind and he flinched. High pitched screams echoed inside of him as he was overwhelmed by the remembrance of many simultaneous occurrences of each member of the Twelve. There was nothing discernable and then it subsided.

"Are you okay?" Trillius inquired.

Jack regained his composure but did not answer.

The gnome shrugged off the odd occurrence and softly said, "We have no other choice, Jack. We have to try. It is the only way."

Jack stared at Trillius for a long moment and then nodded.

Trillius' face brightened and then he walked to the desk, "So where were we, Smitty? Tell me where I can find the Madame or this vampire will drain you of your life."

"She won't see you."

"Of course she won't. Not on her own anyway. We will have to make her want to see us and like always I have a plan."

Chapter 15

Grave News

The voice of Raina was strong inside Abawken's mind and he could sense her anxiousness. He and his friends travelled along a trail within the Amber Woods. Crimson colored leaves covered the ground they walked upon. A cool breeze dislodged others hanging above, sending them floating down sporadically, adding to the layers of foliage underfoot.

"My love, I bring you news," she said.

The sounds around him faded as he linked his mind with hers and responded, *"In elven, my light."*

"My apologies for having to skip your elven lesson for the day. I have discovered the whereabouts of Jack."

"Where is he?"

"I fear he is with Trillius as earlier suspected. Where are you now?"

"Rozelle is leading us to a former associate of the gnome's in Shade Haven, across the border. We are currently in the Amber Woods. We will find whoever took Jack."

"Jack was not taken."

"He is just a boy. Do you think he willingly went with Trillius?"

"Yes, for reasons I do not know, I believe Trillius and Jack travel together. There is something else you must know."

"What is it?"

"Jack is not a child anymore."

"What do you mean?"

"Jack is a vampire."

Abawken spoke aloud in shock, "A what?"

Dulgin, Spilf, and Rozelle stopped to look at the human.

The dwarf said, "What now, Huey?"

"My apologies, I'm communicating with Raina, and...I will inform you all shortly."

Abawken asked within his mind, *"Raina, Jack is a vampire? How?"*

"I'm afraid so. We discovered a hidden tomb meant never to be opened. The twelve creatures inside used the diamond ring that Jack's father gave him. They somehow used the ring as a conduit, communicating and luring the young boy to their lair. I know not what they are using the boy for, but I know it is not for good."

"We will find them."

"Abawken, Jack is not to be trusted. The Twelve are very powerful vampires and it is unknown what they have created in Jack. I fear for his soul. Be careful."

"I will," he paused and then continued, *"Is there a way to bring Jack back?"*

"I am sorry, my love. It is not possible. I will contact you if any other information comes."

"Raina."

"Yes."

"Know you are loved."

"Alluve, Abawken."

The human refocused, instantly feeling the stares of his comrades surrounding him. Dulgin crossed his arms across his barrel armored chest wearing his naturally grumpy look, "Well, Huey, spit it out. We are a millari away from Glendale and something to drink, so hurry it up."

"Raina has discovered grave news."

Spilf stepped forward, "What is it?"

"Jack and Trillius are together."

Dulgin said, "I knew that pipsqueak took Jack. I'm gonna rip that nose off of him and shove it…" Dulgin stopped speaking when he saw Rozelle glaring at him. "Sorry, no offense."

Rozelle stepped forward, "I'm the one going to rip his nose off."

"Now you are speaking my language, sweetheart."

"I'm afraid it is much worse than that," Abawken said.

"What are you getting at, Huey?"

"Jack went willingly with Trillius and—"

"Why would he do that?" Spilf cut him off.

"And, Jack is now a vampire," he finished his statement.

"A what!?" Dulgin yelled.

"Exactly what I said," Abawken stated.

"How did this happen?" Spilf asked.

"We are not certain, but Jack was lured to a hidden tomb deep in the Frost Dwarf keep."

Rozelle said, "So how did Trillius get mixed up with Jack the vampire?"

"That is for us to find out."

Dulgin surmised, "We can gain ground on them since they can only travel at night. We will stop in Glendale to eat a hot meal and then continue."

"I can't believe Jack is a vampire," Spilf said softly.

"Nor can I," Abawken responded.

"The question is, who is using who? Is Jack using Trillius or is Trillius using Jack?" Rozelle proposed.

"My guess is the damn gnome somehow tricked Jack into serving his purpose," Dulgin said.

"It wouldn't be the first time," Rozelle said. "Just not with a vampire."

Chapter 16

Toad's Stool

The town of Glendale had a quaint quality about it. Although the buildings wore the signs of age, with green moss creeping up the sides in the shadier areas, there was a glow about it in the golden hour before nightfall. The amber leaves of the forest shuffled above and the loose ones swirled through the dirt street as the cool breeze swept them up into tiny flurries. Glimmers of sunlight peeked through as daylight waned and the shadows extended, ushering in the night.

"If Trillius and Jack came through this way we will know it," Spilf surmised.

"Only if they stopped. They could have bypassed it altogether, Master Spilf."

"There are a lot of woodsmen in these parts. Perhaps one of them saw something?" Rozelle added.

Dulgin licked his lips, "Stop all of your yacking and let's get a drink and see what these huey's are all about."

The small town was quiet and the few shops were now closed, except for the tavern, called Toad's Stool. Two humans, cloaks wrapped around them, hustled inside the warm hall just before the heroes stepped foot onto the aged wooden deck. The squeak of the swinging saloon styled doors slowly softened as each side came to rest.

Dulgin entered first, splitting the doors open with the palms of his hands and taking a hard gander at the human woodsmen inside. There were a dozen folks spread throughout, some at the bar and others at tables. Several turned to view the dwarf and then returned back to their mead. He walked in, Abawken right behind him, followed by Spilf, and finally Rozelle.

When the gnome entered, Spilf heard whispers at a nearby table where a few humans gathered together. "It's another one of them gnomes," he heard them say. His instincts told him instantly that Trillius had left his mark at this very tavern not too long ago.

Dulgin marched to the bar and bellowed as he walked, "Bartender, this dwarf is thirsty!"

The grizzly bearded man turned and raised his bushy eyebrow. He planted his hands firmly on the bar-top and said, "We don't serve your kind."

"Oh yeah, well, I would think twice about that Huey."

"You bearded folk are nothing but trouble."

It seemed the entire tavern of patrons froze, watching the spectacle take place.

"And you huey's are all alike," Dulgin stared intently at the human for a long second and then followed with, "Except for you Old Max. How the heck are ya?"

The frozen patrons returned to their drinks and conversations.

"Good to see you Dulgin. Where ya been all these years?"

"Ah, keeping bad people from your neck of the woods. So you settled here did ya?"

"Sure did," he said, then spotted the ordakian, "Spilf, good to see you. I see that you are still travelling with this ancient dwarf." He laughed.

Spilf stepped forward, "It appears so. You look good, Max."

"Yeah, much better after leaving Baron's Hall. Don't know why I tortured myself and my family by staying so long." Max stretched to look beyond his two friends and squinted his eyes. "I know he is here. Where is that fearless leader of yours? I can't wait to give him the Old Max bear hug he hates so much."

An uncomfortable silence descended as Dulgin and Spilf exchanged glances and the cold reality flooded back into their hearts.

"Well, where is he?" Max looked at Dulgin who lowered his face in sadness.

"He has fallen, my friend."

"No, it can't be. What happened? I cannot believe it."

"Nor can we, it was only recently and the loss has not settled into our bones as of yet."

Spilf said, "There is a chance that he is still alive, Dulgin."

"Aye, but slim."

"I know that if there is the slimmest of chances with that one then you have good odds he will make it. I am sorry for the loss. Bridazak will forever be in our hearts. Everyone!" he bellowed to the patrons, "Raise your tanks to a fallen hero. Bridazak the Brave!"

Everyone did as instructed, not really needing a reason to drink, but it seemed this tight knit community understood loss. They went back to their conversations and drinks. Rozelle felt uneasy stares directed toward her. She gave half-hearted smiles to those she caught looking her way but they turned away quickly. Spilf also noticed the looks and then sidled up next to Rozelle, "It will be okay. I have a feeling Trillius was here." The female gnome nodded her appreciation and agreement.

"What can I get you, Dulgin?"

"I can't believe you are asking me that. Do you have any?"

Max cracked a slight smile, "I saved some, just for this occasion."

"Grand. Let's have a chug of it."

"Well, a chug is all you will get. I will be right back. Do your friends want anything?"

"Who? Oh, yeah, these light-weights probably want water," Dulgin chuckled.

"A table, some warm food, and a few drinks would be fine, Master Caretaker."

"Master Caretaker? Where ya from, the other side of Ruauck-El?

"Actually, yes. I have travelled from the Province of Zoar, east of here."

"Ah, don't mind this huey, Max. He is a grand fighter."

Max nodded and pointed at a table in the corner, "I'll have Ginny get you your order. Ginny my dear!" he called.

She turned from a table where Spilf had initially heard the whispering, "Yes, Papa."

"Get these travelers some food and drink."

"Yes, Papa."

Dulgin said, "Ginny is all grown up, Old Max. She looks healthy."

"Yep, thanks to Bridazak and you two."

"What brought you to Glendale, Max?"

"Well, it was my brother, Willy."

"You mean Wild Willy? He is still alive?" Dulgin chuckled.

"He actually bought this tavern and then I partnered with him when we fled the Hall. I will be right back. Let me get you your drink."

Ginny followed her father's steps into the back room, leaving the heroes and the bar patrons. The group gathered around Dulgin at the counter.

Abawken said, "It is favorable to have found someone you know."

Spilf responded, "Max is a good friend, but I already know Trillius was here."

"How so?"

Spilf threw a glance at three men at a table, "They seemed pretty spooked when they saw Rozelle come through the door and I overheard them whispering."

"Well, let's find out what they saw, shall we?" Dulgin marched to their table.

The others followed.

"I'm a thinkin you recently had a run in with a gnome," Dulgin blurted.

Spilf whispered, "Well, that is one way of asking." Abawken gave a nod of agreement, unsure how the humans would react to the dwarf.

The three humans turned and a curly black haired man with a short beard said, "Matter of fact, we did, just the other night."

Dulgin looked back at his friends, "He can't be far now."

"Are you friends of his? He stole our money."

Dulgin said, "Figures as much, that gnome is rotten to the core."

Rozelle stepped forward and the humans instantly placed their hands on their money pouches, "Not all gnomes are thieves and Trillius is trying to break his habit. I will give you back what he stole."

Dulgin responded, "It's not a habit missy, it is part of his very soul. He would try to rob the vaults of heaven if he could."

She ignored the dwarf and placed several coins onto the table, "Is this enough?"

"Tucker and I both lost our wages."

Rozelle then pulled out a gold coin and set it gently next to the copper and silver. The human's eyes flared wide.

"I believe that should settle the dispute," she said.

"Indeed it will," he said as he plucked the gold piece off the table. "My name is Tel."

"I'm Rozelle, this is Dulgin, Spilf, and Abawken. We are tracking the gnome, Trillius, and would appreciate any information you can give us."

"Not much to tell. He wandered in the other night and had a drink with us at this very table."

Spilf asked, "Did he come in alone?"

"Yeah, he was alone, but…" Tel paused and looked around.

"But what?" Dulgin said.

Max answered from behind them as he and Ginny brought in the drinks and food and set them down at the table next to the human woodsmen, "Vampires."

"How do you know?" Spilf asked.

"I know 'cause we have dead vamps in the cellar. Hauled in the bodies just this morning when they were discovered at the edge of town along the road."

"And the gnome?" Dulgin questioned.

"I'm afraid he is gone, either escaped, or drained and dumped somewhere in the forest. We have noticed a shift in the woods of late, we initially thought it was the rumors of war, but several folks spotted foreigners that left no tracks and then one of our own was found dead, drained of all his blood."

"Can we see these vampire bodies, Master Caretaker?"

Max smiled, "I'm liking this Caretaker name. Yeah sure, follow me."

The tavern owner led them down the creaky wooden steps to the dank cellar. It smelled of mold and soured wine. The temperature below ground was chilly. Max lit an oil lamp dangling at the bottom and the dim light cascaded around them revealing the vampire corpses on the stone floor. One was missing its head, another its neck, torn to shreds, and the third body had a fist sized opening from the back through the chest.

"Can I hold the lamp?" Spilf reached out his hand. Max gave it to him.

The ordakian slowly brought the light to each of the fallen faces, looked up at the others and said, "None of them are Jack."

"Who's Jack?" Max asked.

"A young human boy who has become a vampire and is travelling with the gnome," Dulgin answered.

"Travelling with the gnome? That is absurd, Dulgin."

"Don't ya know it? We are thinkin that Trillius has something that Jack needs and they are working together."

"Well, no one has seen a young boy in these parts. Why bother with this Trillius though?"

"He has something inside his tiny mind that we need. It could help us discover Bridazak's fate."

Rozelle added, "And Trillius is our friend."

"Ah, speak for yerself, missy." Dulgin stomped back upstairs, "I need a drink."

"Thank you for your hospitality, Master Caretaker."

Rozelle and Abawken followed the dwarf.

Spilf stared at the bodies, "What could have done this to three vampires?"

"It's a mystery that is for certain. I have never seen so many vampires so close together. Their kind are usually solitary hunters so to have a group is a rare thing and why here of all places? Something like this makes me more fearful than any possible war coming our way. Spilf, you need to be careful."

"We will, my friend." Spilf handed the oil lamp back to Max. "I wish we could have saved her."

"Aye, Sarah was a good wife and I know she would be happy that you rescued our sweet Ginny."

Spilf smiled slightly, his heart heavy with so much loss over the years and the ultimate loss of his best friend. The ordakian turned and began his walk up the stairway.

Max called, "Spilf?"

"Yes," he stopped and looked down.

"Is there a war coming?"

"The dwarves are marching, but for your safety, I cannot say where. It is time."

Max nodded and they both headed back upstairs.

The heroes were unaware that Romann de Beaux hid within the darkness of the cellar. He stepped out and perused the fallen vampires at his feet.

He thought to himself, *"I know this Trillius, but who is this Jack? I think it's time I speak with my dear friend, Raina Sheldeen."*

Dulgin raised his stein high into the air, giving his thanks, "You have blessed me this day." He guzzled the Dwarven Ale, trickles of it running through his thick beard, and then slammed the empty container onto the table. "That was delicious!"

The heroes gathered and ate their fill of the food Max and Ginny had brought them. Spilf and Dulgin shared the story of the Orb of Truth, the carrier of the Voice of God, and finally the recent adventure rescuing Spilf's family and the fall of the Dragon God. The townsfolk moved tables and sat closer to listen to the tales.

"We must be off. Our time of storytelling has come to an end," Dulgin pushed his chair out and stood.

Max rose, drink in hand, and said, "To the heroes of Ruauck-El!"

"To the heroes of Ruauck-El!" the entire tavern yelled in unison.

They said their goodbyes and exited Toad's Stool into the dead of night.

The group of four walked in silence, trudging through the fallen leaves of Amber Wood. Abawken heard the heavy thuds of a horse approaching and alerted his friends. A single rider galloped in on an exhausted horse that frothed at the mouth. The human pulled up the reins, "Woah!"

"Well met," Abawken hailed.

"Is the town close?" Panic was in his voice. His lips were chapped and his skin white with red cheeks and nose from the cold air.

"Yeah, a millari or so," Dulgin answered.

"War is coming. Troops are massing on the borderland. I'm warning everyone I can."

"Did you by chance warn a gnome along the way?" Spilf said.

"Nay, but I did see a gnome cross the border earlier today."

This ignited Spilf's voice, "You did! Was he alone?"

"Nay, a cloaked human was with him. I only remember because I have not seen a gnome for many years in these parts. I must go and warn the others. Well met!" The human kicked the sides of his horse and galloped away.

"Did he say he saw them earlier in the day?" Dulgin asked.

"Yes, he did. Why?"

"Vampires cannot travel in the daylight."

"Then who was Trillius travelling with?" Spilf said in wonder.

Chapter 17

The Masquerade

"This place is spectacular, Jack. You won't find any architecture like this in all of Ruauck-El. Did you know that this city was built on an old religion lost in the Bronze Age?" Trillius marveled at the buildings they passed along the street.

"What is your plan, Trillius?" Jack calmly asked.

"The question truly is which plan should I choose? I have so many," the gnome smirked. "But I wasn't finished. The story says that each building was strategically built to face the center. There are five entrances into the city and each main road travels straight to the middle. All steeples were designed from the smallest to the greatest leading to the—"

"Center, I get it Trillius."

"Don't interrupt me, please, but yes, the center. But why you might ask?"

"Because whoever built it wanted to be the center of attention which is why you love this place so much, it matches your personality."

"Mmmm, a witty vampire, but no, that is not why, although a good guess. Stop and look at the cathedral for a second. This entire location was designed to communicate with the gods of old. Even the buildings were fashioned in a way that they were worshipping the gods, ushering in those who came to *that*," he pointed.

A single spire gleamed in the sunlight that stretched hundreds of yards into the air. It appeared as a crystal shard.

"You are correct about the design and its purpose, but it was not for many gods but instead one. The only true God."

"What do you know, young Jack? You are just a boy in a vampire's body."

"The Twelve imparted to me much knowledge of the realm at my conversion."

Jack was suddenly overwhelmed by a flood of memories flashing in his mind. He brought his hand to the side of his temple and then as quickly as it hit him it ceased.

Trillius thought, *"What happened there I wonder? Probably some type of conversion tick he picked up from this Twelve group."*

"Who are the Twelve?" Trillius inquired. The gnome squinted in contemplation. He had seen this 'conversion tick' occur once before but he did not care to press the issue with Jack.

"They were paladins in the old age," Jack said while pushing through the discomfort of the experience.

"Paladins? Those do-gooders are the worst."

"Why is that?"

"Cause they fight for a justice that is corrupt and say they come in the name of all that is good, but in reality they come and mess things up for everyone else."

"Your version of justice is different than theirs."

"This conversation is boring me. We need to find a clothing shop to get you your new attire for the party this evening. You haven't commented on how you like my new look."

Jack remained silent as they walked keeping his thoughts of Trillius' disguise to himself. The gnome was no longer. A six-foot tall human with brown silky hair that came to his shoulders, perfectly cut, stood before him. His face was flawless, like that of a prince, with clothing to match. Trillius did not hide but instead showed off to all. Many eyes stared in their direction, attracted by the influence he flaunted. His velvet clothes and gold buttons made a statement, "I am rich."

"I grow weary of your plans. We should just take what we need and be off."

"I guess there is a first for everything," Trillius shrugged.

"A first for what?" Jack said in disdain.

"For a vampire to be tired. C'mon, this will be fun. Just enjoy it. You lost your childhood so take advantage of this time."

Jack watched the gnome walk away but it was his last statement that caused him to pause. *"My childhood?"* he thought to himself. *"A child cannot help the realm. A child thinks and acts like a child. Those things*

I have left behind for a greater purpose—a greater calling."

The opulence of the masquerade would have made Jack sick to his stomach as a human, from what he remembered of being sick anyway, before he turned to what he had become. *"What have I become?"*

His mind shifted when he watched Trillius make his grand entrance in his elegant gold velvet jacket with platinum buttons. The back tail of his coat hung down to his human formed calves. Jack noticed Trillius had increased his muscle slightly, a common trait for males to attract the woman they sought after. *"Forgive me dad for getting involved with this gnome."* Jack finished his thoughts and then slowly meandered through the throngs of invited guests and costumed servants bringing out platters of food.

Jack observed from the second floor balcony. Down below the tan marbled floor had a single letter emblazoned on top of it in gold—"M". He wanted to rip the ridiculous mask off of his face but Trillius wanted him to blend in. This masquerade symbolized what he had seen as a teenage boy within Black Rock castle; the people pretending to be something they are not. The charade of dressing up, females comparing themselves with every woman that passed by, men nodding their heads to one another as if they were more important than the next. Trivial and worthless in the scope of all Jack had learned and seen. He could smell the fresh blood flowing through the guests around him—the essence inside each living soul he craved. He heard the heart beats, some slow, some fast, as they passed him. The Twelve had taught him to suppress the urge at his conversion. Jack thought, *"Did they teach me or is it just a memory they embedded into my mind?"* Jack fought against the need to kill anyone of innocence. His remembrance of morals remained resolute but if he encountered someone truly evil he would not have a quam about it. Not for a second.

Jack passed by a mirror and saw his reflection for the first time. Normal vampires cannot see their reflection but he had the power to interchange that. It halted him in his tracks, not because of the ridiculous clothes, the vibrant colors of orange and yellow, but his eyes. The mask he donned blocked the intricate tattoos as did the hood covering his head. It was his eyes that captured him. They were not his own any longer. He heard his father in his mind say, *"We have the same grey eyes because you were always destined to be my son."* His father's voice now seemed so distant and it pained him. It had been said that the eyes are the window to the soul and now for the first time Jack questioned if he had lost his soul completely. The separation from his dad in heaven and from God, he could not have imagined. *"I was naïve. Why did I leave you, dad…God help me."*

A female voice jolted Jack from his inner prayer, "Well aren't you interesting. Care to dance?"

The blurry vision of the masquerade behind him came back in focus and there, with an entourage of bodyguards, stood the prize Trillius sought, the Madame. Jack turned to face her.

"We shall dance indeed," he said as he raised his arm for her to take hold.

He escorted her along with her dressed protectors, who blended horribly in as guests, to the ballroom dance floor in the adjacent room on the upper level.

"I have not seen you before. Where do you hale from?"

"Many places."

"Mmm, you are my mystery this evening. I was hoping the party would not be a bore and it appears this night the gods have heard my plea." She snuggled a little closer to Jack.

A band of minstrels with multiple instruments brought the old melodies to life. The floor was packed with partnered patrons in an assortment of colored costumes twirling in unison. They swayed from hand to hand and mirrored each other as the ordained steps warranted for the ancient Muldeenian customs of this dance.

"Do you know the steps?" she asked.

Without a word, he twirled her perfectly into the crowd of dancers. The magical lighting, glowing from the chandeliers above, caused the gold flecks on her basket dress to sparkle. The crowd of onlookers gave a low, "ooohhh," which then transformed into whispers, "Who is that dancing with the Madame?" Jack could hear it all with his vampire senses.

He tilted his head flawlessly as did his partner at the correct beat of the song. This melody was entitled, the Maera, or Mirror in the common, and the movements were to portray the reflection in the dance. Perfect timing was required, but only few could make it appear as if it was truly a mirror image.

Jack thought, *"How appropriate the message of this song for what I seek."*

The Maera was a contest and the pattern would continue until the last dancers were on the stage, where they would end it and be declared the couple of the evening. Spotters, as they were called, would tap couples on the shoulder when they were found not in alignment and were escorted off the floor. Although Jack and the Madame entered late, no one would dare ask the owner of the party to wait.

One by one, couples were tapped out of the competition and soon it came down to two. The music, combined with the tension, the joy, and the excitement of the entertainment was palpable.

Jack could see the intensity in the woman's emerald eyes and the smirk of satisfaction of how far they had come. The Madame's perfectly pinned chestnut colored hair adorned her head like a crown and her curls draped to the middle of her back with a bounce. Diamond earrings dripped from her lobes.

The remaining dancers eventually tapped out. None would know if their loss was due to coordination or the Madame's status. Once they were escorted off the floor, the minstrels shifted the Maera into the finale. Jack and the hostess of the night moved as one. They turned in perfect synchronization, with arms out and their backs to one another, while swaying back and forth and shuffling their feet so their bodies moved in a circular motion. It came time for the face-to-face and in an instant their noses literally touched as they bore into each other. The Madame's eyes slightly flared in shock but they each backed away at the right moment and stepped to the edge of the floor across from one another. They turned to face the crowd. The Maera concluded. A roar of applause erupted. Cheers echoed.

The Madame received her accolades and turned to find her mystery man had vanished amongst the crowd. She half-smiled to those congratulating her, all the while searching for Jack. Never before had she been so afraid and excited all at once. When she looked into those beautiful, yet disturbing eyes she was torn to either fall into them or push away. She was determined to unravel the secret behind this man.

Her bodyguards quickly surrounded her and began to usher people kindly away to give her space. The Madame had her entourage there as a sign to others to show her respect. Most knew of her fighting prowess and her ability to move like a shadow. She loved the rumors about herself that bar patrons spoke of during their drinking festivities. Her favorite was "she was born from the shadow world itself".

"My Lady, I have brought you a well-deserved drink," a new voice said, with eloquence, but still very much Trillius.

He stood just inside her protective circle. The Madame faced him and she did not flinch at his beauty.

"I am not thirsty," she said dismissively.

Before she turned, Trillius quickly added, "It is your favorite. The nectar of Lilliath."

She came back at Trillius strongly, parting the two guards in front of her, stepping into the disguised gnome's face, "What do you know of me? Do not play games."

Trillius smirked, "I am the Prince of Sarsha to the south and have come to pay my respects."

"You are no prince here. Guards, give this so called prince my warmest regards."

"My Lady, surely we can talk in private. I have wealth."

Two chaperones grabbed hold of Trillius as she turned in the other direction, ignoring his plea. She turned finding herself face to face with her mystery man.

"You come and go like a ghost. I must know who you are."

"First, release my Prince."

"What? You are together?"

Jack nodded.

"Guards!" she called without turning. "Bring our prince back to me."

Trillius was brought back, almost carried back by his arms, to his former location and began to run his hands quickly down his jacket to straighten the wrinkles he had received, "Well, about time I am recognized for who I am."

"I care little of who you are and more about your," she paused, turning to look at Trillius, "Who is this man?"

Trillius eyed Jack, unsure of what Jack had said to her thus far, but aware of their little soiree on the dance floor. "This man," his confidence returned, "is my bodyguard."

The Madame chuckled, "No guard knows the art of dancing like that. I will ask you again, who is he?" Venom thick in her voice.

Trillius glanced back at Jack and then returned his focus on her, "He...is the true Prince of Sarsha." Trillius spoke sullenly as if fighting to relinquish the title he wanted to parade around in.

"Ah, I see, and who does that make you then?"

Jack said, "He is my fool, my Lady."

She smirked, brought out a hidden item in her sleeve, which she quickly revealed as a fan, waving it in her face, "Yes, he is a fool indeed and one fool you almost lost this night, my Prince of Sarsha."

"There is always a fool to step into the next fool's shoe. Shall we speak in private?"

Trillius rolled his eyes ever so slightly while trying to maintain a grin of acceptance for his new title. *"Nice one, Jack,"* he thought to himself.

"But of course we can. This way."

Her colorfully clad escorts led them to an antechamber off the main hall. Luxurious tapestries, velvet stitched couches, and armoires decorated the room. Tall mirrors were placed throughout for one to look at themselves from head to toe. Two women were giggling when they entered but were quickly ushered out for this private meeting to take place. Her guards were outside the door to halt anyone from entering, while others laced the inside, standing at attention, ready for any command given them.

"And to what do I owe the honor of hosting the Prince of Sarsha?"

"You have something that I want."

"Oh, I'm intrigued," she waltzed to Jack and ran her feathered fan around his chest, shoulder and then his back, "and what is it that you want, my dear prince?"

"The Quill of Fate."

She paused and looked at him like he was joking and then laughed, "There is no such thing. Who told you I would have such an item?"

"Madame of the Cathedral, we stand in the Host Tower of Tongues. The exact location of where it is said that the races of Ruauck-El began."

"You know your history, but that doesn't answer the question."

"But it does, my Lady. You see this place was touched by the Hand of God when it scattered the five dominant races. God severed the Tower of Insight shattering the idea of having this focal point peak into the heavens itself. New languages were birthed so the races could not communicate with one another and they were forced to spread out. In the wake of their punishment a single shard, the size of a quill was left behind—the Quill of Fate."

Trillius' mouth hung agape. *"How does he know these things?"*

The Madame had stopped fanning herself when Jack spoke of the ancient history of the Cathedral. Only a handful of people within the realm knew of this. She began to wave the feathers again, "You have quite the tale of my home. Who tutored you in your lessons?"

"The Twelve."

She wrinkled her face, "The Twelve? I am not familiar with them. Are they your teachers?"

"Let's just say that they have isolated themselves for quite some time and I am privileged enough to come under their tutelage."

"If," she started, "if I were to have this so called Quill, why would I give it to you?"

"Give or take does not matter to me."

"You are starting to become like your fool over there. What would your intention be with such an item, Prince of Sarsha?"

"I wish to become a King."

"A quill is not needed for such a task. All you need is a hired assassin."

"This is a unique King, a one-of-a-kind."

"Well, I hear there is a vacancy to the north," she mocked and giggled.

Jack unmasked himself, revealing the strange tattoos laced around his eyes and grinned, flaring his fangs.

The Madame stepped back and before she breathed a command to her sentries, Jack had mystified himself. With speed beyond lightning itself, Jack zipped through the room, ripping out the throats of all her guards, and then materialized in front of her once again.

Blood sprayed from the gullets of their bodies as they fell to their knees and gurgled their last breaths. Jack quickly grabbed the Madame by the neck and lifted her up and pulled her in close to his face. Her hands latched onto his forearms to try and pull them away but his strength was beyond her own.

"I am the Vemptukai."

She gasped for air, her eyes wide in horror but fixated on his.

"And I am Trillius. Remember that name, sweetheart. I am not the fool here after all." The gnome, in human form, reached out and pulled a single slivered shard from her hair. "This is exactly what we are here for. Thank you, my lady. And thank you, Jack, for informing me it was a crystal and not a piece of wood we were looking for."

The prismatic bauble had an immense sense of power that Trillius could feel, but he quickly tucked it away and said, "Oh dear, my lady, your ears must be in pain. Let me help you." Trillius quickly looted the Madame's diamond earrings and then turned, "Okay, Jack. Let's finish up and disappear."

Jack brought the Madame closer and lessened his grip, "I enjoyed our dance and *hope* that we can dance again in the future but I will leave that up to you." He set her down gently and she retracted away, holding her throat and heaving in large breaths of air. When she looked up they were gone. She opened the door to the antechamber and the two guards outside were on the floor dead and costumed attendees scattered in all directions. Jack and Trillius escaped in the chaos and the Madame walked briskly away with new guards coming to surround her.

"This is far from over," she said under her breath. "I will indeed remember you Trillius, when I bury you in my cemetery. As for this vampire named Jack, I will find you and we will most assuredly have that dance together but under my terms. The Madame always has the final dance."

Chapter 18

Round Two

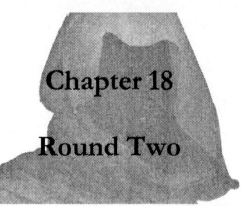

"**D**oubtful we will find any Dwarven Ale in this huey establishment. Too rich for my blood," Dulgin said, hands on hips as he took in the upper class tavern before them.

The day was waning and Smitty's Place appeared quiet.

"Something's not right," Spilf said.

"Agreed, Master Dak. Something is amiss."

"This has Trillius all over it," Dulgin added. "Well, times a wastin."

The heroes entered to find an empty tavern. Not a soul lurked about. An empty stage, the upper level quiet and shadowed, and tables without customers alerted the group to be ready for whatever might jump out at them. The stillness gave off a feeling of somberness.

"Definitely no Dwarven Ale here."

A voice called from a back room, "We are closed!"

"We don't care," Dulgin responded, looked at his friends and then shrugged.

"I said," the voice cutting short when the large human peeked from the doorway and saw the gathered races. "What do you want?" His tone harsher now.

"My apologies, Master Caretaker, we are in search of Smitty Bigglesworth."

"You travel with uncommon races, human. What are you about?" Ricshar opened the door and ten humans armed to the teeth emerged and fanned out in front of him. Their hands were on the hilts of their sheathed long swords.

"Again, our apologies, we only wish for some information and then we will be on our way."

Dulgin smiled, laced his fingers, and cracked his knuckles, "Hey Stubby, do you smell it?"

Spilf whispered back, "Smell what?"

"The next best thing to dwarven ale, a fight."

Spilf sighed and then took a step back to stand next to Rozelle who had a concerned look on her face.

"It will be alright," Spilf assured her with a half-smile. "Dulgin just needs a little exercise. Probably safer if we just stand back here while they...talk."

"Talk?" Rozelle questioned.

"Yeah, talk."

Ricshar spoke, causing the gnome to refocus, "This isn't the visitor center. Now bugger off. I've had my fill of her kind for the day."

Clearly, the human referenced the gnome amongst them. Before Abawken could respond, Dulgin blurted, "Have ya had yer fill of my kind? I'm much more fun than a gnome."

Ricshar bore his eyes into the dwarf, "Clear them out of here," he commanded.

The guards drew their weapons and walked toward them.

"Abawken, I can handle this one myself."

"Indeed, Master Dulgin, but let us not kill these misguided folk."

"Kill? Nah, I'm just going to introduce myself is all, dwarven style," he grinned through his red-bushy beard.

Abawken bowed elegantly, waving his arm for the dwarf to proceed. He then backed away and stood next to Spilf and Rozelle.

Rozelle asked, "Will he be alright?"

"Sure he will," Spilf said.

"Okay huey's, who's first?" Dulgin brought up his clenched fists as they half surrounded him. Two of the humans broke away and held their swords pointed at the others who raised their hands in surrender, taking another step back by the exit.

One human lazily lunged with his sword to intimidate the dwarf. Dulgin unexpectedly grabbed hold of the blade, pulled the human in closer and then walloped him with a tremendous uppercut, sending the fighter backward, out cold. The human had let go of his weapon, which Dulgin then swung and smacked an adjacent guard on the side of his temple with the hilt. He twirled slowly and slipped into unconsciousness. Dulgin let go of the blade and the thud of the weapon echoed in the vacant tavern.

The remaining six thugs' converging on Dulgin shoved tables and chairs out of the way to make more room. Dulgin gave them a hand, grabbing a nearby chair and tossing it toward one, which the human easily pushed aside. The red-head dwarf was upon him instantly with a punch to his gut. "Didn't see that one comin, did ya?" The human slumped to the ground trying to catch his breath.

Another fighter swung his sword downward. Dulgin spotted the attack, turned slightly, hunched, and blocked the blade with the shaft of his axe, slung on his back. A large resounding clank resonated. The dwarf instantly retaliated, spinning on his heel, and then backhanded the human to send him crashing into a couple other guards.

"Come on. Who taught you huey's how to fight, anyway? Was it Fatsy over there?"

The humans could not have understood the history of this dwarf, the many battles he had undertaken, the upbringing among a kingdom of fighters. Dwarves were born to fight and most describe them punching their way out of the womb.

Rozelle spotted a gnome tied up in the far back room, where Ricshar and the others came from. She nudged Spilf and pointed, "It's not Trillius, but I'm certain that gnome knows something."

"I think you are right."

Just then Dulgin fell at their feet, looked up at them, and smiled. "This is fun."

Spilf responded, "Can you hurry it up Dulgin? We need to talk to the gnome in the other room."

"Gnome? Please tell me it is Trillius?" He got back up to his feet.

"No, just hurry it up."

The two humans who held his friends at blade point were on either side of the dwarf. Dulgin glared at the three remaining in front of him but instead lurched to his right, punching the kidney of the unsuspecting fighter and then dropping back to hit the other in his sword arm, deadening it, causing him to drop his weapon. Abawken caught the blade on his foot as it came down and then flicked it into his hand, now holding the tip of it at the guard, who held his arm and grimaced in pain. The other writhed on the floor holding his rib section and groaned.

Dulgin turned to the remaining three. The other men were either out cold or rolling on the ground moaning in discomfort, "Okay Hueys, play time is over. As much as I want to punch each of you in the face, it is time for ya to put yer weapons down and back away. I need to be talkin to the gnome in the other room."

The humans looked at one another, uncertain what to do, fear of the dwarf's skill and strength gripped each of them.

Ricshar called, "Kill that dwarf! What are you waiting for?"

Dulgin growled and then withdrew his mighty two-handed battle axe, "Drop yer weapons."

They instantly obliged and their blades bounced slightly on top of the wooden floor boards. Each of them backed away, hands in the air.

The heroes approached Ricshar.

"Who are you people?"

"That is no concern of yours, huey. Now step aside before someone really gets hurt."

Ricshar could not match the fighting prowess of the dwarf, not to mention the others who accompanied him. He stepped away. Dulgin growled. Ricshar, startled, hastened to exit the tavern with the other guards right behind him.

The heroes entered the back room. In a single wooden bar chair sat a tied up gnome with a blood stained bandaged hand. Several bruises marked his face. The gnome's eyes, a filmy bronze color, focused on the approaching Rozelle. He wiggled his wrinkly nose as if he had a scratch to itch and then said, "Rozelle, good to finally meet you."

She responded, "How do you know me?"

"I'm Smitty Bigglesworth. I kept track of Trillius' friends so as not to be surprised if they ever showed up here."

"What happened here, gnomey?"

Smitty coughed, "Trillius happened. Him and his vampire."

"What did he want?" Spilf asked.

"A ring."

"Why?"

"To aid him in getting what he truly desires."

"And what exactly is that?" Dulgin glared.

"He is going after the Quill of Fate within a place called the

Cathedral."

"And why the ring, what does it do?"

"It is a ring of disguise. Trillius is not a gnome any longer and can change his appearance by mere thought."

"Great, as if it wasn't difficult enough to track him," Spilf sighed.

Dulgin answered, "We'll find him. He always leaves gnome crumbs behind for us to find. Remember, he is still Trillius and a ring won't change his personality."

"Good point."

Rozelle asked, "Is he working with the vampire?"

"The vampire wants something that only Trillius can get him, but Trillius needs the Quill in order to get it. I overheard them talking, along with reading their lips."

"Do we know where this cathedral is located, Masters?"

"Yeah," Dulgin said, "it's a couple day's travel away. It is said to be the first city of Ruauck-El in the Bronze Age, but is now owned by—"

Spilf said it first, "The Madame."

"Yeah, the Madame," the dwarf said with disdain.

"And who is she?" Rozelle asked.

"She is a real treat, that one. Trillius sure knows how to get into some serious trouble," Dulgin added.

"But he has a vampire to back him up," said Rozelle.

"Jack is only a boy child and has no skill in fighting even if he is the walking dead. Vampires only take with them what they knew before as a human."

Smitty interjected, "A boy? That was no boy vampire and he had skills I had never imagined. He moved in the blink of an eye, had the strength of ten men, and his eyes, yes, his eyes—they spoke of lifetimes of experience."

"What do you mean he wasn't a boy?" Spilf queried.

"He was man-size, as tall as the human you are with." He indicated Abawken with a glance.

"How is that possible? What happened to Jack?"

"Jack is what Trillius called him, that is for sure. I have other information you seek."

"Spill it, shorty!" Dulgin leaned in.

"Untie me first and let me live."

Abawken stepped forward, "We are no enemy of yours, Master Bigglesworth. Your choices in life have brought you the consequences you suffer today. Let your choices be for the heart of others once you leave here."

"My thanks," he said while keeping his bandaged hand secured with his now free hand. "Trillius mentioned another item," he paused, "a mirror."

"A mirror? Why, so he can gaze upon his ugliness?" Dulgin squinted, puzzled.

"I know not. He mentioned another name that I am not familiar with but perhaps you are. Dal-Draydian."

All were stunned by the announcement, no one spoke.

Smitty added, "Trillius needs this Dal-Draydian while Jack wants the mirror. Apparently, the Quill of Fate has something to do with Dal-Draydian."

"I am going to kill that gnome." Dulgin clenched his fist and hit his open palm.

"Who is Dal-Draydian, might I inquire?"

"A dragon," Rozelle answered, "A very bad dragon."

Chapter 19

Lake of Fire

Bridazak awoke, no longer within the dungeon of Manasseh. The grim memory of the encounter flooded his mind as he stood. He was bathed in the soft light that emanated from his body, but still surrounded by the soulless darkness.

He whispered, "God, I want to go back. I don't want to be here any longer. I am not strong enough to do this task you have given me."

A warmth touched his back and he turned to see in the distance an amber pulse of light on the horizon of what could only be described as a plain of darkness. He walked toward it.

The semi-circle aura grew the closer he approached and the warmth becoming hotter and hotter. He discerned that it was fire, but unlike any fire he had ever seen before. The flames licked high into the air, but there were shades of grey mingled within the familiar yellow and reds he had known fire to be. Waves of heat washed over him but he was still able to come to the edge of the sea of fire with no harm.

The horror of what lay before him took his breath away. An ocean of naked bodies writhed and glistened in black oil. Flames, not burning any flesh, sprouted from the surface and the people moved in agony, despair, and hopelessness. Faces grimaced as they contorted.

What Bridazak thought to be the sound of fire was actually people gnashing their teeth and growling in their torment.

He whispered, "The Lake of Fire."

A piercing screech of cries rose in unison upon Bridazak's utterance and then faded back to the roaring flames.

Bridazak looked beyond the horrific sight and searched for a way to get across. There was nothing but the same darkness. Just before he sighed, there it was, a glint, ever so slight, but a glint of something none-the-less. Mudd said he would be close once he found the Lake of Fire. He needed to get to the far side.

The ordakian extended his foot out and barely touched one of the tormented bodies that slithered to and fro amongst the others. Something happened upon his touch. It instantly froze in place and he felt the contact burn the body, bringing boils and the hiss of searing flesh. He placed more pressure and it stuck in place with little movement like a wobbly stone. In faith, Bridazak stepped onto the lost soul with all his weight, balancing himself, and realized he could walk on the surface to the other side.

He jumped carefully as if finding the perfect rock across a stream to make his way. The light that surrounded him pushed the flames back as they lapped at the enchanted globe around him.

A third of the way across he started to hear the voices of the people he walked upon. They hissed his name with contempt and anger, "Bridazak."

He made it half-way and then surveyed his surroundings. The hairless, oil-soaked, naked bodies rolled and slithered about at a depth unknown to anyone. Faces writhed in pain and suffering that caused Bridazak to look away. Deep down he knew these images would haunt him the rest of his days.

He took another step and suddenly a hand grabbed his calf. The hiss of burning skin and smell of burnt flesh rose. Bridazak, startled, looked down to see a face with black pupils and razor sharp teeth.

"Abaddon," Bridazak said.

"All those who bow to me know my name," it said, the voice a chilling echo.

"Except for one," Bridazak bit back.

"Are you enjoying my home and all of my guests?" it mocked.

"I can't say that I am."

"You look weaker than the last time we spoke, Bridazak."

"I didn't care for your ruse with my friends."

"Ruse? Oh, that was no ruse but a possible future, Bridazak."

"I don't believe you."

"Beliefs are for children, the mortals of Ruauck-El. Even now your friends search for you and I long for them to find you."

"No, they will not come, not here."

"Oh come now. You know them better than even I. They are coming and I will ensure they find you in the Underworld. Do you think your god will save them also?"

"Of course."

Abaddon laughed, "Did your god save the ones you tread across now upon this lake? Their souls are forever mine. You see, free will can be a downfall and your friends freely search for you."

"No, leave them be!"

The arm released Bridazak, the bubbling appendage dipping below the surface of the writhing bodies.

Abaddon laughed menacingly.

Bridazak ran, leaping to an exposed chest, then to a bald head, and so on. He skipped along the surface as fast as he could. He would pause periodically to regain his balance, arms flailing about as he almost fell.

The voice of Abaddon echoed around him, "You can save your friends. Call on me. Bow to me and I will ensure their safety."

Bridazak dove and landed firmly onto the plain of darkness. He breathed heavily but peered up and spotted the glint he had seen earlier. It was stronger and more prominent. He discerned it was another door. The ordakian picked himself up, looked back, and then made his way for it.

He thought to himself, *"I told Xan that I would be back, but I did not calculate that they would try and rescue me. Would they attempt such a feat? I did. Oh, God protect them, lead them away, and let them never taste this darkness that surrounds me."*

Chapter 20

Qel-Soma

Jack and Trillius travelled many miles and found shelter outside the city for the night within the plains.

"I'm nobody's fool, Jack," Trillius said as he threw his belongings to the ground. "I can't believe you said that to the Madame."

"We have the quill and that is all that matters."

Trillius twirled the slender crystal shard through his fingers on one hand and calmed himself. It was a fragment from the tower at the Cathedral.

"I was expecting something different," Trillius said as he inspected it.

"What is the next step in your master plan?"

"I need to figure out how to use this thing."

"The Great Trillius doesn't know?" Jack teased.

Trillius narrowed his eyes and glared, "As much as I love your company, my dear Jack, your increased wittiness clouds my great mind."

Minutes elapsed. Jack stared at the gnome all the while, not blinking.

Trillius rolled his eyes, "You creep me out. Stop staring at me."

"Perhaps I can help."

"You might know some history but what does the young and impressionable mind of Jack the Vampire know of magic like this?"

"I know a great deal. Have I not shown you? Don't underestimate the knowledge that I have gained."

"Yeah, the Twelve, I know and I'm sure they passed along some real gems to you."

"Qel-Soma," Jack said matter-of-factly.

Trillius paused, "Qel who?"

"She is an old woman that resides in the Crags of Munshire."

"Munshire? That is a cursed land. No one goes there."

"I'm sure you have a better idea forthcoming."

"Don't mock me, Jack. How do you know of this old hag? Wait, I know, the Twelve, right?"

"Qel-Soma has the ability to touch an item and understand the workings as if she created the item herself."

Trillius raised his eyebrows, "My suggestion is that we visit this Qel-Soma."

"You are indeed intelligent. What wisdom you—"

"Enough! I get it. Do you know where she lives?"

"Yes, I had intended to visit her when I acquired the mirror, but it seems we need to see her first."

"Well, good, it all worked out then." Trillius rested his head against the rock in the shallow depression of the open plain and closed his eyes. "Time for this gnome to get some shut-eye. Why don't you keep guard for the night, if you don't mind?"

Jack grinned to himself. He then thought, *It did work out after all. I look forward to meeting you Qel-Soma. The Twelve have told me so much about you.*

"You know, Jack, this has been one grand adventure to be sure, but I don't like going into situations I don't fully know. Care to enlighten me on what to expect here?"

"Death."

"Well, aren't you the reassuring vampire?"

The two travelers made their way through the open alleys of the crags located at a small area within the west simply entitled Munshire. An earthquake in ancient days created the openings in the ground. The earthen veins were mainly slim while others were vast, but all led to the center. The beige and tan colored rock spoke of a dry and desolate land. Jack walked with determined steps as if he had been there before. Trillius continued to look behind them, unsure of his surroundings and noticeably nervous.

"Calm yourself, Trillius."

Just then Trillius spotted the bleached bones of a long forgotten warrior leaned up against the rock in a shady covering. He had a long spear sticking out of his chest. The skull slowly turned and watched them.

"Calm? You want me to be calm in a place like this? Did that just move or am I seeing things?"

"Stay close, little-one. They sense the life you possess."

"They?" Trillius instantly moved to Jack's shadow at his side, peered up at him, and half-smiled with clear fear seen upon his face.

The deeper they went into the Crags of Munshire, the greater the number of dead littered the area. It only took minutes for a mob of the lifeless to gather and begin to follow them.

"I told you this place was cursed. Let's get out of here while we still can. There has to be another way," Trillius pleaded.

"Not until we get what we came for…Qel-Soma. As long as you are with me they will not touch you."

"I don't even want them looking at me."

More creatures poured in through the jagged pathways that were connected to one another like a maze. They pooled in until they could not see past them but still gave enough space for the intruders of their domain. Jack made his way deeper into the Crags of Munshire until finally reaching the center. Standing before them was a massive rock with a split down the middle of it. The line was jagged from top to bottom and increased in size at the lower half. A chilling cold reached Trillius, a cold that went straight to his bones.

"Don't tell me we are going in there?"

"We are going in there."

"I just said don't tell me."

"It won't be the first time I won't listen to you."

The dead amassed from all of the pathways, filling the central reaches. Trillius looked up to see the sun waning and the shadows lengthening. Night would soon be upon them.

"Qel-Soma," Trillius said under his breath, "what a great idea."

Jack heard Trillius but did not respond. He hastily moved into the dark crack of the rock, turning his body sideways to edge through. Trillius right behind him. The gnome's eyes adjusted and he saw clearly the outlines of the walls and the floor.

They emerged into an open chamber filled with cobwebs. Sitting in the middle was a throne made of the same desert rock, mundane and of little architectural beauty. It was the thing that sat on the throne that caused Trillius to stop breathing for a second. Jack approached it.

"What are you doing?" Trillius whispered and his voice echoed.

"Let me introduce you to Qel-Soma," Jack waved his arm out toward the figure on the throne.

"She looks dead to me. Let's go."

"Of course she is dead. I told you there was nothing but death here."

Qel-Soma's skin was old and wrinkled with signs of rotting flesh. Her ears were missing and only a few wisps of hair remained on top of her head. She was clothed in black robes that should have fallen in decay, but remained intact. Trillius could feel the magic pulsing from her.

A sweet sounding voice came into the gnome's mind, *"Come closer little-one so I can see you better."*

"Um, Jack," Trillius called, "um, she is talking to me inside my mind."

Jack mystified his body and transported himself instantly before Qel-Soma. His hands rested firmly on top of hers on the throne armrests.

"You will speak with me directly," Jack commanded.

A covering of finely woved webbing surrounded her entire body, but it was a thin layer. Her eyelids flew open to reveal milky white lenses underneath.

Her voice crackled to life but her lips did not move, "Who dares to enter my domain?"

Jack released her and said, "The Vemptukai."

She wailed so loudly that Trillius had to cover his ears and grimace in pain. It faded and then Jack released his grip. Qel-Soma rose from her seat, her bones cracked from age and the fine dust and webbing cascaded off of her thick robing.

"What do you request of me?"

Jack responded, "You will give the gnome the answer he seeks to the item he holds."

Her head creaked as it moved slowly to gaze upon Trillius, "Bring me your item, gnome."

Trillius produced the Quill of Fate and trepidly walked toward her, placing it into her open palm quickly and then pulling away just as fast. She closed her hand, wrapping her aged skin around the item. Trillius took hurried steps backward to distance himself.

"It has the ability to bring back someone lost. You must know their name and speak it aloud at the place their life was before it was no more. Their soul will be forever linked to yours."

Her hand opened up and she waited deathly still.

"Jack, you mind?" Trillius nodded, clearly indicating for him to fetch the quill.

"She will not harm you."

"Yeah, just the same, why don't you retrieve it?"

Jack only stared and did not move.

Trillius huffed, "Fine, I'll do it."

The gnome cautiously approached then snatched the item and moved away.

Qel-Soma spoke inside Trillius' mind, *"Do not use this item. You will be forever entwined with the soul you bring back."*

"I will be fine. You don't know what I'm capable of," he responded back to her in his thoughts.

"Who you travel with is an ambassador of evil."

"Oh, like you are a fluffy babbit yourself I see?" Trillius mused.

"Betray the Vemptukai and find a way to destroy it."

"I don't even know what that word Vemptukai means."

Jack spoke aloud, "I have one more request for the great Qel-Soma."

The female continued to speak to Trillius in private, *"What happens to me will befall you as well."*

Jack appeared behind Qel-Soma, turned her neck sideways, and he sank his teeth into her decaying flesh.

Trillius, startled, backed away even further. "Jack, what are you doing?" he yelled.

Jack lifted his face away and then ripped her head off. He slung it over his shoulder like trash.

Jack said, "The Twelve warned Qel-Soma to never use her gift again and damned her to this eternal cell. She broke her promise and now I have set her free."

"We were the ones asking her, remember? So you are the

Twelve's enforcer, carrying out their orders? Do they speak to you or are their memories so engrained that you act them out as if you were them?" Trillius asked.

Jack pondered the gnome's question. He did act swiftly with little thought as if he had been betrayed himself by Qel-Soma. She had done what he asked of her knowing the outcome would be her death and yet she complied. *"Perhaps that is what she always wanted to begin with,"* he thought.

Jack responded, "These paladins invoked memories and powers upon me. I speak to them when we are face-to-face. Only you and your dragon speak to one another inside your mind."

"Well, let us be thankful you were able to rid Ruauck-El of such a vile creature," Trillius said. "Now, why don't we get out of here?"

"And where is our next destination, Trillius?"

"We go back to the Frost Dwarf's castle and ultimately to the Chamber of Cleansing."

Jack's mind swirled with the added gifting of this Qel-Soma now coursing through his body. The Twelve had given him the ability to drain the powers of other undead for his own use. Now with Qel-Soma's talent in his grasp, he would be able to understand the magic of the Mirror of Lost Souls once he found it. Trillius would be under the influence of an ancient blue wyrm in the coming days and he would have to be mindful to ensure they gave him the location of the artifact he sought after.

Chapter 21

The Crumbs of Trillius

A regal human with a squeaky voice announced, "The Madame will see you now." He wore a pearl sheened silk robe and adorning his head was a funny looking hat that had a point drooping over his left ear and touching his shoulder. His voice echoed throughout the polished crystal walls of the Cathedral.

The heroes looked at one another and then let Smitty Bigglesworth lead the way into the main hall.

Every step they took resounded in the opulent auditorium, which was the remains of an ancient crystal once reaching high toward the clouds but now a mere spectacle for onlookers entering the city. The old texts speak of a spire that reached the threshold of heaven. Stories are told by the many travelling bards. A pair of guards stood at attention on either side of the entryway. They wore gold plate-mail that covered them from head to toe. The sentries stared through their helmets that shielded their heads and faces.

Spilf whistled, "Wow, quite the place this is."

Dulgin and Abawken didn't respond, instead they looked around and gawked at the opulence of the Cathedral. They were inside a single crystal shard where the open ceiling revealed the blue sky above. Colors of the rainbow refracted throughout the ancient temple. There was an inkling of the reverence that once flourished here in the ancient past but now it was only a lingering wisp of a feeling.

At the end of the great hall stood a raised section with steps leading to the pinnacle. Sitting regally on a gold throne was the owner of the Cathedral—The Madame. Her perfectly placed locks curled in tendrils down her shoulders. She exuded confidence as her arms rested comfortably on the armrests and a sweet smirk on her face as they walked toward her. More gold plated guards stood at attention behind her and at the foot of the steps.

"Welcome home, Smitty Bigglesworth," her voice carried throughout.

Smitty responded with a bow, "My deepest apologies, my lady."

"Why are you here and not in Shade Haven?"

"I have come to beg for your forgiveness. I was found out by the humans and thus the operation has...collapsed."

Her eyes narrowed a bit as she contemplated his statement and then she said, "We had an arrangement, Smitty. I have no use for a washed-up gnome."

Dulgin quickly said, "I don't care about the arrangement you had with long-nose here. We are looking for another of his kind."

Smitty sighed, "I'm so sorry and—"

"Silence!" Smitty stopped and quickly lowered his head. She now knew Trillius was in control of the ring of disguise once belonging to Smitty. Now it all made sense to her. She had heard of the name Trillius before but she knew it to be associated with a gnome. She had gathered the information she desired in mere seconds. "And who are you, dwarf?" she continued.

"Not in the mood, missy. Only thing that matters is us finding Trillius whom we know has recently been through your area."

"Mmm, I see, friends of his are you?"

Rozelle spoke before the dwarf, "Some of us are, yes."

"And others no," Dulgin growled.

"You will not get close to this Trillius, I'm afraid."

"Yeah, we know he is with a vampy who actually is or was a friend of ours."

The Madame stood and her silver sheened silk dress captured many colors in its folds, "I'm intrigued by the variety of this group represented before me. Who are you, travelers?"

Abawken stepped forward, "We only seek information on where they have gone. We have been tracking them for days and hail from the north."

"The North? Manasseh's territory."

"Former territory," Dulgin added. "Compliments of us."

The Madame stood, "You are the ones that felled the greatest Horn King ever to walk Ruauck-El?"

"Well, us and a few others," Spilf said.

"You speak the truth. The hall would have alerted me otherwise." She paused for a second and then said, "I have a proposition for you."

"And what is that?" Dulgin asked.

"This Trillius and your vampire made their way on foot according to my sources and are heading in the direction of a cursed land. A land that not even I would pursue someone into. They stole something of value from me and I would like it back."

"We ain't scared of no land. Name it," Dulgin said.

"The Crags of Munshire."

"Oh, that place, well, yeah, that's not a good place."

"What is it?" Spilf asked.

"A land reserved for the dead. The Crags were cursed in the Old Age and no one enters. Those that do, never return," Dulgin answered.

"Why would they go there?" Rozelle chirped.

"I can only guess to escape with my Quill of Fate, knowing I would not follow."

Dulgin growled, "Nay, that gnome is up to no good. He wouldn't go there unless he needed something and he is using Jack to get him inside. I can feel it in my dwarven bones."

"Not even a vampire on his own could get through the Crags. The dead are controlled by someone within. Her name is Qel-Soma, an ancient wizard that delved too deep into her magic and it betrayed her."

"We better hurry then," Dulgin said. "I don't want the old bag of bones to get to Trillius before I do."

The Madame said, "Retrieve what was stolen from me and I will reward you greatly."

"No reward is necessary, my lady," Abawken said. "We apologize for this intrusion and will be on our way."

"What about Smitty? What are you going to do with him?" Spilf questioned.

"It is no concern of yours, halfling," she quipped with a bite in her voice. "I will reassign him in another town if this information relieves your consciousness."

"It does, my lady," Spilf nodded.

Abawken made a proposal, "If we retrieve the quill and return it, will you spare Trillius and Jack and call off any revenge debt?"

She paused then bowed slightly and grinned, "Of course. But mark my words, my revenge on the two of them will be severe if the Quill of Fate is not in my hands very soon." She stood and then exited through a concealed door at the far wall of the Cathedral.

Spilf said, "Whatever this quill is it must be very powerful. The rumors of the Madame inspire fear to not cross her ever."

"Well that's because them people never met me before. I inspire great fear in everyone I meet," Dulgin said.

The ordakian rolled his eyes.

"Spilf is right, Master Dulgin. The Madame's name has reached my land as well. Best we retrieve this quill intact and return it."

"Whatever, Huey. She'll get her precious item and be back to writing new laws just as soon as I wallop that gnome a few times."

The heroes left in pursuit of Trillius once again.

"Behold the Crags of Munshire," Dulgin waved his arm outward.

"It doesn't look that bad," Spilf chimed.

"Yeah, whatever Stubby. Come on and let's take a look at what's exactly inside."

The four heroes cautiously approached the open rock veins and withdrew their weapons. Sweat dripped from their brows and the smell of decay grew stronger the deeper they went into the crags.

Rozelle transformed into an eagle and flew high into the air above them to scout the region. Her eight foot wingspan gracefully sailed overhead and the occasional screech in the distance reached their ears.

The others began to see the dead laying on the ground and slowed their pace.

"Why aren't they moving?" Spilf whispered.

"Shut it Stubby. We don't want to wake the dead." Dulgin paused and then said, "Get it. That was a good one."

"Yeah, I get it." Spilf rolled his eyes.

More of the dead littered the ground, yet none moved. Various forms of decayed flesh and bleached white bones mingled together.

Looking deeper, they piled on top of each other in layers as if they had fallen like brittle trees in a forest. Rozelle soared in, alerting the group with her hawk screech, before transforming back into her gnome form as she landed.

"They are all dead."

"Well of course they are all dead, missy. We are just wondering when they will become un-dead."

"No, none of them move and there is a vast number of them at the center surrounding a single rock that has a crack in it."

"What if these things wake up all of sudden?" Spilf said.

"I can transform into a larger eagle and carry one of you and Abawken can use his sword to carry the other," Rozelle answered.

Spilf nodded his approval while Dulgin said, "Ah, it's only a few skeletons and zombies, nothing to worry about."

"I saw giants further in and some other larger unidentifiable ones."

"Enough talking, let's find out what crumbs Trillius left behind. Amongst all this death I can still smell that gnome's stench over these corpses."

Within minutes the heroes were forced to start walking on top of the dead. Abawken had Spilf hold onto him while he hovered above. Rozelle transformed into a small bird that fluttered and chirped about. Dulgin marched through the grotesque environment, enjoying each booted stomp, crushing skulls and caving in chests.

They arrived at the center and the huge rock Rozelle had spoken of. It had a single zig-zagged crack that enlarged at the bottom. One by one, they entered the darkness and soon discovered the hollow inside of the immense boulder. Abawken's sword glowed brightly, casting eerie shadows throughout.

"Over here," Rozelle said.

They gathered around a headless, black robed, corpse.

"More crumbs from Trillius is my guess," Dulgin growled.

"Here is the head," Spilf announced a little further away.

"Well, she is a real beauty, isn't she?" Dulgin mocked.

Just then the group started to hear whispers echoing around them. Each of them spun, weapons ready, trying to pinpoint the owner of the voice. There was synaptic energy strengthening and within moments the haunting tones formed into hollow words, "You must hurry. The gnome and the Vemptukai must be stopped."

"Where are they?" Dulgin yelled.

"They are going to the Chamber of Cleansing. You must stop them before it is too late."

"Too late for what?" Spilf asked.

"The gnome carries the Quill of Fate and will use it to entwine his spirit with another." The haggard voice began to fade, "The Vemptukai is going to release the Twelve. You must stop them." The whispers returned and then silence engulfed the heroes once again.

Dulgin finally said, "Why is Trillius going back to the Chamber of Cleansing?"

"Master Dulgin, the question is what spirit is Trillius trying to contact?"

"Oh no," Spilf said while shaking his head.

"What is it, Stubby?"

"Trillius is going to try to bring back Dal-Draydian."

"This just keeps getting worse and worse. I am going to kill that gnome-skull."

"How do you know this, Master Spilf?"

"Come on everyone, he had been talking under his breath for weeks about that dragon. It left a wound inside of him that he won't ever be able to heal from. It is the only thing that makes sense."

"I believe you are right," Abawken whispered as the realization of the situation sunk in deep.

Rozelled chimed in, "Maybe Trillius wants to bring back Bridazak."

All three of the heroes turned to look at her with facial expressions clearly suggesting she was crazy for saying what she did.

"Well, yeah, he probably isn't," she conceded.

"C'mon, it's a race back to the Shield," Dulgin said slapping shoulders along the way to snap them into action to move out.

Chapter 22

Romann's Quest Revealed

Romann watched Raina navigate the empty halls of the Frost Dwarf castle, a place he had visited centuries before. It was very noticeable that the Dwarven kingdom had little troops remaining which told him an army of Dwarves were indeed on the march. The Dwarve's mission was not his own and he had to stop his mind from naturally going to his previous life's military strategizing and refocus on why he was there.

"Raina is a very special individual," he thought. Her confidence was not to be construed as arrogance but instead as someone who understood who they were, what their destiny was, and a power that could almost be seen in the natural. Romann noticed the scar on her chin and wondered how it came to be. She fascinated him, unlike any elf he had ever met. If anyone could help him unlock the curse of Oculus, it would be her.

Romann remembered the loss of Kiratta, his true love, in a time now long forgotten. She was taken from him. The evil of the West Horn King was beyond anyone's imagination, including his.

Raina entered her private chamber and the vampire glided inside without notice. The room was simple in the soft light exuding from the castle walls. Raina sat at a table and looked upon herself in the mirror fastened to the top of it. She grabbed a brush and began to run it through her yellow and white hair.

Romann stood directly behind her. She could not see his reflection in the mirror as he gave none and continued to brush her hair. Romann smirked as he watched her delicate and purposeful movements, then noticed her hand stop in mid-stroke. His eyes narrowed, wondering if she had somehow detected him. Her hand continued and then she finished. She stood and turned, not seeing Romann now hidden in the shadows.

Raina reached for her fur coat and brought it around her shoulders. She spoke, "I prefer to speak outside my private chambers." She turned and exited the room.

Romann walked into the light, smiled and thought, *"She is indeed powerful."*

In an instant he materialized beside her as she strode down the empty hall.

"Forgive my intrusion, Raina."

"Romann, I understand your need for friendship but even you should realize boundaries. Next time knock."

"How did you know I was there?" he asked without waiver.

She stopped and looked into his eyes, "Why are you here?"

"I wish to find out what has transpired in the legendary halls of King Morthkin's keep."

She began to walk again and did not answer. Romann understood that they would speak in private. Raina opened a door and Romann was already inside waiting for her. It was an antechamber just outside the Great Hall.

"We have a lot going on currently, Romann. What are you after?"

"I wish to exchange information."

"I'm listening." Raina moved and sat in a chair. She whispered an incantation and a low fire erupted in the fireplace next to her. She waved her hand to request Romann to sit opposite her.

The vampire sat and said, "Your Jack is now a vampire and I wish to find out more about his recent conversion."

"Jack is of no concern of yours. We will deal with him."

"Oh, is that so? Do you know that this Jack single handedly killed three vampires and turned another to deliver a message? Do you know that no vampire has ever been able to turn another vampire? Do you know that his message was 'the Vemptukai has returned'?"

Raina was unaware of all that he had stated but held her ground, "Jack was a boy who made a bad choice."

"My dear, Raina, do you know what this word Vemptukai means?"

"It is a language from the age before which translates to vampire."

He shook his head no, "It is a dialect only known by a few and your translation is incorrect which alarms me greatly. You of all

148

people understand that knowledge is power."

"What does it mean then?"

"Simply, Vemptukai, is the Vampire King."

Raina focused on her thoughts as his words sank in like fangs into flesh.

Romann asked, "What has transpired in this place, Raina? I must know."

"Jack was consumed by the Twelve," she stated plainly.

His eyes narrowed at this new revelation, "Then it is true. They have created the most powerful vampire Ruauck-El will ever know."

"We are not going to kill him, Romann."

"Tisk, tisk, I have no intentions of killing him, not that I would know how to, to be honest. I require his help along with yours."

"Help with what?"

"To restore what was stolen from me."

"And what was that?"

"Kiratta Green, the helper of mankind."

"You speak of the mystic of the old age. The tomes speak of her falling in the Purge of Magic."

"My Kiratta was involved in a plot of jealousy and was forever entombed within a creature named Oculus."

A flash of realization hit Raina. "Bridazak spoke of a Kiratta that came from within Oculus once he answered the riddle. She is the true Kiratta Green you speak of?"

"Indeed. She is the reason for this state that I'm in."

"Kiratta turned you to a vampire?"

"Nay, I chose that path so I could be with her forever. Her soul is trapped within Oculus, the result of Ravana's revenge against me."

"Ravana, the daughter of the West Horn King?"

"She is the true ruler of the West. She is the daughter of King Oedikus and is more vile and evil than suspected by anyone. She changed me to who I am today."

Raina had known of Ravana's ruthless nature and her abilities as a powerful mystic long before what Romann was revealing to her now but not this last statement. "Ravana is a vampire?" Raina asked.

"She is more than that. She discovered an ancient vile of blood from what she thought was the Vemptukai and consumed it. She transformed into a medusa, a vampiric-medusa."

Raina said under her breath, "I must warn El'Korr."

"So the dwarves march to the west then," he said more as a matter of fact than a question.

She nodded.

Romann said, "I can help your army."

"For what in return?"

"If you help me speak with Jack and break the curse of Oculus."

"There are no guarantees that Jack will help, but I will do what I can."

"That is all that I ask."

Suddenly, Raina's head shifted slightly as if she heard something. Romann did not hear a thing even with his heightened senses and plainly asked, "What is it?"

Raina closed her eyes and seconds later opened them.

"It appears you might have your chance to speak with Jack sooner than you thought. Abawken informed me that your Vemptukai and Trillius are on their way back here."

"Then let us prepare for their arrival."

Chapter 23

Full Circle

Trillius peeked from behind the ice encrusted boulder and saw Frost Dwarf sentries posted at the entrance of the Chamber of Cleansing tunnel. Squads of the blue-skinned fighters marched in the area, guarding their precious home from intruders. Trillius had snuck by this kind before but these were not ordinary dwarves and his short time within their keep did not allow him to discover their specific weaknesses. His ring of disguise wouldn't help at this point as there were too many variables to consider. They would spot the ruse if he chose to be a Frost Dwarf and especially when having to interact with them as he couldn't speak the language. He could try one of the heroes but which one and the dwarves would know they don't travel alone. Trillius ran through the options quickly in his mind.

"Jack," he whispered, "I'm going to take a more direct approach than I normally do." The gnome turned to find his vampire partner had already vanished. "I hate it when you do that."

Trillius brazenly stepped out and walked toward the guards.

"Halt!" one of the Frost Dwarves bellowed.

"Well met," Trillius hailed them and continued to walk closer.

One guard spoke to the other, "It is Trillius."

"Yes, it is I and I wish to pass."

"Morthkin wants to speak with you. We will escort you to him."

"Of course, right after I retrieve something that I lost within the chamber. It will only take a minute." Trillius attempted to step between them but they stopped him with outstretched arms holding silver tipped spears.

Suddenly, Jack appeared behind them, grabbing hold of one dwarven armored shoulder, crushing the plate mail within his grasp. The Frost Dwarf buckled under the pressure, wincing in pain and falling to one knee while trying to grab for his attacker. The other turned and looked directly into the swirling eyes of the Vemptukai.

Jack spoke, "You will continue to keep guard and will not speak of our arrival. Do you understand?"

The dwarf resisted. His eyes squinting in determination before finally submitting to the command, "I understand."

"What are you doing?" the other guard protested through gritted teeth toward his partner.

Jack spun him around, releasing his grip and gave him the same instruction. The protector fell against the will of the vampire and both now stood at attention at the opening, ignoring Trillius and Jack.

The gnome said, "We make a good team."

"I'm hopeful you will keep your end of the deal."

"You can trust me, Jack. When I get my own kingdom, you will be the only vampire I allow to see me."

"Your own kingdom? You are quite confident. What makes you think you can keep any vampire from entering your domain?"

Trillius sighed, "It was a compliment Jack. I consider you a friend."

"You have a strange way of expressing compliments, but I will just say thank you, I guess."

"Come on Jack. Let's get you your precious mirror."

They walked the long tunnel and emerged into the Chamber of Cleansing. The black and grey smoke slowly swirled in the center. Trillius' knees buckled as flashes of memories ignited within his mind. The five dragon entities wanted to be free and he became the conduit against his will. A sudden flash of a dragon eye erupted inside his thoughts and Trillius flinched as if coming out of a nightmare.

Jack caught him and said, "Are you alright?"

Trillius regained his composure, "Yeah, I'm fine. This place gives me the creeps."

The gnome withdrew the Quill of Fate that he had secured within a leather pouch on his belt. The crystal shard fragment revealed no visible power but Trillius knew the capabilities of this item, as did Jack. He edged closer, on shaky legs, to the stone arched walkway that stretched across to the other side.

Jack noticed and could feel the nervousness inside the gnome but remained silent as he watched the fate of Trillius unfold. He remembered the Twelve calling to him, using the diamond ring his father had given, and the pull of their collective voice. A strong pull he could only define as destiny.

Trillius looked around the chamber. The four stations, fashioned into stone pedestals, hummed softly. They cradled the four elements retrieved by Raina and the other heroes weeks earlier. The artifacts set into their positions were like stationed sentinels protecting the room. The vortex that led to the Underworld swirled quietly just below him. His heart thumped loudly inside his chest and he felt beads of sweat forming on his forehead and scalp. He smelled remains of the charred stone from the red dragon's breath weapon. Memories came to mind of the evil mystic, Veric, casting his spell and the turbulent cyclonic air whipping around the chamber. Trillius thought he felt the wind and looked around. His mind brought images of the past to the forefront and he watched El'Korr and Rondee battling the mage. The heroes were scattered around at the different stations that now harbored the legendary gems of power. His heart raced and he thought, *"It's happening again."*

Jack called out, "Trillius, calm yourself."

Trillius suddenly snapped out of his nightmare and looked at Jack. Reality returned to him. He inhaled a deep breath, let it out, and took his first step onto the one-foot wide walkway arching across the chasm to the other side. At the center stood the perch where the five dragon stones had been placed. He visualized the stone that harbored the spirit of Dal-Draydian, an ancient blue wyrm of legend.

Trillius took careful steps and finally reached the center. He climbed on top of the stone pedestal and looked back at Jack who watched in anticipation.

The gnome held the Quill of Fate out, holding both ends with his tiny hands. He took a deep breath and exhaled.

Shakily, Trillius said, "I summon the spirit of Dal-Draydian."

Nothing happened. Trillius swallowed hard, began to look over at Jack, and then the crystal shard started to glow. It was a fierce crimson red, morphing to orange, then fading to a pitch black. A new portal swirled before Trillius, causing his wispy hair to flutter back in the strong breeze bellowing out of the opening. Electrical discharges sporadically shot out of the murky cloud until finally a bolt of lightning struck the gnome. The shard shattered in his hands and he flailed in place, vibrating as the electricity surged through his body. Inside Trillius' mind everything went black.

The gnome found himself walking in endless darkness. No sound came from his footsteps. He spoke, "Dal-Draydian." His voice did not echo.

"What have you done?" the dragon's voice questioned inside the pitch blackness.

Trillius smiled in relief, "I rescued you. We will now be together. Forever."

"You fool!" Dal-Draydian's head zipped in out of the void and suddenly stopped right in front of Trillius' face, unable to approach any further. Its blue scaled head, orange and red hued eyes glared and then retracted.

Trillius confidently clutched his hands behind his back and smirked, "It appears that I am now the one in charge of this relationship, my dear friend. You were the dominant one before but no longer. Your spirit is forever entwined with mine. Your thoughts and memories now submit to me."

Dal-Draydian growled, "I have seen the likes of you perish a thousand times over. When you fall, Great Trillius, and you will fall, I will be there to catch you."

"I'm glad you are such a straight forward kind of dragon. I will rule my own kingdom and you will serve me all the days of my great life. I always said it is lonely at the top, but it appears I will now have some company. Don't fight it, just embrace it."

Dal-Draydian drifted back into the darkness and said, "My patience will endure your lifetime and beyond, gnome."

Suddenly, Trillius opened his eyes and he was being held by Jack at the side of the Chamber of Cleansing. Jack was repeating his name.

Trillius smiled brightly, his eyes focused on something not tangible beyond Jack and said, "I know where your mirror is located. I know where everything is located."

Jack saw blue snaps of electricity spark from his pupils and understood that the blue ancient wyrm was now linked forevermore with Trillius. Jack could only hope that the Quill of Fate somehow garnered the gnome the mental strength to protect his mind enough to hold Dal-Draydian at bay. Trillius could now pillage the memories of the ancient dragon at will but for how long.

Deep down inside, Jack had grown fond of Trillius through their journey together, but Jack also had a destiny that did not align with anyone in this realm. The pull of the Twelve within his mind ushered him toward the singular task of retrieving the Mirror of Lost Souls at all cost.

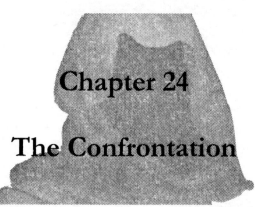

Chapter 24

The Confrontation

Jack lifted Trillius to his feet, "Give me the location of the Mirror of Lost Souls?"

"Not so fast, Jack. I will need to help you get it."

"I can manage without you, Trillius. I do not wish to bring you into harm's way."

The gnome smirked, "The place where your mirror is holds more than just that item and I want to gaze upon the treasures with my own eyes."

Jack squinted and then said, "Let us be off then."

"Fantastic! Another adventure for the both of us, Jack. Adventure just as you have always wanted."

"I have had my fill of adventure. More than a hundred men combined."

Trillius chuckled, "Is that so? I believe your Twelve have had the adventures, my friend. The young innocent Jack had none to speak of, but his escapade upon a bronze dragon and a brief trip to heaven if I recall correctly."

Jack stared for a long time at Trillius. He whispered, "You are right. None of the other memories are my own."

"It's alright. We are currently making up for all that lost time." Trillius noticed Jack turn his head slightly and froze in place.

Trillius said softly, "What is it?"

"It appears we have company."

They both turned to the exit and standing there were Raina and Romann.

Raina looked at Jack for the first time in his altered state. Now a man, but very much a vampire, and her heart broke.

Trillius snarled and growled in pure hatred and ran toward the elven mystic. Raina's hair flared into flames like a lion's mane.

Superheated air surrounded her, forcing Romann to quickly step away and halting the advance of Trillius.

Jack grabbed the gnome and pulled him back and quietly said, "What is wrong with you, Trillius?"

Trillius continued growling and his vision wobbled in and out of focus. He slowly relaxed and began to regain his composure. He looked at Jack, barely able to say, "Dal-Draydian."

Jack understood just then that the hatred the blue dragon felt towards Raina had caused the sudden outrage. She was the demise of Dal-Draydian here at this very spot.

The Sheldeen elf returned to her natural form, ending the heat she projected, and said, "Trillius, I have no ill will toward you."

Jack responded, "The gnome and a sworn enemy of yours are now entwined and for a brief instant it was not his mind but the other inside that came at you."

She nodded and peered over at Romann, concern upon her face. She turned back and said, "I had secretly hoped that it would not be possible."

Trillius quipped, "You know me, I love the impossible, but rest assured 'D' will not be doing that again."

Jack said, "Let us start over. Hello, Raina. Who is your friend?"

"Let me introduce myself, I am Romann de Beaux," he swept his hat off his head and bowed low.

"We wish to speak with you, Jack," Raina said.

Trillius coughed to get Jack's attention raising his eyebrows to hint that he wanted to leave quickly.

Jack said, "We cannot stay long, Raina, what is it?"

"I will speak plainly with you Jack. The Twelve, whatever they have promised, are lying."

Jack paused, shifted his eyes from the swirls to his original steel grey, and said, "I understand things now, Raina. Before I was merely a child but now I understand."

"What is it that you understand?"

"I couldn't be with you and the others because I wasn't ready. It was not my time but now it is. I will see this through, Raina, without you."

"Jack, let us help you."

"Help me? All of you abandoned me. You left me with the

dwarves to fend for myself."

Romann stepped forward, "If I may? You are now the Vemptukai, Jack. I can see that your motives are for the good within the realm. I have come before you to ask for your help."

"You may ask but I direct my own path now."

"We don't have time for this, Jack," Trillius interrupted.

"What is your request?" Jack spoke, ignoring the gnome. Trillius flailed his arms in the air in disgust and turned away, shaking his head.

"My thanks," Romann started, "I was betrayed hundreds of years ago."

"Who hasn't been betrayed?" Trillius scoffed.

Romann continued, "The West Horn King's daughter, Ravana, cursed my beloved for eternity within the creature that is known as Oculus across the Plains of Shame."

"I know the creature you speak of, Bridazak told me, continue."

"Ravana is a twisted version of a vampire and she was jealous of Kiratta and my relationship with her. I chose to become a vampire in order to someday be reunited with my lost love. I believe you are the answer that I have been waiting for."

"What is it that you think I can do?"

"I need you to have Ravana end the curse and release Kiratta from Oculus. You have the power to compel her to relinquish this egregious act."

Jack contemplated this for a second, before speaking, "I will weigh your request, Romann, but I make no promises. I have other matters to deal with."

"Exactly, other matters, now let's get going, Jack," Trillius said.

Raina said, "Jack, El'Korr and his army are marching to the west. They are going to attack the Horn King. We could use your help."

"The dwarve's war is not my war."

"Jack, I cannot change what has happened but can instead recognize the hurt it caused you and ask for forgiveness."

"It's not that simple, Raina."

"But it is," she stepped toward him.

Trillius intercepted Raina, floating up into the air looking at her, face to face, "Our time here has ended. Jack and I are going now." Blue sparks ignited the gnome's eyes. "How do you like my new stature, Raina?"

She stepped back, not in fear, but to assess what she was seeing. She looked at Jack, "The Twelve are evil Jack and they are using you so they can be released. I know that you don't want that and I know that you don't like being used."

"Well, we can all talk another time. Jack and I completely understand how busy you are with your war and all but we have unfinished business to attend to. Now excuse us or not, we are leaving."

Romann stepped forward and Trillius turned sharply at his approach, halting Romann, "I will destroy you where you stand vampire, if you take one more step." Trillius' voice was amplified and he spoke with power and confidence.

"I believe you," Romann backed away.

Trillius then stated, "The Vemptukai and Trillius are united and together, even you Raina, are no match for us."

Raina said, "The greed inside of you will only amplify Dal-Draydian's strength. No amount of treasure will ever fill the gap in your heart. That gap is only filled through relationship."

"You are more correct about that statement than you will ever know. My heart does have a vast gap inside of it and I have already planned to restore many relationships to fill it. One I plan visiting now as a matter of fact. This one from my past has a hot temper but I think he has cooled down since we last met. Time will tell."

At first a low rumble was heard and then felt but it soon increased until finally an intense bolt of lightning struck Trillius and then forked to strike Jack. Raina and Romann shielded their eyes and looked away. When the flash and the thunderous crack ended, they peered back, still partially blinded, to find the gnome and Jack vanished.

"What happened to the meek gnome I once knew?" Romann asked.

"It appears fate has united Dal-Draydian and Trillius once again."

"Who was the gnome referring to in his past?"

Raina thought for a second and said, "I believe it to be a red dragon."

"How do you know?"

"I can't be certain but my guess, since Trillius' focus is on wealth and power, would be a red dragon. It is the closest to us.

"Can you teleport us there?"

"I can but it requires me to research the location which will take too long. I know someone in the area that can help."

"Who?"

"Abawken."

The sheik fighter could hear Raina's voice within his mind as the group walked back toward the Shield in hopes of tracking down Trillius and Jack.

"Abawken, I bring grave news."

"What happened?"

"Trillius has united with the spirit of Dal-Draydian and Jack is more than just a vampire. He is called the Vemptukai, which translates to the Vampire King. They are working together to release the Twelve and are at a place called the Hall of Sorrows."

"Where is this place you speak of?"

"Dulgin will know of it. Ask him now."

Abawken refocused on the lonely dirt road they were on and blurted out, "Dulgin, do you know the location of a place called the Hall of Sorrows?"

The group stopped as Dulgin turned to face the human, "What? Why would you all of sudden ask such a thing?"

"Do you know?"

"Yes, but I'm not interested in any side missions."

"Raina said that is where Trillius and Jack are now."

"Well, why didn't you say so, Huey? It's half-a-day march to the southwest."

Abawken refocused on Raina and delivered the message, *"Yes, Dulgin says it is not far from us."*

Raina responded, *"Do not try to stop Jack and Trillius. They are very powerful. We need to get Jack back, but he feels that we have abandoned him. Abawken, there is still good in him. I know it to be true. We will find a way somehow to bring him back to us. Be careful my love."*

"We will."

Spilf asked, "What is going on?"

Dulgin answered, "We are going to a place of legend, the Hall of Sorrows. C'mon, I'll tell you all about it while we walk."

Abawken added, "Raina told me one other thing."

"What is that, Huey?"

"He used the Quill of Fate. Trillius and Dal-Draydian are now together."

"Damn that infernal gnome. His brain matches his size."

Rozelle said, "Could we get there faster if we had a cart?"

"Yeah, but there are no stables for miles," Spilf said.

Rozelle pointed and the group turned to see an old cart tipped over in the brush. They inspected it, lifting it back onto its wheels.

"It's in decent shape, but we have a problem," Spilf said.

Rozelle answered, "And I have the solution." She instantly turned into a massive war horse.

The others hooked up their rope and the leather straps that remained attached to the cart and began their trek to the Hall of Sorrows.

Dulgin said, "Now we will be there in couple of hours to say hello to Big Nose. It's our turn to surprise him for a change."

Chapter 25

Hall of Sorrows

The strange partnership had brought the gnome and newly transformed Jack to a place called the Hall of Sorrows.

"It doesn't look as scary as it sounds," Trillius said as he gazed upon the entrance of the legendary hall.

"Looks can be deceiving. You, of all gnomes, should know this."

"Well, your mirror awaits us inside but first we must speak with Gaermahn-Shesteeva, the red dragon. Let me do all the talking."

"By all means," Jack responded, as he waved his arm to usher Trillius to lead the way.

The air was dry, the dirt crunched underfoot, and the fine dust puffed out on the sides with each step. A temple had been built inside the cliff wall that stood several hundred-feet high. The once brilliant gleam of marble was now faded, cracked, and in some spots, scorched from a blast of flame. A single entrance into this ancient place of worship led to the vast hall and ultimately to the red dragon's lair.

Trillius turned to address Jack but found he had vanished. He said to himself, "Typical vampire. Scared of a dragon."

The gnome stopped at the entrance, cupped his hands around his mouth and shouted, "Gaermahn!" Trillius stood waiting in the fading sunlight. A sharp edged shadow scrolled across the face of the cliff as the sun hid itself. He called again, "Gaermahn!"

The ground rumbled under his feet and in an instant the head of a red dragon, measuring the size of a small cottage, protruded from the temple entrance. Its eyes were a red flame, ablaze with hatred. It shimmered in the sunlight from deep maroon to soft orange and waves of heat emanated off its impenetrable scale hide. Prominent horns, the length of a man, protruded from its elongated forehead. The mouth of the beast was revealed when it snarled, revealing its purple slithery tongue that crept out between the layers of sharp teeth.

It growled at Trillius, connecting with his mind telepathically, *"How do you come by my name, gnome?"*

Trillius smiled, "I'm Trillius Triplehand and I have a message for you."

"Your name is meaningless and your message is even less than that."

Trillius smelled the foul breath of the creature as the warm humid air encompassed him. He felt his clothing saturate with the odor. His face soured and he covered it with his hands. "Do you not want the message I have for you?" he sputtered.

Flames shot from the dragon's nostrils ending a few feet before engulfing the gnome. The heated air blasted Trillius causing him to close his eyes and take a step backward.

"Are you done trying to intimidate me? I know you Gaermahn all too well or should I say Kezch-etz-akeiv-ekotsch?"

"You speak our language and with the correct inflection. You are no gnome and yet I don't smell dragon blood in you."

"I knew your father, Gaermahn."

The red dragon paused, contemplating the statement, before beckoning, *"Come inside my lair and let us talk in private."*

"What a grand idea. Lead the way."

Trillius searched through the memories of Dal-Draydian as he walked inside the temple, memories that were now his. He blocked the complaints and empty threats of the spirit he had resurrected from the Quill of Fate. They were one, but this time the gnome called the shots. Dal-Draydian was now Trillius.

The gnome could see in the dark as clear as day. He now possessed dragon-sight. A soft orange glow permeated further ahead. He was in the excavated tunnel leading to the actual hall. Trillius stepped forward and stared in amazement at the wonderfully filled treasure room of the great Gaermahn. Gold, silver, and platinum coins were piled in the chamber like prairie hills. Gem encrusted chests, chalices, and chainmail littered the landscape. Long and forgotten items adorned the room of the dragon lair. Mounds of the loot were pushed up against the outlining wall covering ancient carvings of a lost religion. The stagnant smell of metal and dirt filled the chamber.

"You have been very productive, Gaermahn."

The red dragon, the size of a two-story farmhouse in body alone, nestled within his gold laden bed, curled its deadly tail to his side and buried it underneath his leathery wings.

"Trillius Triplehand is the name given a thief. You search for something within my spoils, but know that I don't give, I take."

"Your father, the great red, the feared wyrm of the east, known to all in the Bronze Age and to all the gods before and after him, made this statement about his heir, Gaermahn-Shesteeva, 'He is a spoiled dragon of little-worth'."

The breath-weapon of the dragon unleashed in agonized fury at Trillius. Flames jetted out of its maw with enough force and heat to disintegrate flesh, bone, and spirit. Coins in the vicinity melted. As quickly as it came it receded as Gaermahn cut off the superheated blast of fire. The intense roar ended and silence engulfed the room except for the sizzling metal as it cooled. Trillius was gone.

Gaermahn had taken the Hall of Sorrows as his home centuries ago, after the fall of his father to the east. He fled to the west, the only one to survive, losing his mother and siblings in the time of the Purge. The Mystics of Old hunted and besieged their territory.

The red dragon settled himself, closed his eyes, and tried to block out the memory of that time, but suddenly, his eyes flared open when he heard the tiny gnome speak again, "Your father did not die within the Purge."

"You lie!"

"Five of the greatest dragons sought eternal life and sought out the Lost Mystic within the Veil of Shadows, between Ruauck-El and the Underworld." Trillius' voice echoed throughout the room. Gaermahn walked a path he had made within his treasure chamber and zipped his head behind mounds in search of the gnome.

"These five dragons were betrayed and their spirits were controlled by this mage of darkness. The people of Ruauck-El banded against the Dragon God and each ancient entity was trapped within a single stone and scattered across the realm. The mystic was never seen again."

"Who are you?"

"I am Dal-Draydian."

"Impossible."

"And yet I know everything about you, young Gaermahn. Your father wing-bucked and tail slapped you for every good deed you performed and praised your bad nature. He encouraged you to steal, kill, and destroy. He called you 'Etz-akeiv-tekotsch'."

Gaermahn froze in place. *"I have not heard that name in such a long time. I don't know how but you have the knowledge and insight of Dal-Draydian."*

"Yes, Trillius and Dal-Draydian are now one."

"What is it that you seek in my lair?"

"Nothing too consequential. A mirror."

The great red scoffed, *"A mirror? I have several mirrors, none of which present me with any favor. You can take whichever one you like and then be gone."*

"This mirror is special."

"Of course it is. You would not come within my lair if it was ordinary. Don't belittle my intelligence, Dal-Draydian."

"Where is the Mirror of Lost Souls?"

"I don't have such an item," it responded slowly and calmly.

Trillius pulled the memories of his new partner, "I know it is here because I was visited in a dream from one of the clerics of old. The fool asked me to protect it and revealed to me what it was and where it came from."

Gaermahn narrowed his eyes and said telepathically, *"It is too dangerous, even for the dragons to have in the world. The doorway to the chamber is magically sealed and only I know its secrets."*

Jack was absorbing the broken information of the one-sided conversation. Trillius spoke openly while the dragon delivered his responses via the mind. He listened intently to the gnome, trying to piece together the location of the mirror and how to get it. Other mirrors of various size and decorations could be seen against back walls or partially buried amongst coins and jewelry.

Trillius said smoothly, "I see. The clerics brought you here to protect this mirror, now magically locked within a chamber. They knew that they would die and needed something that would live a very long time, but you are getting older and weaker, Gaermahn. I can take over and release you to have fun in the world. Just relish in the thought of freedom. Imagine ravaging villages, plucking the cowpecks that graze the land, and hearing the screams of terror in the people as you swoop over them."

"I can leave when I choose and I am not required to stay here. The chamber can only be opened by me. The clerics used their dark magic to make certain of this."

"I suppose it requires a phrase from you to open?"

"More than words, Speck."

"Perhaps I should kill you and take the mirror," Trillius boldly stated as he walked out from his hiding place.

Gaermahn chuckled, *"Kill me? The spirit of a dragon and a gnome, kill the Great Gaermahn?"*

Trillius pointed toward the dragon and a blue and white lightning bolt shot out exploding a mound of gold next to Gaermahn. Coins were scattered everywhere and rained down the surrounding hills like water. The cascading sound echoed and then subsided.

The gnome said brazenly, "I missed on purpose, now give me the mirror."

Gaermahn laughed heartily, but stopped suddenly when he felt something on top of his neck. The dragon could not see the vampire that now straddled him. Its eyes widened from the pain as one of its scales was ripped out of place by the tremendous strength now granted to Jack.

Jack said, "Settle yourself great beast or I will—"

Gaermahn did not wait for Jack's message and quickly slammed his body into a pile of gold, rolling over to crush the intruder. It came to its feet once again and looked for the blood as evidence of Jack's death but found nothing.

"I'm over here," Jack announced as the misty vapor of his body materialized next to Trillius.

Gaermahn snarled and was about to unleash its mighty breath weapon, but it froze in place, a visible strain in its jaw and other facial features. Its eyes rolled back in its head and then it plummeted straight down as if it passed out.

"Jack, what did you do? Kill him?"

"Patience," Jack whispered.

Trillius watched as the once fiery eyes opened, revealing cold black irises instead. Its red shimmering scales faded slowly from the head to the tail; the vibrant red now dull. It mechanically turned toward them and approached one stomp at a time. Gaermahn stopped when it reached them and lowered its head in a bow.

The gnome giggled in unbelief, "You turned Gaermahn? No vampire has ever turned a dragon or any creature outside the human race." Trillius was hit with sudden realization and continued, "You mean this entire time you could have turned me?"

"I'm the Vemptukai," Jack answered. "Gaermahn, open the chamber that harbors the Mirror of Lost Souls."

Without a word, the undead dragon, snarled to reveal its prominent vampire fangs as it turned and marched to the back of the hall. It cleared the heavy treasure away with several swipes of its claws. Behind the mound of coins was a door with the symbol of a dragon eye. The deep etchings blazed with a magically vibrant orange hue, which cascaded peacefully over Gaermahn's head, bathing it in its light. The cleric magic that barred the entrance faded as it scanned the undead behemoth standing before it. Trillius and Jack stared as they watched the door crack and crumble. A passageway lay beyond.

Gaermahn backed away. Jack walked to the tunnel. Trillius followed.

Jack stopped and said, "I don't think it wise for you to go any further, my friend."

"My friend? That sounds nice, Jack. I can honestly say that I also consider you a friend."

"I would have never thought you would use the word 'honest'. Do you consider me a friend only because you fear that I can turn you to a vampire?"

Trillius chuckled, "You are more powerful than I had imagined but I have no fear of you. You are still that young boy I met within the Shield. The same child who was searching for his own destiny and, in that, I know you are not one to take destinies away from others. You are a strange vampire Jack but knowing you before your conversion has helped me understand you a little better than most. I hope you find your place in the realm, Jack."

"I have a feeling that you will be gone once I come back. Where is the Great Trillius off to next?"

He paused, "I will come into my own kingdom and help myself to the lost treasures that are in Ruauck-El. I'm sure we will see each other again."

"And what about Gaerhman's treasure? Wasn't there something here that you wanted?"

"Nay, I only wanted to look at it. You can have it. Consider it a gift."

"You are too kind. Well met, Trillius. Your dreams are unfolding. My hope is still for you to find peace."

"Peace is for those poor souls buried in the ground. I'm a young gnome with a whole realm before me."

Jack smirked, "There is more than this realm. I'm not sure you will find anything in this world to fill your heart."

"Oh, my heart is full, I can assure you of that, young Jack. Go on, get your trinket and do whatever you need to do with it. I want to make sure I'm not around. A Mirror of Lost Souls doesn't sound fun to me and you know me, I'm all about fun."

Trillius began to walk away but suddenly turned back and asked, "Jack, do you smell it?"

Jack did not respond and waited with a raised eyebrow for the gnome's answer.

"I smell the spoils of war. No longer will this gnome scratch by with a few coins. I'm now a world-changer."

With that, Trillius skipped off out of sight. Jack turned to face the opening that led to the mirror and thought about Trillius' last comment. *"I'm now a world-changer."*

"So am I."

Chapter 26

The Mirror of Lost Souls

T he darkness surrounded him like a cloak. Jack remembered a time when he feared it as a child. He had only been a vampire for a short time, but his memories seemed a lifetime ago and more a dream than reality. His conscious thoughts weaved back and forth amongst the Twelve spirits' memories inhabiting his body; the fallen paladins who now engrained their lives into his very essence. He could feel the pressure of the task at hand. His mind remembered what the leader of the Twelve had said to him firmly before he left the Shield. *"Set us free and let us join you to rid this world of evil once again."*

There was a soft amber glow emanating from a chamber up ahead, accompanied by an alluring melody. The music seemed familiar but he could not place where he had heard it before. It pulled at his subconscious and Jack hastened his steps.

"This tune..." he thought to himself. *"I know it."*

The charm and curse of the Mirror of Lost Souls beckoned him closer. Jack entered the rough cut stone room and found resting in the back recesses the item he sought. Gold and black steel melted together forming the outer frame of the reflective silver mirror. As he approached the black seemed to move like slithering snakes through the gold.

A whisper called to him from the mirror, "Jack, come to me." It was a woman's voice.

"Jack, come to me," it harkened again.

The music was hauntingly sweet and pulled at his mind, drawing him to stand before the mirror and gaze into it. Jack's face, distorted at first, slowly sharpened as he walked closer to the mirror that leaned against the back wall. The cursed treasure was the size of a human's torso. His image metamorphosed into a ghostlike woman with chestnut colored hair. The woman's apparitional face softened.

"I have missed you, Jack."

"How do you know me?"

"Come closer and you will recognize me."

Jack leaned in a little further. It felt natural for him to follow her instruction.

"Now, we can be together…forever!" Her voice heightened into a frightening screech with her final word. An unseen force pulled and yanked Jack's spirit inside. He was able to look back and saw his body gripping the edges of the Mirror, energy surging through his limbs, and then falling to the ground. Jack looked at his hands and saw the wispy incorporeal substance of a body. Jack thought, *"So, I didn't lose my soul when I was converted to a vampire afterall. My God is for me and is protecting me."*

The ghost-soul that had pulled him in wailed a hideous cackle as she weaved in and around Jack's ethereal form. He was inside the Mirror of Lost Souls.

He floated within the murky mire. Soul after soul soared around him in screams of pain and torment. Jack now knew the secrets of the Mirror because he inherited the power of Qel-Soma, the lich-mage he had killed, and her ability to understand the magic of the item upon her touch. When he touched it briefly, before being consumed by its power, the knowledge of the depths of this lost legend had engrained into him. He was now inside a dimensional conduit of the Underworld. It was a doorway and he had entered it.

Jack could feel the evil within this place. These were once people who walked Ruauck-El but were now forever damned.

"I wanted you dead," the female apparition said venomously.

"Who are you?"

"It was you and your father who ruined it all. I knew you were a curse!" she yelled.

"My father? How do you know of him?"

"You were to be sacrificed to the witch-goddess Bendis."

Jack had never heard of this deity. "I ask you again, what relation do you have with my father?"

The shifty ghost-like image settled and her face softened once again. She suddenly materialized fangs and her face elongated into a hideous creature as she said, "He was my husband!" Then she reeled away and zipped around amongst the other lost souls screaming and yelling as they weaved about aimlessly.

Jack was stunned. He had no memory of his mother and this spirit was claiming to be her. He pushed back the thoughts and felt strongly this lost soul was lying to him. "My mother died at childbirth when having me."

"Nay, your father found out about the sacrifice on the night of your coming and he murdered me right in front of you!"

"You lie. Dad told me my mother died when she gave birth to me."

She cackled and weaved her translucent spirit in circles around him. "Bendis will be pleased now that you are here. You were lost to me but now have been found, my Jack."

"She knows my name," he thought. *"Could she be my mother? Could father have lied to me about her death? No, it can't be."*

The spirit-mother writhed around him and brought her face in front of his and said, "Do you require more proof, my son? When you were two-years of age you fell into the fire and burned your arm."

Jack was at a loss of words. This was true and only someone close to him would know of such a thing.

"Bendis has double-blessed me. She has given me eternal life and now has returned my son."

"No, this can't be right," Jack thought and then the rage built up inside of him as he shouted, "This is a lie!"

She laughed as she flew around in circles and yelled, "I have gained my son!"

Jack soothed his emotion and calmly stated, "You have gained nothing but more pain. I am no longer your son and you are not my mother."

"You cannot leave. No one leaves," she cackled.

The spirit form of Jack lifted away as if being pulled from the darkness by an indiscernible force. "I wish things could have been different for you. You are here because you made your choice. All of you did," he said, falling distant.

"No, you cannot leave!" She tried to chase him down, but the light of his spirit faded to a pinpoint dot until finally disappearing altogether.

Jack's spirit image jetted out from the Mirror of Lost Souls and shot back into his body lying on the floor. Jack jolted awake.

His brief visit within the Underworld was like two magnets repulsing one another. He knew he did not belong there and yet the pull on his very being warred within. Deep down there was a desire to be there and he compared it to the longing he had inside of himself to be in heaven.

Jack laid there and thought, *"Where do I belong? Hell cannot keep me and I have remorse over my decision for who I have become. What am I? Who am I? All I have ever wanted was to be known and now I am known only by what I am now and not what I was. My memories, my knowledge, are now of others…The Twelve. Their souls are trapped, but can I be the one to bring them redemption? Can I be the one that frees people from the clutches of this world? Was this God's assignment for me all along? Surely, God knew I would make this choice and surely He is on my side to help me even in my darkest hour, but where is His presence. He seems so distant. Do not abandon me, Lord. I cannot do this alone."*

The Twelve ignited in his mind as he remembered what they spoke to him before he left, *"You are not alone, Jack. We are here to help you. We will guide the people with you and bring justice to the darkness that has invaded our land once we are freed."*

Jack stood up, approached the mirror, and placed his left hand on the upper corner and his right on the lower corner. The Mirror of Lost Souls shrunk and became the size of his palm. He placed the cursed item inside his tunic, brushed the dirt from his pants, and said, "Let us see where my choices take me next."

Chapter 27

Gnome Economics

Trillius laughed hysterically like a giddy child as he ran out of the Hall of Sorrows. The sun was waning and the shadows of night beckoned. He was relieved about the freedom he now had and the kingdom he would soon build. The vast treasures of the realm awaited him as their new owner.

Trillius fell to his knees outside and yelled into the air, lifting his hands high, "I'm the Great Trillius!"

A gruff voice off to his left said, "You got one thing right. You are great, great at finding trouble."

Trillius turned and his giddiness quickly soured at the sight of the ugly dwarf named Dulgin. Standing next to him was the human fighter, Abawken, and the ordakian, Spilf. Stepping from behind them was Rozelle.

The gnome stood with his palms facing out, "Rozelle, let me explain."

Rozelle stepped forward, "Trillius, what have you done? Why are you doing this? What happened to us? You and me?"

"I was securing our future, darling. You were busy with your forest stuff and well I—"

"Just stop it, Trillius! You can never just tell me the truth. Do you even love me?"

"I think so."

"You think so? You think so!"

"What? Did I say something wrong?"

Rozelle clenched her fists, her face turned red with anger, and she instantly transformed herself into a ten-foot tall black bear and roared in rage. She turned and lumbered away thrashing at bushes and trees along the way.

Dulgin chimed in, "Is there ever a time when you don't say

something wrong?"

Trillius pleaded, "What about me? I was stuck helping Jack the vampire this entire time. It was traumatizing."

Spilf scoffed softly, "I'm sure it was very traumatizing, but I feel much sorrier for Jack."

The heroes one by one crossed their arms across their chests and stared at Trillius.

"Why doesn't anyone believe me?"

Spilf said, "Maybe because you stole the Quill of Fate and used it to bring back Dal-whatever-its-name-is."

Trillius froze slightly, paused, and then said coyly, "Oh, you know about that?"

"Master Trillius, we know about your endeavors with Jack. Where is he?"

Trillius pointed behind him, "Well Abawken, he is in there, but you don't want to go in."

"Don't tell us what to do, gnomey."

"Be my guest but I warn you that Jack is not alone in there."

"Who else is with him?" Spilf asked.

"Oh, just a dragon of sorts."

"Of sorts?"

"Well, it kind of changed since Jack, well, bit it." Trillius tried to imitate fangs by lifting his upper lip to show his teeth.

The heroes' brows scrunched as they tried to interpret what the gnome was suggesting.

Trillius threw up his arms, "Fine, don't believe me. It seems to be the trend these days."

"As much as we would like to see Jack, we are here to find you," Abawken stated.

"Me?" Trillius placed a hand onto his chest. "Don't I feel special? What is it that I can do for you?"

Abawken, Spilf, and Dulgin looked at one another and the human said, "We need your help, Master Trillius."

"Oh, I see, now you need my help?"

"Don't make this a big deal," Dulgin said.

"Oh, but it is and I require two things in return."

Spilf said, "You haven't even heard what we need."

"I don't need to know that right now."

"What are your terms, Master Gnome?"

"First, each of you need to grant me one favor that I can call upon at any time."

"I don't like this one bit," Dulgin said to Abawken.

"You won't like my next request even more, dwarf."

"What is it? Spit it out."

"Second, I want you to say out loud that you need my help."

"What? We just said it."

"No, Abawken asked on your behalf, but I require it to come directly from your lips."

"Why me?"

"I'm waiting."

"I'm going to punch you so hard your—"

Abawken grabbed Dulgin before he could march over and hit the gnome.

"It's a simple request," Trillius jabbed.

Spilf and Abawken settled the dwarf. The ordakian whispered, "For Bridazak." Dulgin looked at him for a long moment and then nodded.

"Well, Dulgy? Can you get past your dwarven pride and ask me personally for my help?"

"I'm only doing this for Bridazak."

"You honor the dead, how nice, I'm sure Mr. B was a fine young Dak."

Dulgin hesitated. He looked at his friends who nodded and encouraged him to say it. Trillius smirked.

The dwarf finally said quietly, "I need your help."

"What was that? I couldn't quite hear you."

"I need your help!" Dulgin yelled. He glared at Trillius wanting to rip the nose off of the cocky gnome and wipe his smug face off.

"Deal. Now what is it you need the Great Trillius Triplehand to do for you?"

Abawken said, "We need to find out if Bridazak is alive within the Underworld."

Trillius giggled, "That is easy. No, he is not."

"There is an item that will discern that for us, Master Trillius."

"Oh, I see. Another item. What is it that you seek?"

"It is called Akar's Looking Glass."

"How interesting." Trillius' eyes squinted a bit in contemplation of the request.

"Do you know of the item?" Spilf asked.

"It is not an item per say, but instead a place. You seek Akar's Tower and inside you will find his scrying pool."

"Where is this tower?" Dulgin said.

"To the far east in the Plains of Glynndle."

Spilf turned to Dulgin, "Have you heard of it?"

"Nay, but the far east will take us weeks to get there, not to mention the border crossings."

"Nonsense," Trillius announced, "I have someone who can help us."

"Someone?" Spilf said.

"I also have an interest in finding some old friends of mine and the Looking Glass will do the job nicely."

"Who can help us, Master Trillius?"

He smiled, "Dal-Draydian."

Just then, the adventurers heard a dragon roar from inside the Hall of Sorrows. They could feel the ground beneath them tremble.

The heroes looked at Trillius with raised eyebrows. Spilf whispered, "Dal-Draydian?"

The gnome did not have to answer as the red dragon, Gaermahn, launched itself out of the opening and into the air, causing them all to duck and shield their faces from the dirt that kicked up. The debris settled and they watched the huge wyrm fly to the west. There sitting on the neck of the beast was the silhouette of a man they could only assume was Jack.

"Apparently young Jack is not up for talking," Trillius mocked.

"Where is he going?" Dulgin said.

"I would say he is going to settle up with the Twelve at the Frost Dwarf kingdom, but that is to the north and yet he flies west. Your guess is as good as mine."

"El'Korr," Dulgin whispered.

"Yeah, perhaps he wants to talk to your brother and join his war party," Trillius said sarcastically. "But we have other matters to deal with, like Akar's Tower. Shall we?"

Spilf stepped forward, "Wait, we also need to have the Quill of Fate back?"

Trillius eyed him curiously, "Why?"

"The Madame. She wants it back."

Abawken added, "If we return it to her then she will call off her search for you."

Trillius smirked, "Oh, you are all concerned for my well-being, is that it? I'm flattered."

"Actually," Dulgin said, "It was more for Jack's well-being. We told her we would help bring you in."

"Ah, love the dwarf-wittiness. Well, we seem to have another problem," Trillius shrugged.

"Where is it, Long-Nose?"

"It's now dust, I'm afraid. I guess the Madame won't be too thrilled about that," he mocked.

Spilf said, "This isn't a game. Don't you care about people? Your decisions have consequences."

Trillius lightened up on his sarcasm and said, "My apologies, dear Spilf. I assure you that the Madame will not harm me in any—"

Spilf became angry and cut him off, "What about Jack? All of your decisions affect other people. Rozelle, us, everyone!"

"Oh, Jack. Well, you boys don't understand. Jack will be just fine, well, he is not fine like the young Jack you all knew before, well, never mind. Trust me, the Madame won't be able to get to him. He is, well, very different now."

Spilf turned and walked to stand behind Dulgin, unable to look at Trillius. The others just stared at the gnome. Dulgin gave a low growl and Abawken had his typical reserved appearance.

Trillius sighed and said, "Listen, I will help you get to Akar's Looking Glass. Let me redeem myself, granted in a small way, and help you to find your lost Bridazak."

One by one they hesitantly nodded agreement.

"Good, now will someone go and get Rozelle? I don't think she is in a talking mood with me right now."

Chapter 28

We Meet Again

The newly transformed Gaermahn Shesteeva soared over the trees and plains of the western land of Ruauck-El. Jack felt the bite of the cold air on his face. He tilted his head back, closed his eyes, and held his arms out wide. Memories of him and the heroes, Bridazak, Spilf, Dulgin, Xan, and Raina, flooded his mind with the thoughts of them all flying on the back of the bronze dragon, Zeffeera. He imagined himself, a boy, being back in that time, but the red dragon broke his revelry, sending a telepathic message to his mind.

"We approach Tuskabar."

Jack surveyed the land. The twinkling lights of the city lay before them along the coast of the Illustrya Ocean. The great walls protected the patrons inside and the lonely spire of the West Horn King towered high into the air as the beacon of Tuskabar.

"Good, fly out of sight of the city in the veil of darkness."

"What are we looking for?"

"Romann de Beaux."

"We will not find a single person while flying."

"He was dressed like a swashbuckler so he must have a ship. Fly over the docks."

Gaermahn did as instructed. Smaller villages laced outside the walls appeared quiet. Wisps of smoke puffed out from thatch roofed chimneys. The city torch lights waned in the late hours and there was calm throughout the town. Taverns had settled, the streets were empty, and guards casually patrolled the walls and inner wards. They flew over the water and hundreds of various sized ships were anchored in the harbor and docks. The water glistened with the soft moonlight.

Jack instructed his dragon via telepathy, *"Fly south along the coast.*

Romann's ship will most likely be hidden."

"How do you know?"

"The West Horn King's daughter, Ravana, is not someone he wants to alert. Let's see if my instincts are right."

"This city smells of death," Gaermahn said in Jack's mind.

Jack did not respond but instead kept his focus on finding Romann. He spotted something seconds later. *"There, a milarri off the coast just past the waves."*

"I see it."

"Land on the coast, remain hidden, and wait for my return."

The galleon creaked and the ropes groaned as it rocked gently back and forth. A mist came over the edge of the railing and Jack materialized on the deck. He surveyed the area. It was empty. The vessel had no crew, nor did he sense any below. He heard the flag snap above with a sudden gust of wind and he could see the pattern of a stitched rose in the moonlight.

Jack strode toward the captain's quarters but stopped suddenly. He turned slowly around and found twenty vampires standing at the ready.

Daysho, dressed in all black, stepped forward and asked, "Who are you?"

Another vamp lurched forward with a shaky finger and said hesitantly, "It's him. That is the one."

Jack recognized the nervous vamp from the forest. He was the one he instructed to go back and give them his message.

Daysho's eyes narrowed and he tilted his head slightly, "So you are this supposed, Vemptukai?"

Jack nodded.

"I'm Daysho, the Caretaker of the Thieves Guild."

"It doesn't look like a thieves' guild any longer," Jack replied as he looked around at the deck filled with hungry vampires. He could sense their insatiable thirst for blood as the night deepened.

"Do you wish to join us?"

"I'm looking for someone."

"And who might that be?"

"Romann."

The red curls of Penelope bounced as she waltzed out from behind the other vampires to stand in front of Jack. Her dazzling green eyes looked intently into Jack's steel grays. She studied the tattoos laced across his face. She suddenly broke away her gaze and walked to the rail of the ship.

Jack felt a connection to her deep down in the recesses of his mind. He could not place how or where he had seen her and realized it was the Twelve's memories. She was of great importance, he was sure of it. He could feel a block within his mind and could only see flashes of her face, nothing more.

She said, "I'm Countessa Penelope de Luz," still not looking at anyone but the ocean. "Daysho Gunsen is the Vampire King. You will bow to him and give your allegiance."

Jack remained silent. He studied them all. He thought, *If she is of importance then how can she believe that this Daysho is the Vampire King. He is nothing compared to my power. Is she testing me?"*

"Bow to me!" Daysho yelled.

Jack slowly took a step toward the assassin and then another. As he came closer the tension increased and the other twenty vampires prepared to fight.

"Halt!" someone called from atop the galleon's tower.

"Romann?" Daysho said as he looked up.

"Do not touch our guest."

"But my grace, this vigilante must submit to the new leadership."

"If you value your life, all of you, then stand down. This is the true Vemptukai."

Daysho growled and was ready to lunge, but Romann was instantly by him, pulling him away. "Stand down, Daysho."

Romann pushed him into the twenty undead and said, "Take him back to headquarters and wait for me."

They took hold of their leader and one-by-one walked to the back of the ship and disappeared into the night. Romann turned and faced Jack.

"My apologies, my King." He bowed low.

"Your love for her runs deep."

"If you speak of Kiratta," he rose back up, "yes."

"So deep that you would create a vampire army?"

"I have found no other way. It has been planned for decades."

"And why are you not leading this army?"

"In a way I am, but from a distance. I only wish to be with Kiratta. Even with an army I am alone."

"What do you hope to accomplish with this army?"

"We will break Ravana's spirit and force her to relinquish the curse of Oculus."

"How does one break a spirit where no spirit lives? She is undead."

"Jack, I am also undead, but my spirit longs to be with Kiratta."

"You as a vampire only live in your memories. Your spirit is lost. You can never be with her Romann."

The captain paused, "Then my memory will be my spirit. Whatever it takes I will be with her. I chose this life to find a way and I believe love is stronger than death."

Jack was stunned by Romann's words and faltered in giving any response.

Romann pressured him, "Will you help me?"

Jack turned into mist and evaporated into the night. Romann lunged for him, but it was too late. He ran to the railing and yelled, "Help me, Jack! Help us!"

Penelope came to stand next to Romann, "My deal with your training of Daysho has just ended."

Romann sighed, "I know."

"That was the true Vemptukai and yet he did not recognize me."

"What will you do now?"

"It appears the Vampire King has evolved even further in power than I once knew, as I also did not detect him until I looked upon him face-to-face. My destiny is to be by his side and I will make arrangements to do just that."

Romann hesitated but finally asked, "Help me. Reach out to the King and ask on my behalf. I will swear my allegiance to you."

She laughed, "The King does not answer to me or anyone but himself. He will do as he pleases and it will please me to help him. It appears that the realm of Ruauck-El is about to experience another great shift in power. I suggest you prepare yourself to choose your side. Your allegiance will be under a new authority, not mine." With that the Countessa vanished into the night. Her haunting voice from far away said, "Choose wisely, Romann."

The age-old swashbuckler, stricken with the curse of blood-hunger, looked out into the dark. He closed his eyes and whispered, "I choose love."

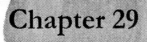

Chapter 29

Akar's Tower

The brilliance of the lightning bolt blinked away as fast as it came, leaving Trillius and the others in a new location than where they had started. Except for Trillius, smoke from the transport wafted from their clothing. The heroes all placed their hands against their temples, fighting against their unsettled equilibrium.

"It will pass," Trillius said.

The smell of burnt dirt and vegetation from the electricity was strong and a visible scorch mark was left on the dry and desolate prairie weeds forming a perfect circle around them.

"Welcome to the Valley of Giants," Trillius said extending his arm out.

"Where's the tower?" Dulgin growled.

"Giants?" Spilf whispered.

Dulgin placed his hand on Spilf's shoulder, "Don't worry, Stubby. It won't be like the last time we encountered Giants when Bridazak concocted that idiotic plan to have you as a decoy. We will save that position for the gnome."

Trillius ignored Dulgin and instead answered Spilf's concern, "The great giants of the Bronze Age ruled this valley and the surrounding mountains and were known as the Gathians."

"Where's the tower, thief?" Dulgin asked again sternly.

"I was just getting to that, Dulgy." Dulgin narrowed his eyes and pursed his lips trying to control his anger. Trillius continued, "Akar built his tower in the center of the Valley of Giants."

"I don't see a tower, Master Trillius."

"Akar was a master of illusion and thus he built his tower so as not to be seen by natural eyes. Like a far-away oasis within the heat on the horizon, the tower could be seen, but then would be gone in the blink of an eye. It shifts in and out of reality."

Rozelle observed Trillius from behind the others. She watched his mannerisms, his speech, and his facial inflections. All of them had slightly changed, she noticed, and yet deep down she felt it was still Trillius. She needed to talk to him privately to get to the heart of the matter and truly find out if he was still there or if it was the dragon manipulating him once again. The unmistakable question blared within her mind, *"Is it Trillius or Dal-Draydian?"*

The trouble-maker, of all trouble-makers, announced with a flourish of his hand, "Behold, the great Tower of Akar!"

A pulse of heat washed over the group and there before their eyes materialized, out of thin air, a stone spire a hundred feet tall. The blaring sun baked the ground at their feet. Like a mirage toying with their perceptions, the hot air around them continually shifted the ancient wizard's home in and out of reality.

"Now, we must hurry before it disappears again," Trillius said as he walked toward it, still a hundred paces away.

The group slowly followed. Dulgin announced, "I don't see a door."

"Oh, you poor creature," he mocked. "Your eyes are not in tune with what is truly there. Follow me."

Rozelle hurried to be by Trillius' side and then stayed in step with him. She asked, "Was there ever really an us?" Rozelle did not make eye contact, keeping her face forward, as Trillius glanced at her.

He smirked, "Rozelle, what do you want me to say?"

"The truth for once in your life."

"Truth? You want the truth? Okay, fine. My intentions have always been about me. I have never waivered from that and that is the truth."

"True enough, but I thought we had something...special."

"You are the most incredible woman I have ever met, Rozelle. Even Dal-Draydian was wrong about you."

She scoffed, "Dal-Draydian was wrong on all accounts."

Trillius shrugged, "Yeah, that might be true about his opinions but his knowledge of the realm is supreme."

"Are you?" she hesitated.

"Still me?" Trillius finished her thought. "Of course, but a better me, and soon to be a king me, and..." he stretched out the last word stopping to face her, "would like you to go with me."

"Go where, Trillius? I don't even know what really happened to you. First, you ran off with Jack, and now you've brought back the spirit of a dead dragon. How do I know you are not lying to me?"

Trillius sighed, "I know that I have not gained any trust as of late, but in time, you will all see my true colors. Albeit selfish still in nature, I can assure you I am still a gnome with a deep passion for what is good."

"Good for your pockets," Dulgin scoffed as he passed by the two gnomes.

Trillius smiled, "You can get far in the realm with gold in your pockets. Poor people have no influence."

Rozelle brought him back to focus on her as she said, "I don't care about gold, Trillius. I care about you. I would rather be poor in love, than rich in misery."

"This is why I need you, Rozelle. You can keep me grounded...well, as much as anyone can keep me grounded. You have done the best."

"I don't want to be your counselor, Trillius. I wanted to be..." she couldn't say the words.

The other members of the party began searching the outer stone wall for a door to enter. Spilf called to Trillius, "How long before this thing disappears?" Spilf's voice trailed off as he noticed the gnomes in deep conversation. He took it upon himself to find the door with the aid of his trusty pick-friends, Lester and Ross.

"Hello, boys. I need your help once again." Spilf spoke telepathically to his animated friends.

Ross screamed and both Lester and Spilf asked, *"What happened?"*

"Sorry, the dwarf scared me."

Dulgin stepped near and peered over Spilf's shoulder, "Yeah, put Lesty and Rossy to use. Tell them if they don't find the door then I will use them to clean the mutton from my teeth."

Another scream blared inside Spilf's mind after Dulgin's threat, but this time from both picks.

"Save us! We are doomed!"

Spilf looked up at his long-time friend and said mockingly, "Thanks Dulgin. You really know how to motivate them."

"I know. Well, they better come through. I've had a piece of meat stuck in my back molars for over a week now." Dulgin proceeded to open his mouth and point into the back recesses.

"We find traps, Spilf. Tell it to go away!" Lester yelled, trying to be heard beyond the girlish screams of Ross. It sounded as if he was falling off a cliff to a horrible death.

"Dulgin, please! Just back away and let them be."

"I'm watching you. Now get to work!" Dulgin walked off to see if Abawken had any luck finding an opening.

"Breathe Ross," Lester was saying repeatedly to try and calm his brother down.

The screams subsided to whimpers, then to stuttered attempts at taking deep intakes of air.

"Are you okay?" Spilf asked.

"I'm okay. I'm okay. I'm…oh my animated soul, I'm not okay," Ross went back to crying loudly.

"He is gone now," Lester tried to console his brother. *"You looked death in the eyes and—"*

"And screamed!" Ross said in a high pitched voice.

"Well, your screams scared it away, my brother," he lied.

"They did?" Ross calmed.

Spilf said, *"The best medicine right now is to focus on locating an opening to this tower."*

"Yes," Lester agreed. *"We can do this, Ross."*

"Just give me some time. Go ahead Lester and I will follow shortly."

"Okay, Ross. Spilf, move me closer. I will take the lead."

A few moments passed as Spilf maneuvered his faithful picks back and forth around the wall of the tower.

Lester said, *"I see something. Move a few feet to your right. There. Hold steady, Spilf."*

"What is it?"

"Ross, help me out."

"Okay. What did you find?" Ross chimed.

"It's symbols of some kind. Do you recognize them?"

Ross investigated and then said, *"Never seen anything like it but it is a code."*

Spilf called aloud to the others, "Lester and Ross found something!"

Abawken and Dulgin approached.

Meanwhile, Trillius and Rozelle continued their conversation.

"Rozelle, I am still trying to figure out my own feelings, but I know that there could be you and I, but it will take time."

"I can't be involved with your acts any longer. The thieving has to stop."

"I don't have to steal anything any longer."

"Why don't I believe you?"

"Rozelle, like I said, it will take time. You will see the great fortune I have come into and that it does not involve picking pockets. Those days are over. I now have the knowledge of one of the mightiest dragons to ever walk this realm and even now, here in this place, at this tower, Dal-Draydian's past lingers like a mark on a treasure map."

"But what if this evil spirit finds a way to get out and take control of you again?"

Dal-Draydian suddenly blared in his mind, *"I will find a way!"*

Trillius did not react but calmly stated with a warm smile, "It won't, Rozelle."

"But what if?" Rozelle pressed.

Trillius gently placed his hands on her shoulders and said emphatically, "It won't." Trillius suddenly looked past her and saw the heroes surrounding Spilf at the tower. "Well, I'll be a dragon-minded gnome. They actually found it."

"Found what?" Rozelle turned to look.

Trillius walked to the adventurers and Rozelle followed.

"What did they find?" Dulgin said.

"A code in a dialect they are unfamiliar with," Spilf answered.

"I thought those pick-heads could read every language out there?"

"It's not a language, ugly creature," Lester said even though Dulgin couldn't hear him.

Spilf repeated what Lester had just said without realizing the derogatory comment at the end.

Dulgin quickly snapped, "Who you callin creature?"

"Lester, he admits he is ugly!" Ross laughed and then Lester soon followed.

"Settle down and describe to me what you see," Spilf said.

"Ross thinks he knows. Go ahead Ross."

"Thank you, my brother. It appears to be a mixture of symbols taken from both the ancient mystic language and the tongue of dragons."

Before Spilf could relay the information, Trillius said from behind them, "How did you find it?"

"Master Spilf, discovered something."

"He discovered the entrance, not an easy task, to say it lightly."

Spilf said, "You can see it?"

"Of course I can. I am the Great Trillius and there is no chest, door, or room that alludes me. The question is how can you see it?"

Spilf stealthily palmed Lester and Ross from sight and then said, "I found something but don't understand it."

Trillius appeared not to notice the thieves' tools in the ordakian's possession and stepped forward to look more closely at the stone wall. "You don't understand it because it requires a combination of two lost languages and the eyes to see the wizard mark. You have the eyes apparently but you don't know the languages."

"But the languages don't say anything."

"Ah, that is the point. Most triggers are from a word or a puzzle to form a word, but this particular one is gibberish."

"You are the one speaking gibberish," Dulgin blurted.

"Stand back, Dulgin Hammergold, and witness the power of gibberish."

The group took several steps back unsure what the gnome was going to unleash or if the ancient Akar wizard had other intentions for intruders attempting to enter his domain.

Trillius gazed at the walled keep intensely and began to whisper. A supernatural tone to his voice carried to everyone's ears as they watched. The sound like that of sizzling bacon intensified as an outline of a door came into view, then the stone faded from existence and there before them all was an opening into the magic-users tower. A unique smell engulfed them like a faint trace of a recently cast incantation.

Trillius turned to the others and said, "Shall we?" The gnome waltzed inside.

Dulgin looked at Rozelle, "Did ye find what the dragon-brain is about?"

She sighed as the others waited for her response. "It's Trillius," she said but even she was unsure if it truly was or if Dal-Draydian was using him. She told the others what they were hoping to hear as she needed to find out his true motives for herself. It was better to have the heroes of Ruauck-El focused on finding Bridazak. Her mission was to find Trillius.

Chapter 30

The Fallen Manasseh

S tanding before Bridazak was what appeared to be a door of some kind. There were no walls to support it and the entire giant-sized entrance was made of flesh. It expanded back and forth like it was breathing. The macabre portal had stitches throughout as if it had undergone multiple surgeries. He peered around to the other side of it and saw the same sewn flesh as if it mirrored itself. It stood resolute and alone on this endless plane of darkness. The handle to open it was a balled fist of white bone and Bridazak slowly reached for it.

"Let's see what's inside the Door of Death."

The door opened on its own just before he touched the knob. Beyond, it revealed a window to another dimension within the Underworld. A misty fog blocked his view, but he heard the distinct sound of a cracking whip and a scream of pain following.

"I trust you, God. I've come this far and believe it to be your leading," he whispered, taking his first step into the chilly vapor beyond. The fog clung to his skin like a wet blanket and he could feel his clothing soak up the moisture.

The sound of the whip's lash rushed into his ears, causing Bridazak to flinch as it startled him. He then heard an all too familiar voice — Manasseh.

"You are weak and pathetic," the fallen king said.

Muffled cries came into focus as the ordakian slowly waded deeper into the mist. Forms began to materialize through the haze. Each step he took brought clarity to the scene in front of him until finally the fog cleared altogether.

"I hate you!" Another crack of the whip resounded.

A twelve-year-old child cowered in front of the imposing Manasseh. Red stripes laced his back and exposed flesh and bone caused Bridazak to grimace in disgust.

"Enough Manasseh!" Bridazak yelled.

Manasseh relented from whipping the child and looked at Bridazak. "It's you."

"Why are you doing this, Manasseh?"

"You are just in time to witness the death of innocence."

Manasseh's jet black hair washed over the shoulders of his beige colored tunic and clung to his sweaty, blood splattered face. His black leather pants and boots matched the color of his heart as rage embodied him. The ebony sheen of the whip slithered back for another lashing.

Bridazak brought up his bow and pulled back the string. The spark of blue light formed as the power of his bow increased. "I came here to save you Manasseh, but I cannot allow you to hurt this child any further."

Manasseh froze from unleashing his whip and looked at Bridazak. "You are a fool just like the boy."

"Come with me, Manasseh. It's not too late. God sent me to you."

A wicked smile came upon the human's face and then he looked at the child and snarled his hatred.

"Don't do it, Manasseh. I will kill you."

A boastful laugh roared, "I'm already dead, Bridazak. Do you not know where you are?" Manasseh focused on the boy and raised his arm to come around for another lashing.

Bridazak fired his arrow of light and it slammed into the chest of Manasseh, launching the fallen Horn King backwards. The whip slid from his grasp.

Bridazak then rushed over to Manasseh. The human sputtered blood from his mouth and in the gaping wound he saw exposed flesh and bone. He was dying.

The ordakian knelt to one knee and shook his head, not understanding the reason for him to come to this dark world, only to kill the one person he felt he was sent here to save.

"I have to kill..." Manasseh coughed and sputtered. "You don't understand...I hate him."

Bridazak watched as Manasseh tried to get up, propelled by pure hate for the boy behind him. He fell back as the mortal wound of the arrow had torn through his chest. Blood gushed out streaming down his sides and stomach. His breathing slowed until finally he had passed and his eyes fluttered closed. Bridazak's head lowered. "I'm sorry for failing you, God."

He heard the child behind him say through tears, "Is he dead?"

Bridazak stood and turned, "Yes, you are safe."

"I want to go home."

"Me too." Bridazak came closer. He wasn't sure but the black hair, pasty white complexion, and compelling steel blue eyes caused him to pause. This child looked familiar to him.

The twelve-year old shivered from shock and said, "I'm so cold."

Bridazak snapped out of it and gently placed his arms around him to bring him some comfort and warmth. He tried to keep the boy in conversation and said, "Where is your home?"

"I don't know."

"I will help you. My name is Bridazak. What is yours?"

"Manasseh."

Chapter 31

Ravana's Tower

"**W**hat is your wish, my master?" said the undead red dragon within Jack's mind.

Jack did not answer as he came alongside Gaermahn petting its scaly neck. The newly converted vampiric beast of the air had hidden within a secluded craggy cave along the coast.

"Do you want me to destroy Tuskabar?"

"Nay." Jack fell silent once again and leaned his back against the dragon sliding down to a sitting position.

"Then what is your command?"

"I'm not sure," Jack whispered.

The dragon suddenly shifted and sniffed the air, *"I smell dwarves."*

Jack stood, turned to face Gaermahn, and said, "Let's take a look at this dwarven army that El'Korr has assembled.

El'Korr stood on a hill overlooking his troops. They littered the landscape as far as the eye could see. Torch light dazzled the terrain in uniformed segments as military leaders ushered their groups into formation. The dwarven king's face was resolute; no fear, no joy, just pure determination. He turned the other direction and walked past his Wild Dwarf bodyguard platoon. Geetock stepped aside as El'Korr gazed upon the city of Tuskabar in the distance. It was known as the Heart of the West and harbored three-hundred thousand souls. He did not want to be in this position where the innocent would be caught between two warring factions. The brutal truth was war is ugly.

"My King," Geetock said, bringing El'Korr back from his

thoughts, "Should we begin our first assault?"

"Nay, let us attack at first light."

A new voice from the darkness said, "I prefer the night."

All the Wild Dwarves rushed around their King defensively as Daysho Gunsen, followed by several other vampires, entered the torchlight.

El'Korr's eyes narrowed, "I know you. You are the assassin who took the head of the West Horn King's mystic, Veric."

"Yes, my name is Daysho."

Geetock whispered, "Undead, my liege." El'Korr waved him off fully aware of what stood before them.

Daysho answered their internal questions, "My gift was immortality for Veric's head."

Geetock responded venomously, "Your gift was eternal damnation."

This caused the other vampires to growl and shift uncomfortably but Daysho raised his hand to halt their discontent.

"We are here to help your cause, Dwarven King."

"What is in it for you?"

"Tuskabar."

"And what if I wanted Tuskabar for myself?"

"It has poor craftsmanship and doesn't suit a Dwarven King."

El'Korr paused and made eye contact with Geetock, "Behind me stands over a hundred thousand fighting souls. We estimate less than fifty-thousand warriors within the city walls. I think we will do just fine without your help."

Daysho laughed heartily, "You know nothing of what is inside those walls."

"And I take it you do?"

"Of course. What you see behind me is a fraction of what I bring. I also have an army. An army of vampires and vamplings ready to do my bidding. It would not be wise to attack my city without getting my blessing. I would hate for your precious human friends to be unfortunately turned to fight against you in the process."

"Are you threatening me vampire? Our clerics outnumber you ten-to-one."

Geetock stepped forward, "This thing has no idea what a Wild Dwarf can do to its kind. Come a little closer, vampire." The other dozen Wild Dwarves stepped forward in unison, hands on weapon hilts, but El'Korr halted them with a hand on Geetock's chest.

Daysho smiled, "El'Korr, let us speak in private."

"No, my Mahlek," Geetock pleaded but El'Korr nodded his approval to Daysho.

They walked into the darkness, alone.

El'Korr spoke first, "What is your end-game, Daysho?"

"I wish to be a king with my own kind and to take what I have worked for my entire life."

"It can't be that simple. I am dethroning evil only to have another evil replace it. How does this benefit the land?"

"You call me evil, but is not evil walking amongst the living as well, even dare say within your very camps? I am just," he paused, "different."

"You will remain in this city and not take any more ground?"

Daysho then asked, "What kind of resistance did you and your army see along your way to the gates of Tuskabar?"

"Little."

"That is because of me."

"How so?"

"I created fear in the hearts of men. I recruited my army while the others abandoned their posts with the looming rumor of your massive gathering of dwarves marching to the west. I have my men, even now, ready at the gates to open them to you."

El'Korr's orange bushy eyebrow rose, "Does the West Horn King have an army inside those gates? What are you sending us into that you are too afraid to take yourself? You need me but for what?"

"You are perceptive, King El'Korr. Your fight is not against the King of the West but instead his daughter, Ravana."

"This I know."

"Aye, but what you don't know is that she is a medusa."

"A medusa?"

"More than that, she is also a vampire."

"A vampire?" El'Korr whispered as one hand went to his beard to stroke it in contemplation.

"She is extremely powerful."

El'Korr responded, "But you appear to outnumber her and yet you still fear her power? One individual cannot take on an army.

What else do you know?"

"I know that I have not had any resistance within the walls. It was easy, too easy. Some of the more brazen vamps have openly turned people out in the streets as even I could not contain them all."

El'Korr chuckled, "And you want me to join you even after you admit your own lack of control."

"Even you cannot control every man out on your field. There is contempt within your ranks against their leaders. You try to keep the peace and yet anger and hate knocks relentlessly at the door. Let us unite and rid this world of one evil and then we can figure out our next recourse afterwards. Let time and action dictate our decisions."

"Is her army under your control?"

"Nay, we didn't want to take too many of hers, so we took the surrounding towns and villages along with the underground patrons of Tuskabar. We cannot be in the daylight and thus our attack must be at night. This is why I came to you tonight. Let us not delay and strike now."

El'Korr turned and began to walk back to the torchlight.

Daysho asked, "Will you join us?"

El'Korr did not answer and walked away. Geetock was at full attention when he saw his king enter the light. El'Korr marched to face his right hand dwarf and said, "Assemble the men. We attack tonight."

The vampires disappeared and Daysho's voice could be heard, "We will be waiting for your arrival."

Jack had overheard Daysho and King El'Korr. It was time for him to meet this Ravana, the Medusa-Vampire, before these armies got to her first.

Gaermahn Shesteeva waited for his master a mile away. Jack appeared in front of him and said, "It is time for you to take me to the city, my friend."

The red dragon responded, *"We will feast tonight."*

"You will wait for my calling and not attack. Feast on the livestock in the surrounding area outside the city."

196

"You keep me from battle. You keep me from my calling. Why, my master?"

"You have many battles awaiting you including this one. Just wait for my command."

"As you wish."

Jack scaled the left-leg of Gaermahn with ease and settled on top of the dragon. It pushed off from the ground and propelled itself into the faint moonlit night. He soared high over the dwarven army and then turned sharply toward the city of Tuskabar.

Ravana's tower was silhouetted against the ocean's reflective water behind it. It was dark and menacing, like a shadow where there should be no shadow. The darkness fed upon the fear that it elicited from the stronghold. It brought depression into the hearts of men. Tonight, Jack would enter this domain of evil and find out the truth of what lay within.

Jack jumped off the back of the red dragon with his arms and legs extended. He glided through the cold air as he plummeted down toward the dark tower.

The Vampire King made his way into Ravana's lair. There were few within the confines of this dark and macabre environment. Two giant-kin in chains waited at the front gate while several hooded monks walked in unison swinging incense and humming a low dirge. The walls and floor were made of black slate and a single entrance into the tower was the only discernible path. The double doors were wide open.

Inside, along the wall, were sparse decorations of battle-ready statues wielding weaponry and shields. At the foot of each statue was a kneeling monk with more incense smoke rising up at the life-like statues.

Jack thought, *"Ravana's handiwork."* Jack moved by the hooded worshipers with ease and eventually found himself before an open chamber, lined with pillars on either side that funneled to the steps of a throne set on top of the dais. Hundreds of candles adorned the steps and the flames fluttered slightly at his entrance. *"Clever,"* he thought to himself as he knew the flames had alerted someone of his presence.

It was confirmed when Ravana spoke and her voice echoed around the room, "Who are you brave-one?"

"My name is Jack," he said as he turned to mist and fell into the shadows.

"You are not the dwarven army's emissary with such an informal introduction? Where does Jack hail from?"

"The Holy City."

She laughed and her cackle was piercing and menacing. "You bring me laughter, Jack. Something I have not experienced in quite some time. Show yourself so that I might have a good look at the patron of the Holy City."

The shadowed pillars laced the massive chamber on both sides, creating a maze for those wandering within the confines, but this was the design that Ravana had wanted, Jack surmised. He could not sense her location as he could with other vampires. He also could easily be turned to stone at one glance of her eyes if he was not careful. So if he were to fight then it would have to be with his eyes closed. Romann's plea suddenly bubbled up in his mind to help him rescue his lost love, Kiratta.

Jack said, "I came to warn you."

"Ah, yes, you wish to be hired perhaps? You are a spy, no, an assassin? Come out so we can negotiate your terms."

Jack spotted a slithering tail go out of sight and now heard the snake heads hissing. Jack threw his voice in another area of the room in hopes of corralling Ravana, "My warning is free of charge." The snakes hissed louder and the medusa made its way in the direction he had placed his voice.

Ravana answered playfully, "I enjoy this game we are playing. My warning is also free, I always get what I want." Ravana said the final words as she slithered quickly out into an area she suspected Jack was hiding, only to find it empty. She growled and then turned back to make her way to a new area of the room. "Jack of the Holy City, you are more than you lead me to believe."

"I will reveal myself upon one condition," Jack said, again throwing his voice in a different area.

"And what is this condition?" she asked as she made her way to the new location.

"You have a prisoner that I wish released."

Ravana stopped moving, surprised by this new revelation, "I was not expecting this but whom do you seek in my prison?"

"This prisoner of whom I ask for is not in your dungeons."

"I grow tired of your dance. Speak the name and why you demand such from me."

"Her name is Kiratta Green."

A high pitched squawk came from the throne as Ravana stood next to it, "Romann sent you. If Romann wants his precious tramp released then he needs to ask for her hand himself."

"Nay, Kiratta will be another victim for my trail of revenge." Jack was unsure why he was saying such things but realized it was the thoughts of the Twelve. They wanted revenge as he pulled on the memories flooding into his brain. Kiratta was the one who had captured the fallen paladins. Jack struggled to concentrate and push the thoughts to the back recesses of his mind.

"There is nothing holy about you Holy City patron. Show yourself."

Jack ushered himself across from one pillar to another with great speed but slow enough that Ravana could see an outline of him. Her eyes flared a bright red to capture Jack within her gaze but he purposely did not look at her. She hissed her discontent.

"Who are you?"

Jack whipped behind her while whispering, "I am the Vemptukai."

Ravana spun to find no one there and then calmed herself. "The Vampire King? Is that so? And why do you want this Kiratta?"

"Give her to me."

"And what do I get out of this?"

"Your life, Mistress Ravana."

She shouted angrily, "I am a King, not a mistress!"

"I am also a King and as kings I had thought we could be more informal."

"I will not give you Kiratta."

"Then I will take her if I must."

"If you kill me then she dies also."

Jack moved the conversation to lessen her agitation, "The

Vemptukai was before your time. How did you become what you are today, Ravana? Only the Vampire King could grant such things."

She laughed, "You are not the only one who grants things to the good patrons of Ruauck-El."

"Then it was the ruler of Kerrith Ravine, the Dark One," Jack stated plainly.

"How do you know of such things?"

"I told you that I am from the Holy City."

"That is a fantasy realm that does not exist."

"I've seen your dark master and I'm not impressed."

"Don't mock my god, infidel," she bit back.

"Your god was unable to protect the Horn King of the North."

Ravana glanced around the room, still trying to pinpoint Jack's location, "Manasseh was weak. Is it true then, that he has fallen?"

"Yes, but the north is now under new leadership."

"Please," she scoffed, "this dwarven king is nothing but a stain on clothing."

"Manasseh also dismissed their strength and look where that got him."

"Do you stand with these band of dwarves outside my domain?"

"I am with no one but myself."

"I don't think it is coincidence that Romann has made demands for Kiratta recently, the dwarven army at my door, and now your arrival."

Suddenly, screams and the military gongs blared throughout the city. Ravana smiled, "Welcome to Tuskabar, King El'Korr."

Just then Jack came out from hiding holding the Mirror of Lost Souls out toward her as he approached. Jack understood the power of the artifact and could see through the mirror from the opposite direction, holding it out in front him. Ravana would not be able to turn him to stone and would be forced to look into the mirror where Jack could actually hold the lost spirit of the West Horn King in his hand to do as he willed. He could crush and destroy the spirit altogether or return the soul back into the body.

Jack halted suddenly when he saw Ravana's image was not there after all. It was an illusion. The true Ravana suddenly knocked the mirror from his grasp and Jack watched the item slide away from him face down.

"Look at me Jack!" she demanded.

Jack closed his eyes and twirled to face her while bringing the back of his hand out to smack the medusa. He hit her squarely but she withstood his strong attack. Jack could not see her smile as she returned the backhand and sent him sprawling to the ground.

"Now you will see my true power, Jack of the Holy City."

Chapter 32

Move In

The mighty force of El'Korr could be heard over a mile away as the thuds of military boots shook the very ground. The unity of this army moved in pure determination as dwarf, elf, and human had the same goal. The races of Ruauck-El had joined forces and something like this had not been seen for centuries. The dwarves led, followed by the humans and elves, and as they came closer to the city walls the troops pace increased in anticipation of battle.

Calls from within Tuskabar sounded alert and soon the clang of the warning bells resounded, but it was too late, as Daysho's vampires cracked open the massive reinforced door, giving El'Korr's army complete access.

Like a sea being held back by a dam, they flooded the streets of Tuskabar. Steel met steel, but Ravana's limited guards could not stop the torrent of intruders.

El'Korr, Geetock, and the rest of the Wild Dwarves stood inside the gate entrance directing the troops.

"Take the walls!" El'Korr commanded, while Geetock pointed troops to move left or right as they came in.

"Not a single arrow was loosed upon us, my King," Geetock stated while still moving men here and there with the wave of his hands.

"I know. I can feel something wrong in my dwarven bones."

"What are your orders for us, my liege?"

"We move upon her tower." He pointed behind them to the looming dark spire with hooked claws that sprang around the pinnacle. Her tower was known as the Ten-Heads. "We will find out what this Ravana is all about once and for all."

"And we will join you," Daysho said as he materialized from the misty vapor along with a dozen other vampires, including a red-haired vampiress. "I have instructed my undead followers to clean up the mess left behind by your men and feed on the freshly killed. They will stay out of the way and hidden so as not to bring confusion to the fray. If any of them attack your people they will answer to me."

El'Korr squinted in contemplation and then nodded, "Geetock, inform Bailo and the other leaders to take the city, round up the citizens, and take prisoners when possible. Then have them converge on the tower."

"Yes, my liege."

El'Korr turned to face the vampire leader and said, "I pray you don't cross me and my people."

Daysho nodded his understanding, "Come, this way, Dwarf King."

"A mirror? You planned on defeating me with a simple mirror, Jack of the Holy City?"

Jack remained on the ground face down, intentionally not looking at the medusa. He focused on the deep shadows amongst the lined pillars. *"She is more than what she appears to be,"* he thought to himself as he vaporized into mist and hid in the darkness. He could hear her hideous cackle as he fled her stone-turning eyes.

"So brazen to come to my home. Don't leave, my dear Jack. We were only getting started."

Jack's voice echoed once again in her lair, "You will fall, Ravana. Before this night ends I will hold your soul in my hand and end your destiny."

"So poetic, Jack of the Holy City—end my destiny will you?" she giggled. "My destiny is unfolding before your eyes. Why are you so bent on my destruction? You don't know me. We should unite and rule together. You will see how merciful I am if you join me."

"Your precious city is being overrun with dwarves as you speak. How will you stop an army?"

"I will embrace them with open arms."

Jack paused for a long while until he finally asked, "Where is your father, Ravana?"

Her voice snapped harshly, "You will not speak of him." The hisses of the brood of snakes escalated.

"From what I have heard, you showcase him to the city patrons on each full moon. Is he not well?"

Jack heard Ravana moving quickly through the pillar maze in search of him. He had found the opening he needed to break down her iron will. The tell-tale glow of her eyes alerted him to her presence and he moved into a different location easily but at the same time he now understood her skills in illusion. Jack scooped up the Mirror of Lost Souls while Ravana moved deeper into her room and then he exited the chamber. It was time to open the wound she protected and uncover the truth.

"Commander Geetock!" A human soldier called as he ran to the Wild Dwarf in the main street of Tuskabar.

"What is it soldier?"

Out of breath he spoke hastily, "The patrons...are,"

"Are what?"

"They are statues."

"What are you talking about?"

Another dwarven soldier came toward them and yelled, "There be stone statues in all the homes."

Without a word, Geetock stormed over to a shop and bust down the door with his armored shoulder. Inside were tapestries that hung from rope. He slid the material away from him as he waded deeper and deeper into the store. He reached the counter and standing behind it was a life-like statue of a shop owner. Its hand was lifted in such a way as if the patron tried to shield themselves from an attack. Geetock's eyes narrowed. Other men surrounded behind him.

"Sir, we are hearing more reports from around the city of the same. What are our orders?"

Geetock whispered, "It's a trap." He turned abruptly and ordered, "Gather the army to the front gates."

"The front gates? We have control of the city, why?"

"Just do it, now!"

"Yes, sir."

As they exited the tapestry shop, they all heard guttural screams coming from deeper within the city that grew louder and louder.

"Sound the horns to retreat," Geetock commanded.

"Retreat?"

"Do it!"

Three burly dwarves raised curved spiraled horns of the great Karketh and blew. A deep tone bellowed forth.

Dwarves, humans, and elves stopped their search of the city or quickly finished off the little resistance they faced along the walls and turned in confusion to look at one another. From all accounts they had taken Tuskabar and yet they heard the horns calling them back. Each platoon leader sounded the retreat though most of them had nothing to retreat from.

Geetock could see hundreds of their men filling the main square from all directions as the call went out. Geetock linked his mind with the other Wild Dwarves and said plainly, *"We must get King El'Korr."* He could feel the others acknowledge his thought and one by one they paired up and began to march into the city toward Ravana's tower and toward the screams of their troops.

A Wild Dwarf halted King El'Korr.

"What is it, Belshed?" El'Korr quizzically asked.

"We need to go back."

"I am not retreating. We are taking this city tonight," El'Korr pushed his bodyguard's hand aside and marched forward.

"My Mahlek, Geetock sounded the horns and he and the others are coming to retrieve you."

"Retrieve me? I'm not a dog-bone, Belshed, and nor will we retreat from something I have not seen with my own eyes."

"Is there a problem?" Daysho asked. His entourage of vampires stood behind him in a pyramid formation.

"No," El'Korr stated while staring at Belshed. "Lead on."

"We have arrived," Daysho said and pointed to the open gate. "Ravana never leaves her tower. She is inside."

As they entered, huge hill giants, frozen in stone, gripped large chains over their shoulders that held the gigantic wooden gate open. The two creatures stood as tall as a cottage and their life-like faces grimaced in mid-stride pulling the chains that now swung loosely. Sounds of metal slightly squeaking with each sway brought an eeriness to the already tense environment.

"Is there a problem?" El'Korr asked Daysho, noticing that the vampire group had halted.

"Ravana has a barrier that prevents us to enter. We will wait for your return, good King of the Dwarves."

"Why didn't you mention that before? I don't take kindly to half-truths."

"It was not my intention to mislead you, but none-the-less, we are unable to enter."

"Figures you would have me do all the work," El'Korr mumbled under his breath as he turned back toward the gate entrance and proceeded inside. His five Wild Dwarf bodyguards followed behind him, weapons at the ready. The horns of retreat blared in the background.

"My Mahlek, where are all the people? This city instead feels like ghosts roaming the streets," his bodyguard said.

El'Korr whispered, "Be ready. Your instincts do not lie. Something is not right, that is for certain. I can feel it in my bones."

Chapter 33

The Curse of Oculus

Romann placed his back against the cold stone-wall and closed his eyes. He longed to feel her presence once again. "It is almost time, my Kiratta," he whispered. His voice echoed down the dark corridor. Romann was inside the lair of Oculus, a cursed Eye-of-the-Deep, where the spirit of Kiratta Green was trapped inside the evil entity.

He knew that El'Korr's army would be attacking Ravana soon but he also knew that Jack was his only hope in saving her and him for that matter. Romann was just as lost as Kiratta. He gave his life, to be undead for all eternity, in the hope of freeing the love of his life someday.

The anger of Oculus rumbled throughout the complex. It knew he was there and would be searching to destroy him if it could. All those who encounter the Great Oculus must answer a riddle or they forfeit their life to the Eye-of-the-Deep but Romann was told by Ravana after she turned him into a vampire, never to attempt to answer because it only worked with the living. It was another stab at his heart from the venomous West Horn King.

Centuries had passed while he searched for a way to break the curse. He knew the only key was Ravana but her death would forever seal Kiratta inside Oculus. His only hope was Jack, the Vampire King, and his ability to turn another vampire to his will. Romann had once prayed as a human but never as an undead. Prayers to a god were foreign to him, as his soul was empty, yet he pondered why his love remained after his transformation. The love he felt burned inside of him like a roaring fire.

Romann's resolve strengthened and he spoke aloud with renewed passion, "I have been placed like a seal over your heart; for my love is as strong as death, its jealousy unyielding as the grave. It burns like a blazing fire, like a mighty flame. I will not rest until we are together again, Kiratta."

The old vampire closed his eyes and remembered her face, her fair skin, the softness of her touch. He remembered watching her sleep aboard his ship in his cabin and the first sun of the day breaking through the small window and streaking vibrant colors across the bed. He liked how it stirred her awake and she would start smiling even before her eyes opened. The sparkle of her emerald eyes was not from the sun but from the joy contained inside her very soul.

Romann suddenly opened his eyes when he heard Oculus come closer and quickly realized he was actually smiling, something he had not done for quite some time.

"I will not leave, Oculus, until I have what I came for!"

A roar bellowed from the mythical creature, followed by a hearty, deep, and evil laugh.

"I am not afraid of you!" Romann yelled.

Oculus responded, closer than ever before, "Kiratta calls for you, Romann."

The swashbuckler vampire mystified and the vaporous being of Romann whisked through a crack in the wall and emerged into another corridor. He transformed back and knew Oculus was now where he used to be. "Oculus, she is mine."

"Bow before me and I will consider your request." Its voice deep and menacing.

Romann, without a shadow of a doubt, understood this foul monster of lore could not do as it stated, "Consider and grant are as far away as you and I."

"I could unite you with Kiratta if you would simply come before me. You would finally be set free and be together for all eternity."

Romann had once thought this to be the case. He had envisioned succumbing to Oculus in order to be trapped inside with Kiratta but his faith in that leap was not strong enough to take that plunge. "I believe in another."

"What is the name of your god?" Oculus asked.

"It is not a god—it is the Vemptukai."

There was a pause before Oculus spoke, ever so slight, but something Romann cued in on, "The Vampire King is a myth and anyone walking in the power of that being is an imposter."

"We shall see, Great Oculus. Even now this so called imposter and an army of dwarves descend on Ravana."

"The fate of Ravana's destiny was dealt with many years ago."

"How so?"

"The prophecy of ancient times pointed to Ravana's father being her demise but she killed that insignificant being and broke the prophecy and entered her new calling as the true West Horn King."

"Where is this prophecy? I have seen much over my centuries but have not heard of such a thing."

"The Lost City, now veiled behind Kerrith Ravine, brought to Ruauck-El words and inscriptions of things to come. The patrons within this city released these prophetic visions upon the realm. Many believed until the time of Separation, until the Silent Years, when Kerrith Ravine created a barrier around it, cutting the life force off to all."

Romann remembered that time, he remembered the followers of the god that reigned during this era. These zealots preached love but the rules that governed this god and its people were not something he wanted to follow. His freedom came from the sea and his ship and his heart to fight for what was good. It was a time of great heroes and a land rich with beauty, but he also recognized the separation of the Holy City and what fell on the lands after the birth of Kerrith Ravine and the Reegs—the shadow demons entered Ruauck-El.

"My destiny is to be with Kiratta no matter what," Romann said.

"Vampires are without destiny. Death is all that surrounds you now."

Chapter 34

The Looking Glass

The heroes were now inside the tower. They were dazzled by the intricate wizard ingredients lining the shelves and tables scattered about. Smells of stale bread, mixed with pepper, caused each of them to wrinkle their noses. No one spoke as they spread out, walking slowly around the furniture where a fine dust had settled.

Dulgin eventually whispered, "Definitely a wizard's place." No one responded as each of them lifted up small trinkets to inspect, blowing the layer of dust off each item. Spilf looked over a porcelain bell that barely tinkled, a vial containing what he thought to be dead flies, and then a long stick with bristles at the end, which he eventually surmised was a broom.

Dulgin picked at oddities in another area on some shelves. One was a vial containing green liquid which he shook violently and sniffed before eventually putting it back after bubbles started escaping out of the cracked cork. He looked around as if he had done something wrong and then went on to look at the other items, but not picking anything else up.

Abawken made his way to a display of books within a glass case. Each one had ancient writing as titles, none of which he understood. They were protected inside and he was unable to find a way to open it.

Rozelle walked with Trillius, who strolled around with his hands clasped behind his back and a cocky grin plastered on his face. He walked as if he owned the place and was unconcerned about the items, but instead watched each hero searching the room until they finally spotted what he knew was the ultimate prize—Akar's Looking Glass.

"How does this thing work?" Dulgin asked.

Everyone turned toward Trillius who in turn shrugged, "Perhaps the one who found the entrance to the tower can discern the artifact before us." Trillius purposefully wanted to find out what Spilfer Teehle was all about. The ordakian had peeked his curiosity when he discovered the invisible portal into Akar's tower. Only powerful mystics or those with dragon-sight could see such things and he knew Spilf was neither.

"Me? How would I know?" Spilf played coy, not wanting to reveal Lester and Ross.

Dulgin said, "Use your pick-heads."

There it was. Dulgin, good old Dulgin, let the beruvian cat out of the bag. Spilf stood there stunned but then quickly fumbled with his words, "My rusty picks are only good for traps and locks on doors, Dulgin." Spilf emphasized the word rusty and Dulgin while looking straight into the dwarf's eyes in hope that he would grasp that he did not want to reveal them to the gnome.

Dulgin stared back and was about to respond but quickly laughed as he caught on and said, "Yeah, well I don't understand your ways. That makes sense. Yeah, doors and traps."

Trillius saw the hidden exchange that only long-time friends would understand between each other, but he had been 'around the village square' several times as they say in the realm and knew that Spilf's thieves tools were more than just rusty instruments. *"Strange that my dragon-sight could not see them for what they truly are,"* he thought to himself as he grinned at the others.

There before the group was a naturally formed stone basin with gnarled smooth wood woven in and out of the rock. Everyone could feel the magic pulsating from the five-by-five foot circular well. Inside was a slow swirling grey smoke with periodic flashes of light below.

Dulgin said, "Well, Trilly, you brought us here so you must know something about it now that you are linked with dragon-brain."

Trillius smiled and said, "I, well not I, but Dal-Draydian, only heard rumors of this relic. If you look inside and concentrate on what you are looking for then something happens."

"Something happens? Well that is a gnome-brainer. Something happens, I will show you something happening in a second." Dulgin walked away.

"Can we do it together or is it a one at a time kind of thing?" Spilf asked.

"Beats me," Trillius shrugged.

Dulgin stormed back, "Sounds good to me. You need a good dwarven beating." Abawken grabbed hold of the dwarf to stop him from carrying out his hostility toward the three-foot gnome.

Spilf went to the rim and leaned over to look inside the swirling murky smoke. The others watched with anticipation and nervousness. A part of Dulgin and Abawken wanted to grab their friend and pull him back since they had no idea what this would do to a person. Deep down inside though they wanted to do the same as Spilf.

"I don't see anything," Spilf announced.

Dulgin and Abawken let out a held breath they did not realize they were holding.

"Wait, I see something," Spilf said excitedly.

They both approached and also leaned in. The smoke dissipated in the middle and there before them was Bridazak. Surrounding their lost friend was complete darkness.

"He lives," Spilf whispered, afraid to take his eyes off of Bridazak to look at his friends. He could sense the relief and joy in each of them. Somehow, Bridazak, the Carrier of the Orb, survived the Underworld.

Bridazak suddenly turned in their direction and looked directly at them and smiled.

"He sees us!" Spilf cried and then began yelling Bridazak's name. Dulgin and Abawken also called to him.

Suddenly, another person came into the picture to stand next to Bridazak. It was a young human boy, no more than a dozen years of age, and he also looked toward them. The heroes could see Bridazak and the child speaking to one another but they could not hear them. The scene within Akar's Looking Glass expanded slowly and then suddenly a bright light exploded behind Bridazak and the boy.

Just then a flash of light erupted behind Bridazak and Manasseh.

They both turned to look, shielding their eyes. It was a tunnel of pure white light and Bridazak knew this was the path to the Holy City of God. It was calling to him within his very spirit.

"What is it?" the child asked.

"Home."

Bridazak looked back at his friends who waited for him to return to them. Their images moved like a reflection within a pool of water. He could see their faces light up with joy upon seeing him. He could not hear them but could see them calling and waving him toward them.

"Who are they?" Manasseh asked.

Bridazak answered, "My family."

"There is another portal," Spilf said.

"Is that the portal he needs to go through to get to us or when he looks at us is there another opening?" Abawken asked.

"What is he waiting for? He looked right at us, dammit," Dulgin said.

They continued to call out to Bridazak which prompted Trillius and Rozelle to come closer and look into the Looking Glass. Trillius thought to himself, *"This is indeed a powerful item to find those who don't want to be found even in the depths of the Underworld."*

Just then Bridazak looked toward them all and smiled, not a smile that revealed joy, but a smile of appreciation. The ordakian then placed his hand over his heart and stared at them longingly.

Dulgin said, "I don't like that look he is giving us."

"What is he doing?" Spilf questioned.

"Master Bridazak is not coming back."

There was nothing left to say. Words were meaningless as several emotions raced through them all, most of all shock. Each of them slowly resigned as they watched their friend, their family member, turn, walk into the light, and vanish with the human boy at his side. The image within the smoky well dissipated and returned to the grey swirl with deep recessed flashes. Spilf fell to his knees and began to sob.

Rozelle clutched Trillius' arm as she witnessed the pain of loss these three long-time friends were experiencing. She longed to be amongst friends that would die for one another, that would sacrifice themselves for the greater good. Trillius looked at her and half-smiled, then turned to the group and said, "I'm sorry for your loss."

This caused Dulgin to turn and glare at him suspiciously.

"Truly, Dulgin. I wished I could have met him."

Dulgin paused and then nodded. The dwarf turned back to Spilf as the ordakian wailed and released all of the pent-up emotion he had been holding onto.

Trillius gave them a moment and walked to the other side of the Looking Glass with Rozelle locked next to him.

She asked shyly, "What about us?"

Trillius quickly responded, "Is there an 'us', Rozelle?"

"I want there to be."

"You have to trust me. I know I have not shown much trust as of late and I apologize for that. If you can't trust me, then any chance of us will only turn to separation." He stopped and looked into her eyes, "Do you trust me?"

She stared longingly into his silver orbs and said, "I trust you, Trillius Triplehand."

A gleam returned to Trillius' face and he grinned wide. He leaned in and kissed her and she kissed him back. He slowly pulled away and then whispered, "Come, let me show you our new home."

Rozelle's face scrunched in puzzlement but at the same time half-smiling in wonderment of what this thieving gnome was up to. She thought, *"Yes, the lust of possessions had always imprisoned Trillius. Am I just a possession to him also?"*

She approached the basin of the Looking Glass and watched Trillius lean into it. She stayed just behind him as the scene unfolded. A brilliant throne of gold laced with runes and gemstones appeared. The dazzling spectacle slowly expanded to show a large audience chamber of polished floors, brass braziers burning red coals, pools of pristine blue water on either side of the room with steam hovering over the top, and glass steps leading up to the seat of importance granted only to kings.

"What is this place?" Rozelle marveled.

"It is called Gheel-Mon."

"Gheel-Mon? The lost city of the Bronze Age?"

"It doesn't look lost to me. Odd, it actually looks well lived in. The question is who is there?"

"How are we going to find it?"

"Oh, that is the next thing to be answered." Suddenly the grey swirl returned inside the well and then shifted again to a new scene. A huge silver dragon came into view. It rested upon a large pile of silver and platinum. Its eyes came to life and looked directly toward Trillius and Rozelle. Rozelle gasped while Trillius smiled brightly.

"Who are you, thief?" A deep voice resounded within Trillius' mind.

He was pleasantly surprised to be able to communicate with the dragon and responded in perfect draconian, *"Gheel-Mon lives."*

The silver dragon lifted its head and narrowed its eyes, *"Who are you and how dare you speak of that evil city?"*

"It was not destroyed. The mystic that betrayed you and your enemies live."

"Who are you, gnome, whom speaks my language?"

"I am Trillius, but I also have another name—Dal-Draydian."

"Dal-Draydian was destroyed—"

Trillius cut him off, *"By the same mystic who betrayed you and the same mystic in whose tower I now stand speaking to you through his Looking Glass."*

"Akar."

"Yes."

"What do you want of me, Trillius?"

"I want the kingdom of Gheel-Mon for myself to put it bluntly."

The dragon scoffed.

Trillius continued, *"You wanted it destroyed and were unable to because of the dragon-bane sword that rests in the center square. The same sword that slayed your kin, the same sword named after the city itself— Gheel-Mon."*

"You know much for a thieving gnome."

"I am a gnome with the mind of a dragon. Dal-Draydian is now enslaved within me. You know of the location of the city. Give me this location and I promise to rid the world of the sword that killed your family."

"It is not a place you can give directions to."

"Then take me there and show me."

"You have piqued my interest and I wish to meet you face-to-face."

"I know where you reside, Kali-Thekquan."

"You know my name?"

"I know lots of things."

"Tell me why you want this city?"

"To be a king of course, why else?" Trillius stepped away from the magical well and the grey smoke returned and cut off the communication.

Rozelle asked, "What happened?"

"The Silver Dragon is going to help us find the city."

She looked at him confused and then he said, "Trust me." Her face lightened and she nodded.

Trillius clapped his hands once and turned to the other adventurers, "Well, I think it is time to go."

"What's the hurry, gnomey."

"Well, Dulgy, it is time for me and Rozelle to go to our next destination and unfortunately I only have room for her so that means you all need to make your own way from here."

"Trillius, we can't leave them out in the middle of nowhere," Rozelle pleaded.

"Rozelle, trust me, these fine gentlemen are well versed in travel and besides, I think they have grown tired of my stay to be honest."

Dulgin nodded his agreement. Spilf was still wiping away tears and Abawken had his arm around him to comfort him.

"Yeah, I think it's a grand idea to part ways," Dulgin said.

"Good, we are all in agreement, see Rozelle?" She nodded slightly and half-smiled.

"I wish to say goodbye," she said. Trillius nodded.

She approached the heroes, "Thank you for all you have done. I hope someday that we can be close friends. I am sorry for your loss of Bridazak but thankful you were able to see him." Rozelle stepped toward Abawken and addressed him directly, "Thank you for being a symbol of what you represent."

Abawken nodded, "Your journey is a process and along your path the destiny residing in your heart will show you this love that I spoke of."

"Rozelle," Trillius spoke softly, "time for us to depart."

She backed away and then turned with Trillius. They walked to the door leading to the outside of the magically enchanted tower. Trillius opened it and an orange sunlight spilled inside.

"Ladies first," Trillius bowed and waved one arm out.

"Thank you," she responded with a smile and took her first step outside. It happened so fast. A dark form walked straight through Rozelle, a shadow creature feared by all of Ruauck-El, a Reeg. She collapsed instantly and Trillius backed away as the yellow glowing eyes of the demon glared brighter and terror gripped them all. More Reegs could be seen outside the tower along with the mythical giants of this valley.

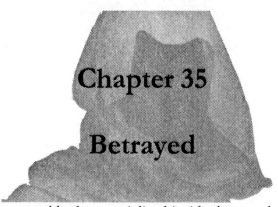

Chapter 35

Betrayed

Jack's incorporeal body materialized inside the antechamber at the top of Ravana's tower. He gazed upon the former King of the West— Oedikus. His lifeless body glowed faintly from spells Ravana had placed upon him. He wore regal maroon furs with enlarged platinum buttons and gold stitching over his fat belly. The corpse of the fallen king appeared peaceful, Jack observed, as he walked around the human propped within a high-backed upholstered chair, his barreled arms resting upon the armrests.

The room was ice cold and Jack could hear the whipping wind outside the balcony that encircled the entire tower. This chamber was completely barren of any décor except that of the puppet Oedikus. For what reason Ravana needed her father in this state, he had no idea, but he knew him to be important to her.

Jack stood in front of him and said, "It is time."

Jack pulled forth the Mirror of Lost Souls, making sure not to look into it, but instead pointing the reflective mirror toward the man. Jack could see through from the other side and he whispered the king's name, "Oedikus."

A wispy image of the robust human sailed forward as if being pulled. Haunting whispers emanated from within the dark Underworld of the mirror. Jack willed it to go back into the host and like a spear it shot forth and into the nostrils of Oedikus. The king's eyes flared open wide and the once lifeless pupils focused. Breathing returned in deep intakes and exhales. Jack lowered the mirror away and shrunk it back to its pocket size once again.

A deep husky voice crackled out of Oedikus' mouth, "What happened? Where am I?"

"I'm here to give you another chance at redemption."

"My Mahlek, I insist that we retreat. Geetock is bringing the others to get you," Belshed said while stepping in front of El'Korr.

The horns of retreat trumpeted in the background, along with clashes of metal and strange screams from his army falling victim to an unseen enemy. El'Korr paused, staring hard into his bodyguard's eyes and then turned to the other Wild Dwarves around him.

"You are no longer just our king but instead the Giimtock, leader of all dwarves. Let us regroup and find out the treachery of this place," Belshed continued. "Your men need you. We need you."

El'Korr could feel the pull of wanting to take Ravana's head and spike it at the front gate but he also felt the heart of his dwarven brethren. Though his mind declared victory was at hand, his mind also brought doubt of the unknown and doubt of the vampires.

The dwarf king nodded and said, "Inform Geetock we are returning to the gates."

Geetock received the message from Belshed. The other Wild Dwarves nodded approval and clasped shoulders in thanks.

Geetock said, "Let's meet our King, find out what is attacking our army, and get out of here."

A new voice penetrated from the outside of the dwarven brigade, a cynical voice, full of malice, "It is too late and we are hungry."

Suddenly, three vampires appeared behind them, grabbing the hair of three dwarves, and pulling their heads to the side to reveal their necks. Fangs sank into the meaty flesh as the vamps sucked their blood. Geetock was shocked but quickly regained his composure and yelled, "We have been betrayed!"

Daysho stepped forward out of the darkness with two other vamps by his side, including the red-head Penelope, "Foolish dwarves. I look forward to draining you personally, Geetock."

Geetock stepped forward with his sword and said, "You don't know anything about Wild Dwarves, undead."

The three vamps who drank of their blood suddenly retracted

and began to cough and gasp. Their hands wrapped around their throats as they choked and gagged. They fell to the ground writhing in pain. Daysho looked confused.

Geetock said, "Our blood contains wild magic and that is not a good mixture for vampires."

Daysho sprung at Geetock with supernatural speed but the dwarf sidestepped him and almost cleaved his head off had Daysho not maneuvered away at the last instant.

"Oh, we can also match your speed in combat," Geetock answered the question Daysho had in his mind.

"Kill them!" Daysho ordered. "Kill them all!"

The Wild Dwarves were ready and already engaging the undead. Hands were cut off as the clawed vampires tried to swipe at the dwarves. The vamps were not accustomed to fighting against an enemy that matched their speed and power and the initial attack was thwarted before it ever began. All fourteen dwarves gathered, backs to one another in a circle and prepared to take on the life-drinkers. The three, who were initially attacked, clasped one hand over their wound as they held back their blood from spurting out. They stood resolute to fight to the death. The vampiric bite had no effect on them other than the puncture wounds.

One of the vamps that had tasted the dwarven blood was beginning to screech with broken high pitched squeals until Geetock swung his sword and severed its head, "Back to the Underworld you go." Geetock looked at Daysho, pointed his sword, and said, "You are next."

Penelope waltzed forward with a wry grin on her face, "You do know the ways of vampires. These young vamps however would know nothing of your kind but the ancient vampires would."

Geetock responded coyly, "Lady vamp first then. I have no problem separating your head from your body."

"You will have a tougher time with me than the others. I'm one of the ancient ones and we were trained to encounter your dwarven kin." Penelope suddenly produced half-moon shaped blades that fit within her hands. The blades were darker than normal metal and ran over the outside of her knuckles as she gripped the custom hilts.

Geetock said, "She wields dark-metal."

"Yes, the metal found in the depths of the forges of the Dark-

Dwarves."

"It will take more than your blades to kill us all."

Daysho stepped behind her and said, "Why didn't you tell me about these dwarves?"

She turned to face him, "I have been groomed from the beginning to serve the Vampire King. I was educated in all facets to train the one to come. Romann de Beaux came to me and said you were to be the one. It is now your time to show us that you are the true Vemptukai. Take these weapons and use them to take their lives."

Daysho slowly understood and an evil grin emerged. He took hold of the curved fist blades. Penelope stepped aside and the assassin vampire glared at Geetock and the other Wild Dwarves.

"Seal off any escape," Daysho commanded. Scores of vampires circled the Wild Dwarves, coming out from the darkened alleys and streets.

Geetock stepped forward alone to meet Daysho. The dwarf slammed his eyes shut, held his breath, and concentrated intently to invoke the wild magic inside of him. Blurred images of Geetock began to emerge from his body and suddenly everyone was looking upon shimmering reflections of Geetock moving back and forth within each other, making it difficult to locate the real dwarf.

Daysho smiled wickedly and approached with cautious steps and blades ready, "I will wear your braided beard on my belt, dwarf."

"El'Korr, Geetock and the others have engaged the enemy," Belshed said abruptly after receiving a telepathic message.

"What are they fighting?"

"My Mahlek, we have been betrayed. It is the vampires."

El'Korr bit back words he wanted to spew forth at himself for choosing the wrong path for his people. This was his fault for trusting Daysho and the blood-walkers. "Where are they?"

"No, my Lord, Geetock wants us to leave and escape. He is giving us time."

"I have already gone against my better judgment and I will not do that again. This ends tonight. We will be the dawn of day against this evil." El'Korr moved quickly through the streets and his five bodyguards followed.

Daysho sliced at the mirrored images of Geetock but each swipe missed. Geetock countered with his sword and likewise did not connect.

"You have lost, dwarf," the assassin whispered.

Geetock swung again, anticipating the undead human to step aside, he launched a jet of flame at the location he suspected Daysho to be. It ignited the vampire's left arm and Daysho reeled away, ripping the sleeve of his clothing off and growling at the Wild Dwarf.

"Ravana will sweep across the north and reclaim what Manasseh lost and then we will dominate the rest of Ruauck-El. You cannot defeat us." Daysho came in hard and furious, slashing at every image he could see until finally hitting the flesh of Geetock. The Wild Dwarf quickly retreated a few steps, clutching his free hand at the open wound on his right side. The dark-metal burned like a cancerous sore and he could feel the poison creeping slowly into him. This wound would not be healed by any magic and would fester continuously until treated with the plant juice of the vorskirr—the dripping willow.

Geetock held his hand up to keep the others from engaging Daysho, "No, I am fine. He is mine."

"Stand down, Geetock!" A new voice, a familiar voice, bellowed from beyond the perimeter of vampires.

The undead wall parted to reveal El'Korr and his bodyguards' right behind him.

Daysho said, "Come El'Korr, let us play."

The dwarven king entered and joined his brethren. He never took his eyes off of Daysho but commanded his followers, "Invoke the Tel-sharouk."

Belshed quickly responded, "My Lord, the Tel-sharouk could kill you."

Daysho said, "I will be the one killing him. Are you ready El'Korr to meet your maker?"

"I am always ready, but today will not be a day of reunion with my fallen brethren, but instead a day of victory."

"Old dwarf, you are truly delusional."

El'Korr turned sharply on his men, "Do it! That is an order."

Geetock reluctantly nodded and the dwarves surrounded and laid hands upon El'Korr. A humming noise slowly became louder as each Wild Dwarf unified into one voice. El'Korr closed his eyes and welcomed the power being bestowed upon him by this ancient clan of bearded warriors.

Daysho was not going to wait and rushed toward the group of dwarves but was quickly repelled backwards as he hit an invisible force field surrounding them.

El'Korr's body began to shake like electricity coursing through him. Foam built up around the creases of his mouth, his hammer and shield fell from his grasp to the ground, and the Wild Dwarves increased the volume of their unified hum.

The sound abruptly ended all at once and King El'Korr dropped instantly.

Daysho tested the barrier and found it to be gone. He looked down at El'Korr and smirked while saying, "I will take all of your heads and dangle them from the castle walls."

"Your treachery ends, Daysho," Geetock coughed, feeling the effects of the dark-metal.

The vampire leader laughed, "By your hands? I think not."

"No, by mine," El'Korr said. His eyes fluttered open and he sat upright. The mighty warrior dwarf stood while picking up his shield and hammer. "I'm ready for you."

The Wild Dwarves backed away and seemed uncertain as to the final outcome of the Tel-sharouk invocation. They quickly witnessed the effects when their Giimtock suddenly flashed forward with quickened speed and slammed his shield into Daysho, sending the vampire flying backward into its crowd of followers. Daysho sprang forward, blades out, fangs showing, and eyes swirling in anger.

Daysho lunged forward but El'Korr spun and came around with his magical hammer, breaking bones in his back upon impact. Daysho snarled at the dwarf. He caught sight of the red-haired Penelope who slowly faded into the night with an evil grin plastered on her face. *"She betrayed me,"* he thought. *"She lured me into this combat."*

Daysho rolled out of the way just in time as El'Korr's hammer cracked the ground where he once was. The vampire leader suddenly transformed into smoke and vanished. The other vamps slowly backed away and one-by-one they also disappeared into the night.

The dwarves watched the area, weapons at the ready.

El'Korr said, "What do you know, Geetock? How many have we lost to the vamps?"

"Uncertain, but there is another evil within this city which caused me to sound the retreat."

"What is it?"

"The medusa witch has turned many of her patrons to statues."

Screams continued to echo throughout Tuskabar along with clashing swords.

"I don't understand. What is attacking our men?"

"I believe—"

Suddenly, a crash of glass jerked the dwarves' attention toward a nearby shop, causing Geetock to stop. Standing before them was a moving statue of what appeared to be the owner. The muddy brown rock moved fluently like skin and a low growl emanated from deep within it.

El'Korr threw his hammer and the head of the creature shattered, toppling rock fragments to the ground. His weapon magically returned to his hands.

"They might not bleed but they do break," El'Korr said, raising one orange bushy-brow.

Geetock chuckled while placing his hand upon his King's armored shoulder but suddenly coughed violently and backed away.

El'Korr rushed to his side to keep him steady.

Geetock waved him off, "It's the dark-metal, my liege. I will be fine."

Everyone's attention was upon them but as Geetock stood upright his eyes locked on something behind them all.

El'Korr saw his bodyguards face quickly turn to concern and he looked in the direction Geetock faced. Others turned that way as well.

Hundreds of walking statues filled the streets and alleys.

"Fall back!" El'Korr yelled.

Chapter 36

Father of Light

"You cannot do this," the Dark Lord spoke. He stood within a chamber filled with bright colored walls that moved fluently.

"It has been a long time, Abaddon." The voice of God responded, while he gazed upon the portal of light where Bridazak and Manasseh stood.

"Why do you protect this Bridazak? He cannot come into my home and take what is not his."

Ignoring his question, God said, "I love his heart. Such strength, don't you think?"

"Manasseh's soul is mine."

"Should I close this portal and have Bridazak save more souls from your Pit of Torment? His heart is strong and could endure a little longer. I wonder how many others—"

"Enough. I will allow this one soul. Take your precious Bridazak out of my domain."

"You are most kind, Abaddon."

The Dark Lord faded away. God gazed upon the ordakian standing at the edge of the portal and waited to greet him with open arms of love, longing to embrace him.

The light encompassed Bridazak and Manasseh as they walked hand in hand. It felt like a father's hug and each step they took elicited a brighter smile as pure joy washed over them.

Manasseh whispered, "I have never felt anything like this before."

An image of a person emerged before them and colors known and unknown sprouted from him like an endless kaleidoscope. "Welcome home, Bridazak and Manasseh. I have been waiting for you."

A huge smile beamed from Manasseh, "He knows my name."

Bridazak said, "He created you. He is your true Father. Go to Him."

Manesseh looked into Bridazak's eyes, "He wants to be with me? He is not mad?"

Bridazak's eyes began to pool with tears as he remembered this same feeling when he had met God. "Go to Him and find out."

Manasseh slowly turned to face the beautiful human that stood before him with flowing green robes that majestically rippled like waves of water behind him. God opened his arms, knelt down to one knee, and smiled brightly. His blue eyes sparkled with the essence of joy and love. The young child rushed into His arms and they embraced.

In Bridazak's eyes he saw the Ordakian Father of God, not a human, as God came to each race in their own image. Suddenly, Manasseh disappeared into a bright light and then Bridazak was face to face with his God.

The Father of Light said, "Thank you for bringing Manasseh home."

"To be honest, I really didn't know what I was doing."

"You know more than you think you know. Come, I have much to tell you."

Bridazak grabbed God's hand and together they walked through an open doorway that wasn't there just a second ago. On the other side, they came into a warm ordakian home. A fire burned in the fireplace but the flames did not crackle but instead giggled. Bridazak noticed the flames were individual fairies. He had never seen anything like this before. They tumbled around the wood, playing and giggling together.

In front of the fireplace was a table with two chairs. On top of the table was the most amazing spread of food—loaves of bread dripping with honey glaze, plump blueberries, and a perfectly roasted brown skinned chicken rested prominently in the center. Steam rose from the bread and meat. A bowl of bright red walnut cherries caught his eye along with clusters of fruit, some recognizable while others caused him to raise an eyebrow. The vibrant colors of the food, the smells penetrating his senses, and the ambiance of the room, overwhelmed Bridazak. On the backside of the table his eyes widened in delight at the sight of two pies with delicately laced strands of crust crisscrossed over the oozing berries inside. There was a perfect sugar glaze on the top.

"Please sit," God said.

Bridazak moved and as he took his seat he noticed there in front of him a prized childhood memory—cinnamon sticks. "These are my favorite," he said as he took one.

"I know."

Before Bridazak snacked on the stick he looked at his God and said, "Thank you."

God smiled and said, "The food is now blessed. Let's eat."

"What do you mean, blessed?"

"You gave thanks."

"I thanked you."

"I created the food and in thanking me you have blessed what you are about to receive."

"Isn't it already blessed?"

"Bridazak, give thanks for all that you do and your journey will be extravagantly wonderful. Giving thanks is another expression of love and it is and always will be about love."

"I'm sorry for having so many questions."

"I love your questions. You can ask me anything, but first let's eat, I'm hungry."

"You get hungry?"

God began to break a loaf of bread, hot steam bellowed from the insides as he tore it open, and then he handed the other half to Bridazak without answering him. They laughed at each other's groans of enjoyment with each bite.

The meal was coming to a close as Bridazak and God leaned back in their chairs and held their full bellies.

God said, "Promise me one thing, Bridazak."

"Anything."

"Don't give a speech when giving thanks for your food. Although I enjoy the colorful stories expressed in my honor, people are starving and want to eat. In those lengthy prayers we have lost many."

Bridazak stared, the seriousness on God's face, but then saw a small glint in His eye. That was enough and suddenly they erupted into laughter, so much so, that they both fell out of their chairs and were rolling on the ground.

Bridazak sputtered through labored breaths, "What...is...happening?" This brought more laughter from them both. This was a joy-filled laugh that Bridazak hadn't experienced in his entire life.

God's laughter slowly resided and he responded, "In heaven, joy and laughter are intensified."

They laid there on top of the patterned rug and slowly quieted. Bridazak wiped away tears that had streamed down his face. He looked up at the wooden ceiling and then focused on several objects falling from the edge of the table. One red berry splattered on his forehead, followed by another and another. Bridazak sat straight up while wiping the red juice from his face and then spotted the giggling flame fairies working together to roll the berries over the edge.

God was also sitting up and each of them locked eyes and began to laugh once again.

The two ordakians propped their hairy topped feet on small padded pedestals that were just a touch lower than the comfortable upholstered chairs they relaxed in. Each of them lazily slouched back in the high-back arched seats and intermittently tugged on their long-stemmed pipes, producing an orange hued smoke bellowing from their mouths and nostrils. The smell of rich tobacco mixed with the orange blossoms of a langerine tree wafted throughout the cozy hovel.

Bridazak drew in a big inhale and then slowly blew the smoke out. He smiled as he watched the swirling mass form into a unicorn and prance around God's head.

"Very good, my dear Bridazak. I'm impressed."

Bridazak raised his eyebrows with pride and slunk deeper into his chair until he heard God exhale a large cloud, which slowly transformed into the likeness of his friends who ran over and began to pet the smoky unicorn form he had just created. Bridazak lurched forward, his eyes a little wider now.

"Do you miss them?" God asked.

Bridazak sat back and said, "Of course but I made my decision. I want to be here with you."

"Do you know the best part about being me?"

Bridazak could tell he was being set up for some new enlightenment, "How could I know?"

"I read the heart of man, their inner being that they cannot even know themselves."

"Tell me what my heart says." Bridazak sat up straight in anticipation.

"Your tears have always pointed to your destiny, Bridazak."

"I wanted to know who I was and what I was meant to do."

"Yes, and do you now feel complete, even with me?"

"I feel complete love."

"You know that this love will never change. It will never love you less nor love you more. My love for you is perfect. But what about you? Do you feel complete?"

"Nay, there is still something missing, like a quest still beckoning me from afar."

"Your destiny calls your name. Your purpose awaits you."

"Waits for me where?"

"Once someone unlocks their identity they now possess the key." God reached out his hand and revealed a golden key.

"What does it unlock?" Bridazak said as he took hold of it and inspected it closely.

God half-grinned and said, "It can now be used to unlock other's identities. Your breakthrough can be someone else's breakthrough but only if you are still in the world."

"Ruauck-El?"

"Yes." God stood up and walked over to a silver chest that Bridazak had not seen there before. "I have something for you."

Bridazak watched as God opened the lid and a brilliant soft glowing light emanated from inside. He pulled forth a leather strap, "This is called the Belt of Truth."

"What does it do?"

"Put it on. You will need it." God turned and then pulled out another item. "This is the Breastplate of Righteousness." It gleamed silver with gold laden etchings.

"I don't wear heavy armor, it is so restrictive."

"Put it on. You will need it." God turned back and another item came out. "This is the Helmet of Restoration."

Bridazak took it and said, "I know, put it on, I will need it."

God nodded and smiled but then turned and took out another item, "These are the Boots of Peace."

"C'mon," Bridazak sighed. "You of all our race know that we don't wear boots."

God raised his eyebrows and handed the footwear to Bridazak. He took them and added it to the pile he had formed on his chair next to him.

"One last item." God revealed from the chest a singular beam of light, like a crystal shard, yet it had no substance.

"What is it?"

"This is a warrior's weapon. You now possess the full armor and no fighter is complete without his weapon. Now, put them on, you will need them." There was a serious tone in God's voice on his last words.

Bridazak slowly picked them up and then placed each item to the appropriate place he was to wear them and one-by-one they mysteriously vanished as if they were absorbed into his very body. Bridazak's eyes widened each time it happened, feeling something inside of him each instance that increased his senses, yet not really understanding what it was.

"Now you are ready and now it is time."

"Time for what?"

"Time for you to go back and fulfill your destiny."

"What if I don't want to go back?"

"Your friends need you."

"You are going to kick me out of heaven?"

"No, I am sending heaven to Ruauck-El. Inside you rests my Kingdom. You will be my ambassador in a foreign land. You will represent all that I am and bring to the people the key to unlock their purpose."

"An ambassador? I'm not one for politics."

"Good."

Bridazak wrinkled his brow confused at his response.

God looked upon him like a proud father. "Now open that door and be united with your friends once again but first give me a hug."

God's arms opened wide and received Bridazak as he flung himself into Him.

Bridazak turned to face the wooden door leading back to Ruauck-El but more importantly back to Dulgin, Spilf, and Abawken. He took a step toward it and reached for the latch.

"Wait!" God said abruptly.

Bridazak turned, "What is it?"

"I forgot one other thing." God reached into his robes and produced a glowing purple ball.

"What is that?"

"Oh, this is very special. It is a Ball of Joy. Catch!"

The ball magically propelled itself and slammed into Bridazak's chest. He didn't launch back upon impact but instead started laughing uncontrollably. Pure joy had entered his body. The laughter subsided but chills ran up his spine and tingled his arms.

"That was amazing," Bridazak said while smiling.

"Release that joy into a world greatly needing it."

"I will."

Bridazak unlatched the door and a brilliant light beyond the threshold engulfed him.

Bridazak fell through the white billowy clouds, the icy cold air biting into his skin and then he broke through to see an immense beige valley. Directly below him was a wizard's tower. He felt as if he knew this place, like he had been here before. His bow materialized within his grasp but he did not have any arrows nor was his weapon strung.

He could feel the darkness within the valley. The sun waned in the distance as it began to set. Bridazak focused on what he thought was shrubs until they appeared to be moving. The tower was surrounded by hundreds of these shambling creatures. He was almost upon the mystic's building when he was finally able to discern what they were—Reegs. The shadow demons glided above the ground, their wispy tails of pure darkness and evil dissipating behind them as they moved closer and closer to Akar's Tower.

"My friends are inside," Bridazak whispered to himself. He knew it. He felt it.

A door opened and a female gnome stepped out but was instantly struck down by one of the Reegs.

Bridazak's bow began to vibrate. He could feel the power inside of the Seeker weapon just like when he was in the Underworld. There was no string on his bow to pull on and no arrows in a quiver to retrieve. He knew they would appear and as he went through the motion of pulling on an imaginary line, he felt the resistance. Suddenly a shaft of light materialized and Bridazak smiled.

"Move inside, Trillius!" Abawken commanded.

Dulgin brought up his axe and readied himself. Spilf backed away, uncertain on what he could do to help.

"I won't leave her!" Trillius yelled back. He was now looking through the shadow creature that had entered the tower. He could feel the dark void of lifelessness inside of it as it emitted a supernatural cold.

Rozelle groaned ever so slightly, causing Trillius to refocus his attention back on her. He lunged for her on the ground just outside the doorway. "Rozelle," he called. Her breathing was shallow and she was barely alive.

Another shadow creature was almost upon him. Trillius launched a lightning bolt but it went straight through it without any effect. He whispered to Rozelle, "This is not our battle, my dear. Time for us to depart."

Suddenly, a flash of light from above pierced the Reeg nearest to Trillius and the evil creature shattered as the light dispelled the darkness. The gnome looked upward and saw what appeared to be an ordakian raining down shafts of light upon the Reegs. He didn't spare the time to figure it out. Trillius summoned the power of transportation and disappeared within the thunder of the lightning bolt, Rozelle along with him.

Abawken just scored a hit on the shadow creature inside the tower but suffered the life-draining power of the Reeg as it retaliated.

Dulgin flanked it, trying to judge when to swing his axe.

Abawken said, "They are affected by a magical blade only."

Dulgin replied, "Then we might have a problem. My axe is not magical."

The Reeg sailed toward the dwarf and Dulgin instinctively brought his weapon to parry. His axe suddenly shimmered and the dark assailant retracted in pain, fearful of it. Dulgin didn't hesitate and brought the axe-head around, cutting through it and watching it shatter and dissipate before their eyes, screeching a horrific wail.

Dulgin looked at his father's axe up close and grinned through his red-beard, nodding his approval, "It's been heaven-touched. Thanks Dah."

"There are more of them coming!" Spilf alerted them as new Reegs appeared just outside.

"Come on! I will take you all down!" Dulgin yelled.

"There are too many of them, Master Dulgin."

"Well, if you have a better idea then let me know. I'm not going down without a fight."

A dozen Reegs soared in toward the opening, but just before they entered, two of them were destroyed by an unseen force from above. The heroes could see spears of light descending and then impacting the shadows, but they could not see where they were coming from or who they were coming from.

Several more were destroyed and then soon the Reegs began to scatter and move out of the way.

"What's happening out there?" Dulgin asked.

"Maybe it is Akar," Spilf spouted.

"If the ancient wizard has miraculously come back from the dead then I'm sure he won't be greeting us with open arms after just busting into his place," Dulgin said.

"Whatever it is, we are thankful, none-the-less, Masters."

More arrows of light slammed into the dark monsters of Kerrith Ravine. The heroes edged closer to the door and tried to peer out to spot their answered prayer.

Bridazak suddenly dropped to the ground, sending the parched dirt up into the air around him. A soft glow surrounded him as he twirled back and forth, side to side, never ceasing to fire his bolts of light.

The heroes tried to focus and get a good look at the dust cloud that surrounded the glowing fighter.

"Bridazak?" Spilf sputtered. "It's Bridazak!"

Abawken and Dulgin looked back at their friend and saw Spilf sporting the goggles he was gifted by the mysterious old man in the forest.

Spilf pointed, "It's him! He came back to us!"

They turned simultaneously and watched as the dust settled and the form pivoted all around firing the magical arrows.

"This Dak is turning my red hair to grey."

"I could use some help, friends!" Bridazak yelled.

"It is him," Abawken whispered.

"Oh, you know what this means? He is going to brag about how many kills he got compared to us." Dulgin sprinted outside and chopped at one of the grey-skinned, eight-foot giant-kin, cutting its leg clean off.

Abawken summoned a rock elemental with a wave of his sword and a command word.

"Hurry up, Stubby! We are getting out of here!" Dulgin yelled.

Spilf edged out and then ran to the middle of his friend's protection. They moved away as one, swinging sword and axe, firing arrows, and clearing a path out of the Valley of Giants. They were back together once again fighting evil side-by-side.

Chapter 37

The Fall of Tuskabar

The Wild Dwarves formed a wall in front of their Giimtock, El'Korr, as they backed toward the front gates of Tuskabar. A sea of statues swelled throughout the streets, pushing El'Korr's army further back. Clanking swords clashed against rock throughout the chilled night.

"We are almost there, my liege," Geetock called as he spotted the gate.

Two-thousand of El'Korr's dwarves had set up a defensive stance and calls could be heard as El'Korr came into the open square, "It is El'Korr!"

Another commander said, "Put your beard into it and push those statues back!"

The statue army flooded into the streets from every building and street but they did not charge. It was like they were holding back and assigned to only usher the dwarves out of the city.

El'Korr called, "Launch the boulders!"

Several responded, "Yes, sir!"

"Continue to fall back!" El'Korr commanded.

They moved as a united group funneling through the front gate. The troops on the wall filed down the towers or climbed the wall on the opposite side to escape the city. Tens-of-thousands of El'Korr's troops stood ready outside on the open terrain. Wooden contraptions were already loaded with giant sized rocks which began to be hurled over the walls and into the city buildings.

"Take it down!" El'Korr yelled.

A thousand elven archers launched scores of fire arrows into the city and at the petrified patrons. The arrows bounced harmlessly off of the statues but ignited flammable material all around. The smell of broken stone and burnt wood soon permeated the area.

The cursed townsfolk and militia of the city of Tuskabar flooded outside. Hundreds quickly grew to thousands and fanned outward.

"Concentrate our boulders at the front gate!" Geetock yelled to several runners who nodded and took off in an all-out sprint to deliver the new orders.

Just then a squad of humans and elves, out of breath, came to stand at attention. They were held back by Wild Dwarves from approaching any further.

"What is it?" one of the dwarves asked. "Why have you left your posts?"

"Sir, we are being attacked by the villages and surrounding towns but they are not people."

Geetock overheard their comments and asked, "What are they?"

Suddenly, seeing the army of statues coming out of the city they pointed toward them, "They are just like that."

The Wild Dwarves exchanged glances and Geetock sent a telepathic message to the others who were spread out, *"We are surrounded by the statue-folk."*

Geetock then alerted King El'Korr who was issuing commands.

"Deploy troops to take them on and position our artillery to fire on all sides," El'Korr said.

"Yes, sir!" several dwarves said in unison.

"Geetock, I have a special job for you."

"What is it?"

"My Lady of the West, the dwarves are surrounded," the cloaked monk said. His face was covered by the shadows cast by the cowl over him.

"Very good. Once we kill the King of the Dwarves then we will convert as many of their human army as possible to fight with us against the other Horn Kings. We will sweep across the north converting all the remnants of King Manasseh's people to our cause."

Just then Ravana felt a presence in her audience chamber behind her. "Go and deliver my orders. I have one loose end to take care of here."

The monk bowed low, "Yes, my Lady." He exited.

Ravana turned and could see that someone now sat upon her throne in the distance. "You are truly daring, Jack of the Holy City."

There was no response as she came closer. Jack's shadowy figure became clearer as she slithered nearer, then he suddenly disappeared.

"Are we going to play this game again?"

"Nay, a new game," Jack responded somewhere in the shadows of the pillared room.

"Jack, your dwarven army has failed. Even now they fall victim to my new army of living rock."

"El'Korr is on his own. I'm here for Kiratta."

Ravana was now at her throne and she sat upon it. Her scaly hands rested on the armrests. The snakes upon her head snapped and hissed. She looked out into the shadowy domain. Jack stepped out from behind one of the pillars and stood resolute. She noticed his distance was too far for her to turn him to stone.

"Come to me, Jack."

"Release Kiratta first."

"It is not that simple. It is complicated."

"It seems simple enough to me. Release her and then I leave and your world domination can continue."

"What if I told you it is impossible to release her?"

"Then I will show you how much worse I am than the army of dwarves. Now release her!"

Ravana stood in anger and yelled, "I can't you insignificant speck of undead!"

She composed herself, "I grow tired of this conversation, Jack of the Holy City."

"Then it is time for action. You will feel the true might of the Vemptukai and your beloved city will crumble under my power."

Ravana began to descend the steps from her throne when suddenly a new figure emerged from the shadows. The heavy set human adorned in majestic furs and a dazzling jewel-ladened crown said, "What have you done my sweet, Lily."

Even the hissing and snapping snakes on her head paused as she gasped, "Father?"

El'Korr's army was surrounded and the living-rock creatures methodically closed in on them. Their boulder hurling ballistae were spread too thin.

Suddenly, a bright jet of red, orange, and yellow flame propelled forth from an unseen source hidden in the air over the city. A tall palace ignited, rock tumbled, and a roaring fire now lingered in several spots.

"Dragon!" El'Korr's men called out.

More jets of flame shot out as Gaermahn attacked Tuskabar.

El'Korr stepped forward, squinting, and said, "Someone is controlling that dragon."

"How do you know," Geetock inquired.

"Red dragons do not attack cities unless they are looking for food. It can clearly see the battlefield and yet it attacks an empty city."

"What do we do if it decides to change its mind?"

"We need to punch a hole in the living-rock creature's defenses and fall back. Focus the hurlers at the north quadrant. I don't want to find out if the dragon changes its mind."

"As you command." Geetock called for more runners to give them new orders.

El'Korr whispered to himself as he looked at the flying scaled beast in the distance, spitting out more flames of destruction, "What are you all about, dragon? Who brought you out of your treasure-hole?"

The ground underfoot quaked, jarring loose dust from above and the sound of cracking stone echoed throughout the chamber.

Jack waited as Ravana approached her newly resurrected father, seemingly unaware of the foundations grumbling, shock still plastered on her visage.

"Father, how is this possible?"

"My dear Lily, I came back for you."

"You can't be real," she began to compose herself as she stopped. "Come to me. Let us embrace."

A sudden flash of her father's heavy ruling and frequent rage-filled fits caused her to step back. "You are a ruse. Jack," she yelled, "you have gone too far!"

"You can end this nightmare Ravana by just releasing Kiratta," Jack said.

Something shifted in King Oedikus at the mention of the imprisoned Kiratta, "What did you do, Ravana?" His voice now deeper and more focused.

"I did nothing. It was your fault."

"Where is she?"

"You loved her more than me. You always favored her."

Jack was uncertain, but it appeared King Oedikus knew of Kiratta, but to what extent?

"You speak nonsense," the resurrected king said.

"Do I? Did you not give her the King's blessing? Did you not shower her with wealth, power, and training in the arts of magic? And did you not give her the hand of the one I loved?"

Oedikus growled, "What did you do with your sister?"

Jack suddenly understood, Kiratta and Ravana were not enemies but blood. The Twelve had flooded Jack with their knowledge at his conversion. In that enlightenment they had revealed hatred toward Kiratta but Jack didn't know why. Their memories were intertwined with his own and deep down he shared this hatred toward her as well. His heart warred with his own mind. The lines of who to trust blurred in an instant. There was no distinction between his memories and the Twelve's and Jack waivered on the heavy decisions he had before him. *"Why do we hate Kiratta?"*

He heard their voices echoing within his brain, *"The witch must be destroyed. She is evil and together we can purge the realm of her existence."*

Chapter 38

Kings

Gaermahn Shesteeva, a great red dragon, now turned undead by the Vemptukai and controlled by the same person, spread its anger and fiery waves over the city. Gaermahn noticed it was an empty city. The pleasure of hearing the screams of those dying and fleeing with their lives had not come. Seeing a building crumble and timber disintegrate could not quench the desire to see the fear in a person's eye and the unique smell of burnt flesh.

The immense beast's thoughts waivered, *"I did as I was told. The city is razed."*

"Shore up our defenses over there!" El'Korr pointed.

A surge of dwarven warriors swelled into that particular area to combat the animated statues. All the while El'Korr's army slowly retreated. They were now engaged on all four sides but the biggest portion of his men were punching a hole through the rock creatures to the north. He had his boulder slinging contraptions focused to target that quadrant but he knew he would have to abandon the machines as they were slow to move and position.

Geetock was by his side and the rest of the Wild Dwarves surrounded their King. Geetock said, "The dragon has ceased attacking the city, my liege."

"Can you see it?"

"Nay."

"Well, there is nothing we can do about it. Our main concern is getting the north opened up. How do we fare?"

"Recent reports have informed us that the living rock is difficult to destroy but they don't have any military coordination. Their only strength is that they outnumber us."

"All the more reason to get out of here and regroup with our other forces."

"Dragon!" several Wild Dwarves called and pointed.

The maw of the giant red dragon illuminated to reveal its position as the power within it increased. It soared toward them.

"Archers, ready!" A commander yelled deep in the ranks. "Fire!"

Hundreds of arrows sailed into the night sky and the few that hit the beast did not penetrate the scaled armor.

Gaermahn unleashed his mighty breath weapon as he adjusted and targeted the section of archers. El'Korr and everyone watched in horror as scores of men disintegrated into ash. The ground was scorched for hundreds of feet as the intense blast of flame burst forth and destroyed everything in its path. They could feel the air whip over their faces as the King of the Air flew past them and soared back out of sight into the dark of night.

"It will have another run," El'Korr said.

"What are your orders?" Geetock asked and then grimaced in pain from the dark-metal poison.

"Your orders are to stay alive. What can we do to heal you?"

"The poison is slow and thankfully I was struck only once. I will be fine. What are your orders?"

"You and I will meet the beast head-on." El'Korr laid hands upon his Wild Dwarf commander, whispered the divine dwarven words, and felt the surge of magic flow through him. Geetock received it as did El'Korr. They opened their eyes and could feel the weightlessness within their bodies. By their own minds they were able to control their elevation and they began to rise.

Geetock yelled down at the other Wild Dwarves, "Get the north opened up and move our troops out!"

They nodded and headed off without delay.

El'Korr walked upon the air as if it were solid ground and positioned himself in a spot where he felt the dragon would strike next.

"Spread out, Geetock."

"We don't know where it will strike from," Geetock said.

"Dragons are intelligent and will most likely go where there is the greatest number of troops. Hold your position and keep a watchful eye for the beast. This one is confident and will reveal itself before it strikes."

El'Korr could now see the overwhelming number of golems below surrounding his army and it shook him to the core. He exhaled with a bit of a growl and refocused his attention on staying alert within the darkened sky. Tall plumes of smoke, ash, and firelight cascaded over the surrounding area from the burning city but the beast of the air was nowhere to be seen.

"My liege," Geetock pointed, "it is flanking our men."

El'Korr turned and immediately charged in that direction. He could see the red behemoth begin to fuel the furnace of fire within its mouth as lava colored outlines formed under the scales on the neck and jaw. Gaermahn released its breath weapon upon the heaps of men below at the same time El'Korr released his mighty warhammer. The screams of the men below reached his ears. The jet of flame was suddenly cut off as his weapon smashed into the dragons head, shattering one of its horns. An ear splitting screech resounded but it quickly reacted and turned flying away into the darkness. El'Korr's hammer magically returned to his hand.

Geetock soon joined him by his side, "My Mahlek, it will be coming back."

"It only got a taste of what I plan to do to that thing."

A new voice entered their minds. It was the red dragon, *"I look forward to your death, Dwarf King."*

"And I look forward to making a new drinking horn from your lifeless body," countered El'Korr.

The two dwarven warriors knew that they were immune to the fire damage of the creature due to their many years of captivity within the curse of the Burning Forest and would use that to their advantage the next time it came in. They had done their job and brought the full attention of the dragon to them instead of the army below. This would give his men more time.

"My liege, there it is," Geetock pointed as it sailed across the moon to reveal itself.

"It wants us to know where it is. They are intelligent but not as wise."

They prepared to meet it head on. They would surprise the creature after it breathed on them with their own counterstrike.

Within moments the ancient Gaermahn unleashed its flame. The searing heat engulfed the dwarves and they shrieked in pain. Geetock suddenly morphed into a giant boulder of rock in front of El'Korr to shield him, as the innate wild magic was triggered inside.

"Dark magic!" El'Korr yelled, gritting through it.

The fire did not affect them but the undead dark magic that was now engrained within it did. Red, orange, and black colors splayed around the rock and then ceased as the dragon passed by.

"*I'm impressed, Dwarf King,*" Gaermahn said inside their minds as he saw El'Korr was still alive.

Smoke from the absorbed fire wafted off of him and the boulder form of Geetock. El'Korr shook off the effects of the dark energy but it had taken its toll on him nonetheless and he felt weaker. It was like something had stolen a piece of his life force and he could only imagine what a direct hit by such a creature could mean. Once again, Geetock had saved his life, much like his lost friend, Rondee the Wild had against the dragon named Dal-Draydian. He pushed aside the thought of losing another friend to a dragon and readied his hammer as he looked to and fro for the beast.

"Where are you?" he whispered.

Suddenly, Gaermahn swooped in and snatched the dwarf from the air with his powerful claws. "*I'm right here,*" it mocked.

El'Korr grunted, losing his hammer from the impact but the magic inside the linked weapon quickly returned it to his grasp. He smashed it into the scaled clutch repeatedly but was unable to get enough leverage to cause any damage.

Gaermahn spoke telepathically, "*I am curious.*"

El'Korr relented his attacks and said, "About how I am going to kill you?"

"*How you are connected to the Vemptukai.*"

"What are you about dragon? This word is meaningless to me."

"*The Vampire King, how do you know him?*"

"You speak of Jack. What have you done with him? Who brought you out of your slumber?"

"*How ironic, I no longer sleep Dwarf King, and Jack, as you say, is now my master.*"

"What? Where is Jack?"

"*He is within the city dealing with Ravana.*"

"Let me go, dragon."

"*Mmmm. Let the dwarf go or enjoy the taste of a royal bloodline? Choices,*" it said sadistically.

"I know Jack, your master, and he won't be happy if you eat me."

"*He will never know.*"

Gaermahn landed on a rocky crag overlooking the battlefield and the fire plumes littering the city. He brought El'Korr closer to his face.

El'Korr said, "Let me die honorably with my weapon in hand and not caged like an animal."

"*I care not of your honor, Dwarf King.*"

"What are you? What have you become? I remember the dragons of old and they fought valiantly in the open knowing their strength and understanding their heritage."

"*I am now undead, with no emotions from the life I lived, and now only longing to fill my desire for blood. I am of the vampire lineage now—the first of my kind.*"

"There was a time that vampire blood only affected humans."

"*I had once thought this to be true before my turning by the Vemptukai—by Jack.*"

"Domosh ki seote te blite."

"*Ah, the dwarven tongue, a language I have not heard in a very long time. I am sorry Dwarf King but I no longer have a soul to be cursed.*"

Gaermahn was about to consume El'Korr when the sudden flash of a lightning bolt struck his body. Blue electrical sparks danced over his scales and penetrated deep into his flesh. The red dragon held its ground as shards of rock underneath broke away at the awkward movement of the heavy creature resting upon it. It turned in the direction of where the bolt came from.

"*Gaermahn!*" a booming voice resounded inside the red dragon's mind.

"*Zeffeera!*"

The bronze dragon maintained its position in the air a hundred paces away, "*It has been a long time.*"

"*What brings you so far from your hidden valley?*"

"*You have something of mine.*"

"*Oh, this Dwarf King is yours?*"

"*Let him go, Gaermahn.*"

"*You are no match for me now, Zeffeera. I am undead.*"

A new voice spoke out from the dark night, "You will release El'Korr now, Gaermahn."

The red dragon turned to see a beautiful female elf with her fluttering robes trailing behind her fly into view. She had a slight glow about her from the magical flight she had summoned through her spell.

He snarled to reveal his vampire fangs, *"Raina of the Sheldeen Elves. It cannot be so."*

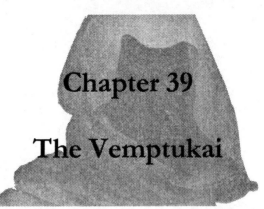

Chapter 39

The Vemptukai

Penelope's red hair glistened and her black leather pants and vest reflected the light as the crackling orange fire roared around her. The destruction caused by the dragon did not phase her countenance. Her focus was on Ravana's Tower that still stood. She had thought Daysho could be groomed into a Vampire King figurehead but the thought quickly evaporated when she encountered Jack on Romann's ship and saw firsthand his power. The intricate tattoos on his face had also shown her the truth; the dialect of the original vampires.

Daysho was unfit for the leadership position and her original judgment was clouded by her thirst to be desired as the mistress of power. Over the centuries her patience had worn thin. When Romann had come to her she jumped at the chance but deep down in her cold, unbeating heart she knew the former assassin would never live up to the standards of the Vemptukai—a true Vampire King. But as fate would have it, her master of the walking dead had arrived and now it was time for them to join forces and for her to take her rightful place by his side.

"But why didn't I sense his presence?" Her thoughts warred inside her mind, but deep down she knew he was the one. *"If the king has the power to block my senses, then what other power does he possess?"*

Ravana, secret ruler of the western lands, had killed her father centuries ago but he now stood before her. The impossible had become possible and her mind raced thinking of how to deal with it. A prophecy had spoken of her father being her demise and by her killing the threat centuries ago it was eliminated but here he was, alive and speaking to her. Ravana suddenly focused on Jack standing in the background.

"You caused this," she declared venomously.

"Shifting the blame does not change the truth of what stands before you now."

"How is this possible?" she asked.

Jack responded, "Today you will release Kiratta."

"Kiratta? All of this for my sister? You have only forced my hatred toward her to increase, Jack of the Holy City. I will never release her."

"I brought the true King of the West back to rule," Jack stated and then nodded toward King Oedikus.

The large human turned toward his daughter and said, "Ravana, you will release her and answer for your treason."

She laughed and the snakes atop her head hissed and snapped loudly in chorus, "Treason? It is you who betrayed your family. You betrayed me. You never loved me."

He took a step forward and gently lifted his hand toward her face, "But I do love you, my sweet Lily."

She swatted his hand away and spun him around. Her face was nestled in her father's shoulder and neck and her snakes slithered around his head. "Jack, the game is over."

"I'm not the one playing games, Ravana."

"You thought bringing my father back could change things but it hasn't." Ravana flared her fangs and buried them into her father's flesh. Blood trickled out of the wounds left behind as she lifted her bloody face away in ecstasy.

Jack walked toward her, now entering her range of turning flesh to stone with a single gaze. "It is over, Ravana."

King Oedikus slumped to the ground lifeless. Ravana stood above her father but her focus turned toward Jack and her eyes flared a bright yellow with sharp black lines laced like electrical sparks. Jack held up his hand and Ravana suddenly jolted back a step and her eyes returned to normal.

"What have you done to me?"

"Nothing. You did it to yourself." He walked closer.

"What is happening?"

"There is power in the blood, Ravana. You drank my blood when you killed your father and now you are mine."

With panic splayed across her hideous scaled face she looked down at her father. She thought it was his blood but now realized he was nothing but a puppet of Jack's.

"But how? Even your blood can't bring someone back to life."

"You are right." Jack pulled out the Mirror of Lost Souls, expanded it, and placed it in front of Ravana's face. Her visage stretched as if the mirror was a vacuum pulling on her spirit. She screamed as the pain and despair bellowed deep from her vocal chords.

Jack said, "You are now under my control, Ravana. You will now release Kiratta from the curse of Oculus. I call upon the soul of Ravana and command it to return to her body now." The Mirror of Lost Souls vibrated and a single translucent spirit in a murky white cloud sprang out and soared around the room. Ravana watched it zip to and fro until finally stabbing her chest. Her hands and arms spread out as if a spear tip had penetrated her body. She gasped for air and stumbled backward rigidly, hands clasping toward her heart.

Jack was beside her instantly and held her steady. She turned to face him, eyes widened in shock, still trying to grasp what was happening.

Jack said, "You and your soul have been reunited."

She sputtered, "I feel so much pain. What is happening to me?"

"Your emotions were one-sided for so long, Ravana. Love and remorse are feelings that have come back to you. Your body is adjusting."

Tears welled up in her eyes as she looked at Jack. "I love him."

"Your father?" Jack asked.

"Romann. Where is he?"

Jack understood and said, "There is no greater love than to lay down one's life for another. Romann chose to lose his life in order to be with your sister, Kiratta."

"No," she cried, "I can't let him go."

"Release her and free yourself at the same time, Ravana. Trust me."

"But I can't. I don't want him to go."

"You must, by your own will or by the command I will give to you. Free yourself of this burden you have carried for so long." His voice was soft but full of authority.

Ravana looked away from Jack. She looked upon her father on the ground. The emotions had surged through her body, mind, and spirit and now had settled back into her like coming home after many years of imprisonment. She gave up the fight within and the image of Romann shattered upon the utterance of her words.

"I…release…Kiratta Green."

Chapter 40

Is This Real?

"You chose your destiny when you took Ravana's bite," Oculus' voice echoed through the halls as he continued to search for Romann. "Without her father the reign of Ravana is supreme. Your quest to free Kiratta failed before it ever began."

Romann tried to ignore the foul creature's words but each syllable pounded against his chest and he clutched at his velvet tunic. There was something stirring inside of him and though his heart did not beat it felt like he was having a heart attack. The grey stone around him blurred and shadows elongated. The voice of Oculus trailed off like someone yelling from a distant ship. There was no time to think as he writhed on the ground in rigid motions of reflex, captured by, and in most regards, intoxicated by the feeling he was having, a physical feeling he had not known for many centuries—pain.

Raina and Zeffeera hovered in the air ready to battle the undead red dragon that held El'Korr hostage. Gaermahn on his own was formidable but now as a fire-breathing vampire it changed things immensely.

Gaermahn spoke within their minds, *"Raina, you and your pet are no match for me."*

"You were a dragon of reason once before and I do not believe you would throw that away now."

"The Vemptukai, Jack, has given me a new reason and my days of slumbering on top of a bed of gold are over."

Raina's face was resolute, "My power has grown also and if you choose to leave now then your life will be spared."

Gaermahn noticeably calculated her words and he was uncertain if she was bluffing or not. Raina had been gone for many centuries and the dragon network of information against mystics of Ruauck-El he once had access to had diminished causing many dragons to go into hiding and isolation. He was willing to test this legendary mystic however. *"Let us embrace in combat."*

"Now, Zeffeera!" Raina shouted.

Another blast of electricity spewed out of the bowels of the bronze dragon. The blue and white arcs snapped forward and struck Gaermahn. Before the red dragon could retaliate, Raina initiated a readied spell and teleported next to El'Korr. She grabbed hold of the Dwarf King and they were both pulled back into her magical transportation spell. In the blink of an eye, Raina and El'Korr now hovered in the night sky out of the immediate harm's way of the vampiric dragon.

"Is that all you have?" Gaermahn hissed back at Zeffeera. He opened his maw and the dark magic of death mixed with the superheated energy of fire shot forth. Zeffeera was blasted back, wings a flame, and descended quickly to the ground all the while screeching in horrific pain.

"You cannot defeat me!" Gaermahn bellowed inside their minds.

Zeffeera fell out of sight below the craggy mountain but several other dragons suddenly rose up to replace her. The various sized beasts shimmered their true colors of bronze, silver, and a single gold dragon, the largest of the flying brigade.

"We brought friends," Raina announced.

Gaermahn shifted from his perch and flapped his wings to gain altitude. *"This is far from over, Raina."*

The sheldeen elf mystic did not respond and allowed the red dragon to leave unscathed as she needed the resources Zeffeera and she had gathered to battle the army of stone. If Jack had turned Gaermahn then that would make Jack his master and there was still the chance they could reach the lost human child.

Raina and El'Korr descended and landed by Zeffeera. She was being attended to by two silver dragons. They were soothing the burnt flesh with the cold breathing power that resided inside of them.

"I will be fine, Raina," Zeffeera said after clearly noticing the look

of concern on her face. *"Take the others and help the dwarves."*

Raina nodded after a long pause and then turned to El'Korr, "Time to end this. Are you ready?"

"I'm a Hammergold. I'm always ready."

Geetock's wild magic raged. Each of his arms formed into bronze hammers and he demolished a living statue creature. Fragments of chipped stone sprang out in all directions. The smell of crushed rock engulfed his senses but he ignored it as he yelled out commands to the surrounding troops, "Keep them back!"

His words alone could not muster the strength to keep this overwhelming number at bay. When one was killed, three more would replace it. The sheer power of Ravana's magical army seemed indestructible. Their losses would be devastating after this was over. Geetock desperately wanted to find his King but he would be unable to do so dead. His goal was to stay alive and kill as many of his enemy as possible along his path to survival.

All of the immediate troops had fallen around him and he was separated from his clan. Geetock swung his weapons over his head in a circular motion. His body was the anchor as the pull of the heavy hammerheads wanted to drag him along with it. He whirled around repeatedly and struck another statue. His momentum did not slow and then another statue crumbled. Geetock yelled as more statues came at him. He was isolated from his army, surrounded, and fighting with all he had. He could feel the wild magic inside begin to boil and soon it would be unleashed. He did not know what magic would be released and at this point he did not care. He would die victoriously and be honored in the realm beyond.

Bright blasts erupted around Geetock as he spun in circles letting the weight of his weapons guide him. He continued to yell, "For El'Korrrrrrrrrrrr!" His wild magic surged and the bright blasts around him melted away as he closed his eyes and let it overtake him. He partnered with the magic. He trusted the power inside of him and gave way to its demands. His hammers continued to strike objects and he felt the energy being released like a fireball from the hand of a wizard. Geetock could no longer stand and he fell to the ground in pure exhaustion. The chaotic battle around him calmed as he readied himself to be launched into the next adventure of eternity with God.

The fighting, the clanking of swords, the cries of dying men, all began to fade and he felt his body rise. "This is it," he whispered.

The voice of his King penetrated his mind, "Stop sleeping. I'm still needing you, Geetock."

Geetock's mind of dwarven heaven quickly evaporated as his eyes flittered open. El'Korr was holding him up, looking into his face inches away. All of his senses came back and with them the sights and sounds of the battle around him.

Geetock saw Raina standing just to the right sending out conjured missiles of energy to splash into the enemies. A huge muscled dragon leg stomped next to him as his focus shifted to the gold dragon smashing statues and then releasing the hot fire of its breath weapon. Geetock watched several living golems melt under the heat.

"Snap out of it!" El'Korr commanded.

"What happened, my liege?"

"Raina brought us our help to escape. You contacted her just in time. Now c'mon before the hole the dragons opened closes up again."

"Is this real? I thought I was going to dwarf heaven."

"Heaven is not ready for you yet."

"Quickly, the dragons above informed me that more of them are coming out of the city. There are too many," Raina announced.

Geetock was on his feet. Sudden blasts from several dragons rained down to clear out patches of the enemy and give El'Korr's army a chance to flee.

The Gold Dragon, clearly the leader of the scaled beasts, remained on the ground and led El'Korr, Geetock, and Raina through the sea of moving rock. Huge jets of flame lit up the area as the mighty breath weapon melted all in its path for hundreds of feet. The scorched gap left behind by the dragon quickly filled in like ants as the statues flooded into the open space.

"There are too many of them. Climb on," the gold dragon said inside their minds.

Without questioning, they each climbed aboard, clutching the legs and standing on the claws. Raina elevated on her own as a gust of wind propelled her upward.

As they rose, El'Korr saw the devastation, worse than he could have imagined. The dragons had cleared an opening at the back and his remaining army was rushing through while at the same time battling the magically cursed creatures birthed by the evil Ravana.

He whispered, "God Almighty help us."

Chapter 41

Your Time Has Just Begun

"Leave me. I have given you what you asked," Ravana said as she stood and faced Jack.

"There is one more thing that I require," Jack responded.

"Speak it and be gone."

"Halt your attack on the dwarves."

Ravana sprang at Jack but he held up his hand and she instantly stopped, stuck fast. She hissed at him, "Never!"

Jack leaned in and said firmly, "End the attack or I will end you."

Ravana softened and said, "Let us rule together. I beg of you. Do not take everything away from me."

Jack walked slowly behind her, "You are asking for good to co-exist with evil."

She laughed, "You claim to be good? You are the Vemptukai. There is nothing good about you other than the perfection of who you are."

"And who am I?"

She turned to face him. Her green scales shimmered from the lit braziers in the room and her emerald eyes brightened. "Perfect evil. All your thoughts and actions move you in purpose of who you were created to be. When a king rules over his people others say he is evil and yet the king brings purpose and value to the land and its citizens."

"You seem to have it all figured out, Ravana."

"As do you, I suspect."

"I only wish to govern myself and no other," Jack said.

"And yet you direct my will as we speak."

"Only to protect myself and those I care about, nothing more."

A new voice entered the chamber. Penelope's red hair glowed in the dim light. "I will help you, my King."

Ravana giggled, "Ah, Countessa Penelope De Luz, the great mythical Advisor of the Vampire King."

Jack was barraged suddenly with memories released by the Twelve in his mind. She had been in service with them. She had counseled their motives, their desires, and their needs. "I don't need an advisor," Jack said calmly, quickly taking control of his thoughts.

"You don't know what you need and that is why I am here," Penelope responded.

Jack said, "Were you not grooming Daysho to be your King?"

Ravana interjected, "Daysho is a pawn, nothing more to Penelope. You will understand soon enough Jack of the Holy City how much of a pawn you will be as well."

Penelope's eyes flared orange, "You are an abomination to our kind, Ravana."

"Is that so? While you have hidden yourself away on your pathetic island waiting for your beloved king, I have gathered an unstoppable army and will put this realm beneath me as my footstool."

Penelope slowly looked away and refocused her attention on Jack, "You are suppressing our bond. Let go and you will feel my call to you."

"I am suppressing nothing. I have a different call on my life and it doesn't revolve around you."

She pressed further, "You feel it even now. The Vemptukai has the ability to sense me."

"I sense everyone and everything."

"The quickening; like your heart coming to life."

As she spoke, Jack could feel the sensation.

"Like the wings of a butterfly touching your skin," she continued.

Her words began to trigger something inside of him. Unknowingly, he had suppressed this feeling around her.

"It is the marker, my King. We are bonded to one another."

Penelope triggered his mind to focus on what was always there. He realized the pattern now and also that it happened only when she was around. Deep down, he did feel a connection, as if they had met before.

She said softly, on queue with his last thought, "You know it to be true."

Jack's brow furrowed, "Who are you?"

They stared at one another for a long while. The silence was loud within the shadowy chamber and then it was broken by a distant roar of a dragon—Jack's dragon.

"There is something different about you, but my time here has come to an end," Jack said.

"Your time has just begun," Penelope countered. "The Vemptukai has returned to the realm once again."

The very moment he received the blood of the Twelve, time had stopped for him. He was now an eternal being meant to walk this realm alone, so he had imagined. No one could possibly understand him except God himself but Penelope's comment rang true. His time had just begun.

Jack turned to Ravana, "You know what must be done. I will not ask again."

"Pray tell what you speak of now?" she mocked.

"End your attack on the dwarves."

Ravana resisted the demand. There was a visible surge of power she fought against internally.

Penelope stepped forward to stand by Jack's side, "Do as he says!"

Ravana, stiff in concentration turned her head slowly toward the Countessa and Ravana's eyes flared to life. Penelope tried to flee her look but it was too late as the curse of the medusa took root inside of her. Her skin began to freeze and harden. There was a noticeable sound of cracking of stone as her entire body transformed.

Jack warp-stepped next to Ravana and grabbed her throat, "Let her go!"

"It is too late," she managed to say.

"Reverse your curse," he growled slowly.

"She is nothing. You and I can rule together."

"Am I now to be your Romann?" His comment cut to the core of Ravana. He had poured salt into the gaping wound.

"I will destroy everything you—"

Jack's body turned to mist and he instantly transported behind her. Ravana's eyes flared wide and her voice was cut off as she saw her beating heart and blood dripping through his fingers to the ground in front of her. Jack crushed the bulbous flesh in his hand and Ravana's green eyes dulled to a lifeless grey. He retracted his arm and the medusa fell to the ground dead.

"I had wanted to save you, Ravana," Jack whispered. "I could have saved you if you had let me."

He walked toward Penelope, strangely affected by this woman, no, not a woman, a vampire, but clearly there was a strange sensation he felt toward her. There was a connection but he was unable to understand it. Instinctively he had blocked whatever it was and now it would not be something he would be able to explore.

Jack whispered, "Why God do I feel abandoned by you? I am trying to help your people and this world. Isn't that why I came back? People are dying around me and yet you give me no insight or help to save them."

The perfect statue of Countessa Penelope De Luz stared blankly at him. Jack reached out and caressed the smooth charcoal grey stone, distraught by what had transpired, and then he vanished.

Chapter 42

Bitter Sweet

"Raina, summon your meteor storm like you did at Blackrock Castle!" El'Korr called to her. Geetock and he were holding onto the massive legs of the gold dragon while Raina flew beside them launching her spells of destruction upon what seemed to be an endless army of living rock below.

"It takes time. Time we don't have and there would be too much risk to our side."

"But those are my people, we must do something," he said, uncertain if anyone could hear him through the rushing wind.

Thousands more of Ravana's army came from the city and the surrounding villages. There was no hope. El'Korr felt the weight of the loss and his actions at that moment. No dwarven king before him had ever fled even if it meant death.

El'Korr commanded the gold dragon, "Take me down to my army."

"It would result in certain death."

"Dwarves do not fear it. Take me down." El'Korr looked at Geetock and his trusted bodyguard nodded his approval. "Contact the others and have them shield-up. The dwarves will make our stand here and now."

Geetock nodded again and then closed his eyes to telepathically reach his Wild Dwarf brethren.

The gold dragon surged toward the front lines, flying just past the clashing weaponry where El'Korr's army spread out to clear a landing path for the beast. The Dwarf King hopped down.

The elite Wild Dwarves came forward, "We serve the Giimtock. What are your orders?"

"We fight. Gather the remaining dwarves and call out to the other races that they can fight or flee as they are led but our kin will not run any further."

All of them hit their chests with their forearm and fist and bowed their heads to the command.

Geetock said, "It will be an honor to die by your side."

"It has been an honor to live by yours," El'Korr said, locking his eyes onto each of them. "It is time, my bearded brothers. Invoke all you have and leave it on this battlefield today for this day we leave our mark on the realm of Ruauck-El. Hell will remember this day and heaven will celebrate our return home."

The sounds of the dying, the clashing swords, and brave roars of fighting men became louder and louder. The line approached and the clutch of destiny tightened.

The gold dragon launched from the area. Dwarves that had once been trying to escape now turned and embraced what lay before them as they heard the horns blaring, calling them to fight. Their leader stood resolute as any dwarf would want. El'Korr represented the very essence of dwarfdom—strength, honor and sacrifice.

Thousands of dwarven warriors lined up and fanned out behind the line of fighters that were slowly being overtaken. El'Korr focused on the statues that swarmed. This was not a normal enemy but instead a group of people cursed by the evil Ravana. He could see the detail etched into the moving rock. Their clothing, now a mottled splotchy grey, moved fluidly, and their faces were sullen, without remorse, without emotion, not knowing what they were doing, or did they? El'Korr shook his head slightly in disgust of what was before him. This overwhelming army of drones made of rock would be his demise, would be his friends' end. Could he have changed this outcome? There was a pit inside of his stomach, a seed of anger toward this dire situation. He hated to see villains win. His last army fell entrapped by an evil deity at the Burning Forest. He thought, *"Perhaps I am cursed."* The Dwarf King was pained by the loss of not this war but of the many people he held dear and the innocent within this curse Ravana had brought upon the people of Tuskabar.

El'Korr turned and yelled to his men, "It is time!"

A tremendous roar from his army shook the very ground. Tens of thousands of stocky, bearded troops were riled and ready to die here and now. El'Korr and his bodyguards moved forward, weapons and shields ready. The stomps of booted dwarves resounded as the mass moved forward.

Raina watched above with the dragons swooping in and out of the enemy ranks to try to slow down the inevitable. "El'Korr, my dear dwarven King, you will be remembered for all time." She turned toward the gold dragon and issued a telepathic command, *"Felloch, concentrate on the statues around El'Korr and call the other dragons for support. We must give them as much time as possible."*

"But even time cannot help them, Raina."

"Just do it!"

"As you wish."

Dragons were contacted and one-by-one they came in hard and fast, issuing devastating breath weapons or sweeping down with claws and tail. Raina continued to unleash her magic upon them with fireballs, bolts of lightning, and energy missiles.

The living statues continued to pour from the city and the surrounding countryside. They even seemed to come up from the ground as if they had laid in wait for centuries. The depth of Ravana's power unnerved even the greatest mystic Ruauck-El had ever known. This created army was always intended to take over another Horn King, perhaps every territory and beyond.

Raina could see these everyday citizens, now turned to stone, fight with sluggish punches, but a hit by one of them would break bone. She even saw women and children fighting. This loss would be felt for centuries. Another blast of energy was issued from her fingertips and she watched the former humans be destroyed as rock fragments shattered and toppled over.

Felloch, the gold dragon, contacted Raina, *"You must see this."*

"We don't have time. El'Korr needs us."

"Raina, look to the west."

She glanced to her left and stopped breathing. In the moonlight, breaking through the sparse clouds in the night sky, were the silhouettes of more statues marching from the shoreline of the Great Illustrya Ocean. These were not the ordinary ones they were fighting now but instead an actual army with shields and weapons also turned to stone. They marched unified in rows upon rows and there was no end in sight as to how many would bubble up from the depths.

Raina looked above, closed her eyes, and began to chant her most powerful spell. With the loss of the dwarves, elves, and human army that had assembled, she would need to destroy as many as possible of the trained enemy troops.

"Kel vas torak-vue sheltite ke-ahmbet!" Sparse clouds overhead quickly gathered together and became dark. She raised her arms overhead and continued to chant under her breath. A flash of lightning struck from within the gathering clouds. Her eyelids fluttered as the sky began to swirl into a vortex and open up. The flashes of lightning increased and the movement of clouds hastened.

El'Korr could feel the shift in the atmosphere and called out above the sound of battle, "Raina is bringing her fire!" He crushed another statue in the head with his shield and threw his warhammer at another.

The Wild Dwarves had gone into a flurry of supernatural movement and were warp-stepping to and fro all the while smashing the enemy to pieces. The mixture of blurred dwarves surrounded King El'Korr in a protective manner. Other dwarves were falling all around them as the animated rock creatures pressed in with their overwhelming numbers. Each dwarf fought valiantly to the bitter end but the carnage around those that remained began to take its toll mentally and the fighting began to slow as the dwarves diminished.

Another bright flash of orange and red burst forth as the gold dragon swooped in and unleashed its fire. The superheated air ignited and blasted a large group of statues, melting them instantly. Those that were directly hit and the others close by were shattered from the intense heat. This gave El'Korr a little breathing room but the sea of moving rock continued to fill in.

A light rain fell and the ground quickly became muddy underfoot. The statue army glistened in the night and El'Korr's magical plate mail shined brilliantly like a beacon.

Thousands of humans and elves had been given the opportunity to escape when the dwarves took their stand. They had broken free of Ravana's grasp for the time being and moved further and further away. Hundreds of dwarves that had not heard the call looked back at the sacrifice of their comrades and soon began to band to together for their own assault on the enemy lines at the rear.

The beginning of Raina's spell was forming as small bursts of flame began to fall from the open vortex of swirling dark clouds. The fiery drops melded within the rain and never hit the ground but each second that passed it increased until the actual fire rain was touching the surface.

El'Korr was suddenly bull rushed by several statues. He fell back to the ground and the swarm was almost upon him until the Wild Dwarves warp-stepped in front of him and pushed them back. Other statues came in from the sides but El'Korr was on his feet and ready for the incoming. He slammed his shield to block one and swung his hammer to smash another. There were too many and he prepared himself to be overrun until a dragon swooped in and propelled the statues away with such a force that they impacted their own right behind them.

The Wild Dwarves regrouped and created a bubble around themselves and their King—their Giimtock. It was a magical force field that kept the enemy out. Silence engulfed them instantly but the echoes of the clashing and screams rang in their ears. Geetock and the others slumped to their knees as they concentrated as a collective group on maintaining this protective barrier. El'Korr watched in horror as he slid his hand down the window and witnessed the mass statue army overtake his dwarven brethren.

"What have you done, Geetock?"

He answered inside El'Korr's mind, *"We are saving you, my Mahlek."*

Raina could not see the battlefield below as her attention remained on the coming devastation. Her emerald, gold-pupiled eyes flared brightly and she began to pull on something tangible, focusing on the open vortex of swirling dark clouds above. An immense light brightened the sky as a huge meteor fell from the opening and soared toward Ravana's true army. In that instant, everything and everyone stopped and watched the ball of rock and fire impact the shoreline.

The earth shook and the concussion blasted all in the vicinity to the ground. Hundreds upon hundreds were destroyed. The ocean water was pushed away by the tremendous force but the sea quickly regrouped and took back what was lost. The crashing waves unified in their distinct rolling lines once again.

Zeffeera contacted Raina telepathically, *"The curse of Ravana is falling."*

The Sheldeen Mystic did not respond but looked down at the battlefield. The living statues continued to fight. *"Zeffeera, you must be mistaken."*

The bronze dragon flew toward Raina, her wings noticeably damaged by the devastating attack of Gaermahn earlier. Her flight was wobbly but Raina knew whatever was causing her to fly to her side must be of importance.

"The edges of the battle lines are reverting to flesh," Zeffeera said.

Raina refocused and through the dim moonlight and the falling rain, she managed to verify what the bronze dragon had reported. The statues were transforming back. Colorful clothing returned and stood out amongst the drab grey matter. She watched as the wave of transformation surged through the ranks.

"Shut this force field off!" El'Korr yelled while watching the semi-globe be covered with the statues as they fought, clawed, and scratched to get inside. The King knew the Wild Dwarves would never do it but he felt compelled to demand it nonetheless. A soft glow from his armor permeated the quieted area he was inside of as the light from outside was cut off.

"No, God!" El'Korr shouted as he fell to his knees, dropping his shield and hammer to the muddy ground. "Do not let my people suffer this loss. Rise up inside each warrior and let them fight with the power of your Kingdom." His head hung low.

The battle sounded distant while inside this protective shielding. Soft thuds resounded inside the chamber as stone fists pounded relentlessly. El'Korr raised his head to look up into the sky. His pleading eyes longed for an answer from God and looked beyond what was in front of him until he thought he heard someone crying in the distance. He snapped back to reality and looked around at the Wild Dwarves who were in deep meditation. He heard the muffled cry again and his head jolted to the left and there at the edge of the shield was a human child in muddy clothes looking directly at him. There was another human, in the flesh, next to the boy and soon all of the living rock transformed into human form. The people slowly slid down from the shield and looked around in shock and bewilderment as if they had come out of a trance. Dwarven warriors slammed up against the bubble and looked inside frantically. A deep sigh of relief came over their faces when they made eye contact with their King.

"Geetock, open the shield, now! God has answered our prayers."

Chapter 43

Freedom

Raina witnessed the transformation of the citizens of Tuskabar below from her vantage point but the new army that had come from the ocean continued to march, this one different from the citizens that were turned to rock. Her devastating spell could not cover the mile of sandy shoreline. She had destroyed hundreds of the stone warriors but thousands more rose from the sea. The militia of Ravana's true strength was only set back by the enormous meteor she had delivered from her spell. El'Korr and the others had no idea what was coming there way.

She cast a new incantation and whispered into the swirling, stormy winds.

El'Korr looked up immediately into the night sky, hearing the voice of Raina in his ears as if she stood next to him. His eyes narrowed and his face grimaced.

Geetock noticed and asked, "What is it?"

El'Korr bore into his friend, "We are not done. Get these innocent people out of here and rally what is left of our army. A new threat marches against us out of the sea."

"It will be done." Geetock started issuing commands and contacted the other Wild Dwarves telepathically.

The jubilee of victory soon quieted as new orders were yelled out and then echoed further away. Relieved faces of Tuskabar's citizens turned to concern and then the urgent need to get out of the area and flee. Dwarves gathered together in scores and began to form ranks as the people squeezed by them. Horns blared to call the men to order. Clerics ministered to others who were injured and some received enough healing to get back in line.

El'Korr noticed former human militia of Ravana's army gathering together to fight alongside of them. They too were victims, but willing to become victors in this war against evil.

Another huge meteorite fell from the open vortex and plummeted upon Ravana's army but it would not be enough to destroy them all. The ground shook underneath at the impact. A plume of smoke, sand, and mist formed and then dissipated.

"Move out!" El'Korr shouted.

Thousands of remaining troops began to march, stomping at each step. The smell of the salty air replaced the crushed stone and mud. A dozen dragons of silver and bronze soared over El'Korr's marching army and each delivered their deadly breath weapons. Flashes of lightning ignited the silhouettes of the impending clash between the two sides.

Scores of flying stone wyvern's broke out of the sea and began to engage the dragons in swarms.

Raina's meteor spell was depleted and the swirling vortex of clouds slowed and broke apart. The sheldeen mystic continued to send her magical power down from the air in the form of fireballs and lightning blasts taking out sections of the oncoming forces.

There seemed to be no end in sight of how many emerged from the ocean.

The battlefield was set as both sides hastened their steps. Dwarves frothed at the mouth eager to engage and the stone warrior's emotionless faces sent a haunting sensation over the living. Both sides charged.

A roar, like no other dragons' in the area, suddenly fell on everyone's ears and the undead red dragon, Gaermahn, emerged from the city with its rider on top. The huge beast warp shifted causing a stuttered effect from those witnessing with their eyes as it quickly approached the impending battle lines.

Jack telepathically contacted El'Korr and Raina, *"Ravana is dead. The city is yours."*

Gaermahn unleashed his breath weapon and the dark magic fire impacted a score of the stone golems, sizzling through fifty, causing them to explode and sending fragments in all directions.

Jack added, *"My final gift."* Gaermahn veered away and distanced themselves from them all, vanishing into the night.

Raina said, *"Where are you going, Jack? We need you."*

"No one needed me before, Raina. It is time that I take my destiny into

my own hands."

Raina sighed and turned her attention back to their enemy. She hurled another ball of fire and it exploded brilliantly, killing several more foes. Her spell power was diminishing and she could not see the breadth of this army to even know if they had a chance.

She thought, *"It is time to find out, Raina."* She flew toward the breaking waves and then hovered above the ocean just beyond the shore. She peered back and saw the dwarves and stone warriors collide in an epic exchange of might. Dragons were engaged in the air. A silver dragon fell to its death covered by the attacking wyvern's. Blood curdling screams resounded as dwarf, human, and elf fell, along with statue warriors crushed by the initial assault. The smell of the sea, rock, mud, and blood mingled throughout the combat.

Raina began a new spell, "Seiveth tol kith-mal." Her eyes flared a bright blue and she looked intently into the dark water. The new vision penetrated the darkness and she saw clear as day the rows and rows of soldiers marching forth. Her heart sank as she could not find an end to Ravana's hand even after her death. There were thousands.

The sheldeen mystic heard distant voices out into sea and her new found sight revealed ships sailing and rowing toward her.

She whispered in unbelief, "Pirate ships?" She then spotted Captain Elsbeth leading the charge. A hundred vessels behind the half-elf captain fanned out like an arrow. One ship on the left caught her attention as she recognized a glowing sword held by none other than Lufra Yasooma. Lufra had come far on his life's journey from her first encounter with him at Yasooma's tomb here in Tuskabar. He had wanted to commit suicide because of the curse placed upon his third generation grandfather and now he charges forward into battle wielding his grandfather's very sword. She smirked as she realized the young boy was granted a ship of his own. Raina, pride welling in her heart, grinned and flew toward the lead ship.

"Captain, permission to board!" Raina called.

"Raina, permission granted," Elsbeth said as she saw the mystic flying down to the deck.

"How did you know?" Raina asked.

"Romann of course. He said there was going to be a fight, we just didn't know what against. Care to enlighten us?"

"Ravana has summoned an army of stone warriors. They were in hiding under the sea but they press on even after she has fallen."

"Ravana is dead?"

"From what I was told, but I have not confirmed this myself."

"What army do you have, Raina?"

"It is King El'Korr and a massive uprising of dwarves, humans, and elves."

A new voice entered the conversation, "Don't forget dragons."

Raina turned and smiled, "Good to see you, Urlin."

"Good to be seen. How can I assist?" The human's tan robes flapped behind him from the wind and his bowl shaped brown hair kept its shape, not budging from the whipping air.

Raina said, "I only wish there were more mystics about. Spell power is what is needed against this foe."

"Do you not know that each ship carries their own wizard? It is protocol for any ship."

Raina's eyebrows sprang upward, "Protocol for militia, not pirates."

Elsbeth responded, "Romann's background is military. He was once the fleet commander of Tuskabar. When he claimed Pirates Belly as his own he ushered in a new era of tactics."

Raina half-smiled and said, "We need to hurry. Urlin, get those wizards ready to unleash their fury. Elsbeth, move your ships close to the shore but not close enough to be boarded. It will be there that you will attack."

Each nodded in agreement and began calling out orders which in turn were yelled from the crow's nest above in conjunction with signaling directions via shuttered oil lamps to neighboring ships.

Raina began to fly away and Elsbeth called out, "Raina, where are you going?"

"It is time I confirm Ravana's death." Then she was gone as the dark of night swallowed her.

Romann had fallen unconscious from the immense pain he felt earlier. He woke and did not know how long he was out. He picked up his velvet plumed hat and placed it snugly on top of his head.

"Something happened," he thought to himself. *"But what?"*

He knew Oculus was searching for him within the tunnels of his lair. It seemed impossible for a vampire to succumb to unconsciousness but it occurred nonetheless. *"Could Oculus be that powerful? No,"* he thought, *"If Oculus caused this then I would be dead."*

Romann wandered, knowing the landscape intimately, knowing where Oculus would hide and wait. He heard nothing, he smelled only decayed bodies lingering in adjacent chambers, and saw no sign of Oculus.

"Where are you!" he called, but received no response. It was quiet—a quiet he was unfamiliar with, especially in this place.

He turned a corner and entered into a large hall where Oculus resided most of its unnatural life. Romann could not believe what was before him, the remains of the Great Eye of the Deep, the cursed Oculus had fallen.

"This cannot be?" he whispered as he slowly entered. If Oculus was truly destroyed did that mean his lost love was finally free, or worse, lost forever? Romann moved to the carcass and began to pull away and toss pieces of the outer shell. A sticky substance laced with intricate black veins stretched and then snapped as he yanked them away in frustration and eagerness to find her.

"Kiratta! I'm here!" he yelled.

He dug into the belly of the creature, rupturing its stomach, unleashing a black goop and the sickening stench of death. The filth covered his hands like tar and streaks of it stained his tunic and breeches but he did not care.

Romann slowed as he came to realize that she was not here. He turned his head left, then right, looking for an answer. Straight ahead on the back wall was what he had hoped for. A message was written in the stone. It was scratched into it.

SHE IS ALIVE. WAIT AT RAVANA'S TOWER.

The centuries old vampire fell to his knees. His bottom lip quivered slightly as he spoke softly, "She is alive."

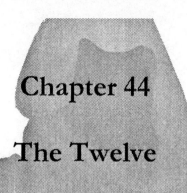

Chapter 44

The Twelve

Jack walked down the corridor holding Kirrata in his arms. Her long chestnut colored hair reflected deep auburn colors from the torch light. Her hair bobbed at each of his steps and her ebony dress swayed as it draped down. He looked at her face, which was soft and alluring, and imagined what her eye color could be. Her cheek bones were well defined. There was a sense of mystery about this mystic of long ago.

"We are almost there. It will soon be all over," Jack said quietly but she did not hear him.

Jack remembered this secret hallway tucked deep inside the tunnels of the Frost Dwarves when he was still a child being led by the diamond ring his father had given him. The Twelve fallen paladins of the Bronze Age had summoned him here. They had changed him into what he was now. Jack could feel their presence heighten as he approached.

The final doorway into the Twelve's resting place opened on its own. Ancient sarcophagi lined the walls in a circular chamber. A single stone pedestal fashioned from the floor was in the middle. His diamond ring still lay on top. Jack stopped at the threshold, not entering. He lowered Kiratta and leaned her against the wall just outside. Her eyes began to flutter, indicating she was coming out of her slumber.

He whispered to her, "Your time has come."

Jack stood, faced the open room and walked in.

The Twelve ignited to life. Crackling of skin and bone echoed as they stepped out from their resting places in unison. Tattered clothes dangled from their frames. They stood at attention, surrounding Jack, who stood next to the pedestal. Jack picked up his diamond ring and twirled it in his fingers to gaze upon it. He fell back into the memory of himself in his room looking at this same ring when fate all of a sudden brought Trillius barging into his chamber. A slight smirk came upon his face at the comical thought and he was thankful for it. It was his memory and not the Twelve's.

The raspy voice of the leader of the Twelve said, "Did you bring us the Mirror of Lost Souls?"

Jack answered, "I have."

"Set it on the pedestal," it demanded.

Jack withdrew the small artifact and extended the mirror into its full length. He placed it face down.

"Break the curse that is upon us and set us free." There was urgency in the voice.

Jack paused and then said, "I am the Vemptukai now. Your orders to me are like the dirt under my feet."

The creature lunged for Jack but was halted by an unseen force. It tried to resist, bringing its cracking lips up in a snarl, revealing yellowed fangs. A growl emerged from deep within.

Jack calmly spoke as the leader of the Twelve continued to fight the compulsion, "It is futile and you know it. Now, before I bring you all your final restoration, I have brought you a gift."

It finally backed away and waited with the others. Ferum, the leader of the Twelve, said in a malice tone, "What is your gift, master?"

"I brought you a young human girl to feast upon after I release you. She is unconscious just outside the doorway."

They bowed their heads slightly, giving silent thanks. "You are most gracious," Ferum said.

"Are you ready for your freedom?"

Jack could feel their heightened anticipation. Centuries they had been trapped.

"We are and we look forward to repaying you with our services by your side."

Jack slowly picked up the mirror. He turned it to face him and called into the depths of the item, "Release the twelve spirits of the paladins of old!"

Haunting screams from inside the mirror bellowed and suddenly dark, murky shadows flew out and zipped about the chamber. They zig-zagged between the vampire paladins until finally one-by-one they soared into them, causing their chests to heave forward.

Jack watched as each of the Twelve began to transform into their original forms in their prime of paladin-hood. Their decayed skin softened and revitalized. Hair grew back, including well-groomed short beards on several of them. Muscles inflated in their arms, chest, and legs as these fully trained warriors connected once again with their lost souls. Each of them looked at one another in amazement and soon smiles of disbelief came upon their faces.

"Let me fetch you your gift," Jack said.

They did not respond as they were caught in the ecstasy of freedom and marveled at their refreshed bodies.

Jack saw Kiratta's eyes for the first time. She appeared to be in a fog from what had occurred but her brilliant wheat colored eyes with a sprinkle of gold flecks sparkled in the torchlight.

"What is happening?" she was barely able to speak.

"It is time to finish what you started, then it will be over."

Jack brought Kiratta's long chestnut hair over her face, blocking it from view. He lifted her to stand and then escorted her inside the chamber. One-by-one the Twelve focused on their gift from Jack and relished the woman's blood they would be drinking. This blood would be the final ingredient to launch their full strength of vampirism. The curse was lifted. Their freedom was now before them.

The leader stepped forward, "Thank you, Jack. The curse of Kiratta is now broken."

The mention of her name caused her to jerk her hair free from her face to look where she was. Her eyes caught the creatures through the strands and she gasped in realization. She broke free from Jack.

Kiratta's hair flared back as if there was a summoned wind and a brilliant glow erupted from every pore of her body revealing her true self to them all.

Stunned, they backed away, shielding their eyes from her.

"Jack has betrayed us! He brought our nemesis to destroy us all. Kill them!"

"I wanted you all to see the light," Jack said playfully as he left the chamber and closed the door behind him.

"Kiratta!" Ferum screamed. The leader of the Twelve tried in vain to leave the room, to shield himself from the brilliance of the mystic who had been the catalyst behind capturing them and banishing them to this tomb.

Kiratta Green levitated a foot off the ground and the emanating light intensified. Screams from the vampires were deafening. The Helper of Mankind, the Ancient Mystic of Lore, spoke authoritatively in a supernatural booming voice, "Hear me, Order of Ferum, the time of judgment has come for you."

A light almost rivaling the sun burned at their skin. There was no place to hide. The smell of flesh sizzling in the high heat of day filled the chamber. Sparks of flame burst forth in patches on their bodies and soon they were consumed. Writhing on the ground, revealing white bone under the bubbling melted flesh, the Twelve's plan of freedom did not come to pass. They were now experiencing a new kind of freedom from Ruauck-El to a place only reserved for those in the depths of hell.

"Jack save us! You will be next. She will come for you!" These were the final words spoken. A pulse of energy shot out in all directions from Kiratta and struck the vampires. One-by-one they shattered into dust. Kiratta collapsed, expelled of all her energy. The chamber went dark.

Raina entered the pillared hall of Ravana's tower. Soft red embers from the braziers produced long shadows but Raina's sight spell allowed her to see through it all in perfect clarity. A statue of a female stood before her and two bodies lay on the ground. A fat human and a medusa.

"You did well, Jack, but one thing you had missed," she whispered. "And now it is my turn to finish this."

In Raina's years as the Sheldeen Elf Mystic she had been groomed with knowledge of the realms and many of the mythical creatures. The answer she had hoped to find to help El'Korr defeat the threat had surfaced. The power of a medusa is severed once the head is cut off. Raina surveyed the area for a sharp blade but did not spot one. She moved gracefully to one of the metal standing braziers and kicked it over causing the embers to splash along the floor.

"Sieknoss-tel-voth," she said and her spell formed the metal rod into a crude sword. The stretching and tweaking of the forming weapon sounded like an out of tune musical instrument.

She picked it up, walked to the medusa, and decapitated it. Raina felt the potency of the medusa dwindle like one of the ancient gems of power that released their energy and faded away. Raina gave a great sigh of relief and turned to leave.

Seconds later, unbeknownst to anyone, the cracking of stone echoed in the chamber. Pieces began to fall to the ground revealing pasty white skin and the familiar red hair of Countessa Penelope De Luz. She stretched out her arms, sending fragments of rock in all directions. "You have a lot to learn, young Vemptukai."

A hundred pirate ships lined the shore just outside the breakers. Each launched ballistae at the stone warriors along with wizards casting devastating spells. Dragons swooped in, breathing fire or landing to attack in shallower parts of the shore along with battling the avian creatures.

Ravana's evil was beyond measure El'Korr thought to himself as he watched intermittently between attacks to see the magnitude of destruction before him.

His Wild Dwarves had set up a perimeter around him once again and he threw his warhammer at will, crushing statue after statue. He was about to hurl his weapon when he saw one of the enemies crumble before his eyes without a single weapon ever touching it. Then another fell apart next to that one and then another. Soon the entire army collapsed and within seconds it was suddenly over.

Each person, whether dwarf, human, or elf, stood quietly in shock. Only the crashing waves could be heard. Moments passed before murmuring started and then tears of sadness and joy. Some fell to their knees in pure exhaustion or to thank God.

Geetock said, "My Mahlek, what happened?"

"Uncertain, but my hope is that it is over."

Raina flew in overhead and announced in a booming magically enhanced voice, "It is finished. Victory is ours!"

This elicited the largest cheer that any kingdom had ever heard. Wizards aboard pirate ships cast spells of fireworks overhead. Dragons roared and landed on the open field. Pirates hooted and hollered.

El'Korr half-smiled, his shoulders slunk a little lower in relief, and he clasped one gauntleted hand on Geetock's shoulder. "Find out our losses and attend to the wounded, my friend. Coordinate our clerics with your team and get your dark-metal wound taken care of."

"It will be done, my Mahlek."

"One other thing."

"Yes, my king."

"Thank you, Geetock."

Geetock nodded with a grin and moved away to start things in motion.

El'Korr, King of the Dwarves, stood there and watched men of all races move chaotically. Commanders issued orders, some followed, while others wandered in shock as the horror of this battle sank in. In war there are truly no winners as both sides suffer the consequences. Even after victory, it becomes a time of remorse, of anger, of healing, but even the healing process can take decades to subside. A deep scar was left in every soul on this very day and though it will be transcribed by travelling bards, the storytellers of the realm, it will invoke different emotions depending on who it is told to. Virgin ears of villages far away will find it fascinating, while a town filled with warriors who contributed to this fight will be forced to remember, and the remembrance will reveal how thin the layer of feelings are that hide underneath. It will indeed be a shallow covering over the hurt buried inside.

"What will I remember this day as?" El'Korr said under breath.

"Indeed," Raina said as she walked up behind him, clearly hearing his words. "What will you remember?"

El'Korr thought long and hard before responding, "Unity."

"An interesting word of choice."

"Raina, I saw on this day, the members of these races uniting together for a single cause."

"What cause would that be?" Raina asked even though she understood what the answer was. It was her way to draw her longtime friend's heart out.

"To right the wrongs of the realm."

"Then we are not finished."

El'Korr turned to face her. His visage hard underneath his orange facial hair and his eyes narrowed. "If King Manasseh and Ravana brought this kind of evil in their wake then we are only half way through this mess. We will regroup and start our plans to attack the south and east kingdoms."

Raina said, "It will be difficult to manage the two kingdoms in turmoil we have now. Let us coordinate our efforts with the other races and solidify this unity you speak of before we send our forces out again. We need to secure the lands we have conquered and make it known to the south and east kings that we are not to be trifled with, otherwise they will be sending their military to attack us."

"Let them come."

She smirked, "Spoken like a true dwarf. Come, let us give thanks to those who have stood by our side and to those who have fallen."

Just then a single dwarf standing nearby, amongst all the chaos, began to recite an old dwarven song. Mud covered him from head to toe and a line of blood trickled from a bludgeoned wound on his head as he released the deep baritone notes. One-by-one others joined him. Some held injured warriors in their lap or were in the process of guiding them to a cleric, but each one stopped to sing.

Raina watched El'Korr soften as he was captured by the voices welling up around him in unison. She appreciated the uplifting yet somber tone that rose in unison from the bearded clan.

El'Korr began to sing with them.

"Praise will ever be on our lips,
Our enemies fall at your hands.
Victory and glory is yours,
You will be praised! You will be praised!
Our battles are already won,
We come to praise thee.
Fill our mugs of ale,

Fill our bellies full.
You will be praised! You will be praised!"

Chapter 45

Friends

Bridazak waited for his friends to join him at the top of one of the lower peaks within the famous Rainbow Mountains—a name garnered from the amazing shingle-layered, multi-colored stone that displayed a prismatic effect from the sunlight. The formerly lost ordakian crossed his arms, leaned against one of the rocks and smiled as they were now clear of danger. "Did you miss me?"

Spilf charged Bridazak and hugged him, "I can't believe it."

Bridazak laughed, "I guess that means yes."

"What were you thinkin' jumpin into the Underworld like that you blundering fool?" Dulgin threw his equipment at the base of a rock.

"Good to see you too, my friend. Abawken, I hope all is well with you."

"It is indeed and even more so having you back in our presence, Master Bridazak."

Each of them set their equipment down and sat in small alcoves away from the chilly wind. Nightfall had completely blanketed them.

Spilf said, "Bridazak, you are glowing. Does that mean...?"

He nodded and said, "Yes."

"What happened? We thought you died," Spilf stated.

"Died? I gave Xan a message. Did he not deliver it?"

Dulgin scoffed, "Yeah, he delivered it, just not as quickly as we would have all liked. I don't like having funerals for people who are still alive."

"A funeral? You had my funeral? Wow, I had no idea. What was it like? Did you cry, Dulgin?"

Dulgin growled and crossed his arms across his chest.

Bridazak said, "I'm just having some fun with you. I missed you all dearly and have a grand adventure to tell you about as I am sure you have the same. I was only gone a few days."

"Master Bridazak, a few days in the Underworld and heaven translates differently in the natural realm. It has been weeks."

"Weeks?" the ordakian was genuinely surprised. "What has happened? I never understood what transpired at the Chamber of Cleansing as I was dealing with Manasseh at the time."

Spilf chimed in first, "We stopped the Dragon God from coming back."

Abawken said, "But with great loss."

"I'm fine, my friends. I am sorry you thought I was—"

Dulgin cut him off, "We lost not only you but Rondee."

"Rondee?" Bridazak sighed and he felt the tears begin to form around the edges of his eyes. Silence engulfed the camp as each of them remembered the battle, the Wild Dwarf sacrificing himself to save El'Korr, and then his funeral.

Spilf asked, "Why did you go after Manasseh? He was evil."

"Was evil. It was something that I had to do."

"But why?" Spilf pleaded further.

"Spilf, I found out it was never about Manasseh. God wanted to show me a different facet of who He is."

"I want to show you a different facet of my fist," Dulgin scoffed.

Bridazak took a deep breath and exhaled, "I found Manasseh in his purest form and brought him home. Heaven. I know that you won't completely understand and I also struggled with the decision I made when I was down there but you have to trust me."

"That human child you were with was Manasseh?" Spilf asked.

Bridazak nodded.

"But why did-"

Abawken cut in, "Masters, let us set camp and get some rest. We have a long journey ahead of us and we can *interrogate* our friend along the way."

Each of them slowly started to unroll bedrolls and prepare their own areas. Bridazak thought to himself, *A long journey ahead of us indeed but not where you think, Abawken.*

"I will gather some wood for a fire," Bridazak said.

Abawken looked at the dak and responded, "It will attract—"

"Not tonight," Bridazak cut him off. "Nothing will harm us this night."

Abawken gave him a long stare of concern and then conceded with a nod.

The four friends sat around the small blaze with a babbit Spilf caught while searching for wood, roasting on a skewer.

Spilf filled Bridazak in on all that had happened; when he was dealing with Manasseh at the Chamber of Cleansing leading up to where they were now. Bridazak listened intently as did the others, all staring at the flames and red embers as images of the events danced inside their minds.

Spilf finished and then Bridazak said, "No one knows then what's happening with El'Korr's army, this Trillius, and our Jack? Very interesting."

Dulgin growled, "Interesting? Bah!"

Spilf said, "What are we going to do about Jack? I mean he is a vampire but he is still Jack, right?"

"I'm uncertain, my friend."

The group went silent and stared deep into the fire. Each of them couldn't fathom Jack in his new state and what led him down this path.

"So you are married now?" Bridazak said, breaking the silence. "That makes me happy. Congratulations. My apologies for missing the wedding ceremony."

Abawken nodded his appreciation and took another bite of food.

The ordakian looked at each of his friends for a long moment. He smirked and then looked at Spilf and said, "I know that your journey has been long and arduous in trying to find me."

"You have no idea," Dulgin whispered.

"I don't but I know that our adventuring is not over yet. It is not coincidence we are in the eastern lands."

Dulgin said sarcastically, "What, now you want us to take on the East Horn King?"

"No, our destination is beyond the borders," Bridazak said while looking intently at Abawken who also returned the stare.

"Master Bridazak, you speak of my homeland, Zoar. But why?"

"I am not exactly sure yet but I am having visions of a place where children starve, sewage runs in dirt pathways, and homes are stacked on top of one another in a maze of chaos. Do you know of the place, Abawken?"

Dulgin responded indignantly, "Please tell me you don't know what this blundering fool is talking about."

"I do know. He speaks of the Slums of Kaldor."

"Great, the slums don't sound like a place where gold reigns and Dwarven Ale runs freely."

"Gold definitely reigns in Kaldor but only through the hands of the slumlord."

"Kaldor?" Spilf asked.

"No, my father," Abawken said.

"Your father is the slumlord?"

Abawken looked off in the distance and said, "Yes, and it appears it is time for his son to return home."

Only the sound of the intermittent crackling fire and the haunting howls of distant winds could be heard as the group soaked in Bridazak's proposed destination.

Dulgin brought out his new pipe and began to stoke the embers and draw in the tobacco. White billowy smoke poured out his mouth and nostrils, fighting through his red beard. "What is our mission then?"

Each of them turned to look at Bridazak and he smiled incredulously.

"Well?" Spilf nudged.

Bridazak shrugged, "Don't know."

"What do you mean you don't know? You just said you had visions of this place," Spilf said.

"I did and I don't know why but I'm sure we will know once we get there."

"You're sure?" Dulgin grumbled. "It was bad enough when Stubby was pointing to a map with his eyes closed to find his parents and now this? I'm going just to see how sure you truly are and I'm thinkin there will be some trouble that needs fixin with my axe."

"Thank you, my friend." Bridazak looked over to the next in line, "Spilf, what about you?"

"Of course you know I'm in. We always said we would go to the ends of the realm together."

"Well, it appears you will get that wish, Stubby. That is exactly where we are going, to the ends of the realm."

"Abawken?"

The human looked at each of them, slightly tilted his head in contemplation, and then said, "Master Bridazak, I know not the reason of your visions but the destination we seek does not conform to any other type of community known to Ruauck-El. This place will challenge the very core of your heart and mind and wants to devour every soul that enters its domain."

Spilf asked quickly, "What do you mean, devour? Is this place filled with demons or something?"

"In a manner of speaking, yes. You will see things that will disturb you but know that it is the way of the people. We must tread quietly."

"You mean, sneak in, right?" Spilf said.

"Indeed. My father will not allow us to be there under normal circumstances."

"What about Raina?" Bridazak asked as he poked at the fire.

"I will contact her but what I do know is that she will most likely be joining us."

Bridazak continued to push the embers around with the stick, not making eye contact with Abawken. He was slightly smirking and he caught Spilf noticing him. "Abawken," Bridazak said, "What do you know of Kaldor?"

"He is a myth."

"I like a good story," Dulgin said as he had another tug on his pipe.

"It is written in our ancient texts that Kaldor was a human with the lineage of a Djinn, a spirit race, masters of air, earth, water, and fire. Kaldor was a great warrior that journeyed to the realm of the Djinn and vanished. Some say he is being held captive still to this day while others refuse to believe he even existed and that it was merely a story told to children."

"And what does Abawken believe?" Bridazak asked.

"I know not, Master, nor does it matter what I believe."

Bridazak's eyes shifted from the human to the scimitar lying beside him, which clearly made Abawken uncomfortable as he responded by quickly snatching up the weapon, getting up and stating, "I will take first shift." The tan-skinned fighter entered the outer perimeter of darkness and disappeared.

"Interesting story," Spilf said.

"I'll tell ya an interesting story, Stubby. Did you ever hear about the dwarf named Gunther and the legendary Cat's Eye of Fuldunn Gorge?"

"No, I haven't, but—"

"Well, I'll tell ye about him then and know this, Gunther Stronghand is not a myth."

"Yeah, well it is getting late and —"

"There he was, standing at the edge of the gorge. Now this gorge was only known by the Timber Dwarves within the pine forest of Tethnon..."

Bridazak's focus wasn't on Dulgin's history lesson but instead on why Abawken had not disclosed the full truth of Kaldor. He didn't know himself the story of Kaldor but it was evident from his many years of reading people that Abawken was withholding information. Bridazak thought, *"No worries, my friend, you won't be doing this alone. God is leading us all to your homeland for a reason and the myth of Kaldor has something to do with it."*

Chapter 46

Fate's Kiss

"I am unsure if Jack is the one that destroyed the Twelve but I am sure he had a hand in it."

"Raina, how are you certain?" Morthkin, the former Frost Dwarf King asked; another crunch sounded under his boots as he stepped further into the scorched chamber.

"Powerful magic beyond the capabilities of any vampire or any existing history of the Twelve caused this."

The smell of burnt flesh and the charred remains filled their senses as they perused the room for further evidence. Morthkin wrinkled his nose in disgust.

Xan raised an eyebrow and said, "Have we ruled out the gnome factor? Trillius?"

"Trillius was last with Abawken from what my husband has relayed to me. Both Trillius and Rozelle have not been seen, but knowing the gnome's nature, he would steer clear of this place. I suspect he used Jack as far as he needed him and then departed to further his own interests, my best guess."

"And a good one, as I agree," Xan concluded.

Morthkin's deep voice resonated, "What of the mirror?"

"With Jack I surmise and hopefully locked away where no one can find it," Raina responded.

"Should we pursue this vampire?"

"No, we must let Jack go for the time being. Chasing after him will only push him further away. He is on his own journey now and must come to terms with his decision."

"May God help him," Xan said.

"May God help us all. Come, we need to seal this room and then I must prepare to meet my husband's family."

"Are you sure you don't want me to come along?" Xan asked.

"No, if things change then I will contact you. El'Korr will need you by his side as he secures the northern and western borders. Besides, from what Abawken has told me thus far the meeting of his family will not be a warm welcome."

"It must be because you are an elf and he is human."

"Nay, I don't think that is it. My husband seems to have a different opinion than his father from what he has told me."

"Opinions of what?"

"His father is a king so I imagine it has to do with the way he rules his kingdom."

"He can't be worse than the Horn Kings of Ruauck-El."

Raina half-smiled, "No, of course not. I'm sure it is just a simple misunderstanding within the family unit."

A Frost Dwarf sentry entered and said, "The first of El'Korr's army returns. They have been spotted marching through Marauder's Pass."

General Morthkin announced, "Prepare for their arrival and send out a greeting party to find out more information."

"Yes, sir!"

Romann stood in the moonlight on the balcony of Ravana's Tower. Several nights he had come out but never left the confines. The tower felt like a tomb. His hunger for blood had been forgotten and his only thought was of Kiratta. He clung to the message on the wall of the fallen Oculus. It was etched in his mind, "SHE IS ALIVE. WAIT AT RAVANA'S TOWER."

Romann placed his hands on the railing, leaned over, and watched the rag-tag citizens of Tuskabar attempting to rebuild their city. Fires still burned throughout and the echoes of men calling orders to lift massive stone blocks resounded in the distance. The vampire sighed as he let out a long breath. He cared not for the city. He cared not for himself. Centuries of torture over the loss of his love had been well hidden but now cracks had begun to show.

He whispered, "I know not time in my undead state but where are you?"

The soft voice of Kiratta echoed in his mind. "Romann?" It sounded so real to him but he feared to turn around. He could not handle the disappointment of not seeing her with his own eyes. "Romann," the voice called again but with a softness of relief deeper within. Then it was there, the sense of a human inside his chamber. He could smell her.

Romann said, "I cannot turn around. I dare not in case my mind tricks me."

She lightly touched his back and Romann instantly froze. His eyes fluttered shut and he held his breath.

"It is me, my love," she said.

He could not hold fast any longer and in an instant he turned, "Do my eyes mistake me? Is it truly you?"

"Yes," she was barely able to speak. A single tear trickled from her eye.

Romann caught it on the tip of his index finger with lightning speed and rubbed it into his skin with his thumb.

They embraced and time stood still once again for them as they had no intention of releasing one another.

Kiratta spoke, her voice muffled as she nestled into his velvet jacket, "I never gave up hope."

They both pulled away and looked deep into each other's eyes. Romann started to look away but she grabbed his face and pulled him back in.

"Don't," she said.

"I have changed."

"Appearance, yes, but never your heart."

"Kirra, I…"

She kissed him. He kissed her back. Their love had endured the ages, had never failed them. This surreal moment was longed for, hoped for, prayed for, and now it was happening. They rested their foreheads against one another, eyes closed, hands clutching each-others clothing.

"Nothing will ever come between us again, my Kirra."

"Romann, we would have been united in the eternal home."

He pulled away and looked at her, "No, I condemned my soul when I willingly asked to be turned to a vampire. My soul was cast into the depths of hell. It was my price to buy me more time in hopes of bringing you back."

"I will walk through the fires of hell to find it then," she said.

"Not even the great mystic, Kirrata Green, can retrieve such a thing."

"We are together, here and now, and whatever time we have will not be wasted in self-pity or remorse. You did what you had to do."

"What then, you are saved from one curse and yet you find yourself in another?"

"Stop it, Romann. We will find our way."

"You are human, I am vampire. You will age and I will never sleep."

Kirrata looked at Romann intensely, a determination in her eyes, "Then turn me, my love."

He grabbed her arms, "Never!"

"You must so we can be together, forever." She turned her head to reveal her bare neck more prominently. Romann flinched away in disgust and let her go.

"Don't deny me this request, Romann."

"You knew what I had done. How can you ask me for such a thing?"

"Over the years, at times, I could see you through the eye of Oculus, I could hear your words as if you stood next to me but it was part of the curse. The torture of seeing and hearing you was painful. You did what you thought was best for me, Romann."

"It is ironic that what you hated, hunted, and killed is what I have become."

"I have had many centuries to think about this decision."

"As have I but you know not what you ask, Kirra. This curse is beyond imagination. Everything is a daze, clarity of color dissipates, and the thirst for the living, well, it took me years to control it."

"I will learn as you have. There is no other way. Let us make Ruauck-El our eternal home. Let us sail away on your ship and never return."

"Kirra," he caressed her cheek, "you are so beautiful. Let us talk later of these things but for now enjoy your freedom. We cannot rush this decision."

She paused, "Yes, of course. Forgive me."

"No need to ask for forgiveness. I am so enamored by your

presence that I neglected to ask if you are injured."

"I am tired. I have been plagued with nightmares since my return."

"You are safe now." He brought her in close and hugged her.

Kirrata said, "How did I get here? It seems I am battling my memory of things."

"You and Jack left me a message in the Hall of Oculus. Do you not remember this?"

She pulled back, a confused expression on her face, "Jack?"

"Yes, a vampire, a very powerful one. He saved you. He found a way to break Ravana's curse. You have no memory of him?"

"No. I remember bits and pieces of waking inside of a nightmare. An ancient tomb filled with the undead. I summoned the rays of the sun to smite them and cast them into the pit of hell but then I blacked out and awoke to find myself here. It seems so real but my memory fails me."

"It is late. We will talk in the morning. You must rest. I will watch over you."

Romann ushered her to the canopy bed he had prepared for her before she arrived. The clean linens smelled of the spring air and the mahogany frame was finely polished. He pulled the bedding down and she scooted between them as he brought them back to envelope her.

"Thank you, my love," she said softly. "I still can't believe that I am here, with you."

Her eyes drifted and she fell asleep. Romann watched her for many hours. All of his past memories with her strengthened. She laid before him, no longer a distant thought, but instead as the real Kirrata he had fallen in love with.

Jack stood at the far end of the room, watching Romann watch her. He had overheard it all. The reunion of this lost couple had strengthened his mind and the decision he had made against the Twelve was justice served. Now that Kirrata had destroyed them, Jack no longer allowed them to manipulate his mind as he compartmentalized their thoughts. The ghost memories were hushed and now he was, *"Alone,"* he thought. *"As it should be. I was alone in my childhood, alone when I returned from heaven, and now alone for eternity. It is my fate."*

Jack's feet mystified and he slowly approached Romann, whose back was to him.

"Romann," Jack whispered.

The vampire turned quickly, bearing his fangs, but withheld when he saw who it was. "You return. I am forever in your debt. Ask of me anything and it will be done."

"Romann, I have heard your prayer and have come to answer it."

"My prayers have already been answered," he said as he looked down at Kiratta.

"It is the unspoken prayer."

"Jack, I thank you," Romann said as he bowed to one knee. "You have returned what I never thought possible."

"Never thought possible? You fought for this so you must have thought it possible."

He stood back up, "It was a manner of speaking, nothing more."

Jack smirked, "I will give you something that you truly thought was never possible."

"What more could I want now? Kirrata is all that I want and need."

Jack smiled and brought forth the small decorative Mirror of Lost Souls from inside his tunic. He then expanded it to its full size and said in an authoritative voice, "I call for the soul of Romann de Beaux."

Romann took a step back, his legs now against the bed, uncertain of what was happening. A small translucent entity zipped out from the hidden dimension inside the mirror. It howled throughout the room. Romann watched it closely. Jack gazed at the swashbuckler vampire of Pirates Belly and saw the wonder within his eyes, the wonderment of a once concealed treasure chest finally being broken open to reveal its contents.

Kirrata stirred awake causing Romann to glance in her direction. As he brought up his hand to comfort her he felt the sting of the ethereal force penetrate his chest. He heaved forward as if someone had stabbed him in his back and he gasped for air. His eyes widened and fangs extended. Romann then collapsed to the ground and Kirrata sprang to his side.

She said in a venomous tone, "What did you do?"

Jack remained silent and reduced the mirror back to its portable size and tucked it inside his shirt.

"Romann, can you hear me?" She turned back to Jack, "He is convulsing. What have you done to him?"

Jack said calmly, "He is fine. Better than fine."

Kirrata returned her attention to her love, "Romann? Speak to me."

He finally rolled over, clutching his stomach. What she thought to be convulsions was actually her vampire lover weeping. Romann was struggling with words through the crying and Kirrata leaned in closer to try to understand them.

"Thank...you..." Romann was saying over and over as his speech was gurgled through his tears.

Jack stepped forward and said, "Kirrata, I am uncertain if he can hear me so I will inform you."

"I know you but from where? Your voice...it is familiar. What is happening!?" she demanded as she stood.

"Romann will now live out his days as a human and—"

She cut him off, "Impossible."

"Just listen. He will live out his days as a human but he is still a vampire. The curse of the vampire can never be broken."

"I don't understand. How is this possible?"

"His soul has returned and he will live as his original self but he will be sensitive to the vampire thirst once again. You must help him cope and in time he will re-learn the control he had before."

"I—"

"Do you understand?"

She nodded, looked down at Romann, and then returned her focus back to Jack but he was gone. Kirrata sat next to her love and wept with him.

Jack rode through the air atop of Gaermahn. He closed his eyes and felt the wind whipping against him. He envisioned the sensation like an invisible force giving him an embrace.

"Where to next, my Master?" the undead dragon said within his mind.

"Where do King's go, my friend?"

"To their Kingdom."

"Then that is where we shall go."

"Do you have one in mind, Master?"

"Several but one in particular. Head toward Kerrith Ravine."

"Bold move, Master."

"We won't be travelling to the dark realm itself but I know of a vacant kingdom at a place called Black Rock."

"I am unfamiliar with the name."

"Not to worry, it is a place I am well acquainted with. I look forward to meeting our neighbors in the area of Kerrith Ravine. I am feeling…inspired."

Chapter 47

A New Adventure

Dulgin rolled on the rocky pathway in hysterical laughter. His arms and hands hugging his armored belly and at times he would try to point toward Spilf.

The ordakian had had better days and his red-bearded friend was enjoying this particular moment a little too much.

Bridazak and Abawken were off to the side with hands covering their mouths to attempt to block their own smiles. Eyebrows were lifted, cheeks were raised, and shoulders bobbed.

"Why am I the only one not laughing here?" Spilf said tight lipped as a slimy, milk colored substance slid down from the top of his head and splashed onto his shoulder. Spilf was covered in the translucent goop.

"Spilf...Spilf...baahaahaahaa!" Dulgin tried to say something but went back to laughing hysterically, rolling this way and that.

The dak slowly brought up his saturated hands and sparingly began to wipe it away.

"Is it turning green, Abawken?" Bridazak pointed while nudging the human with his free elbow.

"What do you mean, green?" Spilf asked concerned.

Dulgin sat up and was finely able to speak, "It's the air. It will turn green and then it stains everything. Bahahaaahahahaaa!"

"Help me!" Spilf said frantically.

Abawken and Bridazak threw their water skins but then backed away. Spilf quickly started using what little was there to get the substance off. He stripped off his clothing down to his loin cloth and used the inside material to wipe off the residue left behind on his skin.

"It's too late!" Dulgin pointed.

Spilf could not see that his hair had turned a mildew green along with patches on his neck and face area. His hands had also succumbed to it.

"Why me?" Spilf said resignedly and plopped to the ground.

Dulgin stood, "Oh Stubby, how I needed to laugh again. I will never look at you the same. Your face was priceless."

"Yeah, so is your face," he tried to counter. "All I wanted was an egg. Stupid birds."

"Ye don't go offloading the birds of Rainbow Mountain. I told ya them ass droppings are nothing but trouble."

Bridazak stepped in and said, "So let me get this straight. You were finishing the morning guard shift and thought you would pilfer one of the nests you spotted on the rocks above us?"

Spilf nodded, clearly not having achieved the plan his friend had just laid out. "This is worse than when I ate those strange dried berries the old man had at the farm in Sheraton."

"Those were—"

"I know, Dulgin, don't say it," Spilf snapped.

The dwarf laughed heartily once again. "This is a close second to that event, truth be told."

Morning had come and each of the heroes were frightened awake at the panicked call of Spilfer Teehle running and scampering through the maze of boulders down the mountainside as a flock of birds pursued him out of the nesting area above. Their wingspan was twice his size and one of them could have easily scooped him up and sent him flying to his death below. He had dodged and weaved each of their attacks and his friends saved him with their readied weaponry and met the barrage of the feathered ones known as Gimlings. They are not hostile creatures like the Varouche but instead are numerous in their population in the ranges and are a food source for the wyvern's and giants that roam these parts. They are not a colorful sort and range from ugly to uglier in most regards. They do however produce a variety of colored eggs. A special secretion covers the outer shell as it is laid. The air changes the initial clear substance exactly like what transpired with Spilf. This phenomena hides the avian shelled offspring as it blends in with the Rainbow Mountain pigmentation.

"I need to find a river to wash this stuff off."

Abawken said, "No river will help you unfortunately. It will naturally fade over time."

"How long?"

Abawken hesitated to answer.

Spilf said loudly, "How long?"

"A month."

"A month?"

"Maybe two."

"Two? Oh, for heaven's sake."

Dulgin said, "Didn't you always tell me that you wanted a colorful life like mine?"

Spilf punched Dulgin across his jaw and then stormed off. Dulgin did not expect the attack and froze for a second. He reached his hand up to readjust his jaw and massage it back into place.

"Good one, Stubby. We just need to work on your strength. The next time you hit me like that I better lose a tooth." Dulgin looked at Bridazak and Abawken and stated plainly, "Been teaching him that one for a while. He's a good student."

Bridazak smiled and looked out over the sand dunes of the east. The Rainbow Mountains were the borderlands to the Eastern Horn King and the outer realm of Ruauck-El. The gold sea of sand appeared breathtakingly beautiful from this distance but the harshness of this land would soon be known by them all.

"This is my home; the desert," Abawken stated as he stepped beside Bridazak. "At the base of this mountain we will find water, the last of it for quite some time."

"Abawken, I just want you to know that we are with you."

"Of course, why do you say this?"

"Sometimes what is not spoken should be spoken."

Dulgin said behind them, "You are starting to sound like Huey over there with your spoken should be spoken crap-talk. Why don't you two get your things together and while you're at it pack up Stubby's stuff cause I don't think he is coming back for it."

Abawken, Dulgin, and Bridazak all heard Spilf's heightened voice just behind some larger rocks.

"What do you mean you can't help me?"

A softer, feminine voice responded, but they could not make out the words.

"I don't know where they are and I don't care!" Spilf resounded.

One-by-one they came around the bend to find Raina in full sand-dune attire. Leather bracers were tied in place, locking in the long-sleeves of her beige tunic. Thin layered tight fitting boots clung snugly to her breeches. She had a small backpack with several water skins attached and a walking stick rested against a rock next to her.

"Ah, there you are," Raina said as she stood from her seated position.

Spilf was splashing in the water trying desperately to wash the green splotches off his body. This was a watering hole, one of several in the immediate area. Fresh water bubbled up at the base of the mountain range and just a few strides away started the endless sea of sand.

Abawken rushed in, hugged his wife, and kissed her.

"Get an inn," Dulgin scoffed as he headed by them and pulled out the water skins in his pack. He began to refill them. "Hey, Stubby, did you miss me?"

Spilf shook his head and exited the pool, water splashing everywhere.

Raina looked at Bridazak and said, "I'm in awe by what I see standing before me."

"Good to see you too, Raina."

"In all my years, in all my teachings and learning, the Underworld was only reserved for the dead and yet you walked those lands and have returned."

"Well, I can broaden your knowledge a little more."

"I would like that very much so. We missed you dearly, Bridazak, and it is good that you are home."

Bridazak acknowledged her with a warm smile as he walked past. She reviewed his stature and his equipment as he strode by.

She said, "A bow with no arrows is a seed without water."

Spilf chimed, "He doesn't require arrows any longer, my lady."

Bridazak filled his water skins and peered back, "A gift to me while in the Underworld."

"I do very much anticipate hearing your story but first let me give you an update of the lands."

Each of them took a seat, finding shade where they could as Raina began to inform them of the happenings in Ruauck-El.

"El'Korr returned to the Shield. He will send word from the throne there and direct his troops accordingly. He will strategically set up camps along the eastern and southern borderlands. With the fall of Ravana we have seen a tremendous increase in willing souls to our cause. Some remnants of Manasseh's and Ravana's military are embedded in keeps and castles but for the time being they are without resources and have walled themselves in. We will not waste our time bringing their walls down and in time they will have to come out of hiding. El'Korr has set up stations to watch those areas and will attempt diplomacy to hopefully bring them into the fold. His focus is to strengthen what we have achieved thus far before moving on the other Horn Kings. There has been no sign of Trillius, Rozelle, or Jack in the last weeks. Romann and Kirrata have decided to stay in Tuskabar and are taking a leadership role in the rebuilding and planning of their future and the city."

"Future?" Dulgin scoffed. "He's a vamp. They don't have futures."

Raina responded, "This one does."

"Kirrata Green?" Bridazak questioned.

Raina smiled, "It seems your fated meeting with the curse of Oculus triggered events that we are just now witnessing the fruit of. Kirrata is Ravana's sister and long before all of what has transpired Romann and Kirrata were lovers. Bitter jealousy was the root of all we have seen in the west."

Dulgin said, "There must have been some good fighting and I missed it. Dang it! This is all because of that infernal gnome."

Raina said, "One other thing, Dulgin, your brother instructed me to tell you to stay out of trouble."

"Bah," he shook his head, "trouble follows me like a shadow. Just look at who's around me now." The dwarf gestured toward Spilf.

Bridazak stepped forward, "I believe we are ready for a new adventure. Abawken, lead the way."

"My pleasure, Master Bridazak." The human held out his arm for Raina. She immediately clung to it and they walked side-by-side.

Spilf and Bridazak then followed, leaving the dwarf last.

Dulgin said, "Sure, I'll take your things, my lady. No problem. Looks like I'm just a servant on this crazy adventure." Dulgin changed from the common language to dwarven as he mumbled on after grabbing Raina's backpack and walking stick. He trudged into the sand and the further he went the slower he got.

"Great, another adventure with sand in my boots," he said under breath. "Raina!" he called out, "Can't you summon that dragon of yours?"

Spilf yelled back, "Zeffeera is resting but I'm sure she can summon some horses or ponies."

Dulgin stopped dead in his tracks, squinted hard at the ordakian, who was smiling triumphantly. "Shut it, Stubby! We're walking."

Coming Soon...

Book #4 of the Horn King Series:
The Sword of the Elements

The heroes of Ruauck-El find themselves once again pitted against the evil of the realm. Abawken takes his friends into the desert land of his upbringing, the province of Zoar, but finds himself caught between family, friends, and destiny.

Meanwhile, Trillius and Rozelle get wrapped up in something bigger than even they could have imagined as Trillius' insatiable thirst for power and wealth blinds him to the truth.

And what of Jack, the Vampire King? New adventures will arise as he walks the haunted halls of his past within Black Rock castle.

From the Author:

Thank you for reading my latest book, The Vampire King. I truly hope that the stories invoked in these pages have spurred you to reflect upon your own walk in this amazing world we live in. I call your adventurous spirit to rise up and pursue your destiny. You have been prepared for this day and it is time for you to be fully alive. There is a place deep down inside each of us that calls us to our purpose. It is time to heed the call and take a step of faith toward what you were always destined to do. Now go forth and change the world.

Please leave a review on Amazon, Barnes & Noble, and Goodreads for those who are looking for a great series to read. Your review does matter. Please contact me directly if you would like to. I am available on Facebook or you can contact me via my website, www.braewyckoff.com.

Blessings, and may your light shine bright and blind your enemies.

ABOUT THE AUTHOR

Brae Wyckoff is an award winning and internationally acclaimed author, born and raised in San Diego, CA. He has been married to his beautiful wife, Jill, for over 22 years, and they have three children and four grandchildren.

Brae has worked in Hollywood as an actor and performed in plays and dinner theater. He travels the world with his wife training and equipping people in the ways of Jesus Christ and has ministered to thousands. He has an international ministry called The Greater News where he reports on supernatural miracles happening around the world.

His first book, The Orb of Truth, won Best Christian Fantasy Award for 2013 and has been voted #1 in several categories, including Best Indie Fantasy Book, Epic Fantasy Worth Your Time, and Fantasy Book That Should Be Required Reading.

The Orb of Truth audiobook, produced by Highland Pictures, is available on Amazon.com, audible.com, and iTunes.

The Dragon God (sequel to The Orb of Truth) has been voted "BEST New Epic Fantasy" and rated "TOP Fantasy Book".

In addition to writing the Horn King Series, Brae is the host of Broadcast Muse blog talk radio program, featuring interviews with authors, artists, and world changers such as Academy Award winner Peter Berkos and #1 Best Selling Author, William P. Young, of the Shack.

www.braewyckoff.com